MW00710494

Marlene,

I hope you enjoy the story!

Rob.

SAPO

by

Robert Beatty

Ecopress
Corvallis, Oregon

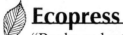

Ecopress

"Books and art that enhance environmental awareness"

1029 NE Kirsten Place
Corvallis, Oregon 97330
Telephone:1-800-326-9272
SAN: 298-1238
Email: Ecopress@compuserve.com
World Wide Web: http://www.peak.org /~cbeatty/

Also available from Robert Beatty:

Journey of the Tern ISBN 0-9639705-8-5

Printed on paper which is 60% recycled, 10% post-consumer.
No elemental chlorine was used to create the paper (ECF).
ISBN: 0-9639705-4-2
LCCC: 96-083915

Printed in the United States of America

10 9 8 7 6 5 4 3 2 1

SAPO

The Programmer

-7-

The Laboratory

-71-

Sendero Luminoso

-139-

Sapo

-197-

The Courier

-285-

PART ONE: The Programmer

CHAPTER ONE

Death is usually a surprise.

When death begins, it is seldom recognized. A virus enters the body and a cell goes awry; a brake pad wears down and a traffic light turns yellow. The death process is initiated and life goes toward it unsuspecting.

Young Henry Beaufort drove sleepily down the Detroit street in his old Volvo. His body was numb from thirteen hours in front of a computer screen, but his mind buzzed with display algorithms and search routines, refusing to let go of the day's work. Henry's brain was like a pit bull – once it sank its teeth in, it would hang on until the job was done. Even when he wasn't thinking consciously, his subconscious would tug the problem around.

He called this "background processing." Inspiration would often come to him in the shower, after a good night's sleep, or while driving down the highway. Intricate source code and elegant flow diagrams would process themselves through the pages of his mind.

He flicked on his turn signal, glanced at the mirror, checked his blind spot and pulled onto the entrance ramp of the highway.

Henry worked an odd schedule. Even though he was now thirteen months graduated and working in the "real world," the college routine – and many of Henry's adolescent habits – remained. Three years of scrabbling for computer time in the university computer science lab had ingrained these strange hours into him. He started at three in the afternoon and normally left the office well after midnight. He liked these hours because he could work undisturbed, had the computer to himself, and didn't have to explain to anyone why he didn't have a date on a Friday night.

To look at him, you would have thought Henry had spent too much of his childhood with his little face pressed up against a computer screen, and too little time growing up. This night Henry wore his usual clothing: polyester pants, patterned shirt, and white sneakers. His short reddish brown hair stuck in clumps to his head, giving him a striking resemblance to a rusty Brillo pad on top of a pear. His socks were the wrong color for his pants. You could see the crew neck undershirt in the v-neck of his shirt. The sleeves of his jacket were too short and his belt didn't quite hold up his pants. But when you put him all together into a single picture, Henry Beaufort *fit*. He was color-coordinated and fully accessorized in a sort of *alternative neo-nerdism* style that was quite acceptable to members of his ilk.

Four o'clock in the morning. Empty six-lane highway.

He drove in the left lane at a steady seventy-four miles an hour, exactly nine miles over the speed limit, which is what he allowed himself. Just fast enough not to irritate anyone else on the road but not so fast as to attract the attention of the police.

A silver sports car zipped past him on the right. It looked like a Mazda RX-7, but by the time he focused on it, the car was in front of him and pulling away.

He automatically turned on his blinker and moved out of the fast lane. A wave of regret poured through him when he realized that once again he had gotten in somebody's way; he had forced the other guy to pass him on the right. It never occurred to him that seventy-four miles an hour might be considered "slow."

Then two large cars zoomed past, one on each side. A dark Continental on the left, and a green Bonneville on the right. Both going around a hundred miles an hour. "Geez!" he said. "What's the rush?" He moved all the way to the right, into the slowest lane, hoping to be safe there.

An instant later he was slamming on the brakes.

The three vehicles were sliding every which way in front of him. The Continental had hit the Mazda, spinning it out of control like a destabilized rocket. It ricochetted off the concrete wall, then bounced back and clipped the Bonneville. Henry plummeted toward the chaos.

At the last second he yanked the wheel to the left. His screeching Volvo jerked, cut loose and careened sidways into the Bonneville with an explosion of shattering glass and crumpling metal. The Bonneville rammed into the wall. Henry's car bounced off and spun back into the highway before coming to a rest.

Stillness.

Henry tried to move. His seat belt wouldn't let him go. He couldn't get the door unlatched, and his window wouldn't open.

Am I bleeding? Do my legs work? Maybe I've got broken bones and I should just sit here and wait for the ambulance.

Peering through the cracked windshield, he couldn't see much in the darkness. To his astonishment, he didn't feel hurt, but he figured that people in the other cars must be. He finally found the catch on his seatbelt and released himself. He crawled through the open sunroof. His legs seemed all right, though they shook uncontrollably.

Crouched on top of his Volvo, he got a view of the scene in the flat light of the streetlamps. The Mazda sports coupe was mangled into an incredible shape, like a ball of tinfoil. The Bonnevillie was smashed up against the concrete wall. He couldn't make out the details of the Continental, which had stopped in the middle of the highway about a hundred feet away.

He crawled down the windshield and over the hood, then stepped onto the pavement and looked around, wondering what to do. The road was deserted. No other traffic. No bystanders. No emergency vehicles coming. Everything dark and still.

He approached the Bonneville. Its rear quarter panel was caved in where the Mazda had clipped it. Its side was crushed where his Volvo had slammed. The driver's side window had been smashed completely out of its frame and lay now in the lap of the driver, who sat with his head slumped forward.

Henry's heart was pounding, and his legs continued to wobble. But he inched forward to the driver's door, which was pulverized beyond recognition. He didn't even try to open it. He reached through the broken window, grabbed the man's shoulders and pulled. He knew this wasn't the smart thing to do, but he was desperate to get the man out of the car. Henry pulled again, lifting the driver by his arm pits. The broken glass tumbled off his lap. That's when Henry saw that the man's legs were missing.

He dropped the body.

A spasm recoiled through his stomach. He turned away in a panic.

Dizzy, he stumbled around his Volvo. He didn't want to look in the other vehicles. He was scared of what he would find.

He unlocked his door and got in, realizing how stupid he had been for climbing out the sunroof. The door wasn't jammed, it was just locked. His windows weren't even broken. Now he was scared to death, but at least he was thinking straight. He picked up his car phone, something he should have done immediately.

With trembling hands, he dialed the highway emergency number.

The passenger door jerked open and somebody swung into his car. "Hang up the phone!"

Next to him sat a young woman. "Hang up the phone!" she ordered him. "Put it down!"

Not knowing why, he followed her command. She wore faded jeans and a well-traveled brown leather jacket. She had a lean build, dark ruddy skin and long black hair. Her foreign accent was slight but palpable.

"Where did you come from?" he asked.

She banged the car door shut. Incredibly, the door worked perfectly, though he'd seen it was dented on the outside.

"Listen," the woman said. "I don't have time to explain. Just drive."

"Drive?"

A hundred feet away, the driver's door of the Continental opened. Henry looked at it in amazement.

"Yes! Drive!"

"I can't just drive away from this!"

She looked back, checking for something.

When he followed her gaze, he could see the headlights of two more cars. They seemed to be approaching very fast. And they didn't have the flashing lights of police cars.

"Go!" she told him.

"But, what's going on? We can't just leave the scene of an accident! *Where* did you come from?"

Henry could now hear in the distance the howl of emergency sirens. He had lived in the city long enough to know that they were still a long way off.

Meanwhile, two men had stepped out of the Continental and were striding toward his Volvo. Henry was flabbergasted that so many people were appearing on a crash site where he'd presumed everyone was dead.

She interrupted his confusion. "If you don't drive," she barked at him. "They'll kill us both!"

As the two men from the Continental came closer, the woman pulled a gun from the pocket of her leather jacket.

Henry's hands were still shaking. He noticed hers were not.

When the two men were less than ten yards away, he saw that they also had pistols. The headlights of the approaching cars glared in his rear-view mirror.

He turned the ignition key. The engine started immediately.

"Drive!" she screamed.

He stomped on the accelerator. The Volvo leaped forward, tires spinning. As the two men split apart, the car's bumper caught one of them. He rolled up over the hood, smashed into the windshield and flipped out of sight.

Even as Henry struggled to control the car, he found his eyes glued to the rear-view mirror. He thought he saw a body on the ground. Accelerating away from the scene, he watched the headlights of the other vehicles grow smaller. They must have stopped near the other man from the Continental, who seemed to be waving his arms and pointing toward the fleeing Volvo.

He also saw, farther behind, the flashers of a paramedic vehicle or police car.

"Just keep driving," the young woman said.

He turned his eyes forward. He wasn't going to argue with her. Although she hadn't yet pointed it at him, she still had the gun in her hand. He sped down the deserted highway, amazed that the old Volvo could take such a collision and still do eighty miles an hour.

Could this woman, he wondered, have been driving the silver Mazda? It seemed impossible that she'd survive such a wreck, but where else could she have come from? She didn't act scared. Was that a Spanish accent?

The way she was sitting made him think she was hurt. She kept shifting her weight to the right, even when she turned to the left to watch behind them. Then, in the flare of a streetlight, he saw a dark stain on the underside of her left leg.

"Where do you want to go?" he asked her, in as neutral a tone as he could muster. He decided he would drop her off at any convenient location, just to get her out of his car.

"Anywhere they can't find me . . ." she muttered.

As he was about to suggest a police station or a hospital, his passenger threw herself to the floor. He saw then the flashing lights of squad cars coming from the opposite direction. They were undoubtedly responding to a call about an accident a few miles up the road. They flew past and were gone.

"What's going on?" he demanded.

She gave him a long look as she climbed back onto the seat, seeming to reach some quick conclusion about him. She kept the gun turned away. "Those men back there are after me."

"I guessed that much," he said. "And the police are after you, too?"

"No. But there's no sense in getting the police involved in this. I don't trust them. Either way, they'll slow me down."

"Look, we just got in a terrible accident. The police *have* to get involved!"

"The accident was nothing. It was the only way they could stop my car."

"Stop your car? You mean that wasn't an accident?"

"No."

"They hit you on purpose?"

"Yes."

"Why?"

She shrugged. "I don't know. Maybe they were out of bullets."

He thought he saw a hint of an ironic smile.

"What?"

"They had to get me out of the car," she went on, as if these were simple facts that anyone could recognize. "They should have just followed me and called the others, but they were too greedy for the kill. They wanted the credit."

"For catching you?"

"For killing me."

"Why do they want to kill you?"

She gave him another assessing look, but she had one hand pressed against her temple as if she felt dizzy. "I shouldn't talk so much."

"But why would anyone want—"

"Because of the package," she snapped, "the package."

"What package?"

Henry's words were lost in the wail of a siren. The woman

dove to the floor again as more police cars raced by. He watched them disappear in his rear-view mirror. How many police cars do they need for one accident? Maybe there was something else going on, too.

He didn't like her on the floor. Not that he enjoyed having her in the seat either, but he definitely didn't like seeing her crouched there like that. She looked like a jaguar ready to pounce. And he was the only goat around.

He checked his rear-view mirror again. When the police were out of sight, he said, "It's OK now."

She didn't answer. In the strobe-like flashes of passing streetlights, he saw her crumpled on the floor with her head against the seat. She still held the gun, but she was unconscious.

CHAPTER TWO

He pulled onto the shoulder and stopped. No cars were approaching from either direction.

The nearest streetlight gave him just enough illumination to study his passenger. Her shoulders rose and fell jerkily with her breath. Her black hair fell tangled on her shoulders. In the weak light her reddish skin looked as dark as the understory of a forest. Even unconscious, she had a lean, muscled grace like a large cat. He wondered how badly she was hurt. Was she going to bleed to death in his car? He saw she'd already left a stain on the seat.

He closed his eyes a moment, trying to get oriented. Though his hands still trembled on the wheel, his pit-bull mind had latched onto this problem. What's going on? Who's chasing her? Why doesn't she want to go to the police? She doesn't seem to be carrying anything, other than the gun. So what's the package? Doesn't she need a doctor right away?

He was torn between calling the police station, grabbing the gun, shaking her awake to demand an explanation, and running like heck.

A few minutes passed. His brain replayed the skidding cars, the crash, the advancing men with pistols. He heard the crunch as the man crumbled the Volvo's hood, and he saw the curled form on the pavement in his mirror.

Another thought occurred to him. Had he killed that man he hit? He knew he had fled the scene of an accident–excusable, he thought, because guns were being waved around–but if he'd actually *killed* that man he was guilty of manslaughter! Would the police come after him? Had the officers in the squad car noticed his Volvo as they sped by? Did they know about him too?

And what, meanwhile, should he do about this woman and her gun?

Without making a conscious decision, he turned the engine off and pulled the key out of the ignition. Cautiously he leaned over and picked the gun out of her hand. It was lighter than he thought it would be, almost like plastic, but he knew that was impossible. Holding his breath, he reached over her head, unlatched the glove compartment and slipped the gun inside. With a muffled click, the glove compartment closed, and he locked it with the key.

Her eyes opened–a flash of black–and they were staring back at him with the violence of a predator.

Startled, he yanked his hand back and tried to hide the key.

"What did you do with my weapon?" she asked, made suddenly anxious by its absence.

He couldn't think of an evasion. "I locked it in the glove compartment."

"Why?"

He didn't know what to say. The real answer, of course, was because it frightened him.

"Why did you put it in your glove compartment? I'm not going to shoot you."

"That wasn't, uh, obvious to me."

She smiled. Pulling her wounded leg after her, she climbed into the seat and checked the highway around them. Satisfied that they were safe for the moment, she turned to him again. "I'm not kidnapping you. I just needed to get out of there. The weapon was for them, not you."

He'd seen, as she'd eased onto the seat, that the dark area was spreading rapidly down her jeans. How could she be so coherent now, a minute after being unconscious?

"Were they really," he asked, "going to kill you?"

"Us. They would have killed you too."

"But, why me? I didn't do anything!"

"That was not, uh, obvious to them," she said. He could see she meant to smile again, but she winced.

"You're losing a lot of blood," he observed. The comment sounded stupid as soon as he'd made it, as if he'd told General Custer there were a lot of arrows sticking out of his chest.

She nodded, looked down at her leg. "I need some bandages. I can't hold out much longer just sitting here."

"You look weak." Another brilliant comment, he thought to himself. "I'll take you to the hospital."

He jumped when she put her hand on his arm. "No," she said. "No."

Exasperated, but wanting to help her, Henry said, "What *do* you want me to do then?"

"Take me somewhere safe."

He started the car and drove. The streetlights blinked rhythmically by. In a moment she had passed out again.

The guard at the gate of Henry's apartment complex didn't wake up when Henry drove into the parking garage and took his normal spot. The garage was full of cars and empty of people, as usual at this hour. Unlike New York, Detroit did sleep now and again.

He got out of the Volvo, went around to the passenger side and opened the partially damaged door. The woman's limp body had rolled to the side, onto her wounded leg. The buzz of the fluorescent lights was the only sound.

Suddenly he lost his nerve. What was he doing? He had killed somebody! He had to go to the police! He should be driving to the station to turn himself in.

Why did that thought terrify him worse than what he was doing now?

Stalling, he turned the woman to take the pressure off her leg. At that point he saw blood all over the seat, and he pulled his hands away from her. Was she dying? Who was she? What made him think she wasn't a common criminal?

Detached from him, his mind computed the variations like an algorithm. Soon it informed him that he definitely did not want to go to the police, nor did he want to drop this woman half-dead and against her will at the hospital. The police would be looking for them—both of them—at the hospital. She had known that. Take me somewhere safe, she had said. Therefore he had come to his apartment, which was the only place he could think of. Nothing ever happened at his apartment.

He leaned over to pull her out of the car. Once in the apartment, he would somehow get her leg bandaged and stop the bleeding.

"Is that you, whiz kid?" a voice called.

He slammed the door and turned.

"You been working late again?"

Jimmy the rent-a-cop was approaching from behind the car on the other side. Since Henry was one of the few people who drove through his gate between twelve and five each night, Jimmy had grown rather fond of Henry. And Henry had to admit that Jimmy came as close to being a friend as anyone else he knew.

"Yeah, been working on a big project," Henry said.

"Why didn't you wake me up when you came in?"

"Didn't want to bother you."

"Aw, man, you know I'm not really sleeping, my eyes are just closed. Wow, what happened to your car?"

From the back, Jimmy had a view of the car's cracked-up side, though he couldn't see the full extent of the damage.

"Ah . . . somebody slammed into me, hard, in the parking lot at work. . . . "

"That's a drag, man, you gonna sue?"

"I don't think I can sue," Henry said, his mind suddenly filling with a hundred thousand database records from the no-fault insurance system he had infiltrated a few years ago. He flushed his mind, irritated by the useless information. That's when he noticed Jimmy peering through the back windshield at the passenger seat.

Jimmy's lips were just about to form a question. An answer jumped into Henry's mind and he blurted it out.

"That's my date," he said.

Jimmy turned to him, surprised.

"Yeah," Henry rushed on. "I met her at the bar. She's drunk though, really drunk."

Jimmy peered again. "She looks unconscious."

"Well, not quite."

"C'mon, she's passed out. What's she been drinking? Since when do you go to bars, whiz kid?"

"Just looking for some company," Henry muttered, embarrassed, and came around to stand in front of Jimmy to block his view.

Jimmy backed up a bit. "Yeah, need some company. I know how that is."

"I'll take care of her. I don't want her getting scared, though, Jimmy, you know what I mean?"

Jimmy's face changed, as he suddenly realized he was intruding, blocking the path between a man and his lay, a sin in any social context.

"Sure, kid," he said, nodding. "I just wanted to make sure you're OK. I'll get back to my post." Jimmy was speaking in a conspiratorial whisper now, moving slowly backward. Then he turned and hurried away, glancing over his shoulder a few times. Before he disappeared round the corner, he gave Henry the sign of the fist and a big lecherous grin.

Henry Beaufort lived in a studio apartment in an older complex on Woodward Avenue in downtown Detroit. He was a little embarrassed by the disarray of his place. Bed unmade. Socks and underwear on the floor. Unwashed plates in the kitchen sink. Books and papers scattered everywhere. A mess around his computer. Yesterday's pizza box sitting on the desk. Luckily, his new guest didn't seem to mind. Unconsciousness tends to make one miss the little things.

Having no other place to put her, he laid her on the bed. Her leg left a smear of blood across the bedspread. He looked at his hands. Blood. He glanced back at the door. Blood. Carpet. Blood.

She began to wake. "What's happening?" she said, bewildered. In her state of semi-consciousness, her accent was heavy and her words barely understandable. Then she slipped into a language he took to be Spanish. "¿Qué esta pasando? ¿Dónde está mi Glock?"

"We're in a safe place. I need to fix your leg."

"Bandages."

"Right!"

He ran to the bathroom, opened the cabinet over the sink. Band-Aids. No good. He opened the other cabinet and pulled out a bunch of towels.

When he returned to the other room, she was unbuckling her belt and trying to push down her pants. The tight jeans stuck on her bloody leg where the fabric was ripped. She grimaced in pain. He dropped the towels at the foot of the bed, sat beside her and helped her peel away the denim. When the jeans were bundled around her knees, she lay down again, exhausted.

He grabbed one leather boot and yanked on it until it came free. Then he wrestled with the other one. She remained vaguely aware of what he was doing, but was not strong enough to help him. Once her boots were off, he removed her jacket as well, to get it out of the way. He saw then the empty leather holster under her left arm. He rolled up the tails of her shirt, a slate-grey silk. Next he pulled the jeans off and tossed them on the floor. Her legs were long and dark, the left one smeared with blood from her panties to her ankle. Gently he turned her so he could find the wound. By dabbing away some of the blood, he could see that the laceration cut across the back of her thigh and ended at her buttock.

He ran into the kitchen and grabbed some dish towels, which were thinner and softer than the bath towels. When he returned, her eyes were closed.

He sat beside her. Not knowing any better, he pressed the cloth to her wound and tried to soak up the blood. He couldn't help observing how tautly her legs were muscled. Flustered, he tried to touch only the wounded thigh, not the cheek above it.

Her eyes burst open. "What are you doing?"

"I don't know," he admitted. "I've never done this before."

"Get cool water, alcohol," she told him. Her eyes closed again.

"I don't have any alcohol. I've never cut myself like this before. I'm just a computer programmer!"

She didn't open her eyes, but for a moment her face relaxed. He thought she almost smiled. "Just water then, programmer. Don't worry, I'm not going to die on you."

Fetching a bowl of water, he dampened one of his dish towels and washed the wound, ultra-conscious of each touch and the pain that jerked her. She held herself steady, gripping the bed. Once he had cleaned the wound, he started dressing it. As he worked, she raised herself slightly so he could wrap the towel around her leg. She showed him how to make a compress and tie it in such a way that it would stay in place. She spoke softly, and with confidence. She had obviously done this before, for herself, and for others.

When they had finished, she lay still again. Her eyes fluttered shut.

He sat on the bed beside her. Henry didn't know what to do next. He was sure she was going to die.

"Don't worry, programmer, I'll be alright," she whispered and fell asleep.

He heard a siren go by. The sound turned his head. Though he was nowhere near the accident anymore, and probably no one had seen him except the men from the Continental, he was convinced the police would catch up with him. He had broken the law, and they were the police–they were *supposed* to catch him. For that reason, he ought to turn himself in.

He looked back at her. He had never had a woman half naked in his bed before. He decided he wouldn't turn himself in just yet. He would wait until morning.

He wanted to help her. He didn't know where she was from, or why those men were after her, but he somehow felt she was on the right side. Perhaps it was because she hadn't shot him in the head.

He got some fresh water and tried to clean the blood off the carpet with a towel. After failing miserably, he decided to clean the kitchen. Then he cleaned the bathroom. Then he shoved the pizza box into the wastebasket and straightened out the mess around his computer. He went to the window and looked outside. He could see a few cars going down Woodward Avenue. He looked hard, for a long time, but nothing seemed out of the ordinary. A police car would drive by every once in a while, ignoring the apartment complex. His apartment seemed like a different world, a world where nothing terrible could have happened.

He crossed toward the bed. Her worn leather jacket lay on the floor where he had tossed it. He knelt down beside it, hoping she wouldn't wake up.

He reached into the first pocket. Nothing. Second pocket: wad of twenty-dollar bills and two full boxes of bullets labeled "9mm". Inside pocket: wallet and American passport.

He opened the passport and read the name. Jetta Mendoza Santiago. If she's American, he thought, why the weird name and the accent? The pages of her passport were crowded with stamps: Brazil, Colombia, Peru, Argentina, Bolivia, Chile, Nicaragua, El Salvador, South Africa, Egypt, Saudi Arabia, Turkey, Northern Ireland, Germany. In the wallet he found several driver's licenses, including a Florida license, a New York license, and an international license, all in different names. He found more money, American hundreds and Brazilian cruzeiros. He also found a list of phone numbers, some other numbers that he couldn't identify, and a bunch of credit cards from different countries.

He took a blanket out of the closet and laid it over her. He sat on the floor next to the bed awhile, looking at her, wondering who she was and what was going to happen.

When his restlessness faded a little, he pulled off his sneakers, sat in his reading chair—a comfortable recliner—and went to sleep.

CHAPTER THREE

When Henry woke the next morning, his mind had solved one part of the problem.

It was a crucial question: What did the police know about the accident? Were they looking for him? Did they know this woman, Jetta Santiago? There was only one way to find out. The night before, he'd supposed he would turn himself in. Now he had another idea. Not just yet, he thought. Not just yet.

The woman still lay on her stomach, head turned to the side. She had pushed away the blanket, revealing her legs and dish-towel bandage. Her black hair fell across her back. Studying her face, he noticed for the first time the fine scar on her left cheek.

He went to the bathroom, brushed his teeth, and thought about his plan while he showered. His idea frightened him. He had never done such a thing before. He had never even thought about doing it. But now he had a reason.

He put on fresh polyester trousers, a v-neck short-sleeved shirt and sneakers. It was Saturday, so he didn't have to go to work. He sat down at his desk, a few feet from the sleeping woman on the bed. He hit the master power switch and waited for the PC to boot up. He clicked on the Office Building icon, and waited for the modem to dial. The sound of beeps and static soon fell silent, and a login prompt appeared on the screen. He logged into the computer at work with his user name and password.

He worked for a group of six men. They called themselves an "investment firm." In truth, they would watch for a troubled company, swoop in with excessive amounts of other people's money, take it over and tear it to shreds. They could usually turn a company around in six months. If they couldn't turn it around, then they'd break it to pieces and sell it. Either way, they made money. They depended on Henry, not only to run their own computer system, but to supply them with market information, company profiles and access to the internal databases of their latest target. Henry was the only one who really understood the computers.

He checked the phone book to find the listing for the police station closest to the scene of the accident. (He refrained from thinking "scene of the crime.") When he found the number, he took its first six digits and issued the following command to the prompt:

TROLL 664-898?

Troll was a program he had written. It was really very simple, just a few lines of code. It used the company modems to call every local phone number that began with 664-898. The question mark was a wildcard. The computer filled in the wildcard with the digits 0 through 9, automatically calling ten phone numbers in sequence.

Originally he had named the program Troll because it reminded him of trolling for walleye with his dad in Lake St. Clair, dragging hooks through open water, hoping to catch something. Later it occurred to him that the word had another meaning: it was a name for an evil, cave-dwelling creature. He liked that coincidence. It reminded him of the fantasy game *Dungeons & Dragons*, which had fascinated him during his college years.

The office computer used an operating system called UNIX, known for its arcane language and its incredible power. Because he wasn't in the office, he couldn't actually hear the modems dialing. But a few minutes later, the computer gave him a report:

```
664-8980    NO CARRIER
664-8981    NO CARRIER
664-8982    NO CARRIER
664-8983    NO CARRIER
664-8984    NO CARRIER
664-8985    NO CARRIER
664-8986    NO CARRIER
664-8987    NO CARRIER
664-8988    NO CARRIER
664-8989    NO CARRIER
```

He frowned. Not what he was looking for. The phrase "no carrier" meant that the number either was not in use or that it represented a fax machine or a voice line. In any case, it wasn't a computer.

Henry knew that when a new office building was constructed the phone company assigned it a block of phone numbers. Usually at least one of these numbers would be dedicated to the computer, and so having the voice number for a building could usually lead him to the computer's number. Of course, the police might do things differently.

He wondered how large the police station was. Did it perhaps have more than ten numbers? He issued a new command:

TROLL 664-89??

The computer went away for a while. He knew it would require a long time, perhaps thirty minutes, to complete a hundred calls. He was glad he was the only one who ever looked at the phone bills. His bosses hadn't put him in charge of phones, but he normally took care of such administrative tasks by default. These tasks were considered quite menial by his high-energy, high-rolling employers. Without really appreciating what he did, they tossed such matters at him.

"What's going on?"

The voice made him jump. He turned around to look at her.

She was sitting up and staring right at him.

"What's going on?" she repeated. She sounded a little confused, perhaps even frightened. He didn't detect any anger in her voice, only a strong desire for an immediate answer, which he knew was in his best interest to provide.

"We got in an accident last night, remember? You told me to take you some place safe, but not the hospital or the police, so I brought you here."

She was looking around, gathering in the setting. "Yes, I remember," she said slowly. "The programmer."

He nodded. "Right."

She twisted to look at the back of her thigh. She put her hand on the makeshift bandage. "You did a good job," she noted. "I couldn't have done much better."

Probably not, he thought. You told me exactly what to do. You just forgot.

"What are you doing there?" she asked again.

"I'm working on the computer," he said, not really telling her anything she hadn't seen for herself. He had learned long ago that the harder he tried to answer someone's question about computers the less likely the person was to understand.

"Yes, but what are you doing?"

"Well, I'm trying to get into the police station to see what's happening."

"Trying to get into the police station?" She didn't understand or she didn't believe him. He was not distressed. Other than his employers, there weren't many people who expected much from him.

"I want to know if they're looking for us . . . me, really. I just want to know if they're looking for me . . . whether I should turn myself in."

"Don't turn yourself in," she said immediately. She stated it like a general principle, to be followed in any and all situations.

"Why not? If I've broken the law, I should turn myself in, and I know, actually, that I've broken the law."

She didn't dispute his legal assessment. But she said firmly, "Police can't be trusted."

"Where do you come from?" he asked.

"It doesn't matter where I'm from. Police all over the world are corrupt. It's the nature of the beast."

Moving the wounded leg slowly, she slid over on the bed for a better view of the screen.

"So you're trying to crack the police computer?"

"Yes, but I don't know if it will work."

"Won't they have passwords?"

"Sure, but I haven't even got that far yet. I need a phone number first."

She nodded and studied the screen.

It surprised him that a person who carried a gun would also be interested in computers.

"What does 'no carrier' mean?" she asked.

"That means it's not the right number." As before, he gave the simplest possible answer. His bosses were seldom interested in the means of access, only the significance of the intelligence he gathered.

"What does it mean, though? No carrier. Carrier for what? Carrier for the modem signal?"

Surprised again, he explained. "The carrier is the signal on the other end of the phone. When the modem calls, it puts out a signal and attempts to negotiate a communication protocol. If there's a compatible modem on the other side, using the right baud rate, then it can establish a link."

"It finds a carrier."

"Right."

"What if it's a regular line and somebody picks up?"

"They get a weird noise in their ear and put the phone down."

She smiled. "But if it's a computer . . . then you're in luck ."

"Right."

"And your modem must automatically adjust the baud rate to match the other computer."

Who was this woman? he wondered. And why were they having a conversation about computers? Her bare legs hung down off the bed.

"How does your leg feel?"

"It's stiff, but I don't think it's real serious."

"It seemed serious last night."

"I lost a lot of blood, but I'll be OK."

"Then what are you going to do now?" This, he thought, was what they should really be discussing.

She shook her head. "They're on my trail. I need to keep a low profile."

"But who's after you?"

"I don't know."

"You don't know?"

"No," she said. She looked down at her leg, then moved it slightly to see what would happen. She flinched in pain.

To Henry, it seemed like she was telling the truth. She really *didn't* know who was pursuing her. But he had no experience with liars other than the men he worked for.

"You want something to eat? To help get your strength back?"

She nodded. "Yes, that would be good."

He went to the kitchen. He found the refrigerator empty. Two ancient frozen waffles in the freezer. Nothing in the cupboards except his never-ending supply of Mountain Dew. He didn't have anything else and he never needed anything else. Mountain Dew, pizza and McDonald's encompassed his entire diet.

He didn't even have any coffee to offer her. She seemed like the kind of person who would want coffee. South American, Columbian, perhaps. The hint of long *e*'s in her short *I*'s; the rolling *r*'s. Was she part of a drug ring? He wasn't sure he wanted to know. Earlier this morning he had felt calm, and somewhat in control, especially after he had started working on the computer. But now his mind was swimming again. Drugs. Police. Accident. Guns. A probable dead man. A beautiful woman. It was enough to make him nauseated.

"I'm sorry, I haven't been to the grocery store in a while. I've been busy lately."

"That's alright." She lay down.

"I'll go out and get us something on the corner. You stay here?"

"Yes, I'm staying, programmer."

"Why do you call me that?"

"I don't know your name."

"Why don't you ask?"

"In my line of work, it's considered rude. In fact, it's a good way to get shot."

"Oh. Nevermind."

He grabbed his keys, scurried out of the apartment, and locked the door behind him. He took the elevator to the street, then walked a block until he came to the McDonald's. The cash register lady recognized him and smiled.

"Hello, Henry, how are you today?"

"I'm fine," he muttered, avoiding eye contact. He glanced around the place. Sometimes the police came in here on their break. They must be looking for me, he thought. There's probably an APB out for my arrest. I've got to keep a low profile. Where'd I get that phrase?

"You look kind of down, today, Henry, what's the matter? Your hard disk get soft?"

"Ah, no. . . I've just been working on an important problem." He rattled off his order. "I didn't have time to eat last night," he added to explain the quantity.

She fetched and bagged the items, took his money and counted out the change. "Don't work too hard, honey," she smiled as she handed him the order.

"No, I won't." He took the bags and darted out.

Back at his apartment, he noticed that his guest had grabbed her jacket off the floor and tucked it behind her on the bed. Did she realize he'd rifled the pockets? She gave no sign; she was staring at the computer screen.

During this time the computer had methodically checked each of the one hundred numbers. As it worked through them, it displayed each number on the screen with the phrase "no carrier." All except one.

"I think you've hooked a fish," she said.

He hurriedly set the McDonald's bag beside her, and then sat down in front of the computer.

664-8992 CONNECTED AT 9600 BAUD

"That's what we're looking for!" he said, unable to hide his excitement. He hit Control-C to disconnect and stop the program. Then he issued a new command:

CALL 664-8992

"Is that the police station?" she asked as she pulled food out of the bag. She handed him a Sausage McMuffin, which he took and began chewing right over the keyboard.

"It could be, but not necessarily. That's what we have to find out."

"But if it connected, then it must be a computer, right?"

"Right."

He waited for the modem to dial and re-connect. Suddenly the screen went blank, paused, and changed:

UNIX 3.2.4: SOUTHFIELD STATION: STATE CRIMINAL DATABASE. LOGIN:

"That's it!" he cried. He couldn't help himself, he had to get a Mountain Dew. He ran to the kitchen and popped one the way a construction worker cracks open a Miller. He was on a roll.

"What do we do now?" she asked, as excited as he. "This is surprisingly good coffee, by the way."

"Colombian mocha," he muttered. I *knew* she was a drug dealer, he thought to himself, but his attention was on the screen. His fingers were flying. The operating system was UNIX. The mission was penetration. He had done this before.

Jumping over to the command prompt on his own system, he issued a new command:

KNOCKER

"What are you doing now?"

"I'm running a password tester."

"Where did you get that?" she asked, obviously surprised such a thing existed.

"I wrote it," he said. "It's no big deal. It just tries a list of user names and passwords."

"Why do you call it Knocker?"

"Because it knocks on the door to see if the system will let me in."

He watched the program try a list of user names against the

login prompt. After the first three, the police station computer interrupted the program and disconnected the line:

MAXIMUM INVALID LOGINS EXCEEDED. NO CARRIER.

"Shoot!"

"What's happened? I thought 'no carrier' was bad."

"It hung up on me. The system administrator of this computer has a pretty good sense for security. Most of them disable the feature for limiting the number of unsuccessful logins because it's annoying to the users. He's obviously a little more concerned for security than the average administrator."

"What next?"

"We'll try it again."

He had already learned quite a bit about this new system. He now knew the phone number, the operating system, its version, and the competency of the system administrator. He had a new idea. He called and reconnected.

UNIX 3.2.4: SOUTHFIELD STATION: STATE CRIMINAL DATABASE. LOGIN:

He typed "UUCP" at the login prompt.

It let him in immediately. "Bingo!"

"You got in?" she asked. "How did you do it? Who's UUCP?"

"I figured the police station probably used UUCP to communicate with other police computers. The FBI used to use UUCP, so police stations did too. It's obsolete now because it's being replaced by the new network protocols, but a lot of these guys still have it on their system. It comes standard with the UNIX operating system software."

"But what's UUCP?"

"It stands for UNIX to UNIX Copy. It's for transferring files over the phone lines between different computers. It's a simple way to set up a crude wide-area network."

"But isn't that a security risk?"

"Any connection to the outside world is a security risk. But a good system administrator will set it up so that all UUCP files go into a harmless public directory on his computer where they can't do any damage. You see, he can't shut down UUCP without shutting down his access to the outside world, but he can restrict what UUCP can do inside the machine. That's the defense."

"What about this guy, did he do that?"

He tried issuing a few commands, but the system ignored him. "Yup. See, he's got us stuck in the public directory. Normally, I wouldn't be able to do anything from here. This guy's pretty smart."

"It is a police station, after all."

"Sure, but you'd be surprised how bad security is on most systems. Administrators have better things to do. They're normally too busy with all their other duties to worry about this kind of junk."

"Are we stuck now? Is there anything else we can try?"

"We're just beginning," he said. "Now the fun starts." He took another bite of his sandwich and a swig of soda while he contemplated the screen. He glanced over at her. She was staring at him expectantly.

He listed some files, changed directories a few times, then listed some more files. He meandered through the system, browsing various file lists. He picked up the soda for another big swig.

The plan formulated in his brain like the moves of a master chess player. He set down the Mountain Dew and returned his fingers to the keyboard. There was a trace of a smile on his face.

"You've got it, don't you! You've figured it out!"

He started writing the program, his fingers moving so quickly that individual keystrokes could no longer be heard, only a rush of noise. A few minutes later, he stopped abruptly. He looked at the screen and smiled. Checkmate.

"What did you do?" she wanted to know. She tried to lift herself to see better, but she winced and stopped immediately.

Henry was impressed with her interest in what he was doing. Most people couldn't have cared less about the technical details. He felt like he had a new friend, or at least a partner: a partner in crime.

"Tell me!" she demanded. "How did you do it?"

"It's not done yet."

"But you've got it. I can tell by the look on your face. What did you do?"

"I'm still waiting."

"But what did you do?"

"I laid an egg."

"What?"

"A cuckoo's egg."

"I don't get it. What's a cuckoo?"

"A cuckoo is a bird."

"So what."

"The female cuckoo lays her egg in another bird's nest. The nesting mother doesn't recognize it as an alien egg, so she incubates it, hatches it and raises it as her own. When the baby cuckoo grows up it kicks out the other birds and takes over the nest. I laid a cuckoo's egg."

"How?"

"You see, sitting here in the public directory I can't really do anything. Even if I write a program, I don't have authorization to run it. There are security daemons that protect the critical parts of the system from tampering."

"How did you get past them?"

"There's a program called Cron on computers like this one. The Cron runs the programs that are scheduled to work in the background, like system accounting programs, backups and month-end reports. The Cron is a system daemon, so it has free access to the entire system at all times. The system trusts it completely and will let it do anything it wants."

"But wouldn't a program that important be protected?"

"Sure."

"Well, how did you get to it?"

"There's a couple of holes. Sometimes the system administrator is smart and he patches up the holes. Other times he doesn't. This guy knew a few of the holes, and patched them, so I couldn't get in, but he missed one."

"Yes?"

"Every UNIX system is shipped with a text editor program called VI. It allows you to edit text files."

"Like a word processor."

"Right. VI used to be all the rage back in the eighties. Now it's old news. It still ships with every UNIX system, but hardly anybody uses it anymore."

"But if it came with the system wouldn't the security daemons control it just like everything else?"

"Sure, 99 percent of the time they do, but there's a bug."

"What sort of bug?"

"Well, the VI editor has a neat feature. Imagine you're typing along and something goes wrong, like the power goes off or your terminal locks up. Normally you would lose the contents of your file. But with the VI-editor, when you boot it up again it automatically detects the fact that there was an abnormal termination and asks if you want to save your previous work. Most people just press Enter, which is like saying, 'Sure, put it in the normal place.' But if you type in a filename the VI-editor will write the file anywhere you want."

"Anywhere? Doesn't it check with the security daemons first?"

"Nope. There's the bug. Creates a hole big enough to drive a truck through, if you know about it. So I wrote a program that tells the system to create a new user account called 'Smith' and give him full system privileges. Then I broke out of the VI-editor. Then I restarted it. It asked me where I wanted to save my previous file."

"On top of the Cron file! That's how you laid the cuckoo's egg!"

"Right. It's incubating as we speak. In a few minutes, the system will run the imposter Cron, which in turn will run my program, create a new account and provide us with system privileges."

"Write down the command to provide system privileges to the Smith account," she said, gesturing to the pad beside the keyboard.

He picked up a pencil, then paused. "Write it down?"

"Yeah, you typed it so fast I couldn't see it. What does it look like?"

"That's easy." He issued the command to print the program:

```
LP -DHOMEPC /USR/TOOLBOX/MAKEROOTACCOUNT.C
```

"How many programmers are there where you work?"

"Just me."

"You run the computer by yourself?"

"Yup."

"You manage the entire system alone?"

"That's what I like about it. It's my own world. No one to tell me what to do. No one to get mad at me. In my own system I'm God. I can do anything I want."

"What else do you have in there?"

He shrugged. "Everything. A backwards encrypted dictionary. Mockingbirds. Imposter daemons. Trojan horses. Worms. Various patches and bug breakers. That sort of thing."

When the printer ejected the page, she grabbed it and studied the program. "What can we do on the police computer with system privileges?" she asked.

"Anything we want. We have total access. We could destroy

their entire database if we wanted to. Of course, I just want to see what they know about me. That seems fair, don't you think?"

He logged out.

"What are you doing?"

"It's time to lie low for a while, in case someone's watching us. Since it's an automatic process and not normally used by a human being, the UUCP account would never stay on for more than a few minutes, so I logged out and disconnected. We'll wait for the cuckoo's egg to hatch."

He turned to her with a smile on his face.

"Do you have any drugs?" she asked.

His stomach constricted. He saw drug lords–international cartels–gunfights in the streets–kids crazed on crack. He knew he shouldn't have gotten involved with this woman!

"Drugs? What sort of drugs?" he stammered.

"Any sort of painkiller. Tylenol or something. My leg is hurting pretty bad. What's so funny? Why are you laughing?"

CHAPTER FOUR

When he returned from the drugstore he gave her three Tylenol tablets and offered to apply a new dressing. She lay on her stomach as he pulled the bloodstained towels away. The wound had stopped bleeding. He applied liberal amounts of alcohol to it, then the bandages he had bought, which were much better suited than the dish towels.

"How did this happen?" he asked. He had to say something to get his mind off her naked body. He tried to listen while he wrapped the adhesive tape around her thigh.

"I don't know. All I remember is the car door exploding off its mountings and knocking me into the passenger seat. It's not too serious."

"It looks horrible to me, but I don't know. I'm not a doctor. You should go to a doctor."

"You're doing fine, programmer. Don't give up on me now."

He smiled at the way she put it, and at the realization that she needed him. It had been a long time since anyone had needed him for much except hacking.

"What do people call you?" he asked. He was careful not to ask for her real name.

"Jett."

"As in the color of your hair?"

"Sort of."

"Do you think we're safe here? I mean, do you think they're going to find us?"

She paused, seeming to think through the possibilities. "I think we're totally invisible. As long as we don't move, they can't find us."

"Really? You think we lost those guys that were after you?"

"I think so. Unless they got your license plate number. Then they could track us down."

"Oh . . . Could they get my address from that? Are they federal agents or something?"

"No, but they have plenty of resources. We can't underestimate this enemy."

He had finished with the tape. She turned onto her back, and he draped the blanket over her legs.

As he carried the bloody towels to the kitchen to throw them away, he thought about his options. He could call the police and explain everything: how he got in an accident, then tried to pull a guy with no legs out of a car, then ran somebody over, then fled the scene, then harbored a fugitive for the night. This option didn't appeal to him. Even without Jett's general suspicion of the police, he imagined a terrifying number of laws they might charge him with breaking.

On the other hand, he could order her to leave. Now that he had helped her, she didn't seem disposed to hurt him. Besides, her gun was still locked in his glove compartment. If he forced her to, she would probably take off and leave him alone. He would never see her again. He didn't like that option either.

There were too many unanswered questions, he told himself. Besides, he wanted to help her. *It was exciting.*

He reviewed what he'd learned by snooping in her jacket. Jetta Mendoza Santiago, her passport said. Was that her real name, or merely one of the fake names she used? Why were those guys after her? How did she get such muscular legs? And where had she learned to dress a wound like a field medic?

Too many questions, he noted again. "Let's see what's happening on the computer," he mumbled and went back to the screen.

She pushed herself up again, studying every command.

As he worked, he paused every once in a while to list the people who were logged into the computer, just to make sure nobody had discovered him running around the system. Eventually he found his way to the main database, and since he had system privileges, the security daemons provided access without challenge.

He scanned through the previous night's accident reports. He found the record immediately.

"That's it," she muttered, but they were both already reading.

The police report described the scene of the accident, the vehicles, the drivers and passengers, the extent of damage, the type of injuries, date, time. It said two cars were involved: a silver Mazda RX-7 and a green Bonneville SE. Two deaths: one man found in the Bonneville, one man found on the highway, presumably the driver of the Mazda since its door was missing and there was no one inside.

Both men had been identified. Both were employed by Jensen-Bishop Pharmaceuticals. The Bonneville was a company car. The Mazda was a rental. No other vehicles or individuals were mentioned, though the officer who filed the report indicated that it was strange for the driver of the Mazda to be thrown so far from the vehicle. Autopsies were pending.

They studied the report for a long time, taking in the details.

Henry was trying to figure it all out. Obviously the blue Continental and the other cars had escaped before the police arrived. And it made sense that they would find the driver of the Bonneville. But who was this other guy, the guy they found on the highway? "Was he really driving the Mazda?" Henry asked himself.

"I was driving the Mazda," she said. "I rented it at the airport."

"Who was the guy on the highway?"

"The man you ran over."

His heart flipped. "I didn't mean to kill him!"

"I know you didn't," she said gently. "But those two guys were going to kill us. Believe me. You should be glad it happened the way it did. And it looks like the police think he was driving my Mazda."

"Won't they check who rented it at the airport?"

"They may. Even if they do, they won't be able to trace it to me."

He didn't ask how that was possible. She must have used one of her fake IDs. He guessed that wouldn't be difficult when renting a car, assuming you also had fake credit cards. He'd forgotten to check that. He remembered she had a lot of cards, though he hadn't looked at the names on them.

"So," she concluded, "the police have a nice little accident to take care of, and they can wrap everything up, and then it's done. At least we don't have to worry about *them* anymore."

Henry gave a sigh of relief. That was indeed good news. Then he thought again. "Who *do* we have to worry about, then?"

"Jensen-Bishop Pharmaceuticals."

CHAPTER FIVE

"I need my Glock," she told him.

He had heard her mutter the term before, and the meaning was clear enough. "Why? What do you need the gun for?"

"They'll find us sooner or later."

"You said we were invisible."

"I didn't realize it was Jensen-Bishop."

"Who's Jensen-Bishop? What does some pharmaceutical company have to do with all this?"

"That's the competitor."

"Whose competitor?"

"My client's." She watched his face change, and then she smiled. "I'm not a drug dealer," she assured him.

"What are you, then?"

"I'm a courier. I deliver things."

"Like what?"

"Whatever they pay me for. It could be anything."

"Give me some examples."

"I deliver special packages for large corporations. Blueprints, secret plans, oil field maps, new software, financial reports. Anything that absolutely can't fall into the wrong hands."

"Why not just send it by registered mail? No one's going to tamper with that."

"It depends on what the stakes are. When you're talking about this kind of money, tampering with mail is a pretty minor offense."

"You think people would risk a jail sentence to–"

"People would kill for it. We're talking about projects involving millions, even billions of dollars. With those kinds of stakes, things get serious real quick. These people need a guarantee that their package will get delivered safely, to the right person, and at the right time. No mistakes. So they call me."

"How long have you been doing this?" he asked, mystified.

She thought a moment, not quite sure how to answer the question. "All my life," she said finally.

"Do you work for a company?"

"No. Companies are corrupt. I work for myself."

"Do you ever get caught?"

"Maybe for a little while, but I never fail to deliver the package. That's why they call me."

"I guess they pay a lot."

"If it wasn't important, they'd use commercial carriers."

"Who are you delivering for now? What kind of package?"

"Are you going to get my Glock?"

"No."

"Why not?"

"I don't like guns. They make me nervous."

"*Not* having it makes *me* nervous. I'll get it myself."

"You don't know where I've put it," he countered, trying to mislead her. "You were unconscious when I brought you up here. Besides," he added more sincerely, "you shouldn't move around on that leg."

"I'll manage." She appeared to have no doubt that she could find the gun wherever Henry had hidden it.

"OK," he sighed. "OK, I'll go get it for you. Then will you tell me what's going on and who you're working for?"

She nodded.

Excited and worried, he grabbed a jacket out of his closet, having learned from her how useful jackets could be for concealing guns and other paraphernalia. He took the elevator down to the garage level.

At the car he found more to alarm him. The daylight showed far greater damage than he'd noticed the night before. He was amazed he'd been able to drive the car home. Besides the crumpling on the right side, the front bumper was ripped partway off, the grill broken, the hood dented. He wondered how he managed to convince Jimmy he'd had a fender-bender in a parking lot. Or maybe Jimmy wasn't convinced? What did Jimmy know? Who else had seen the car in the garage this morning?

Furtively, he took a screwdriver from the trunk and scraped some of the green paint off his car until he realized the task was hopeless. Then he noticed something stuck in the recess beside the right headlight, which was bent out of position. He pulled out a small piece of blue cloth. He found another shred clinging to a raw edge of metal: fine wool. Going upward, he found something else. He picked it out of the windshield with his fingernails: a tuft of hair, bloody skin still attached.

He dropped it in horror.

He got in the car, started it up. He checked to make sure no one was around, then drove to a new parking space at the other end of the garage.

He unlocked the glove compartment, stuck the gun in his coat pocket, locked the doors and started back toward the elevator at the other end of the garage.

A black-and-white squad car came around the corner. It rolled slowly toward him. The engine noise echoed from the garage's bare walls and ceiling.

The gun seemed to weigh thirty pounds in Henry's jacket pocket. He was sure it would fall out, but he didn't dare put his hand in to steady it. That would tip off the police for sure. He pretended to be looking at the ground as he walked toward the elevator.

When the car was alongside him, it stopped.

He pinned his eyes to the floor, but he could hear a voice from the car begin talking on the radio.

Henry hesitated. Desperate to know, he looked up. There were two uniformed officers in the car. The one in the passenger seat was using the radio. The driver was staring directly at Henry. Their eyes locked.

Henry looked away.

He pushed himself forward.

He walked toward the elevator without looking back. At each step he expected to hear the sound of a car door opening or the blast of a loudspeaker: "Police, freeze!"

A quarter of the way to the elevator. Half way to the elevator. He heard the police car move forward, crawling past the parked vehicles.

He supposed the officers were studying each car. He mentally calculated how long it would take them to reach the Volvo. Though he quickened his pace, he didn't dare run.

At the elevator he pushed the button. He thought he heard the police car stop.

His back to the garage, he watched the floor indicator: 8 . . . 7 . . . 6 . . . 5 . . .

He heard the police car's doors open.

... 4 ... 3 ... 2 ...1... G.

The elevator doors parted and Henry stepped in. Turning, he saw the officers at the far end of the garage, stalking cautiously across the concrete floor. They were examining his Volvo.

One of the policemen swiveled to scan the length of the garage. He was staring directly at Henry when the elevator doors shut.

G ... 1 ... 2 ... 3 ... 4 ... "Geez, come on!" It was the slowest elevator ride of his life.

Finally he reached his floor.

The doors didn't open. *They've trapped me!* his mind screamed.

Then the doors opened.

He ran down the hallway, unlocked his door and hurried inside. He shut and locked the door behind him.

But the woman was gone.

He had a surge of resentment. I get in an accident, kill somebody, have the police hunting me, all because of her, and now *she* decides to leave!

"I'm here," she said tentatively. She crawled out from under the bed, stiff-legged and serious.

"What are you doing?" he asked, bewildered.

"I heard somebody running toward the door," she explained. "This is as far as I could get."

"It was just me!"

"Then you run like a horse," she complained.

"The cops are downstairs."

"What?"

"The cops are after me. They're looking at my car. They saw me."

"Did you get the Glock?"

"What good is that gonna do? You can't shoot the cops!" He paused. "Can you?"

"Did you *get* it?"

"Don't worry, I got it!" He pulled it out of his pocket, and handed it over.

The two of them knelt on the far side of the bed–as if it could protect them, Henry thought.

"What are we going to do?" he asked, terrified.

"Are you sure they're coming up here?"

"Yes! They were looking at my car!"

"And they recognized you?"

"Yes! Of course! What are we going to do?"

She pulled back the slide half way and checked the chamber. Then she pressed the magazine catch and pulled out the magazine. "Seventeen rounds, spring down and ready to roll. There's nothing like a good Glock 17 when you need one."

"What are we going to do?" Henry stammered.

She slammed the clip into the handle. Making no allowance for her wounded leg, she stretched for her leather jacket on the bed and pulled it over to her, then wriggled into it. From the pocket she took one of the boxes of cartridges Henry had seen the night before: P-type 9mm. She opened the box and counted.

"How do you know they recognized you?" she said tightly.

"They did! What does it matter? They did!"

"How do you know?"

"They looked right at me!" he screamed.

She paused, waiting. "And?"

"They looked right at me!"

"Cops always look right at you. It's the nature of the beast."

"You don't think they knew who I was?"

"Not necessarily."

There was a knock at the door.

Jett hit the floor, pulling Henry with her.

"Is there another way out of here?" she whispered.

"Just windows. And we're on the ninth floor."

"No fire escape?"

"No."

"Did they know you were running?"

"I thought they did . . . I don't know!"

Somebody pounded on the door.

"Southfield Police!" the officer shouted. He rang the doorbell. Then he pounded again.

Panicked, Henry wondered if he'd left a trail of blood in the hall when he carried her in last night.

"Listen, programmer, if they come through that door, there's no sense fighting them. We'll tell them what happened."

"We will?"

"I jumped in your car after the accident and pointed my weapon at you and told you to drive. You're my hostage."

"I am?"

"But they won't come in unless they have a warrant or probable cause. They don't have probable cause unless they recognized you and you ran."

"I didn't run!"

"Did you lock the door when you came in?"

"I think so . . . "

The doorknob turned.

The fugitives watched the knob rotate one way, then the other, praying.

Had he remembered to wash Jett's blood off the outside knob?

The entire door shook as the policeman on the other side tested its strength with his shoulder.

Henry crouched against her. "If you tell them you're holding me hostage you'll be in more trouble than ever," he whispered.

"I owe you. You seem to forget you saved my life, programmer."

"My name's Henry."

They continued to hunker down after the noise at the door stopped.

After several minutes of quiet, she gestured for Henry to check the window. He crawled over and peeked outside. With another gesture from her he became bold enough to stand and look down. The police car was pulling out of the garage and onto Woodward Avenue. Her instincts astounded him. "They're leaving!" he cheered.

She didn't answer. The crisis over, she collapsed on her back on the floor. She made an odd spectacle in leather jacket and panties. The gun lay loose in her hand.

"That was close," he said as he sat on the floor beside her. "That was *too* close!" he sighed.

"Henry."

"What?"

She was studying the ceiling. "Henry. I kind of like the name, that's all. You must have had a nice mother."

Henry appreciated the compliment, and he was sure his mother would have felt the same. He thought of returning the favor, but what could he say about a name like Jett?

He was feeling rather brave now. "I kept my part of the deal," he said. "What about yours?"

He felt he understood her reluctance to talk about her "clients" and their "packages." he wouldn't share his computer password with other people either; it would be unprofessional, to say the least, not to mention risky. But he wasn't about to let her escape the bargain she'd agreed to. If she told him, they would be more like partners.

She didn't deny the deal or ask him what he meant. She merely smiled a little at his persistence. "I'm making a run," she said, "for Dracon Industries."

"A run? A run from where to where?"

"I was in Manaus when they hired me to bring their package here."

"Where's that?" he asked.

"It's a port city on the Río Amazonas."

"The Amazon River. As in South America?"

She nodded. "Brazil."

"You speak Portuguese?"

"Sim, e você?"

"What?"

"Yes, and you?"

"No, I don't know any languages or anything like that."

She turned her head to look up at him. "You know UNIX, don't you? It's *way* more "foreign" than Portuguese. And what were you writing that program in? The language called C, wasn't it? You must know a dozen other computer languages. Don't be so modest. You know a lot of things I don't know about. But, of course, you're going to teach me."

"How do you know about C?" he asked, astonished she had even heard of the computer language, let alone able to recognize it.

"I've just picked up some here and there."

"What other foreign languages do you know?" he asked.

"English."

"Very funny."

She shrugged. "French. A little German. Spanish, of course. Most of my runs go between the States and South America."

"Have you worked for these Dracon people before?"

"No."

"Why is Jensen-Bishop after you?"

"They must be after the package. No one is ever after me personally."

"What's the package?"

"It's whatever I'm delivering."

"I mean this time! You promised to tell me these things."

"I don't know what's in the package."

"Oh."

"I told you the name of my client. I told you where I came from and what I'm trying to do. I'm trying to get to the Dracon Building on Grayfield. I have to deliver the package, but I don't know what it is."

"Well, what do you *think* it is?"

"I have no idea."

"Wouldn't you like to know?" he asked.

"Sure. I don't like a black box package and I don't like running blind."

"What's that?" he asked.

"What's what?"

"Black box. Running blind."

"A black box is a package like the one I've got now, where I don't know the contents. And running blind means the client doesn't fill me in on the situation. So I don't know what's going on. I don't know who or what to look out for. I have no profile on my potential enemies or intelligence on their position. I don't like running blind. It's stupid."

"Why do your clients make you do it?" he asked.

"Sometimes they don't even trust me. They're stupid. But then, if they weren't paranoid they wouldn't have called me in the first place."

"Is your package from Brazil?" he asked, still trying to figure out what it was.

"I would imagine so. That's where they hired me, but sometimes they change countries a few times before they make the final run into the States."

"What could be so important?"

"I don't know."

"But you're risking your life for it! And what about this

company, this Dracon Industries? They don't care anything about you!
You're risking your life for them too!"

"That's what I'm paid to do," she said.

"Well, where is it?"

She didn't answer.

"Do you still have it?"

She didn't answer.

"Do you plan on making the delivery? After all of this?"

Still she was silent, watching the ceiling.

"OK, then, what are you going to do next? Tell me that,"
Henry said.

"I want to take a shower. Can you help me?"

Henry Beaufort was frustrated. This was like a computer
problem he couldn't figure out, a problem his mind would keep
tugging at until a solution somehow appeared. He understood, of
course, why she was being tight-lipped. Under the circumstances he
would be too.

"Yeah, I'll help you to the shower," he said. "But can you
stand up?"

Leaning on his shoulder, she limped into the bathroom. She set
the gun in the empty soap tray. While he fetched towels from the
cabinet, she took off her leather jacket and tossed it aside. When he
turned around she had taken off her shirt. The upper half of her body
was naked, exposing her smooth dark skin, small breasts and taut
abdomen. The muscles of her chest, neck and shoulders were pulled
tight across her collar bones.

"Sorry," he mumbled and averted his eyes in embarrassment.

She turned on the tap, then bent and pulled off her panties,
gingerly avoiding her wound. "Don't worry about it, Henry," she said.
Across her muscled side he noticed a long jagged scar. "You know, I
think a bath is going to work better than a shower. I'm feeling a little
lightheaded." She slipped into the tub and reclined. The water level
slowly rose past the mound of black hair between her legs, then up her
stomach and over her breasts. In a moment she handed him the Glock
17. "Here, you watch the door."

Not in all his life had Henry Beaufort ever had a full-grown
woman lying naked in his bathtub. He took the gun and sat beside her,
accepting the temporary responsibility of defending them, but he found
it difficult to watch the door.

CHAPTER SIX

How had the police found out about him? That's what he wanted to know. How did they know to come to his apartment complex? Why were they checking out his car? And, most importantly, what did they find?

He helped Jett out of the bath. He gave her his robe and helped her limp over to the bed where she could rest her leg.

"Are you hungry?" she asked. She seemed to have forgotten that the police and an evil pharmaceutical company were after them.

"Are you hungry again?" he asked, astounded.

"Sure. Aren't you?"

"No, well . . . maybe, but aren't you worried about what's going to happen?"

"I've been thinking about it, but that doesn't make me any less hungry. In fact, it makes me hungrier. You got any pizza?"

"You like pizza?"

"Sure, don't you?"

"Absolutely, but . . . nevermind. I'll order some."

"Great."

"Then we'll figure out how to get the package back."

"You don't have it?"

"It's in the car."

"The Mazda?"

"Yes."

"Why did you leave it there?" he asked, a little surprised that a professional would forget the package in the car.

"Don't worry. It's hidden very well. They'll never find it. I didn't have time to get it, and I wouldn't have anyway. I was pretty sure I was going to get caught. In fact, I thought they were going to kill me. It wasn't until I saw you walking around that I thought I had a way out. At that point there was no going back for the package. I knew it was better to leave the scene, and come back for it."

"But the cops have it now!"

"Sure, but they don't know it. They don't really have it unless they *know* they have it. Don't worry, we'll get it back."

Henry picked up the phone and dialed the number he knew by heart and ordered a pepperoni and mushroom pizza. He shook his head in disbelief, thinking about the way she said "we". We'll get it back, she said.

While they were eating their pizza, Jett looked up at him. "Tell me about UNIX."

"What?"

"Tell me about computers."

"What do you mean?"

"I want to learn."

"You do? Why?"

"I might need those skills someday."

"Well, it would take a long time to teach you. I don't know where to start."

"Tell me about the Orange Book."

"How do you know about that?"

"I've run into it on occasion. It's always left me mystified. I've been hindered on many a run because of that thing."

"The Orange Book is a set of computer security procedures written by the Defense Department. Its real name is the C2 Trusted System Security Level, but most people call it the Orange Book, since its first edition was published in an orange cover. The book describes everything that is necessary to meet the requirements of a secure system."

"Do you follow it?"

"Sure, and much more. C2 is just fundamentals."

"Fundamentals?" She was visibly surprised.

"Sure, the Defense Department knows that. C2 is just the foundation for a secure system. A system is never better than its system administrator."

"Are you telling me you can get into a C2-protected system?"

"Sometimes. It depends who's running it, and who ran it before him, and how careful the users are . . . and, of course, how bad I want to get in."

"I thought you said you were a programmer."

"I am."

"And?"

"I work for an investment company."

"And?"

"And sometimes I collect information on our next target."

"And what does this 'information collection' entail?"

He shrugged, nervously. "All sorts of things."

"Like trollers and password checkers?"

"Sometimes."

"Did you write those all by yourself?"

"Yes, though I get a lot of programs from other people too."

"From who?" she asked, as if surprised he knew anybody.

"Why do you say it like that?" he asked, offended.

"I didn't think you had any friends."

"Why do you say that?" It was basically true, but he wanted to know how she knew it.

"The phone hasn't rung since I got here."

"Oh."

"So, where do you get these other programs?"

"Other programmers."

"Very funny. Other programmers where you work?"

"No. I told you, I'm the only programmer there."

"Where then?"

"On the Internet."

"What exactly is the Internet?"

"It's a network of computers. Computers all over the world are connected to it. Everybody on the network has an address, and we exchange electronic mail. I have many friends out there, from all over. We help each other with our programming problems."

"You've never met them?"

"Sure, I've met them."

"In person?"

"Oh, no."

"Why do you help them, then? And why do they help you?"

He thought about this a moment. He wasn't sure. It had always been that way. It was part of the unwritten credo of the programmer: help your fellow programmer. You help others and others help you. That's just the way it was. Being intrinsically allied with all other programmers, Henry sometimes felt pangs of guilt for breaking into protected systems. He knew that if anyone on the other side ever found out that he broke in, the programmers there would get in a lot of trouble from their management. That's why he worked so hard to make sure no one ever detected him. "I don't know," he said.

"Tell me about the security features required by the Orange Book."

They ate their pizza and they talked. Long after the pizza was gone, they kept talking. Eventually they moved over to the computer and he showed her things. He taught her the command syntax as well as the file structure of UNIX. He lost himself in the details of his art, delighted to share himself with someone, especially somebody as beautiful and intelligent as Jett. Though she considered herself a novice, she seemed to absorb the knowledge quickly. He stopped holding back. He forgot that she said she didn't know anything. He demonstrated with great pride all the elegant facets of the UNIX operating system. There was a certain beauty in its power. He warned her also of its pitfalls: where it became messy, or difficult or unreliable. Day fell into evening, and they worked long into the night.

The police did not return. Henry and Jett decided that a witness must have seen a "white Volvo" at the accident and the police had been sent around to ask routine questions of all white Volvo owners. They laughed at themselves.

Near midnight they ran out of Mountain Dew and knew instinctively that it was time to go bed, or they would have to order Chinese take-out.

Henry pulled the sheets down, then helped Jett climb into his bed.

"My leg is starting to feel a lot better," she said. She set the 9mm on the nightstand next to the bed, then pulled her shirt off. She lay down and rested her head on the pillow. "Where are you going?" she asked when he started walking away.

"Just over here," he said, pointing to the chair.

"Is that where you slept last night?"

"Yeah."

"And you were going to sleep there again?"

"Yes, of course."

"Don't be silly, Henry, get your butt over here."

"What?"

"This is your bed. I'm not taking up *that* much space. And I'm not kicking anybody out of their own bed. If you don't want to sleep in the same bed with me then I'll sleep on the floor."

"It's not that . . ." he mumbled helplessly.

"What's the matter? Come on. I don't bite."

"OK," he agreed finally. He kicked off his shoes, pulled off his shirt and sat on the edge of the bed.

"Off with 'em!" she demanded. "I know you don't sleep in your pants."

Finally he pulled off his pants and got quickly under the sheets. The light went off.

He lay quietly, staring up at the ceiling.

"Ow!" he screamed. It felt like somebody bit him.

"I lied."

CHAPTER SEVEN

"What are you up to now?" she asked when she woke up in the morning.

Henry was sitting in his Star Trek boxer shorts and his striped socks, staring at his computer screen. Lying next to a strange woman all night and wondering if the police were going to arrest him had caused Henry to suffer a restless night. He turned to his computer for sanctuary.

"I was just thinking about something," he said.

"What are you thinking about?"

"I've got the solution to our problem."

"What problem?"

"The car."

"The Mazda?"

"Yup."

"You found it?"

"I think so."

She wrapped the sheets around her torso and crawled excitedly toward the end of the bed. Henry had accessed the police database again, and found the impoundment records. The report for the silver Mazda RX-7 was on the screen.

"Impoundment Code 15," he said.

"Where's that?"

"I don't know. I'll look it up." He typed several commands to search through the data files. Then he paused. "Oh no . . ."

"What's wrong?"

"Somebody just slowed the system down. Something's happening." He typed a command to see what the system was doing:

PS -EF | MORE

He read the list of processes that flashed across the screen.

"What's going on?" Jett asked him.

He didn't answer. He issued another command.

WHO

He studied the list of user names, and noted that the user Calahan had just logged on.

"Henry, who's Calahan?"

He issued another command:

FINGER CALAHAN

He read the output:

LOGIN NAME: CALAHAN

IN REAL LIFE: JOHNATHON RIELEY CALAHAN, SYSTEM ADMINISTRATOR

DIRECTORY: /

SHELL: /BIN/SH

LAST LOGIN: SAT JUN II 08:24

"Yikes!" Henry hit the Ctrl-D. "Emergency exit!" he cried. The modem disconnected and knocked them off the system.

Henry stood up and paced around. "Geez, that was close!"

"What happened?"

"I noticed the system slow down. I checked to see what was happening and saw that somebody had started a backup. The system administrator had just logged on!"

He jumped into the text editor on his own system, typed a million miles a minute, then saved the program, and exited. He issued the new command:

PEEK

"What's that do?" she asked. "Henry, you type too fast!"

"Sorry. It calls the police station computer every few minutes, logs in as UUCP and checks to see if Calahan is on the system. If he is, it leaves. If he isn't, it logs into the Smith account and beeps to get my attention."

She smiled, amazed. "Is that all?" she asked sarcastically.

Henry glanced back at the screen, wondering what was going to happen.

"Do you think he's on to us?" she asked.

"I don't know."

"Did he detect us?"

"I don't know. I don't think so, but I can't tell until I get back in, and I can't go in until I know he's gone."

A few minutes later the computer beeped.

He sat down again, and went to work. He tried to explain everything he was doing. At times he stopped and pointed out a particularly tricky piece of syntax.

He checked various logs and history files in order to figure out what Calahan did while on the system. "Looks like he just logged in, started a backup and left. We lucked out. He didn't see us."

Henry issued a new command:

SHOULDER &

"What's that do?"

"It looks over my shoulder for me."

Jett frowned. "I don't understand."

"The only person who can detect me is the system administrator, and I know his name and I know what terminal he comes in on, so I wrote a program to watch everyone who logs into the system and warn me if it's him. That way I don't have to keep looking over my shoulder, wondering who's watching me."

"Wow. How did you find out where he was?"

"I checked the personnel files."

"Really? You can do that?"

"I can do anything I want, until I'm detected . . . "

"But your Shoulder program will warn us!"

"Right. No sense taking chances. Now, let's get back to the RX-7. Where's Impoundment Code 15?"

He changed to a different directory, then brought up the facilities database. He didn't bother to use the menu system. He accessed the data files directly. He got a list of all the police stations and their support buildings. Impoundment Code 15 was on the list, along with an address.

"There it is!" Jett cried. "You're a genius, Henry, a genius! We can go get the car tonight, after it's closed!"

He whirled around in panic, not realizing what he had gotten himself into. To him it had been a puzzle to solve. It was something *virtual*, rather than *physical*. "You want to break into a police impoundment area?" He gasped.

"Sure, why not? It'll be easy."

"Has it occurred to you that it's illegal?"

"Has it occurred to you that everything we've done since Friday is illegal? Hacking into the police computer system isn't exactly Eagle Scout material!"

"But they'll catch us!"

"No, they won't. You leave it to me. You may be the expert on passwords and computers. I'm the expert on barbwire fences and security guards."

She jumped out of bed and pulled on her clothes. Her leg was still sore, but wasn't slowing her down anymore. She plopped herself down beside him. She pointed at the screen. "Show me how you did that," she demanded.

Later that afternoon, after they had spent many hours discussing computer systems and programming, they got back into the accident report database. They found the new report which indicated that a witness had indeed spotted a "white Volvo with a male driver" at the scene. That information shed more light on the strange fact that one of the bodies was found several dozen yards away from the car.

Henry stared at the screen in shock. His eyes focused on a single phrase: *possible homicide.*

A flood of worries poured over him. What was he doing? Had he forgotten that the police were after him? Had he gone out of his mind?

He had to turn himself in! He had to leave the country! He had to drive his car off a cliff to destroy it! He didn't know what to do, but he had to do something!

Jett put her hand on his shoulder. She could see the tremble in his finger tips as they hovered in shock over the keyboard. "It's OK, Henry. Don't worry. They don't know it was you."

"But they were here and they saw my car. They're going to arrest me."

"You don't know that." She put her arm around him. "Don't get all screwed up inside. Just think it through. This is no different than one of your computer problems. You just have to learn to think on your feet."

"How come you're not scared?"

"I am scared, but I've got more experience at this than you. I think we can get through it."

"But how? How can we?"

"First we have to get the package."

"But why? What does that matter?"

"The package is everything. We have to get it, or we'll never get out of this mess."

"OK, what do we have to do?"

"We go to the police station tonight, after dark, and we get it."

CHAPTER EIGHT

About eleven o'clock that night, they ventured out of the apartment together. Jett was wearing her boots, jeans, and leather jacket. The jeans were blackened with blood stains. The brown, cowhide jacket looked like it had been around the world a couple of times. She wore the leather like a warrior wore armor.

She was taller than Henry, and thinner. When she moved, she padded softly and noiselessly. She scanned the area around her, checking details, sensing things he could not. For now, the Glock remained hidden in its holster under her arm.

They went down to the garage and found the car.

"At least they didn't tow it away," he muttered and opened the door for her.

He drove slowly, doing everything he could to avoid the attention of a cop. He figured that getting pulled over for speeding would put a slight kink in their plans.

They rolled like gangsters past the police station, taking the lay of the land, the position of squad cars, lights, fences, gates.

There were seven police cars parked outside. Tall chain-linked fence around the impoundment yard. Locked gate. No guard.

Following Jett's instructions, Henry turned down the seldom used street that ran behind the station. She indicated where he should park next to the fence.

They got out. Approached the yard. A row of heavy bushes grew dense around the fence, blocking the view from outsiders. They pushed their way through the branches and looked in.

When he gazed across the vast grave yard of criminal vehicles, Henry's chest constricted.

"How are we going to get in there?" he asked, noticing the barbwire at the top of the fence and the powerful lights flooding the yard. "We can't get over the fence." In the distance he could make out the windows of the police station.

"I'll go over it."

"Over the fence? It's ten feet high!"

"That tree limb over there is twenty feet. We win."

"You can't climb that tree in your condition!"

"I think I can do it."

"But you're hurt!"

"I'm not hurt that bad. You want to do it?"

"No."

"Then, I'm going to do it. You stay here. Keep a look-out."

"For what?"

She was gone. Disappeared. Her black hair, and dark skin and leather jacket seemed to blend into the night and then she was invisible.

He heard her climbing the trunk of the tree, moving onto a limb.

He scanned the yard, looking for guards. The flood lights cast white light and long shadows over the imprisoned cars and trucks, creating an eerie scene. He strained to make out the shapes of men moving inside the police station. If they were to glance outside they would see her. Having lived all his life in the city, he never thought he would ever hope for *fewer* street lights. Darkness was now an ally.

She dropped to the ground on the other side. He heard her groan.

"I told you," he muttered quietly.

The brightness of head lights hit him.

He dove to the ground.

The car turned onto the street and drove toward him.

He crawled over to the back tire of the Volvo and hid.

The unknown car inched along, its tires rolling audibly across the gravel and broken concrete of the old, poorly-maintained street.

Large vehicle. He could hear the engine. The driver slowed to a stop.

Henry waited.

The car rolled forward again, then pulled up beside the Volvo.

Henry scanned the impoundment yard. Where was Jett? He couldn't see a thing. For all he knew they had caught her already. Then it hit him: Getting into the fenced yard was easy, just climb the tree and drop in. How was she planning to get out?

The car remained stationary.

Quiet.

What was it waiting for? He crawled as quietly as he could to the back of the Volvo, then peered over the trunk.

Blue Continental!

He threw himself to the ground. The bile rose up and burned his throat.

A door opened, then a second.

He held his breath.

Their shoes touched the street. Keys jingled. The Continental's lights went off by automatic time delay. They walked around the Volvo.

He scrambled under the car on his belly. He knew it was a stupid and desperate thing to do, but he couldn't think of anything else.

Now he could see the pant cuffs and shoes of two men. They walked around the Volvo, checking to see if it was locked, looking into the windows, and recording the license plate number. Then they moved toward the impoundment yard.

They stopped by the fence and looked inward through the bushes, their backs to Henry and the Volvo.

"What do you think?" one of the men said softly to the other.

"I don't see her."

"You think she's here?"

"I know she's here. That's the car."

"Whose is it?"

"I don't know, but that's the car. It must be one of her men."

"I thought she works alone."

"Looks like she's got herself a friend to help soak up the bullets. I don't know, but I do know she's here, just like Aaron said she'd be."

"She left the package in the Mazda then. You think the cops got it?"

"Nah, she would've hid it. If she's half as good as they say she is, then they would've had to tear it down to find it. Unless it's a drug bust or homicide investigation, they're not going to tear down the car."

"Where do you think she put it?"

"I don't know. Wheel well. Maybe under the battery."

"Under the battery? I've never heard of no woman getting under the hood of a car."

"Welcome to the nineties, buddy. Get used to it."

"What are we going to do when they come out?"

"When they come over the fence, you take her and I'll take him."

"We shoulda brought the Browning."

"We can't be lurking around a police station with a rifle. If we get picked up now, at least we have permits for our revolvers. Self defense. No problem. But a .308 in the back seat? Now that's a problem. You've got to think about these things."

Henry heard a sharp click, then saw a small flash of light.

"Don't light that cigarette, you idiot."

"Oh, sorry. Just a habit when I'm nervous."

He snapped the lighter closed. The two fell silent again, waiting.

"If you're worried about missing, then use the Volvo for a rest. There's no shame in that. I don't trust this bitch any farther than I can throw her. It's going to be a long shot, and you can't afford to miss. I'm sure she's armed. If she gets a shot on you you're dead."

"Oh, great, thanks a lot."

"Just don't miss," he said.

"You really think she's that good? What's all this *Shining Path* stuff, anyway? Are we gonna have to go to South America now and fight terrorists? I don't think she can be as good as Aaron and them say."

"You want to take that chance? Quiet, there she is!"

The two men darted back to the cars and hid behind the Volvo. One of the men pulled out his pistol and laid his arms across the hood, using it as a rest to aim his shot.

How is she going to get back over the fence? Henry was wondering. He was only a few feet away from the goons, but there were a dozen things running through his mind. It's just like solving one of your problems, Henry. You've got to think on your feet. That's what Jett said. She forgot to mention that he'd be lying on his belly.

"Quiet . . ." the guy in charge was telling the other. "Just wait until you get a clean shot . . ."

Henry could barely breathe. He peered from beneath the car. He could see her through the bushes. Jett was climbing the fence! She scaled the chain link like she had done it a hundred times before. When she reached the top, she stopped and began the precarious and careful work of insinuating her body through the barbwire strands.

"Now?" the shooter asked. Henry could feel the man's nervousness as he adjusted his weight and took aim.

Henry unclipped the mechanical pencil from his shirt pocket. "Take your shot, buddy."

Henry jabbed the pencil into the shooter's leg.

The shooter screamed in surprise and pulled the trigger. The sound of the gun exploded in Henry's ears.

Perched atop the fence, Jett turned, drew the Glock and fired.

The bullet thudded into the shooter's forehead. He crashed to the pavement. He stared at Henry under the car as blood poured down his nose. Henry stared back at him, terrified. The man was dead.

Jett leaped off the fence. She hit the ground with a roll and an audible groan. She slipped behind the trunk of the tree. Weapon ready, waiting.

The other man pulled back, slunk around the front of the Continental, got into the car and drove away.

The wail of sirens rang from the police station as officers poured from the building and squad cars rolled. Code 411. Shots fired.

"Henry! Where are you?" Jett was screaming whispers as she ran toward the car.

He squirmed out from underneath.

"Drive!" she screamed.

His head jerked back when he slammed the accelerator to the floor. The tires spun and the car careened into a one-eighty as he whirled the wheel.

CHAPTER NINE

The Continental went one way. The Volvo went the other. The police spotted the Continental and went after it.

Later the police would search the back street. They would find the body of an adult male Caucasian with a 9mm round in the center of his forehead and a mechanical pencil stuck in his leg.

Henry and Jett drove for miles. Then they found an alley and pulled out of sight.

"Did you get the package?" Henry asked.

"Yeah, I got it."

"Were those the guys from Jensen-Bishop?"

"Yeah."

"They must want this thing bad."

"That's an understatement."

"You killed that guy."

"I can't figure out how he missed me! He got the first shot! He had me pegged!" She shook her head in exhilarated astonishment. "I think I just used one of my nine lives."

"The pencil is mightier than the pistol . . ." Henry laughed.

"What are talking about?"

"I got him in the leg."

"From under the car?"

"Yup!"

"Wow! Now that's a trick I've got to learn!"

"Where'd you learn to shoot like that?"

"I've had lots of practice."

"What do you mean?"

"I practice a lot. That's what I mean. I shoot at the range."

"Yeah, but you were sitting on top of a barbwire fence, and it was dark, and you got that guy with one shot even though he was hiding behind a car!"

"I told you: I practice a lot. Besides, Henry, I had help. He didn't have a chance against us!"

"What's the Shining Path?"

Her face went white. "Where did you hear that?"

"Those guys said it. What is it?"

"It was a long time ago."

"But what is it?"

"I don't want to talk about it."

"Is it some sort of gang or something?"

"No. It's not a gang."

"What is it?"

"Henry."

"OK, fine. What are we going to do now? Can we go back to the apartment?"

"No. They have your plate number for sure now. They'll find us there."

"Who? The police or the Jensen-Bishop goons?"

"Maybe both."

"Both? What are we going to do?"

"First we deliver the package."

"Now?"

"Absolutely."

"It's the middle of the night! I thought you said you have to deliver it to the Dracon Building. Won't it be closed?"

"Not for this it won't."

"What do you mean?"

"If our adventures thus far are any indication, this package is important enough that–"

"–What?"

"Well, let's just say that I think mom and dad are going to be waiting up for us."

"But what can it be?"

"Let's just deliver the package. Then we're done."

"Where's the Dracon Building?"

"It's up on Grayfield."

He nodded and started the car. "I know where that is."

The Dracon fortress had been built in the transition zone between affluent upscale developments and broken-out abandoned buildings. Standing on its granite threshold one was as likely to see a clean-cut man in a thousand dollar suit as a ragged woman pushing her belongings in a shopping cart.

Great grey walls sloped upward and away from the granite steps. Its windows were high up and narrow, seeming to pierce through the thick walls like arrow loops of a castle. No designs or detailing decorated the austere concrete exterior. No fastigiated top or structured setbacks, only a complex antenna and a large satellite dish. The massive building was formidable, a fortress against the decay around it. An archetypal example of post-modern prison style.

"Boy, I bet *they* have C2 security," Henry said as he stared upon the intimidating structure.

Jett scanned the streets and alleys, looking for enemies.

"What do we do now?" he asked.

"We go in."

"How?"

"Front door."

"What? You want to just walk up there?"

"These are the good guys. If they're there they'll see us and let us in. If they're not, then we'll leave and come back in the morning. I have a feeling they're there."

"Why? I don't see any lights inside. The place looks dead."

"Too dead."

"OK, we'll give it a try. If it doesn't work, then we'll find a place to hide."

"Agreed."

He drove up to the front entrance. They got out of the car and ascended the granite steps to the steel and glass front doors. They weren't the designer doors of department stores, though. The glass was at least an inch and half thick and the steel reinforced with heavy rivets.

They stood before the doors.

Jett glanced up at the cameras in each corner. She nodded. "They'll see us."

"How will they know it's you? Do they know you?"

"Not my face, no, but they'll figure it out."

After a few minutes, a security guard approached the other side of the glass door.

A glint of light reflected off a wall. Henry turned. A police car slowed to a stop in front of the building.

The guard pressed a button and they could hear his voice

electronically: "What do you want?"

"I have the package."

"Just a second," he said.

That's all? Henry wondered. "I have the package?"

The guard pressed another button. They could see his lips moving like he was talking to somebody else, but they couldn't hear him and they couldn't see who he was talking to.

"Look behind you," Henry whispered to Jett.

Jett turned slightly and spotted the police car. Stopped on the street. Watching. Waiting.

The glass door opened.

"Come on," the guard told them.

They went inside and followed him through a cathedral-like lobby to an elevator. He didn't say anything to them. They didn't say anything back.

There were many buttons on the elevator control panel. The largest buttons were the numbers 1, 2, 3, 4, 5, 6, and 7 but there was an entire alphanumeric keyboard. Henry watched the guard press the access code, then "2."

The elevator moved down.

Down? Henry thought. We're going down? Isn't "2" the second floor? Why are we going down?

The door opened.

When they stepped into the corridor the smell of surgical disinfectant entered Henry's nostrils. Hospital smell . . . White walls. Tiled floor. Fluorescent lights. Quiet beeping of an IV pump. The hum of computer terminals. Everything told him he was in a hospital. Except there were no patients. No wheelchairs, no candy-stripers, no flowers for sick people. Just a long ominous hallway, lined with closed doors. Henry wondered what was inside those rooms.

A group of four men came down the corridor. Two men in business suits. Two uniformed security guards like the one that had escorted them. The guards didn't look like normal rent-a-cops–retired police officers or young guys that couldn't get into the police academy. These were the cream of the crop. Professional all the way. They carried tonfa sticks, police radios and revolvers. They stood like soldiers stand.

One of the suits said, "You got the package?"

"Yes," Jett replied.

"Let's see it."

"Code."

The suit looked perturbed. He did not move. His silence repeated his demand.

"I need the code," Jett insisted.

Henry didn't know what was going on.

"Who's this?" the suit asked, gesturing toward Henry.

"He's my partner."

"We were told you work alone."

"Tough job."

"Let's see the package."

"I need the code."

Finally he turned to one of the guards: "Go get him."

"Yes, sir," the guard replied curtly, pivoted and walked down the corridor.

A few minutes later the guard returned, walking a few steps behind another man. He wore a long white lab coat over his shirt and tie. He had bright, icy blue eyes sunken deep into dark, wrinkled recesses. He carried with him the air of authority, a look in his eyes that suggested everything and everybody was an on-going scientific experiment. He had the kind of face that would do nothing but twitch a little as he gripped a trembling rabbit, shaved off a patch of its fur, and injected it with toxin. As he approached Henry and Jett he stripped bloody surgical gloves off his hands and looked up at them with annoyance. His eyes darted quickly from person to person beneath his shaggy white hair as he ascertained why the guard had requested his presence.

"Yes?" he asked, looking back and forth expectantly between Jett and Henry.

"I have the package."

"Good. 82931." It was a receiving code. He said the numbers quickly and from memory. This man was smart, Henry realized. What else had he memorized? What was he thinking about when he looked at Jett?

She reached into her jacket and pulled out a package wrapped in brown paper. It was badly flattened, heavily wrinkled and thoroughly wet. She handed it to him.

He took it. Then he walked to a small table several yards away.

The security guard and one of the suits followed closely behind him, protecting him, or perhaps the package itself.

"Who's the girl?" he asked softly as he pulled apart the brown paper.

"She's the courier."

"I didn't know it was going to be a woman."

"Traymore said she was the best."

"Where's she from?"

"I don't know. He hired her down there."

"She doesn't look American."

"No."

"South American?"

"Looks like it."

"What about him?"

"He's unexpected."

"Odd."

"What do you want to do, doctor?"

Henry watched as the doctor tore open the paper, and pulled something out of a plastic sample bag. He held in his hands a large, perfectly preserved, strikingly-colored bird. Henry had never seen a stranger looking bird in his life: bright green back, glowing cinnamon breast, heavy black bill, blazing cobalt-blue crown. Strangest of all was the tail: long, slate-blue trailers, each one ending in a circular formation of feathers.

Gazing down at the bird, the doctor smiled. He read the identification tag around its leg.

After a moment, he turned to the guard. The doctor's words were soft and final. "I need them, so take them alive." Then he picked up the bird and walked away.

"Yes, sir," the guard replied.

"Henry!" Jett screamed. She grabbed Henry's arm. She yanked him to the elevator. The corridor exploded with motion. Everybody pulled out guns. A guard clutched Henry's jacket. Jett moved forward. She seemed to embrace the attacker, then he collapsed to the floor. She drew her automatic and started shooting. Two guards fell immediately while the others took cover and returned fire. Rounds flew in every direction, ricochetting off the elevator walls.

Henry slammed his fist onto the **CLOSE DOOR** button.

CHAPTER TEN

"I thought these were the good guys!" Henry screamed.

"I thought so too, Henry. I'm sorry. I don't know what's going on. I'm running blind."

"Aren't these the guys who hired you?"

"Yes. Dracon Industries. And they knew the code."

"Wasn't that the right package?"

"He seemed to recognize what it was. I thought I saw him smile."

"But what was it?"

"It looked like a bird."

"A bird? How could a bird possibly be worth all of this?"

"I don't know."

"Why capture us? What did we do?"

"I don't know."

"And what do they want us for? We delivered their darn package. This isn't fair!"

She wasn't listening to him. She was holding down the **CLOSE DOOR** button. She had already pressed the emergency stop button several times. She stared at the complex control panel, wondering what else she could do.

Seeing her effort to concentrate and figure a way out, he stopped talking. He realized for the first time that there was a dead man lying next to him. Security guard. Something stuck through his neck.

Henry picked himself off the floor. Trembling. Weak. Think on your feet, he told himself.

He stumbled over to the control panel.

"Henry, can you figure this out?"

"What's the plan?"

"I don't have one yet."

"You make a plan. I'll get us there."

"We need to make them think this elevator is going down. Then we'll go up. We only have a few minutes. Soon they're going to find a way into this thing. Can you do it? Can you make us look like we're going down even though we're going up?"

"I'll try," he said.

He faced the panel. The buttons blurred before him. He put his hand out to the wall, found Jett and used her for support.

"Come on, Henry," she whispered gently, urging him. "You can do it."

"I'm working on it," he said. He hated working under pressure. He needed time to think things through, to let his mind do its thing. If he had a night to sleep on it he knew he could do it.

The control panel consisted of three areas: a section of buttons for controlling the normal movement of the elevator, a section for emergency and maintenance functions, and below those, a compact alpha-numeric keyboard.

Henry had watched the guard on the way down. Without even realizing it before, he had recorded the keystrokes in his brain. But what good were they? He could figure out what each keystroke did, but he couldn't figure out how he could make the elevator do what Jett wanted. He needed to control the display independently from the actual movement. But the darn thing didn't even have a screen! How was he supposed see what he was doing? He was running blind!

"Come on, Henry."

"I can't figure it out. I can't see anything. No command prompt. No nothing."

"Forget computers, think of something else."

"Modem."

"What?"

"It's like issuing AT commands to a modem when you're not in echo mode." It snapped into his mind like a stroke of lightning.

"Henry."

"I'm working on it."

He knelt down and his fingers started flying across the tiny keys. The solution was simple. And his magic poured from him.

Finally he pressed the "1" key.

The elevator started moving upward.

"What about the display?" She glanced up. The display showed them going down. "Fantastic!"

The elevator stopped.

"What's happening?"

"We're at the first floor. You want the doors open?"

"Get to the side. There may be one guard up here even though they see the elevator going down."

Once he had taken her advice and pressed himself into a corner as best he could, he pushed the button.

The doors opened onto the lobby.

A dozen guards awaited them, weapons drawn.

Henry reached out and pressed the button. A slug went through him.

He went down.

Another round hit him.

The doors slid shut.

He was dizzy. He was already lying flat, but he felt like he was going to fall over. A feeling of vertigo overwhelmed him. He shut his eyes, then opened them. The floor seemed to be moving. It's an elevator, stupid, of course it's moving, he thought to himself.

Then the elevator began to spin.

Jett dropped to her knees. "Henry! Henry, can you hear me?"

The elevator was quiet now. Its thick steel walls blocked out the commotion.

She sat with Henry in silence.

One of the rounds had struck him in the forearm. The other hit his chest, shattering cartilage and diving deep between his third and fourth rib.

She picked him up in her arms and held him.

"Henry," she cried desperately, pressing her hands to the wound. Blood welled up around her fingers.

She took off her jacket, and tried to tie it around him. It wasn't working. Blood kept pouring.

"Jett . . ." he said faintly. "What's happening?"

"You've been hit, Henry. In the chest. It's serious."

"I can't feel anything . . . "

"Good. It would hurt bad if you could . . ."

He whispered something.

She couldn't hear it. "What did you say, Henry?"

He didn't repeat it.

"Henry, I couldn't hear it."

"Armageddon."

"What?" It didn't make sense to her. She held him closer. "What did you say?"

His eyes closed and he slumped in her arms.

CHAPTER ELEVEN

Jett set Henry down, laying him flat on the floor of the elevator. She wasn't sure whether he was alive or dead. Exhaling a deep, ragged breath, she braced herself against the possibility of losing her new friend; she knew she must prepare herself for the battle ahead. She squatted on her haunches, and put her back to the wall. She held the matte black Glock 17 pistol in her hand.

In the seconds when the elevator doors opened and closed –and Henry got hit–she had emptied her seventeen round clip. Now she needed to reload. Taking cartridges out of the box in her pocket, she began pushing them against the magazine spring. She knew that she hit and probably killed five of the attackers. As for the rest of her rounds, she could not be sure. After a dozen or more shots from a 9mm automatic, even Jett tended to lose control. The recoil and noise made concentration difficult in high stress situations. She realized now that on her last several shots she hadn't been aiming. She had blindly showered the corridor with as many bullets as possible–just to defend herself and Henry. Long ago her father had taught her the "defensive barrage" as a valid technique: creating a heavy barrier of fire to deter enemy advance. After she left her father she disdained this method. She preferred to take aim–albeit rapid aim–on a specific target and fire, rather than shooting randomly; at first she got fewer shots, but once she had developed the discipline to remain calm under fire, she could aim and fire almost as quickly as random shooting–and her shots were deadly, not just frightening. Only under the most desperate of situations did her self-discipline deteriorate. Once the seventeen rounds were loaded into the magazine, she slammed the clip into place, pulled back the slide, and looked down at Henry. "You deserved better than that, my friend. Forgive me for not foreseeing the danger. Whether I live or die in the battle to come, I'll take down as many as I can."

She didn't know what had happened or why. She had been hired to do a job and she did it. Why at the last second when the package was delivered would her client turn on her? Who was this doctor? What sort of laboratory was he running? Why did he want them? She knew that when they forced the elevator doors open, she would once again find herself in a do or die situation. She had already decided she would fight, fight to the last. She waited, facing the door, with her weapon in hand.

PART TWO: The Laboratory

CHAPTER TWELVE

The black glass of Pearl Tower pierced upward out of the silver and grey skyline of New York City. Robert Pearl sat at his desk. His lawyer sat in the leather chair in front of him.

"As president of Pearl Research, Robert, you have much to lose from a divorce. I'm not sure I can make any guarantees. I have to tell you, it would be a bad move, for you and the company."

"I'll tell you the simple truth, Jack. I just don't want to be married to her anymore."

"I know that you haven't loved Janet for a long time, but may I ask why you want this divorce? Is there another woman, I mean do you want to get re-married or something? Financially, this is just not the smart thing to do."

"Yes, I know," he agreed. "No, I don't need the divorce for anything like that. I'm not even seeing anyone. My wife is, of course. Has been for a long time. I'm just tired of it. I want a fresh start."

"I understand, Robert, but as your attorney I have to advise you against it, especially right now, at least with what else is happening. We need stability. A shift in ownership would really mix things up. At very least, it would worry some already very nervous investors."

Robert's mind stuck on the phrase "shift in ownership." He never imagined that his company would ever be threatened in such a way, from within. He always knew that his venture could fail, but he thought failure would result from his own mistakes, or lack of commitment, or the forces of the market. It never occurred to him that his desire for freedom—freedom from his wife—could play a factor in the success of his company.

The attorney sat before him begging him not to make the choice. It would affect the attorney's pay check, and his lifestyle, as surely as it would everyone else's. And staring back at Robert, he had that sympathetic look in his eyes that said: "Don't do this, my friend.

You don't know what you're getting yourself into."

The phone rang.

Robert picked it up. His secretary told him that the president of Farlan Corporation was on line one for him. He looked at Jack, indicating that he was going to take the call and that it would be just a moment.

He pressed the button. "Robert Pearl."

Robert paused, listening.

"Yes, I've heard of your company. I believe we met at last year's Research Conference."

Pause.

"Yes, I've heard of her."

Pause.

"I'm not sure she would want me to discuss it . . . She used me as a reference? Very well, what do you need to know?"

Pause.

"I've used her services many times, since about '92."

Pause.

"Yes, she's reliable. Very. We don't use anybody else for work like that."

Pause.

"No, she's not with a firm. She works alone."

Pause.

"Yes, she's experienced in that sort of thing. You wouldn't want to meet her in a dark alley."

Pause.

"South America?" Robert rolled his eyes at Jack, getting a little bored with the interview.

"I don't think that would be a problem for her . . . she was born there."

Pause.

"No," he said, his face becoming more serious. "No, she's not a communist. That's ridiculous. Listen, Jim, I've given you my opinion. I've got to go, I'm in a meeting . . . She is not associated with that organization, and I doubt she ever was. Like I said, she works alone?"

Pause.

"No. You don't need to ask her. Don't even bring up Peru. She doesn't like to talk about it. Where's this delivery to?"

Pause.

"Expensive? Yes, of course she is."

Pause.

"That's too low. I don't think she'd consider it. Don't insult her, Jim. Try Federal Express . . . No, I'm not joking . . . If it's important, use her. If it's not, don't. It's that simple."

Pause.

"No, I don't know where she is. I've not spoken with her in several weeks."

Pause.

"Normally in Manhattan. If she's not there, I would imagine she's making a run, but I don't know that."

Pause.

"Yes, I'll tell her you're looking for her . . . OK, thanks, Jim. I'll see you at this year's conference."

He put the phone down.

He stopped a moment, thinking about something.

The attorney looked up at him. "You OK?"

"Sure," he shrugged. He put the phone call out of his mind and turned painfully back to the subject at hand. "I hear what you're saying, Jack. I'll think about it. Try to come up with something. Get it all ready. Do what you can to protect us. I know it's stupid, but I might have to do it. I'm sorry."

Jack nodded compassionately. "Alright," he said and stood. "I'll be in my office if you want to talk." He let himself out.

Robert remained at his desk, alone in his office. Behind him, the skyscrapers of New York reached to the horizon.

He wanted to talk to her. The phone call had only served to remind him. Especially now, he wanted to talk to her, to see her, even if just for a little while. Pearl Research didn't have anything for her to deliver. Sure, there were things that needed to get places, but none of them demanded the security that she provided. It was personal, and he knew it. He had promised himself last week that he wouldn't call her for personal reasons. If he needed her, he needed her. If he didn't, he didn't. It wasn't right to play games, not with her.

He shook his head, put his elbows on his desk and rubbed his eyes. The sun was setting on the city. The golden light cast long shadows across the buildings and the streets. A bank of heavy midnight blue clouds moved in from the northwest, threatening a thunderstorm. The last time he met with her had been weeks ago, and it had been storming.

She had come into his office and stood before him drenched from the rain. She had just come in from the street and rode the elevator to the top of the Pearl Tower to meet him. They laughed at how wet she was. He offered her a towel and watched while she dried her long, black hair. The dampness of the rain glistened on her lips and eyebrows.

He asked her to sit down and he sat across from her in one of the leather chairs instead of at his desk.

He offered her a drink, and she accepted.

He poured a second for himself and they drank together. They spoke of the way the sunlight had been cutting through the clouds in the minutes just before the storm. They spoke of the traffic in the city, and how it seems to get more frantic just before it starts raining. For a few minutes they were normal people, a man and a woman spending a little time together. Did she feel that, too? Then, of course, he started talking about the new project, and the importance of the package she was to deliver. She had spent enough time working with Robert Pearl to know him and trust him. She listened to his explanations almost casually, without her usual second-guessing. She didn't need to read between the lines. She didn't need to bring out the negotiation techniques associated with a new client. When she gave her price, he never questioned it. Had it been his imagination that she enjoyed his company that night while the lightning flashed around them?

His heart pounding, he picked up the phone and held it a moment, hesitating. Then he pressed his secretary's line. "Julie, would you see if you can get hold of Jett. Try to reach her through the normal channels. . . but . . . please indicate that it is not urgent."

"Alright, I'll find her. Anything else?"

"No, that's it for now. Have a good evening, Julie."

"Good night, Mr. Pearl."

CHAPTER THIRTEEN

Mary Olsen wasn't happy. Her parole officer told her she couldn't see Kelly and Jamie for six months. How was she going to "clean up her act" if she couldn't see her kids? How was she going to stay off the crack if she couldn't get herself happy? And she wasn't going to be happy unless she could see her kids. It was a vicious cycle designed to destroy her; she was convinced of it.

"All those pigs hate me," she decided and threw the empty Scotch bottle at the pavement. The bottle shattered with a satisfying sound, rendering that particular parking spot a land mine to the next set of tires. She stood from the curb, using the parking meter for support.

She stumbled down the sidewalk, grumbling as she went. She stopped often and held up the wall with her hand.

Somehow she lost her way and got into a bad neighborhood, a place with no burned out buildings, no abandoned stores, no overflowing dumpsters. Everything was clean and bare, providing no sustenance or shelter to her. She couldn't even remember the last liquor store she saw, let alone the alley she knew was a good place to sleep. She seemed to be surrounded by banks, office buildings, and skyscrapers. How disgusting, she thought. Not a thing around here. She turned around and headed back the way she thought she came.

She was looking for signs, anything to tell her she was headed toward her alley. She went down what she thought would be a shortcut. She stopped, confused. An eerie feeling crept up her spine. *That's not it.* Then she saw a sign, painted in hobo-lettering on the alley wall:

 "I don't remember seeing that before."

She stared at it. "Why should I be quiet?" she asked the wall, ignoring its advice.

She kept walking, convinced that the alley was a shortcut to the part of town she wanted to get to. All she wanted was her own alley, her own mattress, a comfortable place to crash. She crossed through a second alley, wondering why there weren't any doors on this building. Just grey concrete walls. Nothing at all. She hobbled on, ignoring the sign painted in red on the ground:

#####

"Unsafe place, my eye!" she mumbled, and proceeded angrily. There wasn't a thing around here. What could be unsafe about it? There weren't no dogs, no cops, no gangs, no nothing.

Then she saw a sign that she could not ignore:

She stopped and studied it. "I wonder how old that is?" She looked around. *Danger? I don't see anything.*

Nevertheless, she believed it. She hurried on, checking behind her often, wondering what dreadful thing had happened there. Inexperienced travelers might be kind of easy about jotting the "unsafe place" symbol around. Practically any place was unsafe if you were inexperienced. But the danger sign was serious. People didn't fool around with that. Something really bad must have happened. She pressed herself forward.

Her feet made a crunching noise. She looked down at the ground: glass. Somebody had broken a bottle. The shards of shattered glass lay in a sparkling circle.

"That was me," she remembered with relief. She had come full circle. She had simply started off in the wrong direction. Anybody could make that mistake.

She began walking home, to her alley. She kept thinking about the huge, concrete fortress that she had seen by the danger sign. "It's like a desert over there," she mumbled. Nothing to eat, no place to hide, no garbage cans, nothing to do, nobody around at night. Scary.

She found her alley finally, grabbed the blanket she had hidden in the air conditioning vent of the adjacent building, and curled up on her mattress. It wasn't a bad place to sleep, not at all. It kept her out of the rain. There weren't any losers around, no pigeons to crap on her, and it was pretty quiet. "Can't beat the price," she smiled and shut her eyes, pleasantly numb from the Scotch.

She felt four hands grab her. She woke up instantly and started swinging, mostly just flailing. Somebody was shining a big flashlight in her face and she couldn't see what was happening. Then her clenched fist met a jaw and she heard it crack. "You bastard!" she screamed, spurred on by the satisfaction of hurting one of her attackers. She grabbed somebody's throat. Then somebody whacked her arm with a stick. She fell away, cowering.

They pulled her onto her feet and started dragging her. She wrestled with them until they dropped her and she hit the pavement. She scurried away. They grabbed her again. She swung, but they caught her fists. Then one hit her in the head with something. She went down.

They picked her up again and dragged her toward the vehicle.

What was that? A police car? An ambulance? The men opened up the two big doors in the back and threw her in. There wasn't a bed. There wasn't anything, just a steel floor. A van? The last thing she remembered was screaming at the top of her lungs.

CHAPTER FOURTEEN

Robert Pearl walked into his Long Island home and found it empty. His wife didn't have a job, but she wasn't at home either. She often left for days at a time. She had long ago stopped pretending. She never admitted she was sleeping with another man, but she came and went on her own schedule and seldom informed him. He set down his briefcase, hung up his coat and went into the kitchen to make himself some dinner.

He watched the news while flipping through *Research & Development Magazine*. After getting his Ph.D. in human physiology from Stanford, Robert had started working for Merck. He entered the company as a lab scientist and quickly worked his way up the R & D ladder. Eventually, they asked him to manage the operation. Then Bristol Myers Squibb hired him as their VP of Research and Development. He held that position for five years, turning phantom stocks into real stocks, and earning his way onto the Board of Directors. Then he pooled his assets, pulled his allies together, and formed Pearl Research.

Though many admired Robert Pearl, most analysts considered his venture both dangerous and inappropriate for the conditions of the market. Everyone knew that the age of small, independent research firms was over. Small firms had been replaced by huge, multi-national corporations. Small companies didn't have the resources to compete against the giants.

But Robert Pearl set out to do just that. He built his organization with the aid of a few extremely loyal friends that he had attracted from all over the industry. Then he staffed his labs with young, ingenious, incredibly inexperienced scientists. Kids fresh out of school. Kids that had no experience in corporate politics and the old scientific paradigms. Kids that didn't know any better than to invent new medicines.

Within six months Pearl Research had patented a new herpes drug that sold through a distributor. It took the market by storm and rocketed Pearl Research into the pharmaceutical arena with great fanfare. Eight months later they followed up with a vitamin supplement which became part of the daily regimen for many hospitals. Every analyst in the industry predicted that Pearl would go public within the year.

It didn't. Robert Pearl held onto his interests. He rewarded his technicians and partners handsomely, pouring an incredible, almost irresponsible, percentage of the profits into their salaries. He issued private shares in the company to all his top people, those that had started with him and stuck by him. Those that believed in his dream. All the rest of the company's assets he kept for himself, putting them in his and his wife's name.

He often wondered what went wrong with his marriage. He couldn't remember the day it went bad. One day he just woke up and realized it. His wife was sleeping next to him. He looked at her and realized that he didn't enjoy her company, hadn't touched her in months, hadn't thought about her. At the time he hadn't even known that she was seeing someone else. He found out about that later.

His Irish setter came over to his chair and pushed its nose under his hand.

He smiled and rubbed his hand over the dog's head.

The setter encouraged his efforts by putting its paw on his thigh. Of course it didn't realize that its claws were digging into his worsted wool suit, not to mention his worsted human skin.

His secretary had mentioned that afternoon that she couldn't get hold of their normal courier, and that if he needed a special delivery she would find a different firm. He had shaken his head. "No, I just wanted to talk to her," he admitted. In his corporate world, thinking about Jett was dangerous, and talking like this was almost reckless. Despite the fact that his wife had somehow won the alliance of his last secretary, and her betrayal still hurt him, Robert couldn't help from trusting his new secretary. He liked Julie Banks. Top notch professional. Good friend. If he couldn't trust his own secretary, then who could he trust? A secretary sees everything, knows everything, does everything. And she had the right to know that he was thinking about Jett as more than just a courier.

Robert wondered where she was. He couldn't stop thinking about her. He hadn't seen her in a long time. Was she in South America again? She told him she was born there and had "clawed" her way out. She returned only on business, only when she had to. When she was "home," she preferred to be in New York. She seldom spoke Spanish in front of him. She had worked hard to master American English. He hardly even noticed her accent anymore. Years ago she had asked him to help her become a U.S. citizen. He remembered that experience fondly now.

He missed her. It was that simple. He had missed her on other occasions, but this was the first time he had ever attempted to contact her for purely personal reasons. He realized he was crossing a line, moving into a territory that would disrupt everything he was used to, everything that was expected of him. He analyzed himself ruthlessly. What are you doing? What's going to come of this? Are you infatuated?

He had hoped that something would happen in the company labs that would require her services. Unfortunately, nothing had been coming out of his labs in quite a while. It was going on six months now and no new patents had been applied for. The flow of cash was starting to slow down. Soon the flow would reverse itself completely. Money would pour out of the company as fast as it came in.

Health care was big business. The research and development of new drugs was one of the most turbulent forces in the American economy. Drug companies, especially new ones with bright futures, were hot items on the stock market. They were analyzed constantly, whether they were being traded or not. And they competed with each other on the most direct terms.

He had heard of labs stealing each other's ideas, intercepting each other's correspondence, doing anything to gain the advantage. Of course an advantage this year seldom carried over to the next. The drug market fluctuated, changed shape, changed direction. A new company would come out with a new drug and wreak havoc on the old structure. Then an even newer drug would hit the scene and change everything around again. The only thing that was constant was change. And cancer research.

On occasion he heard that a firm's key shipment had never arrived at its destination. Or that a technician carrying test samples in his car got in a weird car accident. He even heard about an armed robbery of a computer disk. The disk had contained the DNA sequences associated with a cure for Alzheimer's disease. Those were facts. But did the thief know what he was stealing? Were the shipments intercepted?

Foul play was seldom discussed openly among the elite of his industry, but everyone suspected it, and perhaps some used it when the stakes were high. Robert Pearl wasn't sure who did what or how. He just knew there were rumors.

When he was on the brink of a new discovery, he wanted to make very sure that it was not hindered by outside influences, and he certainly didn't want to endanger the well being of his associates. That's why he chose to hire a professional courier when necessary. And Jett, though an independent, was the most professional courier he knew. He trusted her implicitly.

He wondered, now, whether those rumors could be true. Had Jett encountered some sort of foul play? Is that why she hadn't surfaced in weeks?

CHAPTER FIFTEEN

When Mary Olsen woke up she was clean. What happened? she wondered. Her skin felt tender, like somebody had scraped her whole body with a pumice stone. Somebody had stolen her clothes and put her in a stupid gown. She looked around the hospital room. Is that what it was? There was something strange about it, but she couldn't figure it out. She was lying in one of the room's two beds. Everything around her was white and sterile. She turned her head and looked over at the other bed.

A young woman with dark skin and long black hair lay there, her eyes closed. What's wrong with her? Mary wondered.

Mary tried to sit up. She had a terrible headache. There wasn't any aspirin around. In fact there wasn't even a table. The room was empty. Four white walls and two beds. That was it.

She looked at the two steel doors. One had a window, but she couldn't see through it.

She looked up at the fluorescent lights on the ceiling. Disgustingly bright, she thought. Where am I?

She had been in a rehab facility enough to know this wasn't one. This place reminded her of a hospital, but there wasn't enough equipment. And hospitals didn't shut doors. Did those bastards throw me in a mental institution?

She was hungry. She wanted a cigarette. And she had to piss.

"Hey!" she screamed. "Somebody! Hey!"

An electronic voice came over an unseen speaker: "What do you want?"

"I need to take a piss!"

"The door on the left leads to a bathroom," the Voice said.

"Fine. Where am I?"

The Voice did not answer.

"Well that's about as good as a kick in the head," she grumbled as she threw her feet onto the floor and ambled over to the bathroom.

Afterward, she went to the other door and peered through the mirror-like glass. "Somebody better clean that window," she said. "Can't see a thing through it."

She walked along the bare wall, then meandered over to the other bed. "Hey," she said. "You awake?" She nudged her. "Hey, girl, you awake?"

Her roommate did not respond.

"You awake?" She hit her a little harder.

Nothing.

"Looks like you're going to be fun company," she complained. Then she looked up at the unseen Voice: "Hey! My roommate's dead! I need a new one!"

CHAPTER SIXTEEN

Jett reached for her Glock 17. She couldn't find it. She opened her eyes.

She gazed around at the white cell. Where was Henry?

Was Henry dead? The memories dropped onto her like gigantic spiders and crawled through her brain until she shut her eyes, tightened her face, and held herself very still. Little tears of pain struggled to flow from her eyes but she wouldn't let them. She tightened herself, pulling her fingers into a fist, bracing herself against the despair.

She regained her composure, slowly replacing her grief with anger. Anger was a useful emotion, she knew, an emotion she could use to survive.

She opened her eyes again. She couldn't remember how they had overwhelmed her. Maybe they filled the elevator with anesthetizing gas. She couldn't remember anything after Henry went down. She remembered seeing the poor kid lying on the floor, not knowing what was happening to him. She tensed herself against nausea. She knew in her heart that she had led him to this demise, and it sickened her.

Looking around, she surmised that she was still underground. There was a basement-like dampness in the air and no windows to the outside. She remembered the many steel doors lining the corridor of the Dracon Building. Did each one lead to a cell like hers?

She was in no immediate danger. She was not severely injured or in any pain. She wore a standard hospital gown. They had re-dressed the wound on her leg. She was disoriented, and a little hungry, but otherwise whole.

She turned her head and looked over at the other bed.

"Howdy," the woman said. She was a friendly looking woman in her late thirties with shoulder-length brown hair, brown eyes and a permanent dull grin on her face. "How you feelin', girl?"

"Alright, I guess," Jett said. She tried to sit up.

"The food ain't bad here, but they don't bring enough of it.

There ain't no booze or TV. I'm glad there's somebody to talk to finally. I've been talking to the geek running the voice box, but that gets old quick. He's not much of a congregationalist."

"Where are we?"

"I donno. Loony bin I think."

"Loony bin?"

"Insane asylum, sanatorium, brain clinic, house on the hill, whatever you want to call it, you know, men in white coats. They all got white coats, except the big guys."

"The big guys?"

"The guards."

She nodded, remembering the guards. "How long have you been in here?"

"A few days now . . . I think. I don't really know. They feed me good and there ain't nobody stealing my stuff, so it ain't that bad, really."

"Did you say there was a voice?" she asked. She scanned the surface of the ceiling looking for a speaker, microphone or camera. She could discern nothing. If they were there, they were well hidden.

"What are you in here for?" her roommate asked her.

"I'm not sure," she replied, but didn't elaborate.

"Me neither. I was doing pretty good, then all of sudden the goons picked me up off the street. They threw me in here. It's a kick in the head, but at least they feed me good."

"Yes, that's important," Jett agreed and put her bare feet on the cold floor.

"I wish they would let us smoke. I'm dying for a cigarette. Most places at least let me smoke. Even the rehab let's me smoke. Better addicted to nicotine than crack, I guess they figure . . . though from what I've been told nicotine is a lot worst for you than crack, it just takes longer."

"That's one way to look at it," Jett agreed. She walked slowly to the door, examined its frame and hinges. There was no door knob or handle. She noted the one-way glass. She touched the concrete wall. Cinder block. Nothing special there. She looked up at the lights. Fluorescents hanging from a white ceiling.

She went into the bathroom. Sink. Toilet. Shower. Cinder block ceiling. No shower curtain, towels or other amenities. What she would have given for a soap-on-a-rope. The rope would have come in handy for strangling the next guard that came through the door.

"Hey, you OK in there, girl?" her roommate said from the other side of the door.

"Yes, I'm alright, thank you."

She washed her hands and face, even though they were already clean. She looked into the mirror. Her eyes were bloodshot and red. Had she been crying?

Why had they spared her? she wondered. Why hadn't they killed her? What were they planning to do with her? Where was Henry? Was he still alive? Was he locked in a cell like this one?

She returned to her bed and lay down. She shut her eyes and lay her arm over her face, trying to relax. How long had she been in here? Would anyone be looking for her on the outside? She realized that no one would even notice she was missing. She lived alone in her Manhattan apartment. As usual, she was a thousand miles from there. She didn't have any friends. That's why she liked Henry. He didn't have any friends either.

No one would miss her. She had no social circle, no upcoming family events, no romantic evenings planned, nothing that would indicate to someone on the outside that there was something wrong and that she needed help.

The last "social event" she had participated in had been to sit down with a client and have a few drinks in his office. Sure, she enjoyed it, but it wouldn't stick in his mind as anything significant. She was pretending they were friends; he was being polite. It was a sorry excuse for a social life.

She just wasn't a social person. She traveled too much, worked too much. There was too much junk running around her head, too much in her past to burden someone with. Henry befriended her, and look what happened to him.

Again, though, her thoughts turned to that afternoon in Robert Pearl's office. It had been a wonderful talk, quiet, relaxed. She remembered the wetness of her clothes, her tangled hair compared to his well-groomed perfection. She remembered the purple clouds hanging over the tower, the strokes of lightning flashing across the panes of smoked glass. They sat quietly, absorbing the sensations of the storm. For a little while they shared a piece of the changing universe.

Of course Pearl was the president of a thirty million dollar company. He wasn't going to be sitting around wondering where his courier was. He had more important things to be thinking about, his wife for one thing.

She remembered when Pearl mentioned that he was married. He didn't say anything negative, or anything positive. He just said he was married, but Jett thought at the time that there was something significant in that. Over the years she had seen quite a bit of Robert Pearl. Never for a long time, but sometimes they just sat and talked. They talked about anything, everything, whatever was going on. She always enjoyed that.

He dealt with her as a professional, almost a partner sometimes, making it clear that she was important to the success of his project. He explained things and spoke to her as an equal. He was unpretentious, unthreatening. The many powerful men she had met in her work were very closed people. Robert, on the other hand, treated her like a human being, almost warmly. She liked that immensely.

"Hey, girl, you bring anything in here with you?"

"What?" Jett opened her eyes and turned to her roommate, whom she had all but forgotten.

"You bring anything with you?"

"Like what?" she asked. Jett was thinking about her 9mm.

"Smokes. You got any smokes?"

"No, I don't. I'm sorry."

"I don't understand why they don't let us smoke. It's just a cigarette!"

The door opened.

Jett jumped to her feet.

The guard stopped immediately, prepared for an attack. Behind him, there were two others like him. "Are you going to cause trouble?" he asked. He was looking at Jett.

"¡Claro que si, pendejo!" she spat at him.–Most definitely, you jerk.

"What'd you say?"

"¿No le enseñaron Español en la escuela de brutos tontos?" –Didn't they teach you Spanish in stupid-goon school?

"You better not mess with these guys, girl. They'll take you down hard!"

Jett ignored this. She stared back at the guard, almost

challenging him to approach her.

"Just cool yourself down," the guard said, putting his hands up in a conciliatory manner. "We're not going to hurt you. Just calm down."

Jett did not respond. She stared back at him, measuring him as an enemy.

Another guard entered the room. The door remained ajar behind them, held by a third.

The first guard took a step toward her.

"Sit on the bed," he suggested. He was trying to be as non-threatening as possible.

She realized that they had gotten her into the room against her will. She didn't even know how they did it. They probably drugged her. They could, of course, drug her again, tie her up and do anything they wanted to her. She forced herself to sit.

"Looks like she's going to be OK," the guard said over his shoulder.

The guard holding the door motioned to someone in the corridor.

The doctor to whom she had delivered the package came in. His facial skin was pasty dry beneath his white hair and white mustache. He walked toward her wielding a syringe.

"Don't worry, girl, it's just vitamins," her roommate said, seeing her fear.

Despite her plan to remain calm, Jett panicked. She punched the guard in the throat.

The guard went down immediately, choking like he was going to die.

The doctor ducked away, allowing the two guards to charge past him.

Jett leaped to the other side of the bed.

The larger of the two guards tossed the bed aside and grabbed her.

She kicked in his knee. He went down in agony.

The third guard tackled her to the floor, her head cracking against the tile.

Guards poured in from the corridor. Suddenly there were three men on top of her. They held her down. She struggled furiously, kicking and punching and biting. She could not overpower them.

Finally, they picked up her entire body. For a moment she was dangling in mid air between them. She twisted wildly. They dropped her. She slammed painfully to the floor. They grabbed her again. They forced her onto the bed, then clamped her wrists and ankles to it.

The doctor approached once again. His rubber gloved hands touched her and she flinched away. They held her arm firmly, as he thrust the needle into her, and pushed the contents of the barrel into her vein. He rubbed the area with alcohol, and departed quickly with the guards close behind.

The lights went out.

Jett heard her roommate turn toward her. "You handled that well," she said.

"Thanks. I thought so, too," Jett replied.

CHAPTER SEVENTEEN

When the lights came back on, Jett realized that the clamps on her wrists and ankles had been removed.

"You up, girl?" Mary asked.

"Yes, I'm up," Jett said. "Did they come back in?"

"What, last night?" Mary said.

"Yeah," Jett said.

"I was dead to the world. I'm used to getting rained on, and traffic going by, and people kicking me. All this still and quiet is unnatural, but I sleep like a log."

"Me too," Jett said. It was her father that had taught her to sleep light, to sleep on buses, and under porches, and sitting in the jungle waiting for the next patrol to come by. Even when they were at home he never let her sleep more than a few hours at a time. He would come into her room and wake her up, just to make sure she could get back to sleep again and be alright in the morning. "Get used to it," he told her. "It's the way you're going to live." Like a cat, she learned to sleep a few hours at a time, usually during the day, so that she would have the energy to prowl through the night. Yet, just as her roommate had described, she too slept soundly through the night, and she did not remember anyone removing the clamps.

"What's your name?" her roommate asked.

"Santiago," she said, using the name on her U.S. passport. She wanted to see how much her captors knew about her. Were they listening? Would they think the passport was real? She didn't have a U.S. passport for her real name. She would have never gotten into the country with her real name.

"Santiago?"

"That's a lovely name, but you don't look like a Santiago."

"I don't? What does a Santiago look like?"

"Well . . . I don't know, but you don't look like one. Aren't you gonna ask me my name? It's Mary, Mary Olsen. You got any kids?"

"No. I came here with a friend, though. His name is Henry. Have you heard anything about him? I think he's in here, too."

"Henry? No, I've not heard anything about a Henry. Sorry 'bout that. These guys are real bastards. We can't even make any phone calls. I got two kids. One boy, one girl. The government won't let me see 'em. They says I'm a drug addict."

Jett didn't reply to this.

"I wish they'd hurry up and get in here with the grub!"

Just as she spoke, the door opened, and a medical assistant arrived with two trays of food. The guards stood at the door behind the assistant. He walked forward. He had been warned of the occupants. His tremble caused Jett's orange juice to spill onto the tray.

"That's alright," Jett said and took the tray from him.

The assistant turned and left quickly. The guards shut the door behind him.

In the "days" and "nights" which followed, the "institution" put Jett and Mary Olsen through a battery of tests. They drew samples, took blood pressure, listened to their lungs, looked in their ears and throats. Each day they injected into them a syringe full of blood serum they said was "vitamins." Most of the time, it was the white haired doctor who performed these tasks, though sometimes his assistant did the work under his supervision. It slowly became evident to Jett that the white haired doctor was in charge of everything. The orderlies, the medical assistants, even the guards deferred to him. Whatever he said was treated like an order, no matter how he said it.

When the doctor came around each day he was usually accompanied by the medical assistant who had spilled Jett's orange juice. He would stand behind the doctor and hold the tray of equipment. He would say nothing and never lifted his eyes to look at her. Jett managed to count eight used and four unused needle cases on the tray and concluded there were at least twelve "patients" on that floor.

She knew better than to ask questions. They would always be ignored and she realized, too, that they would betray the fact that she was still thinking about how to get out. There was no sense tipping her hand. She decided she wouldn't talk to them anymore until she had a plan in mind.

She tried many times to figure out the purpose of their tests and what they were injecting into her. She covertly read each of the bottles on the assistant's tray, but they had anticipated her interest and covered the labels. Each bottle was identified with only a number.

One day the doctor did not come. The medical assistant came alone.

The guards stood at the door while he worked through the tests and multiple injections that he had seen his mentor perform a dozen times before.

"Where's your boss?" Jett asked quietly.

He started when she spoke. The guards had warned him about her. He was a young man, and not as experienced as the doctor. His fingers trembling as he unwrapped a vial. He tried to ignore her.

"Where's your boss?" she asked again, her voice low, unthreatening, and serious: something that could not be ignored.

"He's not here today," he said as he opened up the mercury sphygmomanometer.

She raised her arm to let him wrap the blood pressure cuff around her. She turned slightly, and his hand grazed her side, touching her breast through the hospital gown.

"You OK? You seem a little on edge," she said.

After injecting her with the blood serum, he prepared to inject her with a clear liquid. She studied the vials. The labels had been covered with paper sleeves. She could not read them.

"I'm fine," he said, a little irritated by her attention, and very nervous.

"I know you're new at this. Everybody's got to learn, right?"

He pulled the needle sheath off the syringe. She raised her sleeve, exposing the back of her arm. He dabbed it with a swab of alcohol.

"If you mess up, I won't say anything," she said.

He didn't answer. The more he thought about not making a mistake, the more likely he would.

"Do you know if my friend Henry is alive?"

When he stabbed the needle into her, she jerked her hand and knocked the bottles off the tray. One fell to the floor and shattered.

Thinking it was an attack, the guards rushed forward, ready to subdue her. She glanced down at the shattered bottle. The break had caused the numbered sleeve to tear apart, but failed to expose the real label underneath.

The guards surrounded her.

"It's OK!" the assistant told them, waving them off, embarrassed that his fumbled use of the needle had caused the accident.

He picked up the shattered pieces of the vial, wiped the floor with a cloth, and left the room in silence, praying that his boss would not hear of the incident.

During the night she tried to stay awake, and for a while she succeeded. She sat in her bed in the pitch dark with her eyes open and listened. She listened for Henry. She listened for anything. She heard the grumbling of generators, the whine of an elevator motor, and the screams of monkeys. At first she thought she had fallen asleep and dropped into a nightmare. But she was still fully awake. Somewhere, there were monkeys. Live monkeys. And they were screaming.

CHAPTER EIGHTEEN

On Friday, the Philadelphia Human Physiology Conference let out early. Five hundred suited men and women flooded out of the convention center, filled cabs, and headed for the airport. They were all going home to their friends and families. Pearl walked slowly out of the building, waving occasionally to passing colleagues bidding him farewell.

"See you next year, Robert!" they would call out amiably.

"Thanks for the tip! I'll fax you a copy of the results on Monday!" said another who had exchanged some ideas with him during the week-long conference.

"Call me," winked one of his female colleagues as she passed. She was just joking, of course. They had been good friends for ten years. She was the best microbiologist he had ever worked with.

Robert's mind was elsewhere. He flagged a cab.

"Take me to the train station," he told the driver.

He didn't ask himself what he was doing. He didn't want to ask himself. He knew he wouldn't like the answer. He just bought the ticket and got on the train.

Three hours later the train had traversed New York, gone under the Hudson River via the Lincoln Tunnel and come up on Manhattan Island at Grand Central Station, nowhere near his office or his Long Island home. He walked to 42nd Street and caught a cab. He remembered when they applied for her passport: Jetta Mendoza Santiago. 15th Floor, Suite 1A. Wallren Building. 1313 Broadway. New York, NY 10010.

He met the uniformed doorman.

"Sure, I know her," he said. "You a friend of hers?"

He nodded. "I've not seen her in a while–" he started to say.

"–She's been gone all month!" the doorman exclaimed. "She's quite often away on business, but she's not usually gone this long."

"Do you suppose she's overseas?"

He shrugged. "I wouldn't know. Seems like she'd let *you*

know."

"Does she have any other friends around here? I'm from the other side of town."

The doorman thought about that question for a moment, then wrinkled his mouth, "Not that I can think of."

"You sure? It's kind of important."

He thought again, then shook his head. "Sorry. I don't recall her hanging around with anyone. Beautiful lady, but kind of a loner. Hey, just a second, OK?"

"Sure," he said and waited while the doorman went into the Wallren Building.

A hundred people walked by while Robert wondered what he was doing in this part of town. He was glad there was little chance somebody would recognize him. If they did, he had no excuse for being there. He hadn't even bothered to think one up. He was just there, looking for some woman about whom he knew very little–except that he liked her.

The doorman returned. "Hey, I just talked to the guy at the desk. He said she hasn't picked up her mail since the fifth of last month."

"The fifth?"

"Yup. So it's no wonder you haven't heard from her. She's been out of town for a while."

Robert Pearl was sad. There wasn't any other way to describe his feelings. He was just plain sad. He missed her. He wanted to see her. He nodded to the doorman, and began to turn away. Then he stopped and turned back. He put a twenty dollar bill in the doorman's hand. "Thanks." He couldn't think of anything to say, so he turned again to leave.

"You know somebody's watching you?"

"Excuse me?" Robert stopped and turned back toward him. "What did you say?"

"There's a guy over there and he's watching you."

"Behind me?" Robert asked, without turning.

"Yup. Hey, you in trouble?"

"No. No, I'm not," he frowned. "I don't know why anyone would be following me."

"Well, he's gone now."

Robert turned and scanned the other side of the street. "Where did he go?"

"He went into that deli there. You see it?"

"Yes, I see it. You sure he was watching me?"

"No doubt about it. Then he realized I spotted him. That's when he went into the deli. He'll be ducking his head behind a newspaper soon."

Robert put his leather gloves on and started walking down the street.

Eventually he flagged a cab.

He would be getting home hours later than he should. It never occurred to him to call his wife; she wouldn't be home anyway.

He wanted to get into Jett's apartment. He wanted to walk through it, see how she lived, see what sort of books she had on the shelf. Would they be in Spanish or English? He imagined she would have maps on her walls, maps of all the places she had been. He imagined she would have an expensive, well-kept suite, a place she would sleep in only now and again, and call home, but never really love it like a home. She wouldn't have a cat or a dog, or any house plants; she wouldn't want anyone in her place to take care of such things while she was gone. She wouldn't have an answering machine or a cordless telephone; they were a security risk. The wall coverings in her rooms would be somber. The furnishings would be expensive and elegant, yet simple and practical in design. She made enough money from his company alone to maintain the Manhattan apartment, and another in Tokyo if she wanted.

Yet, he didn't think she had another apartment somewhere else. She wanted to make her home in the United States. Sometimes she talked about it, and he was always left with the impression that she was glad to get out of Peru, glad to get away from whatever she left there. She never said those words explicitly, but he was always left with that thought. He wondered what would happen if he went there, to Peru. Would he find any trace of her? He laughed at himself.

CHAPTER NINETEEN

"What's all the new equipment for?" Mary asked as the doctor plugged the Datascope into the wall socket. He proceeded to connect the topical sensors to her wrist, temples, throat and chest. He flipped on the power switch, and watched her heart rate, blood pressure and pulse pressure appear graphically on the scope's screen.

"Wow! That's quite a box. What's it for?" Mary asked.

He used an alligator clip to attach the lighter-sized box to her sleeve. The Datascope would use RF telemetry technology to track her vital signs, even when she moved away from the bed.

Jett watched with fascination as he put the equipment together. She had learned much in her captivity, much that her captors were not aware of. She had found the cameras in the ceiling. She had silently measured the sound of the elevator and determined she was on the third floor underground. When the assistant brought him paperwork, she had secretly watched the doctor sign his name: Dr. Raymond D. Caldwell.

Caldwell set up the polymer sensors to pick up Mary's epinephrine levels in real time.

He had already inserted a catheter into Mary's chest, just below the collar bone, into which he inserted a needle and a clear plastic tube. The tube ran to a Horizon IV pump with membrane keys and a LCD readout. The readout displayed the rate as it pumped. Two small bags of clear liquid and one large bag of milky liquid hung from the IV rack.

With guards standing by, he left the room and returned rolling in another piece of equipment. Jett wasn't sure what it was. She didn't recognize it. The brand name on the main unit was "Zoll", but that didn't mean anything to her.

"What's that?" cried Mary seeing the strange wires and electrodes protruding from the thing.

Caldwell plugged in the machine and waited. Jett could hear the spin up of a hard disk, the static snap of a CRT coming on, and what sounded like the charging of a high-voltage electric coil.

"This might smart a little when I first connect it," the doctor said to Mary, ignoring her fear.

The moment he touched her, the electricity jolted through her body, instantly forcing her arms and legs rigid as she screamed.

He hurriedly flipped a switch on the Zoll's control panel to stop the charge. "Set a bit too high, I think," he said to himself. He turned a dial, turned it on again, and watched her heart beat register on the screen.

"God, what are you doing?" Mary cried. "What is this thing?"

"It's for your own protection. It's a transthoracic pacemaker that I've modified to include external electrodes for cardiopulmonary resuscitation. If something goes wrong, it will automatically give you a little jolt. Don't be alarmed. It will help keep your heart regular."

"What's going to happen? My heart's fine!"

Nobody answered Mary's question. Caldwell left the room, and the others followed him.

During the night, while the lights were out, Jett slipped out of bed. She took out from under the mattress the piece of broken glass that she had found on the floor and ferreted away after she broke the drug vial. She crept over to Mary's bed. She disconnected the tube that ran from the IV pump to the catheter, then used the sharp edge of the glass to cut it. She reconnected the new end. She returned to her bed and hid the twenty inches of tube under her pillow. Later she would transfer it to a better spot.

The next morning Caldwell returned with his guards and assistant. He checked and recorded a few measurements in his log, then turned his attention to Mary Olsen.

"What's going to happen to me, Doc?" she asked.

"Nothing out of the ordinary," he said. He sat on the bed. He picked up an ophthalmoscope from the tray and checked her eyes. He held her face while he inserted the tongue depressor into her mouth. Then he examined her ears with the otoscope. After the cursory examination, he turned to his medical assistant.

"She's in good shape. I think we're ready to begin."

"Begin what?" Mary wanted to know.

"Nothing to worry about," he told her as he pulled a small glass vial out of his lab coat. This was the first vial Jett had seen that didn't come from the tray. It contained a yellow-green liquid. He shook the vial, tipped it upside down, then drew the liquid into a 1cc hypodermic syringe. As he filled the syringe, Jett read Caldwell's upside-down handwriting:

phyllomedusa bicolor – Sapo solution 1%

Within seconds the syringe was filled and he slipped the vial back into his pocket. Jett returned her eyes to her lap and memorized what she had seen.

"What's that slimy stuff, Doc?" Mary asked. "It doesn't look too good for you!"

"Nothing to worry about," he said. "Just vitamins." He picked up her arm and thrust in the needle without hesitation.

"Ouch! Doc, you need to take some lessons!" Mary complained.

"Just be quiet a moment, will you!" he snapped at her. He grabbed her shoulders and looked straight at her. "Stop your drivel and tell me what you're feeling, now!"

"Why? What should I be feeling? What is that stuff you put in me?"

In the minutes which followed, everyone watched her. Her face flushed red. She began to sweat profusely, especially from her forehead. She rubbed her brow, and glanced over at Jett. Mary's body seemed to take on a wholly different appearance. It seemed to be radiating heat and energy. Mary was moving slowly, like she was sick to her stomach, but Jett could see the muscles in her arms and legs dancing with minute agitation.

Mary's hand rose to her chest, as one who is having a heart attack. "I'm feeling a little tight, Doc."

"Don't worry, Mary. That's to be expected. What else are you feeling?" He glanced at the Datascope and the medical assistant monitoring it. "Are you getting all this?" he shouted.

"Doc, I'm burning up! I'm feeling really tight. My heart . . . It's pounding like it's going to explode."

"One thirty," the assistant said.

"Doc, what's happening?"

"One hundred seventy five with arrhythmia."

Caldwell noted the redness of her arms and legs. "Severe capillary dilation all over the body," he remarked coldly, seemingly unaware that his patient could hear the running dialogue of her condition.

Mary bent at her waist. She put her hand on her stomach. For a moment she panicked, tried to get out of the bed and run, but the guards grabbed her. She gasped and vomited violently. Disgusted, the guards withdrew. She fell to the floor, urinating, defecating and crawling away from them. The mass of wires and tubes pulled taught.

"It's alright!" Caldwell was telling everyone in a loud, authoritative voice. "It's to be expected." But he was obviously surprised.

Mary crawled around the floor on all fours. "Motherhelpme, Motherhelpme, Motherhelpme," it came out like the snarl of a rabid dog. Then she spat something unintelligible and started shouting like a woman possessed. She was in another world, her mind totally blitzed. She started leaping up and down, like a baboon. She growled ferociously, and lashed at the guards like she had claws.

"Heart rate: two twenty three! Pressure change is off the scale, Doctor."

Mary's body went into violent convulsions.

"Doctor, her heart is fibrillating!"

Mary's legs and arms flailed.

The assistant reached toward her, to help her.

"Don't!" Caldwell ordered. "The Zoll will do it!"

Just then the Zoll kicked in, sending a massive shock through her body. Mary screamed and went rigid, then fell limp. The pattern on the Datascope scrambled, like it couldn't pick up a sensible signal. The Zoll kicked in again, then twice more, until it had finally stabilized her heart.

"One fifty five and dropping . . ." the assistant was saying, sweat pouring from his brow. "We almost lost her, Doctor."

"Did you see that epinephrin level?" he said, exhilarated by the experiment and ignoring his assistant's comment.

Mary's heart rate slowed. She gasped repeatedly for breath. She crawled toward Jett's side of the room and gazed up at her with pitiful, uncomprehending eyes, like an animal being tortured. Jett moved off the bed, dropped to her knees and embraced her.

"It'll be over soon, Mary," Jett told her.

"Santiago . . ." Mary muttered.

"Just hold on . . . I'll take care of you." Mary seemed to

understand these words. She held onto Jett with great strength, shaking all over.

"Don't let them hurt me anymore, Santiago."

Jett held her, and pressed her hand to her head, and said soothing words to her. All the while Caldwell watched them, and his assistant took notes.

CHAPTER TWENTY

"No, I've not talked to her in two months," Robert Pearl told the caller. It was the president of Farlan Corporation again, asking about Jett. "I've not seen her."

He paused while the caller tried to persuade him to tell her where she was.

"It's not that I'm not telling you. I truly don't know. I wish I could find her. I have a job for her myself, after yours, of course . . . No, I don't think she's there, and even if she was I wouldn't know how to reach her . . . No, she doesn't go there except on business . . . . Very well, I'll keep that in mind. Goodbye."

He hung up the phone.

"That guy's persistent!" Jack exclaimed. The corporate attorney shook his head and smiled. "I wonder what's going on over there."

"A little too persistent for my tastes," Robert said.

"Sounds like a jerk."

"A jerk that needs something delivered."

"Why doesn't he get somebody else to do it? There are other special couriers."

Robert nodded, but he hadn't really heard what Jack said.

Jack noticed this. "You still worried about her?"

He hesitated, then nodded.

"Hey, Jett's a tough cookie. She could beat the crap out of both of us. What could happen to her?"

"Yeah, you're right."

"I'm sure she's alright. She's probably down in Tahiti lying in the sun, getting a nice tan and drinking margaritas while she looks at the young bucks half your age."

Robert smiled. "Yeah, you're probably right, but somehow that doesn't make me feel any better, Jack."

They laughed together, then Jack took the opportunity to shift gears. "Have you thought any more about your home situation?"

Robert nodded morosely.

"Do you think a reconciliation is possible?"

"A reconciliation? No. Continued estrangement, yes, at least for a little while, but no reconciliation. So many things are up in the air right now anyway. I wouldn't want to do anything yet, not yet."

"When's the last time you saw her?"

Robert's mind rushed forward in panic. Was it that obvious that he was still thinking about Jett? Or was Jack asking about his wife? "I saw Janet last week before I went to Philadelphia for the conference."

"Not since?"

"No. Why?"

"I just wonder what she's up to."

"What do you mean?"

"I mean, as your attorney I need to be prepared for certain possibilities, and warn you of them."

"Like what sort of possibilities?"

"I don't know. Have you ever thought that *she* might divorce *you*?"

This surprised Robert. "Why would she do that? She would stand to lose too much."

"Not if she went about it right."

"What do you mean?"

"Have you had any social involvement with . . . other women?"

"No," Robert said, which was the truth, unless thoughts counted.

"All I'm saying is that if you decide to do something, then be discreet . . . If you decide to do something."

"Like what?" Robert asked. *What's he getting at?*

Jack shrugged. "I don't know. Just be careful. She doesn't want to be married to you any more than you want to be married to her. If I know Janet, she'll use any opportunity she can."

"Don't worry. There's no chance anything like that is going to happen. Now, can we get on with more interesting subjects?"

Jack smiled. "Sure, boss, lead on!"

"Good. What about this investment firm? Did they send you a proposal?"

"Sure did, the day after we talked to them. Impressive."

"What was the bottom line?"

"You really want to know?"

"Absolutely. That's the only reason I got them in here. You don't think I really want to sell the company, do you?"

Jack shrugged. "I thought maybe you were getting tired of it, or maybe looking for a little working capital."

"I wouldn't share anything with those vultures. What'd they offer?"

"They have thirty million in T-bills waiting. Thirty million cash. Flat out."

"*What?*" He was stunned. The company wasn't worth half that, judging by its most recent financials. He had built the company himself and had made a personal commitment to get it through its slump, and *even he* didn't believe it was worth thirty million. What sort of information were these guys working with? "Thirty million?"

"That's what it said. I was astounded when I saw it."

Robert Pearl started to laugh.

His attorney looked back at him, at first puzzled, then started to laugh with him.

"Did you ever think we'd be running a company worth thirty million dollars, Jack?"

"No, and, frankly, I'm not sure we do."

"Well, somebody thinks so!" he laughed.

After a while, Robert brought his laughter under control and gathered some of the paperwork on his desk.

Jack stood up. "Well, it's been fun. I'll see you later. I got a two o'clock I'm late for."

"I'll talk to you later, Jack," Robert said. He picked up his pen and turned to the first document in the pile.

As Jack opened the door on his way out, he stopped. He was frustrated with his inability to figure out what his boss was thinking. It should have been obvious to him, he realized, but it wasn't. "Well, what should I tell them?"

Robert smiled. "Tell them we're insulted by such a low offer."

CHAPTER TWENTY-ONE

That night, long after her watchers had turned off the lights, Jett slipped out of the bed. Reaching beneath it, she removed several of the metal clips from the wire frame. Then she crept through the darkness to the bathroom, opened the toilet tank and hid them inside.

Back in her bed again, she lay still, listening, thinking.

She knew Caldwell was working on something and he was using them as his guinea pigs. What's he trying to figure out?

Her thoughts turned to the green liquid in the vial. *Phyllomedusa bicolor - Sapo solution 1%.* That was the key to everything. But what was it? Phyllomedusa bicolor. At that moment she would have given anything to have Henry and his computer to help her. Phyllo . . . all she could think of was those thin, flaky layers of pastry she used to get at the bakery down the street from her apartment. Bicolor? Two colors? What has two colors? Two color bread? That didn't make sense. What's Medusa? Some Greek myth about snakes. Yeah, that made a heck of a lot of sense in this context! She gave up and went to sleep.

The next morning she woke when the door to her cell opened. Caldwell, his assistant and three guards entered. Caldwell walked straight over to Mary's bed where she lay unconscious. He checked the Datascope. "A faint sixty," he said, shaking his head. "Catatonic, just like the last one."

Jett lay quietly and watched. They left as quickly as they had come. Jett waited, expecting something to happen. She was frightened. What was going to happen now?

Eventually she got up and retrieved the food the guards had placed at the door. She ate sitting on her bed, watching Mary. Nothing was happening.

Later that afternoon, Jett paced the room, then did the regimen of exercises she had designed to keep her mind and body healthy in captivity. Every once in a while, she glanced over at Mary, wondering if she would turn into a giant bat or something.

The next morning, Mary woke. "What's happening, girl?"

Jett moved over to her bed. "How do you feel?" she asked. She pressed her hand to her forehead. She felt a little warm, but that was all.

"I feel great. And I'm hungry. Feel like I ain't ate in a week!"

"It's been three days," Jett told her in happy agreement. She went over to the door and retrieved the plate of food lying on the floor. She sat on the edge of her bed while Mary wolfed it down.

Soon Mary regained her strength. Life in the cell returned to normal. Days turned into weeks. Each day, the medical assistant would come to their cell, perform a short examination on Mary, record her vital signs and draw blood. The guards brought them food three times a day. The rest of the time they were left alone.

Jett could cope with fear, with physical danger, with life and death struggles. But she couldn't cope with the boredom. She tried to find things to do. She did her exercises. She thought about Henry, wondered what he was doing, hoped he was alive and healing from his wounds; her leg wound had healed long ago. She invented difficult games to play. She fantasized about life outside the cell. She would have given anything for a weapon. Not so much to kill her captors anymore, but to give her something to do. She would have given herself goals, then practiced until she reached those goals. She remembered the last time she went to the range. She put five groups of five into a two inch circle from fifty yards. She wanted to beat that. If she had a weapon to practice with, she would work it down to a one inch circle, then a half inch circle. It would give her something to focus on, some goal to obtain. But day after day the boredom gripped her mind, like a migraine that never went away.

One day while pacing back and forth across the room, she realized that she could very easily go completely insane. Already, Mary had drifted into a sort of drug-induced dementia. Jett had to be careful. She had to keep her wits about her or she could lose herself. Then a peculiar thought occurred to her. She had an idea. It wasn't a weapon and a target, but it was a goal, and if she obtained it, it might someday provide her an advantage.

She went to the wall and began walking the room's perimeter. She pushed the beds and all the other equipment out of the way. She walked and walked, her right shoulder rubbing constantly against the wall. Sometimes she would run, then she thought it might add a nice touch if she screamed a bit. She kept it up for a long time. Running, screaming, flapping her arms.

"What's gotten into you, Santiago?" Mary asked, bewildered.

"I'm just going for a little walk!" Jett replied.

"I'm getting exhausted just watching you!" Mary complained.

"Then don't watch!" Jett laughed.

"Very funny!"

Jett continued her lunatic antics.

Finally the electronic Voice spoke to her. "What are you doing in there?"

She wondered, would it be better to answer or not answer? Better not to answer, she decided.

"Stop that," the Voice ordered. "Stop that!"

Smiling, she did not stop. She started jumping on every second step and hooting on every third, and flew around the room like a total idiot.

On occasion she would have to stop and rest, but she would stop only for a short time, then she would continue. She devised new and exciting variations of her game. She would jump up and down on the bed, tear apart the sheets, push the bed around the room and sing songs.

Finally the door opened.

She jumped off the bed and started walking around the perimeter of the room again. She walked quietly, her arms slowly flapping–like the wings of a crow in flight. She avoided the open door and anything that might be construed as threatening. She remained mute.

Carefully protected by his guards, Caldwell walked into the center of the room and watched her for a while.

Perplexed, Caldwell asked, "What are you doing?"

"She's acting like an idiot, that's what!" Mary volunteered.

"I didn't ask you," Caldwell told her.

"Why are you acting like that?"

Jett replied, but didn't stop moving: "At first I thought I'd go for a little walk. Then, because it was such a nice day outside with the sunshine and all, I thought I would fly! Would you like to join me, Dr. Caldwell?"

"How do you know my name?" he asked, a little unnerved.

"Everybody 'round here knows your name, Dr. Caldwell! You're going to be famous!"

Caldwell glanced with accusatory malevolence at his guards. Their expressions denied everything.

He turned back to her. As if he wasn't sure what was going to happen, he said, "Please stop."

"Alright!" She came to a sudden halt three inches directly in front of him. "How are you today?" she chirped.

"I'm fine. How are you?"

"Are you married, Dr. Caldwell?" she asked, her voice about three octaves higher than it normally was, and animated in such a way that under any normal circumstances an observer would conclude she was insane.

"No, I'm not. Are you?"

"Nope! Nope! What about you?"

"What about me what?"

"Are you married?"

"I said I was not. Why?"

"I just wanted to know. That's all! That's all!"

"Did you want something? Is there a reason you are trying to attract attention?"

"Yup! Yup!"

"What was the reason?"

"What's happening?"

"What do you mean, 'what's happening?'"

"Why? What? Where? Who? When?"

"You're not making any sense, I'm afraid."

"Macaco?"

"I don't understand."

"Macaco?"

"I don't know what that means."

"Am I a monkey? Should I start masturbating on the glass?"

"I don't think that will be necessary."

"You turned my friend Mary into a baboon for a day!"

Despite himself, Caldwell smiled. "A baboon?"

"You killed her! You killed her!" she yelped into the sky and started laughing.

"Nobody killed me, Santiago!" Mary cried, frightened by the

turn in the conversation.

"No, I've not killed her," he shook his head. "That was a long time ago. Don't worry about that. I wouldn't do anything to hurt Mary. I care deeply about all of you. I'm trying to help her, trying to save her. She's very sick."

"What's wrong with her? What's wrong with her?"

"She's sick. I'm trying to save her."

"Am I sick too, Dr. Caldwell?"

"Well, not yet, but you might be someday."

"What about the monkeys?"

Caldwell frowned. "The monkeys?"

"Are you making monkeys?"

"No, I am not. I'm trying to help people."

"What about the monkeys?"

"What monkeys?" When she asked this strange question, Caldwell glanced with anger toward the guards again. They stared back at him in confusion. They didn't know what was happening.

"Shock the monkey!" she screamed and leaped into the air.

Caldwell jerked back, startled.

She started singing at the top of her lungs: "Don't you know you're going to shock the monkey! Fox the fox! Rat on the rat! You can ape the ape! I know about that!"

No longer suspecting that she had devised some elaborate trick, he was now sure she had slipped into oblivion. He backed away from her.

She hopped onto the bed. "Cover me when I run! Cover me through the fire! Something knocked me out of the trees! Now I'm on my knees!" She fell to the floor, dramatizing the song. "Monkey!"

Slipping out of the room, Caldwell gave his orders: "Let her run herself to exhaustion!"

Jett's "insanity" provided her with some useful information. Shut in her cell, she craved information more than anything. More than food, more than space, more than a real look at the sun, she wanted to know what was going on.

Her schizophrenic episode had not elicited the conflict in Caldwell she had hoped for, but had given her some clues to the nature of his experiment. First, he had been nearly as frightened and perplexed by her behavior as the guards. She could see his mind working through the catalog of mental disorders he had learned in school. A psychiatrist would have known immediately how to deal with her. He, on the other hand, did not. This meant that he was not a psychiatrist, and therefore not experimenting on their brain functions, which meant she could trust her perceptions and her objectivity. This relieved her, for without them, she would be lost.

She had learned that Caldwell was studying something physiological rather than something psychological. When she observed him working with Mary, Jett had noted his willful disdain for his patient. His bedside manner was not that of a practitioner. She concluded that he must be a research scientist, perhaps in pathology or epidemiology.

Next, she learned that there was indeed a connection to monkeys. Each night she thought she heard them, perhaps two or three different species, but she could not be sure that was the sound she was hearing. Now, though, after seeing his reaction to her wild song, she was sure. Those were monkeys she heard screaming each night.

There was no doubt in her mind that the song had struck a nerve. She thanked Peter Gabriel for the lyrics, lay down in her sheetless bed and went happily to sleep. Goodnight, Henry. If you're still alive, I hope you're doing alright. Today we won. It was a small battle, but we won.

CHAPTER TWENTY-TWO

The next morning, Jett got up but Mary didn't.

"Come on, rise and shine!" Jett called to her. Jett's voice was lofty and loud, impinged with the slur of insanity.

Mary grumbled and turned away from her.

Slightly amused, Jett went to the bathroom and went through her normal routine. When she returned, Mary was laying face down.

Jett walked over to the bed and sat close to her. "What's wrong?" she whispered as she touched Mary's head. She could feel the sweat in Mary's hair. "They're going to bring our food in pretty soon."

"I'm not hungry," she muttered and pushed her face into the pillow.

"Not hungry? You eat like a horse. You feel OK?"

"Yeah, leave me alone."

Jett returned to her bed. That wasn't like Mary at all. Normally it was Mary that was pestering her, wanting to talk about stupid things, wanting to play dumb games, complaining about not having a cigarette. "Mary, you want a smoke?"

"Don't make me gag!" she groaned.

When the medical assistant arrived that day he began his normal examination, but when he checked the lymph nodes at her throat, he paused. "How do you feel today, Mary?"

"I feel like crap!" she barked hoarsely.

The assistant nodded. That didn't surprise him. He proceeded with the rest of the examination. Jett noticed him glance over at the plate of untouched food sitting by the door. That didn't surprise him, either.

That night Mary woke Jett out of a sound sleep. "I'm burning up!" she cried. "Help me! I'm burning up!"

Confused, Jett made her way through the darkness over to Mary's bed. She put her hand on Mary's arm. Her hand jerked away, immediately repulsed by what she felt. Mary was a corpse, as icy cold as death itself. "Help me! I'm burning up!" Mary whispered into the darkness.

Not knowing what to do, Jett returned to her bed and tried to go back to sleep, listening to Mary's gasps.

During the next week, Mary developed a thick, pneumonic cough. She slept through the days, ate little, and spent a lot of time in the bathroom; her legs were so weak Jett had to help her.

Finally, the medical assistant summoned Dr. Caldwell.

When he arrived, Mary was staring up at the ceiling, totally miserable. Her eyes were swollen and tired. Purple splotches had erupted on her arms.

Caldwell sat beside her. He checked the lymph nodes in her armpits, then opened her mouth, noting the white sores inside. "Candida infection," he said calmly. "Did she complain of a sore throat?" he asked the medical assistant without looking at him.

"Yes, sir, she did."

"What's her temperature been averaging?"

"One zero one."

"Any other complaints?"

"Blurred vision, nausea, headache."

"Probably cryptococcosis. Do a lumbar puncture."

He put his stethoscope on her chest. "Fluid in the lungs," he noted absently, as if normal pneumonia was the least of his patient's worries. He turned to his assistant. " Take a sputum sample and a blood sample. Look for pneumocystis carinii, get me a T-4 lymphocyte count, and test for viral antibodies."

In the days which followed, Mary's condition rapidly deteriorated, and Jett watched in horror. Each morning Caldwell would arrive, perform his examination, issue orders to his assistant, then leave without another word. He never even looked at Jett. Jett was a rhesus monkey to him.

Then, one day, Caldwell approached Jett with a vial of green liquid and a syringe.

CHAPTER TWENTY-THREE

She knew it wasn't the smartest battle she ever fought. It was pointless to struggle. But she couldn't help herself. She saw that needle full of green poison coming her way and she panicked. Her instinct to fight overwhelmed her. She threw herself from the bed and went for the door.

The guards grabbed her, struck her repeatedly, dragged her back to the bed and held her down. Caldwell stuck the needle into her. The needle pierced a vein. She felt the serum seeping into her bloodstream. She followed the painful, razor sharp sensation flowing toward her heart. Her heart began to pound. She became acutely aware of her pulsing blood. The serum stormed through her, dilating every capillary in her body.

Her body flushed with heat. She burned from the inside, sweat pouring from every pore. Her heart thumped heavily, becoming so immense and powerful that she screamed. Every blood vessel in her body swelled to a fantastic pulse. Her stomach cramped and she wrenched in pain. She felt as if wild animals were passing through her, trying to express themselves through her body.

"Strap her down, you idiots!" Caldwell called from across the room. "Why didn't you idiots strap her down?"

She hissed like a cornered cat.

One of the guards grabbed her wrist. He tried to force it into the strap.

She found that she possessed phenomenal strength. She forced her arm upward, resisting him easily. The green serum had made her strong, incredibly strong. And her senses were ultra-acute. She could see, hear, feel everything. She could hear the air rushing into the struggling lungs of her captors. She could feel their heart beats through the hands that clenched her. She could sense Caldwell's fear as a predator senses the fear of its prey. Everything around her seemed intensely vibrant. She wrenched her arm free.

The guard looked up at her, astounded.

"Get her arm!" the other one told him.

Her hand went under the bed and came out with a shard of glass. She raked it across his face. Blood flew. She dove away and landed on the floor.

She rolled beneath the bed and came out on the other side. She stabbed the sharp metal clip into the guard's testicles.

The third guard grabbed her, but she leaped up, and in one powerful twist of her body wrenched herself free.

Shocked, the guard grabbed her again.

She hit him in the chest so hard she broke his rib. She possessed strength she had never had in her life.

She charged the door.

Caldwell jerked away from her in terror, thinking she was coming after him.

She sprinted down the corridor.

She heard his cries: "Go after her, you idiots!"

The laboratory was rushing by her at phenomenal speed, and she was absorbing everything. Every door, every window, every detail snapped into her mind. The sounds in the corridor had brought many of the other prisoner-patients to their doors. They couldn't see through the one way glass, of course, but by standing close to their doors they could hear a little better what was happening outside. Any noise, any commotion, brought hope of rescue. Against one of these small windows pressed a boyish face–Henry's face–staring out into the corridor. He couldn't see Jett, but he knew Jett would be able to see him. Jett's heart soared.

"Henry!" She screamed his name at the top of her lungs, trying to give him some hope that–at least for the moment–she was alive. The guards were right behind her. She couldn't afford to stop. She kept running. As she ran she glimpsed the layout of rooms and corridors. She ran past offices, storage closets, computer centers, blood labs, cages. She stopped. She darted into the room with the cages. She was greeted by the scream of a hundred monkeys. She screamed back at them, every bit their equal.

She grabbed a shovel and slammed it into a guard's head, knocking him backward. Then she smashed into the cages. She opened them, and overturned them, and screamed for the monkeys to escape. The creatures went wild, fleeing their cages with great joy, diving onto everything.

She found a vent cover and tore it off the wall with her bare hands. The sheet metal screws popped beneath her strength.

A half dozen guards poured into the room and were immediately inundated by the chaos of a hundred frenzied monkeys.

She slipped into the air shaft and crawled. She wasn't tired. She should have been exhausted, but fear and the power of the drug drove her on. She had never been more alive.

As she crawled through the ventilation system, she experienced a strange hallucination. Boars and other wild creatures were running down the shaft with her. Walls were on fire. Ceilings were raining. She became a wild cat, and she ran with the speed of a jaguar through the jungle. She came face to face with a giant tapir. Seeing the death in her cat eyes, it turned and fled.

She came to a set of intersecting paths: up, down, right and left. Placing her back against one wall and her feet against the other, she chimneyed up a vertical shaft, moving with the agility of a gibbon up a tree.

She could hear everything. Every word in the building came tumbling through the shaft and into her drug-enhanced ears. But she could not discern hallucination from reality: "Phyllomedusa bicolor. . . take her down! . . . she's in the shaft! . . . test lab on the third level . . . seven bioactive peptides . . . tachycardia . . . sauvagine, phyllokinincaerulein, pituitary-adrenal axis . . . capillary zone electrophoresis . . . shut it down! . . . upstairs! . . . watch the elevator! . . . get in there!" And no matter what she did, the boars kept running, running with her, running through her, and she became their stampede.

She smashed a vent cover and leaped into an empty office. She threw herself to the far wall as the door opened. A guard entered the room, a gun in his hand. She pounced upon him and wrapped the plastic tubing around his neck. She yanked it back and brought him to the ground in one motion. Then she twisted the tube until he didn't move anymore.

She picked up the weapon, a Diamondback Colt .38. In a single habitual motion, she popped the revolver's cylinder, counted the cartridges, replaced the wheel, and cocked the hammer. She ran out of the room.

The guards in the lobby rushed toward her. Then they saw the gun. They stopped. She shot one before he decided what to do. The second guard pulled his weapon and fired, but by that time she was gone. She had slipped into an alcove. She aimed and blew a hole through his neck.

She ran for freedom, sensing a dozen more guards running up the stairway, coming down corridors, converging on her from all directions. The thick glass doors that led to the street stood before her. Stupidly, she fired at the glass, thinking her bullets would smash through it and make a clear path for her escape. Precious time wasted.

The bullets punched white spider webs into the impenetrable glass. She ran headlong into a virtual brick wall. The guards surrounded her. She had used every ounce of her strength, every secret weapon, every clever trick she knew. There was no escape.

CHAPTER TWENTY-FOUR

The brown Dodge Dart sat parked at the curb. The day before it had been sitting in the parking lot across the street. That's when Robert had noticed there was somebody in it, waiting.

Robert put the keys in the ignition and started his car. He pulled onto the road, checking his rear view mirror. The Dodge pulled out a few cars behind him.

Just as a test, he turned abruptly.

He found himself in the parking lot of a small shopping mall. He got out of the car and went in.

He lingered in the bookstore just inside the mall's main entrance. He picked up books and pretended to be interested in them. He walked to the back of the store, between the aisles, as if searching for something specific. But his eyes were looking through the front windows, waiting for the man from the Dodge to walk by.

"May I help you?" asked the clerk.

"Ah . . . no, I'm just looking for something," he said, hardly realizing what he said.

The attractive clerk smiled. She was quite a bit younger than he was, but judging by her behavior she wasn't completely appalled by him. Robert wore a long dark coat and a handsome suit. He cut a rather attractive figure and was obviously affluent. "Perhaps I can help you find it," she said.

"No, I mean, I'm just browsing."

"Alright," she said. She smiled pleasantly and turned. "If you need anything, just say so."

"Yes, thank you."

She left him alone in the "Women's Health and Sexuality" section where he had been standing.

He leaned against the bookcase, and once again, he laughed at himself. What was he doing? Did he really think there was somebody following him? Wasn't that a little ridiculous? Obviously, he had seen too many spy movies. His worries over Jett had him hysterical. For the tenth time, he reproached himself for his continued fascination with her. *What do I care? he told himself. I don't even know her! So we've done business together a couple of years, we're friends, we had a few drinks together and a pleasant conversation or two. Her personal life, her whereabouts, have nothing to do with me. They're none of my business. Besides, I'm married, and this is ridiculous. I'm infatuated with some woman I don't even know, and probably wouldn't like if I did. In fact, she's probably a Peruvian terrorist or something! I've got to forget about her! She's driving me crazy!* He decided to leave the bookstore.

He walked quickly from the back of the store, keeping his eyes to the ground in hope of avoiding further embarrassment. He just kept walking until he got to the front.

"Hey, somebody was looking for you," the sales clerk said to him.

He stopped and looked up at her.

"Somebody was looking for you," she repeated.

"When?"

"Just now, when you were in the back of the store."

"Who was it?"

"Some guy, cop or something. He was asking about you. I told him I saw you go into the mall."

Robert stepped toward her. She looked back at him directly and without averting her eyes. Why did she do that? he wondered.

She shrugged. "You seemed like you were sort of hiding out, so I didn't want to give you away."

He was astounded. *Was I hiding out? Who am I hiding from? Who's looking for me?* "Thank you," he said, bewildered but appreciative. He looked at the young woman in a new light now. The way she had covered for him. The way she had protected him. He had gone so long estranged from his wife that the slightest alliance or gesture of friendship became profound.

She saw his hesitation to leave and continued the conversation. "Who was that? He seemed like a real slimebucket," she said. She had short brown hair, hazel eyes and a pleasant face.

He shook his head. "I don't know. I think somebody's following me." This was the first time he had said that to anyone, the first time he had admitted it to himself.

"You don't have to think about it anymore. I saw him!"

"OK. I wasn't sure before."

"But why are they following you?"

"Why." He repeated her question. He was asking himself the same thing. "I don't know," he admitted. He stood there thinking for a few seconds, looking out into the mall. He half turned to leave, then stopped and turned back. "Hey," he said gently. "Thanks a lot, you saved me."

"It's OK. I thought you were in some kind of trouble. Besides it was kind of fun. I'm lying for a good cause for a change."

"Yeah," he agreed with a smile. "What's your name?"

"Elizabeth," she said. "Elizabeth Miller."

"I'll see you around, Elizabeth. Thanks again."

He got half way out of the store.

"Hey!" she called.

He stopped.

"That's not fair! What's your name?"

"If I told you that, I'd have to kill you, Elizabeth," he said.

She smiled and laughed.

CHAPTER TWENTY-FIVE

Jett lay on the bed, staring at the ceiling. Quiet now. No more violence. No more fighting. No more movement. She stared into space. Three days had passed. Quiet.

Caldwell stood over her. He probed her abdomen with his cold fingers. "Pain here?"

She shook her head with the slowness of a lobotomy patient.

The thermometer beeped and he took it out of her mouth.

Too heavy to hold up, her eyelids fell shut. Her body was limp beneath the clamps that held her wrists and ankles to the bed. Three days had passed since the guards had subdued her. In the end she had given up. Her father had told her many times that she should not fight battles she could not win. She hated her father.

Three days had passed and she had not moved. She had not fought her captors, or screamed at the speaker phone, or bit Dr. Caldwell. The old Santiago was dead now.

"Has she been eating?" Caldwell asked the medical assistant.

"No, nothing," he said.

Caldwell nodded. "Has she been saying much, doing anything?" he asked. He was talking about her like she wasn't there.

"She can't move, of course, but she hasn't complained."

Caldwell looked at her.

Her face was withdrawn, almost anemic in appearance. Her eyes were closed.

"In order for her to stay in the experiment, I need to observe her motor skills and her activity level," he said. "After I leave, take off the clamps."

One of the guards stepped forward. "Sir, you sure you want to do that?" He still had a bandage around his thigh where she stabbed him. Four of his friends were dead because of her.

"I need to observe her under normal conditions. I need to record the full array of responses."

"But, sir, she's dangerous. She's proven that."

"We can't leave her like this. Her muscles will atrophy," the medical assistant said.

"And that will throw off the measurements," Caldwell agreed. He turned to the guard with irritation: "Just keep clear of her. Make sure everything is locked down tight. That's what you were supposed to be doing before. You screwed up. I'm not going to let your screw-up ruin my experiment. You understand?"

"Yessir," the guard mumbled.

After the medical assistant and the doctor left, the guard remained behind. He pulled out his gun and jammed it into her shoulder, wedging the barrel under her collar bone. He leaned close to her. "I don't care what the doc says. If you even move when I release these clamps I'm going to blow your shoulder off your body. It won't kill you. The doc won't let me kill you, but it won't be too pleasant, either. You like your shoulder, bitch?"

She didn't answer. Her eyes were closed.

He released the clamps one by one, keeping the gun pressed against her at all times.

"You even move, bitch, and I'm taking you out!"

She did not open her eyes. She did not move.

Once he had detached the clamps, he stepped away from her. He steadied the gun on her as he walked backward toward the door.

He shut it and locked it.

Jett lay on the bed. Quiet.

CHAPTER TWENTY-SIX

Midnight in the laboratory. Dark cell. Silence.

The sound of the guard's heartbeat echoed in her ears. She had heard it clearly. She had heard the movements he made and the air moving through his esophagus. She had felt his rough fingers against her skin as he unclasped her. She had smelled his sweat, an odor of fear.

Her own heart beat slow and heavy now. The blood pounded through her veins like oil pushed by a diesel engine. The green drug that had excited her initial escape-attempt had come to an equilibrium in her system, but it had not worn off. While her "flight reflex" had diminished, the sensory-enhancing effects of the drug had become more profound over time. Every sense she possessed was heightened. Her reflexes were sharp. The incredible flow of adrenaline surged through her.

It was the most difficult battle she had ever fought in her life, to hide her strength and feign weakness. It took all her mental fortitude to appear defeated and submissive while the thought of Henry's survival encouraged her and the powerful drug coursed through her veins. The hallucinations of animals had diminished, but deep, lurking images remained. Whenever she shut her eyes she was swept into the never-ending flow of an immense, golden brown river. And the river gave her power.

She slipped out of bed, and walked through the darkness to Mary Olsen's bed. Mary was going to die. Of that Jett was sure. The last few days had been torture for Mary. Each day worse than the one before. Her tongue had swollen up with white ulcers. Purple splotches and open sores covered her body. She was weak, emaciated and constantly nauseated.

Jett sat by her bed, waiting, thinking.

She looked at the white-tiled wall of their cell. There on the wall, Mary had scratched a symbol:

"What is it? Why did you draw that?" Jett asked.

"It's for you . . . not me," Mary gasped.

"What is it, Mary?"

"Don't give up."

Thinking of that, Jett made her decision.

She reached down and unplugged the machine that was helping Mary breathe. She pulled off the oxygen mask. She yanked out the IVs. Mary didn't struggle. She seemed to welcome death and she went to it silently, almost thankfully.

Jett pulled the IV pump off its mounting and opened it up using a metal clip from the bed as a tiny screw driver. Within minutes she had it in pieces. She collected what she needed.

She went into the bathroom. Behind the door she found the sheet metal grate which covered the access hole to the shower's plumbing. She pulled out the metal bar she had collected from Mary's IV pump. She used the bar as a large screw driver to unthread the screws, then she used a section of the IV rack as a crowbar to pry off the panel.

She worked in complete darkness, doing everything by memory and by feel. She felt the edges of the hole behind the access panel. It was a rough opening, about twenty inches by twelve inches, bordered by the sharp edges of ungrouted tile.

She explored the inside of the hole with her hands. She found the two-by-four construction beams, the plaster wall, the edge of the shower, the PVC water pipes.

She put her head into the hole, then tried to squeeze in her shoulders. Her arm caught the edge of the tile. Her skin tore. She hardly felt it.

She wedged herself into the hole, first one shoulder, then an arm. Then she tried for the next shoulder. It wouldn't go.

She was stuck. She couldn't fit. She became frustrated and pushed hard. But unless she could somehow reduce the breadth of her shoulders, the hole was too small for her to fit through.

At this point she had three choices: She could pull herself out, put everything back together and wait for another chance to escape. She could give up and wait for death to come. Or she could try option number three.

CHAPTER TWENTY-SEVEN

She was wedged half way through the hole. Three options stood before her, all bad.

In the end she thought about Henry and she thought about Mary. That decided it for her. She was not just going to escape, she was going to come back and destroy these bastards.

She twisted herself around so that her left shoulder pressed at a right angle to the tile wall. Then she found the opposite wall with her feet. She measured the distance and gaged the force that would be required. She knew it would take a lot, perhaps more than she had.

She held her breath, clenched her teeth, coiled up her legs and shot them straight out against the opposite wall. Her shoulder slammed forward, hit the wall and popped out of the socket. Her body slipped through the hole. She fell upside down and bent in half on the other side.

Swimming in intense pain, she righted herself. She grabbed her dangling arm with her right hand, then slammed her shoulder against a pipe to pop it back into place. She knew that these things would have been impossible without the drug inside her. She would not have had the strength to dislocate her shoulder, then put it back again. The pain would have been unbearable.

She grabbed onto the pipes and started climbing.

She knew from her lunatic escape run that there were fourteen patient rooms, seven on each side of the corridor, and that she was in Room 13. At the end of the corridor, on the other side of Room 14, was the main laboratory. She started moving in that direction.

She crawled between floor and ceiling, following the path of the pipes and electrical conduits. She saw many things that she knew might be useful to her, wire and nails and pieces of wood. Some of these she collected, but she knew also that she must hurry.

She passed the pipes that led into Patient Room 14. She kept going.

When she reached the next set of pipes, she wedged herself into the cranny that led down into the room and kicked out the access panel with her feet. She wiggled through the hole and found herself under the over-sized wash basin in the test lab.

For a moment she paused, stunned by the array of ultra-sophisticated equipment that surrounded her. A hundred tiny light-emitting diodes. The solid green "power light" of computers. The blinking red lights of modems. The orange lights of multiplexers. The multichromatic flashes of a spectrophotometer. The eerie cast of green terminal screens. The tiny lights seemed alive.

Beside her, a green liquid recondensed in a complex set of glass refluxing coils. Beside it sat an electron microscope, a rack of test tubes, a dozen Erlenmeyer flasks and half as many graduated cylinders. She picked up a maroon-colored reagent sitting on a table. She noted a bottle of liquid nitrogen, vacuum pumps, and an array of steel cylinders: helium, argon, hydrogen.

Four HP 1090 liquid chromatographs were running through their automated testing processes, analyzing the contents of a vial, each one transmitting information into the Chem Station next to it.

She read the title of the book sitting on the lab table: *Isolating Peptide Link-groups with Liquid Chromatography.*

Pulling herself away from the equipment, she checked the room's doors. One was labeled "GC/MS" and led to another lab. The other led to the corridor.

She used a large Bunsen burner cylinder to smash the lock off a cabinet. Then she checked each of the drawers. In the first drawer she found logs, medical charts and a few text books. In the next drawer she found scientific sample bags. Sample bags. Where had she first seen a plastic sample bag? But she wasn't looking for sample bags. She checked the next drawer, then the next. Finally she found the drawer she was looking for. Ignoring the hemostats and forceps, she picked up a ten inch No. 4 scalpel handle and tore it out of its plastic sanitary pouch. Then she found a No. 10 blade, tore it out of the foil wrapper, and attached it to the handle.

Biological sample bag . . . she kept thinking about it. She went back to that drawer. All the answers were in this lab. First she found a book. It was a thick, hard-covered volume: *The Birds of South America.* She picked it up and leafed through it. It contained plates and descriptions of different birds. Why did this seem important to her? Why would a place like this have a book on South American birds?

She searched the drawers. Nothing. She found a small refrigerator. She opened it: blood samples, chemical solutions, human organs. She shuffled through the contents. Then she noticed something that wasn't human. A frog. Preserved in a jar. It was a strange looking little creature, unlike any other frog she had ever seen. Though its legs where brownish and decorated with white spots, it consisted primarily of two colors: bright green and bright blue. What made the frog truly striking was that it had a head shaped like a snake. Then she saw what she was looking for: the bird. The bird she had delivered to Caldwell weeks before. It was still in its sample bag. She stuck it in her gown pocket. She knew the bird was important. The "package" was always important.

She heard the jingle of keys in the corridor. She ducked behind a lab table as the guard opened the door and walked into the room. As he reached for the light switch, Jett moved swiftly. The light never came on. The keys hit the floor. Then came a gurgling sound. Blood began splattering onto the floor. She had raked the scalpel across the guard's neck. He stood now, stunned, unable to comprehend what had happened to him in that instant, unable to scream out, unable to breathe. She heard the air sucking in and out of his incised esophagus. Moments later he collapsed.

She moved forward cautiously.

He seemed dead. The corridor seemed empty.

She took the Diamondback Colt and his keys, then moved immediately into the corridor. She noted the layout of the doors, then smashed the plastic light switch in the corridor with the butt of the Colt. If she had to share the corridor with somebody, she preferred they couldn't see anything. Working from memory, she moved to the other side of the corridor and down to Room 5. She used the keys to open the door.

"What's happening?" came a frightened whimper.

"We're on the run, Henry!" she whispered to him.

"Jett?"

"Come on!"

Within seconds he was holding onto her.

" I'm glad to see you, Henry! I thought you were dead! Are you OK?"

"After they shot me they put me in this room. They treated my wound. It was just like being in a hospital, except I couldn't get out and they never answered my questions. I didn't know what was going on!

Then I heard you in the hallway!"

"Yeah, I remember. I saw you! Come on, we have to go!"

They moved hand in hand through the darkness back to the laboratory. Jett forced Henry into the hole that she had climbed through.

"Is this how you escaped?" he cried, dismayed by its narrowness. He was thicker than Jett, and much less strong.

"It did the job. Get in there and climb upward!" she told him. "Based on the sound of the elevator, I think we're on the third floor underground. So just keep climbing!"

Pushed by her urgent commands, he did as he was told. Whenever he paused to catch his breath, she pushed him. "Keep going!" The climb through the darkness was painful and frightening for him. Only her forceful whispers drove him on.

Eventually they reached the main floor, but she told him to keep going. She wouldn't make that mistake again. The well-guarded, thick-glass lobby was impenetrable. Once at the level of the second floor, she kicked out an access panel and they tumbled into a small room. As they hit the floor, there was a flash of bright white light and a loud crashing sound. Jett scanned the room, not knowing what was happening.

"Thunder and lightning!" Henry said with a giggle. "Come on!" He led the way toward the window on the other side of the small office.

Smashing the window and climbing onto the sill, they dropped to the pavement below.

They found themselves in an alley.

"What's that?" Henry said, pointing toward a symbol painted on the alley wall. Then Jett saw the hobo sign, similar to the one that Mary had used:

Don't give up. That's what Mary had said. Jett stood barefoot, wearing nothing but a hospital gown, wounded, and clenching the Colt. She grabbed Henry's hand and laughed with joy. They were about to run for their lives into the dark safety of the city when they heard something behind them.

CHAPTER TWENTY-EIGHT

When Robert Pearl walked into his office the next morning, he set down his briefcase, hung up his coat, and sat at his desk. Still no news. He had tried everything. He had contacted everyone he knew. He had even hired a private investigator, one that a colleague had recommended as reliable and discreet. And, of course, expensive. Robert didn't care. His whole company was stagnating and his marriage was in a dive, but he was thinking about Jett.

The phone rang.

He picked it up. "Hello."

"Robert, this is Jack."

"Hi, Jack, what's up?"

"You got a minute?"

"Sure, come on up."

Five minutes later the corporate attorney sat in front of him. He brought with him the head of Research and Development and the Chief Financial Officer. They were stolid men, in a somber mood. They sat squarely in front of him.

"We have some concerns," Jack began.

"All three of you?"

They nodded.

"What's wrong?" Robert asked.

No one said anything. No one knew what to say. Everyone, including Robert, was looking at the Chief Financial Officer.

"Tell him, Sol," Jack said.

Sol adjusted his glasses nervously.

"Just tell him," Jack urged.

Earl Myers, the R & D man, didn't move an inch. He waited for Sol to speak.

"We're going into the red next month," Sol said.

It was the beginning of the end. Once they started losing money, everything would start going down hill. Investors would avoid them like the plague. Banks wouldn't lend to them. And because they weren't producing any new drugs, they would just hemorrhage cash until they were completely out of it. Then they would die.

It had happened to a dozen companies just like his.

Robert put his hands to his face and rubbed his eyes. "How bad?"

"One hundred fifty thousand, maybe one seventy five," Sol mumbled, staring at the floor.

"What do we have coming down the pipe?" Robert asked. He didn't look at him, but the other two men knew he was addressing Earl Myers.

"Not much. We've got that new antacid going on the shelves next week, but there's twenty others just like it. We're maybe five percent more effective, but that's not going to do much for us. Bristol is going to squeeze us out sooner or later."

"What about the cancer research?"

The three men lowered their heads in anguish. Success in cancer research was Robert Pearl's dream, and while Pearl Research dedicated a significant portion of its budget to it and had contributed important scientific papers to the field, they hadn't come up with a single marketable product.

Finally, Earl Myers had to reply to the question that their CEO had so often asked. "It's just too slow, Robert. We don't have anything. We're not even close. Whenever we think we might have something, we find out that it's a dead end. Our cancer research is a twenty year project."

"It's not going to help us out of this," Jack said, urging Robert to pull himself into the present reality of the situation: Pearl Research was going out of business.

Robert leaned over his desk and put his head in his hands. He covered his face.

The three men sitting across from him heard a sigh come from him. They waited.

"What's Quinlain doing?" he asked. Quinlain was the anti-herpes drug that he had invented personally, and which he had founded the company on.

"It's holding steady . . . good sales . . . still no competitors . . . but it's not enough."

Robert Pearl did not look up. He did not reply. His mind ran through a thousand possibilities, a thousand wrong decisions, a thousand mistakes, a thousand things he should have done differently. He saw the entire history of his company in the darkness of his closed eyes. He scanned through the images like an investigator scans through pages of a microfiche. He searched the pages looking for one thing: where he had gone wrong.

Finally, after a long time, he cleared his eyes, and looked at his loyal partners. "Jack, we're going to have to cut our spending. We've got to hunker down for a while. No new hires. No new equipment. Cut everything we've got."

"Hunker down for a while?" Jack asked.

"There's no end in sight," Sol said. "I mean, the projections don't look good. Unless something starts happening, we're not going to make the end of the year."

"Maybe we should start laying people off," Earl Myers suggested.

"We're not laying people off," Robert insisted. "We're a team. Either we're going to make it or we're not. I'm not going to start bailing people. We'll just hunker down and ride out the storm. Earl, how do you feel about having some company down in the lab?"

"Company?" Earl said, confused. "What kind of company?"

"Me."

"You?"

"As Sol said, we've got to make something happen. I don't know how to do that sitting behind this desk. Give me a lab coat, maybe a beaker or two . . . then at least we'll go out fighting."

CHAPTER TWENTY-NINE

Robert worked late in the lab that night. He reintroduced himself to equipment and procedures, remembering the old days. He found an empty desk for himself beside some of the junior technicians. The news that the CEO of the company would be conducting research spread through the department and out into the corporation. The rumors that the company was going out of business soon dissipated, replaced by this new development. What did this mean?

Under Robert's recommendation some years before, the Research and Development Department was set up as a number of independent teams, each team working toward a specific goal. He thought about asking each of the Team Leaders to assemble the next day and present a concise overview of their project. He would then review each of the projects and take over the team that he thought most promising. As president of the corporation, this would be expected. But Robert had another idea.

He wanted his hands on the equipment. He wanted his eyes on the scientific papers. He had been in the world of corporate finance and marketing for too long. It was time to get back to basics. He spent the rest of the afternoon and evening catching up on the technical details, scanning text books and reading recent publications. The next day he would show up in one of the labs, present himself to the team, and say, "Put me to work."

He arrived home exhausted. The exhaustion reminded him of the old days, working all night, trying to cram for exams. It felt like a new beginning. And, as with all beginnings, there was fear and there was hope.

He sat in the chair facing the TV, his mind spinning with physiology and long molecular chains. He noticed that his wife had come home while he was gone and she had taken some more of her things. She didn't pretend to live there anymore. She and her lover lived on the other side of town. When the phone rang he picked it up.

"Mr. Pearl?"

"Yes," he said. He didn't recognize the man's voice.

"You asked me to call you if I found anything interesting."

"Oh!" It was the private investigator. "Yes, go ahead. What is it? What did you find?"

"Should we talk over the phone?"

"Sure. I don't think anyone else cares what I'm doing."

"I wouldn't be so sure about that, sir."

Robert paused. "What do you mean?"

"You know you're being followed."

Robert's heart began to pound. "No."

"You must have known. That guy's not that good. Amateur clod hopper."

"What do you mean?"

"The guy tailing you. He doesn't know anything about the business. If he did, I wouldn't be talking to you on the phone about it —whether you thought it was safe or not. The truth is I just don't think that guy's clever enough to get into your lines."

"What are you talking about?"

"The guy following you. He's been right on you for a few days now, ever since you hired me."

"But I hired you to find the woman, not to watch me!"

"Yes, I know, but as I said, this guy's clumsy as a grasshopper in golf shoes. Every time I see you, he's there. Haven't you noticed him?"

"I suspected, but it seemed too far fetched. I wasn't sure."

"Well, be sure. He's there. Believe me."

"I do, but why would someone be following me?"

"I thought you might be able to help me with that one. It's not the IRS or the mob or anything like that. They may not be the most imaginative folks, but at least they're professionals."

"I don't know who it is."

"Alright," the P.I. said, wanting to relieve his client of that worry. "I'll find out. It's piqued my interest. I'll take care of it. That's not why I called, though."

"It isn't?"

"No. You asked me to the watch the hospitals."

"Yes."

"An E.R. doc named Lemmick admitted a Jane Doe into

Masterson Medical Center about an hour ago. Could be your girl."

Robert's chest got tight with excitement. "What makes you think so?"

"The database described her: long black hair, black eyes, Hispanic descent, athletic build, scar on left cheek."

"I'll meet you there. Where's the Masterson Medical Center?"

"Detroit."

Robert paused. "Detroit?" He made a decision. "Alright, I'll meet you at the airport."

CHAPTER THIRTY

"Mr. Pearl," the private investigator said as they shook hands at the airport. "The plane leaves in about fifteen minutes."

"How did you ever find out about this?"

The investigator smiled proudly. "I got rid of my police scanner. I'm high tech, now! I got myself a computer last year. I can tap into any public database in the country!"

When they arrived at Detroit Metro Airport, they caught a cab to the hospital. It was dark and raining. The cab driver complained that it had been raining all night. With trench coats hunched around their shoulders, they ran together into the hospital emergency room. From there they made their way into the I.C.U. Each of the rooms were visible and accessible from the central nurses station where the two men stood.

Jett was curled up on a bed in the closest room. A nurse was attending to her, cleaning the dirt and blood from her face. She had already cleaned and bandaged the wounds on her feet and arms. Jett's hair lay across the bed, tangled into a mess like it had dried that way.

Robert studied the image. Jetta Mendoza Santiago was lying asleep right in front of him. He was sure it was some sort of hallucination. He was sure that as soon as he moved toward her, the stunning image would disappear. So he did not move.

The physician arrived in the I.C.U. He appeared as if he had just come on the shift. He was making a round through the I.C.U, although he was obviously busy with other patients as well. He didn't appear to be concerned about Jett's wounds. They were under control. He was staring at the EKG monitor above the bed. Even Robert recognized the fact that the rapid beep-beep-beep of the machine was going far too fast.

The physician looked at the nurse. "What's she on?"

"Excuse me, Doctor?" the nurse looked up at him.

"We need to test her. She's on something, something strong. Coke? Crack? Never seen anything this potent. Who brought her in?"

he asked the nurse.

"She came into the ER a while ago, on Dr. Lemmick's shift. The police picked her up. Jane Doe."

"Jane Doe?"

"They found her in an alley with only a hospital gown on."

"A hospital gown? She's a mess. She's running a heart rate of one fifty steady."

The nurse nodded. "Yes, I know, that's why I wanted you to take a look at her."

"Did you check our floors? Are we missing anyone?"

"No, we're not. I called."

"What about the other hospitals in the city?"

"I called them, too."

"What about the Psychiatric Center?"

"They wouldn't say."

"They wouldn't say?"

"Confidential."

"Get them on the phone. I'll talk to them. What did the blood look like?"

"Still working on it."

"You say she's been here a couple of hours?"

"At least."

"And she's been like that the whole time?"

"Yes."

"Get her an IV. We're going to have to do something about the heart rate."

"Yes, Doctor."

As he was about to walk away, he noticed the tiny brown spots on her arm. He picked up her arm up and looked more closely. Track marks. He shook his head and walked away.

"Is that her, Mr. Pearl?" the investigator asked.

He nodded. "You've done well," he said.

"I know. Isn't it great? Got her from New York without ever leaving my office. What are we going to do now? Should we tell them who she is?"

Robert didn't answer. He was watching her.

" What's wrong with her?" the investigator asked.

"I don't know." Robert said.

CHAPTER THIRTY-ONE

The next morning Robert Pearl arrived at the hospital to find that Jett had been moved. Her new room was under the guard of a uniformed police officer. As Robert approached, he noticed a plainclothes detective sitting on a nearby bench, scribbling notes in a small notebook. The detective looked up.

Robert paused.

Seeing his hesitation, the detective stood up and walked toward him. "I'm Detective Johnson," he said. "You know this woman?"

"What's going on?" Robert asked.

"I just heard you ask the nurse about the Jane Doe. You know her? Can I see some ID?"

Robert thought a moment. He did not move.

The detective waited impatiently for him to decide what to do.

"What's she done?" he asked the detective, glancing at the officer at the door.

"Who are you?"

"I am a business acquaintance."

"What sort of business?"

"She's a courier for my company."

"What company is that?"

"Pearl Research."

"And who are you?"

"Robert Pearl."

The detective had been writing everything down. At this point he stopped and glanced up at him. "Robert Pearl?" he repeated.

Robert nodded.

"And you know the woman?"

"Not well, but I do know her. What's happened?"

"Is that one of your men out there?" the detective asked Robert, gesturing down the corridor toward the lobby.

Robert was confused. "Out where?"

"Out there, in the parking lot," the detective said. "There's been a couple of guys hanging around here all morning. Blue Continental. Those your men?"

Robert shook his head. "No, I've got a private investigator, but he works alone."

The detective raised an eyebrow. "Private investigator? What's he investigating?"

"He was looking for her."

"What for?"

"I wanted to see her."

The detective smiled. He liked Pearl. He seemed like an honest man, almost to a fault. This was something he seldom encountered in his profession. Everyone had something to hide. If anyone else had given him a smart-ass comment like that he would have slammed the son of a bitch up against a wall for it, but Pearl was telling the truth. The detective didn't push it.

"How'd you know she was here?"

"P.I. found her."

"What's her name?"

"Jetta Mendoza Santiago. What's happened to her?" Robert asked.

The detective wrote her name in his notebook as he spoke. "The Central Station got a call about a 192. Dispatched a car. When the officers arrived on the scene, they found a mob of slugs surrounding her."

"Slugs?"

"You know, drunkards, street people, bums, that sort of thing. I don't know what they were looking for. She didn't have anything on her worth stealing. She was practically naked. Nothing but a hospital gown. She was banged up pretty bad. Hands, knuckles, feet, knees: all bleeding."

"How come she's under guard?"

"She killed somebody."

"Killed?"

"Killed. The gun was lying right next to her. We found the victim in the alley, too. We don't know who he is. Looks like some sort of security guard. There was definitely a struggle between them. We're still investigating."

"How'd she kill him?"

"Bullet in the forehead. That normally does the trick."

Robert was stunned. In all his life, he had never had personal contact with physical violence. All of a sudden he knew somebody that had actually killed somebody.

"It was a .38 revolver. Nice piece. One of those Diamondback Colts. God knows where she got hold of that. It appears she only fired once."

"Then you're saying it was self defense."

"I'm not saying anything. I'm just collecting facts. Juries decide that sort of stuff. We've got to ID the victim. Up till now we've been making a lot of guesses. We can't even figure out what happened after she popped the guy. Looks like she had some sort of drug OD. By the time we got there the slugs had stripped them both—clothes, wallets, shoes, everything. The only things they left were two bodies, the gown, and the gun. Nobody would touch the gun. Until you came along, nobody has come to ID them, either. Now we hear there may be another suspect, a male Caucasian in his early twenties, but we haven't been able to find him."

"Can I see her?"

"Yeah, I'm going in with you."

Robert agreed and they walked into the room.

The hospital bed was empty.

Jane Doe had escaped.

PART THREE: Sendero Luminoso

CHAPTER THIRTY-TWO

Henry sat down at the personal computer in Jett's apartment in Manhattan. Sitting in that chair, in front of a computer monitor, with his fingers on the keyboard, he felt alive again. He experienced a sort of ecstasy–the feeling of coming home after long absence, of possessing power after long enervation. It all came to him, a great rush of strength and happiness: he was once again in his element. He began typing, exploring, determining the strengths and weaknesses of the system, figuring out what he could do with it. He took a long guzzle from the cold Mountain Dew Jett set beside him.

A guard had discovered them in the alley as they escaped the laboratory. Jett had turned and fired. Her nervous system ignited with the burst of adrenalin into her body. Suddenly, she exploded into a fit of convulsions. She fell to the ground, vomiting, her body shaking violently. Henry didn't know what to do. He tried to hold on to her, to help her, but he was terrified. She could barely communicate with him. She seemed to understand what was happening, but he did not. All he knew was that they had done something to her in the laboratory. As the crowds gathered and the sirens began wailing around them, she gave him the sample bag containing the bird and told him to run.

Later he would track her down in the hospital. She was locked behind closed doors, and he had no idea how to contact her. He knew that he dared not make a connection with her. She had told him to run, and he knew he must stay away. Even as wondered what he should do, he saw her stumbling down the sidewalk outside. She had broken the glass and crawled out a window.

Since Dracon knew Henry's home address from the wallet, Henry and Jett knew they could not go there, even for a night. Not to mention the fact that they were *both* wanted by the police now. But since Jett never carried her Manhattan address, *her* place was relatively safe. Wearing clothing she stole from the hospital, they spent the night in a Detroit homeless shelter. Jett begged some change and made a few phone calls, reporting that her credit cards were stolen. They were replaced within 24 hours. With the credit cards she bought plane tickets, clothing, and everything else they needed.

Henry had barely noticed the details of Jett's apartment when they walked in. The first and only thing that he wanted to do, now that he had escaped the laboratory with his life, was log in to his computer. Only then, would he believe he was safe again.

The arm where he had been shot was still a little sore, but much to his relief, he had regained the dexterity in his fingers necessary to type. There was a little tingle in his wrist once in a while, but nothing that really bothered him. He checked the settings on the modem, then told the computer to dial up the computer in his office in Detroit. He had no idea what was going to happen. After such a long absence, anything could happen. His bosses would have assumed he was a milk carton kid–dead or missing–so there's no telling what they would have done. Or maybe they would have figured he just skipped town. They might have hired somebody to take his place. Who would they get? Who would run *his* system? Of course, as long as nobody screwed it up, his system would go on for a long time. Everything was setup to work on automatic.

Henry waited for the modem's beeps and static to turn silent. After a few seconds the screen displayed his familiar login prompt:

WELCOME TO BEAUFORTLAND! LOGIN IF YOU DARE:

"Hot dog!"

Jett came in from the master bathroom, drying her long wet hair. It seemed to Henry like she had spent most the morning in the shower, like she was washing off the dirt that the laboratory had put on her soul. It seemed she was using the shower to recuperate, physically and psychologically, from their imprisonment. Now, fresh and clean, she was more alive, more dangerous than ever. "What's happening?" she asked.

"I've got a login prompt!"

She nodded, knowing the significance of that. "Be careful when you go in there, Henry."

"What do you mean?"

"Just keep on your toes. Make sure your watch programs are running. You don't know what's happened since we've been gone. This thing isn't over yet."

"Sure, yeah, I know that," he mumbled as if he was a little irritated by her obvious statement. In truth, he wasn't sure what she was talking about.

He entered his user name and his password.

Looking over his shoulder, Jett asked, "What's the password?" When they first met, she wouldn't have even asked the question, because she knew he wouldn't tell her.

Now, he didn't hesitate: "Armageddon."

She smiled. "That's what I thought. I thought you were going to die, too."

He entered the password. He was immediately rewarded with the familiar login data:

LAST SUCCESSFUL LOGIN FOR ROOT: SUN JUNE 12 20:21:57 EST 1994

LAST UNSUCCESSFUL LOGIN FOR ROOT: JUNE 23 9:13:52 EST 1994

SCO UNIX SYSTEM V/386 RELEASE 3.2

"Why is it telling you all that?"

"That's a security feature. See, it tells me the last time I logged in successfully, and the last time I tried but entered the wrong password. I can look at that and see immediately whether somebody's been messing around with my user account."

"Have they?"

"Well the last *successful* login was the night we hacked into the police computer. That means nobody's been in since then. That's good. But the last *unsuccessful* login was after that date. That means that somebody was trying awfully hard to get in and failed."

"Your employers."

"Right."

"Is the system OK?"

Henry was already checking. He was running programs, browsing directories, looking for any signs of trouble. He had pages of electronic mail waiting for him: messages from his pals out on the Internet wondering why he had fallen off the edge of the electronic earth, the system reminding him to change his password, colleagues asking him questions. Otherwise everything was normal. He looked up the computer's history records: nothing out of the ordinary except a power outage a few weeks before. The system had run on battery a while, then when the battery began to run out, it shut itself down. When the power came back on, the system brought itself back on line. All of this had happened automatically. This pleased him, and he felt a new affection for his long time friend.

Henry heard a click behind him. He turned. Jett was shoving a Glock 17 into the holster under her arm. Just like Henry and his computer, she, too, had a security blanket. She leaned over and took a swig of his Mountain Dew.

"Where'd you get that?" he asked, surprised. "Didn't they take it away from you in the laboratory?"

"This is my extra. Keep it under my pillow in case of emergencies."

"Nice."

"I miss it." She pulled it out again, pulled back the slide and checked the chamber, just for her own satisfaction. Then she thrust it into the holster again.

"Yeah, I know what you mean,"

Jett sat down in a chair next to him.

"What are we gonna do?" he asked her.

Her mind seemed to walk slowly through the chain of events, each event punctuated by a question: "First a guy named Traymore hired me to do a routine job: deliver a sealed package from Manaus, Brazil to Detroit, Michigan. Deliver it quickly, secretly and with full security. Full price. No questions asked . . . All this was routine, nothing new."

"What about the attack on the highway, remember, when you first met me?"

"Even that wasn't out of the ordinary for this kind of work. I've dealt with aggressive competitors before. In the end we delivered the package to the drop point."

"That's when we saw that Dr. Caldwell creep," Henry said.

"He knew the drop code, so I gave him the package," Jett said. "The bird."

She nodded. "Caldwell opened the package and saw the bird inside. Then he gave orders to capture us and everything went crazy.

The bird's the answer."

"But what's the question?" Henry wanted to know.

She went into the bedroom and returned, carrying the plastic sample bag that they had stolen from the laboratory. She sat down again beside Henry, studying the bird in her hand.

"What's so important about that?" Henry asked.

"Somehow the bird is related to Dracon's research," she said.

"But why did they capture us?" Henry asked.

"And they captured Mary and many others like her, people off the street, homeless folks that other people wouldn't miss. You were wounded, but the rest of us . . . they were using us for their experiments, like rats."

"I thought I was in some weird hospital most the time," Henry said. "Not until I heard you screaming in the hallway did I really understand how much trouble we were in. I still don't understand why they experimented on you but not me."

"You were severely wounded. They needed to bring you back to full health before you could be useful to them. Once you were healthy, then they would experiment on you."

The thought of this gave Henry a little shiver. "Nice guys . . ."

"What were they doing to us . . ." Jett was thinking it through. "What did they inject into Mary and I? Why did Mary die?"

Henry shook his head. He didn't know. "They're working on some new concoction, some drug," he guessed.

"But what are they researching?"

"Yeah, why are they using human beings for test subjects? Why don't they model it on a computer first?"

"They were in a hurry, using unwilling human test subjects . . . it must be something incredibly powerful, something that's worth the risk . . . something exceedingly profitable . . ."

And the questions kept rolling. They had escaped the physical confines of the laboratory, but in many ways these questions were a far more formidable prison.

"What's going to happen now?" Henry asked. "I mean, you haven't been well since we escaped. What's going to happen to you? Are we going to get some help?"

Even as he spoke, Jett's face began to change color.

"What's the matter?" Henry asked.

"Nothing, I'm OK." She began to stand, but stumbled.

Something gripped her and she gasped. Her hands went out to the arm of the chair and to Henry to steady herself. The next second she was on the floor, vomiting onto the Persian rug. The pain surged down her back with a scream. Her pupils dilated, and every blood vessel in her body became visible, her temple pounding like it was going to burst.

Henry stood, terrified, not knowing what to do. Then he knelt down beside her. He tried to help her, to hold her, but it didn't seem to matter. She mumbled, whispered, and hissed. Then her mumbles turned into strange growls. Her whole body shook, limbs trembling like a dog having a bad dream. Wild animals seemed to be running through her. Herds of them. A thousand hoofed-feet running. A thousand screams in her head. She reeled suddenly, like the apartment had started revolving and she had to keep her balance. Her eyes shut. Her body fell limp on the floor. And there was utter stillness in the room. Frozen, Henry watched the thump-thump of the blood vessel at her temple.

After a while, he sat beside her, bewildered. He didn't really do anything for her during this terrifying attack. He didn't know what to do. This was the third attack since they had escaped. Whatever it was they put inside her, it was still there. He could sense its potency lurking within her. Perhaps there was no escaping it. Perhaps Jett was going to die like Mary died . . . but he had to find out what it was, he had to try.

CHAPTER THIRTY-THREE

Henry found his way down to the lobby. The doorman helped him wave down a taxi. He told the taxi driver to take him to the New York Public Library, one of the largest reference libraries in the world. He walked into the main lobby and gazed around, bewildered. Where would he start?

"Hello," a smartly-dressed man said from behind the information desk.

"I'm looking for a book–" Henry started.

"–Well, we've got nine million one hundred eighty nine thousand four hundred and eighty nine volumes to choose from. Approximately."

"Approximately?" Henry asked with all seriousness. "You don't know for sure?"

"Was there one in particular you were interested in?" the librarian, a little miffed, asked.

"Disease."

"I beg your pardon?"

"I'm looking for information on disease research."

"Ah, yes, I think I can help you with that. What disease?"

"I don't know."

The librarian looked upon him incredulously.

Henry shrugged. "All of them."

"Young man, you really must have more of an idea than that. I mean, puh-lease, the library isn't an amusement park you can just meander through like a child. You must have a research plan. Otherwise you have no hope at all of finding the information you are looking for."

"Not necessarily," Henry said and left quickly.

Half hour later, with the aid of an Egg McMuffin, a bag of Nacho Cheesier Doritos, and, of course, a Mountain Dew, he was back in Jett's apartment working on her computer. She was sleeping in the next room.

He used the modem to call up his office. Then he used that computer to access his Gopher System, which would root out information that was spread sporadically across the worldwide Internet. He soon found himself browsing the latest information in Medline at the National Library of Medicine.

And so it began. He tried the obvious things first. He did searches on the key words Jett had given him, including *sapo* and *phyllomedusa bicolor*. After the medical libraries came up empty he tried the words against an ornithological database. Nothing.

Eventually he started reading about diseases, human physiology, and pharmaceutical research. Cocaine 1860. Aspirin 1889. Cyanamide 1905. Typhus Vaccine 1909. Development of insulin 1922. Cortisone 1936. Morphine unknown. Penicillin 1941. Discovery of DNA structure 1951. Polio vaccine 1953. Measles vaccine 1954. AZT 1986. By the end of the day, his head was spinning, so he logged off.

Not unlike many other human beings, Henry found normal classroom education ineffective to the point of boredom, but when motivated internally, he absorbed information easily and found true comprehension. And Henry came to realize that day that there was no better motivation in the world than fear. All that he read and learned that day he would retain for the rest of his life. Unfortunately, the only important thing he learned was that the Library of Medicine could not possibly answer his questions.

The sheer volume of medical data available was overwhelming. When he looked up Jett's symptoms in the medical files it seemed she had at least half the diseases listed. He realized, too, that the information in the library represented the entire history of medical knowledge. What Dracon was doing at the laboratory wasn't history. It was the future.

The next day he researched the recent publications of the Center for Disease Control. His efforts soon drowned him in a deluge of statistics. More than a million mortalities a year due to heart disease, more than 40% of all deaths in the United States. Cancer deaths increasing. So-called "conquered diseases" increasing due to poor vaccination practices. The steady flow of information poured over him and into him, until he came upon a single word that caught his attention: ethnobotanic.

The exact sentence was: "Although most pharmaceuticals are produced and marketed as 'synthetic' drugs, many if not most have natural and often ethnobotanic derivation." Ethnobotanic? What does that mean, he wondered.

He read on. Quinine, cure for Malaria, derived from a tree used by Peruvian Indians. Pilocarpine, a drug used by ophthalmologists, sap from a Amazonian tree. Vinblastine, a cancer treatment, derived from ground up rosy periwinkle. Taxol, ovarian cancer, pacific yew tree. Ginkgo extract, ancient medicine used today for asthma and allergic inflammations, $700 million dollars in annual sales. He thought about that figure. $700 million. Ample motivation for just about anything.

A quarter of all prescription drugs sold in the United States have plant chemicals as active ingredients. About half of those drugs contain compounds from temperate plants, while the other half contain compounds from tropical plants. According to one recent study, the value of medicines derived from tropical plants–that is, the amount the United States spent on them–was more than $6 billion a year.

He kept reading. Only about 5,000 of the world's 250,000 recorded plant species had been screened in the laboratory to determine their therapeutic potential. There were over one hundred commercial drugs on the market derived from natural sources. In most cases, these drugs were not discovered by accident. Indigenous people had already been using them. An ethnobotanist is a scientist who studies the medical application of plants by indigenous cultures.

A blur of drugs started filling Henry's mind: Aspirin, Morphine, Curare, Taxol. . . what next? Where would the next drug come from?

He closed the file and logged off.

Ethnobotany.

The discovery of a natural medicine made sense, but he still didn't know what the medicine was, or even the disease it was meant to cure. That's what he had to find out. Somehow, the bird was the key to everything.

For a little while he tried to forget about it, let his mind noodle it around in the background. He went to check on Jett. He found her awake and up, moving around her apartment like everything was OK. They ordered Thai and talked long into the night.

The following day he returned to the library while Jett rested. He approached the same librarian he had before.

"Birds."

"Birds?" he asked. Then he laughed. "Don't tell me: 'All of them.'"

"You got it."

A few hours later he found himself in the ornithology section, a dozen books strewn across the table. He wasn't even close. Over nine thousand species of birds on the planet. He couldn't find it. He looked at plate after plate, trying to match the bird to the pictures. It was like playing that game "Which one of these pictures is different." Except that there was nine thousand of them. He went home discouraged.

That night, with Jett at his side, he installed *Audubon's Birds*, a CD-ROM of bird life. They browsed its pictures and sounds excitedly, but quickly discovered that it contained nothing similar to their bird. There were over eight hundred species of birds in North America, but their bird wasn't one of them.

During the course of the day, Henry had noticed that many if not most of the references on birds cited the American Museum of Natural History as their source. He had an idea. "Where is that?" he asked Jett.

"The American Museum of Natural History is right here in New York."

The following day they took a taxi to Central Park West and walked into the museum. They found the curator and asked her if she could identify the specimen.

"That's not a North American species," the curator said immediately. "I don't know what it is, but it's not from this country. Where did you get it?"

Jett took over. "We had it in one of our labs. We couldn't identify it. They sent us over here."

"I'm afraid I can't help you. If it was a warbler, I might be able to do some good, but I'm not up on my Neotropicals."

"Neotropicals?" Henry asked.

"Birds from the New World tropics."

"South America?" Henry asked. "Do you know anyone that might be able to help us?"

"Jay Sullivan. That's your man. If you can find him."

"Jay Sullivan? Who's that?" Henry asked.

"He's our ornithologist. He's very knowledgeable about Neotropical species. I've seen people give him a single feather from Ecuador, and he's identified the species of the bird without so much as a second thought."

"Where is he?" Henry asked.

"There's the problem."

"Problem?"

"Finding him."

"What do you mean?"

"He's usually in the field. Most people don't even realize he works for this department, including him, I think."

"And he's out now?" Henry said.

The curator frowned. She leaned forward. "Not exactly."

"What do you mean?" Henry said.

"We just pulled him back."

"Back from where?" Jett asked.

"He was doing field work in Costa Rica. His grant money ran out, so we had to pull him back. Had no choice. We had to order him."

"Order?" Jett repeated.

"Our 'requests' were ignored. You wouldn't want to see him right now even if he was here. Sullivan's not a man to be around when he's angry."

"What did you do?" Henry said.

"I told him to use his vacation time."

"Did he go?" Henry said.

She nodded. "Thank God. There would've been trouble otherwise."

"Where did he go on vacation? It's important that we get hold of him," Jett said.

"Yes, I can see that. For Jay Sullivan the quality of a vacation is measured by the number of days he goes without seeing another human being."

"Where did he go?" Henry asked.

"He's in the back country of Yosemite National Park."

"In California?" Henry said, disappointed.

"I'm afraid so."

"When is he due back?" Jett asked.

"Monday, supposedly. We'll see. Sometimes he just goes for

a while, doesn't come back, doesn't call anybody."

"And you say he could identify this bird?" Jett asked.

"I don't know anybody else who could."

"We'll be back Monday," Jett told her.

CHAPTER THIRTY-FOUR

At one point during the weekend, Jett went out to get take-out Chinese food for them. In the elevator on the way back up to her apartment, a series of cramps palpitated through her abdomen. She leaned back and closed her eyes, tightening herself against the pain. She dropped the brown paper bags and the white cartons inside spilled across the elevator floor. Then the cramps gripped her and threw her down. She couldn't help screaming.

Her body tried desperately to vomit, to expel whatever evil was inside her, but there was nothing in her stomach to throw up. Her heart began to pound. Her blood rushed through her veins. Her eyelids fluttered like an epileptic. She grabbed at the wall to hold herself up, but she fell.

After several minutes, the pain subsided and the retching ceased, leaving her with a feeling of strange euphoria. Her senses were piqued. She could hear the idle conversation of an old couple in one of the rooms down the hall, through several walls, a hundred feet away –obviously impossible. But it was happening.

A few minutes later she found herself waking from unconsciousness on the floor of the elevator. When she picked herself up, she discovered that her clothes were stained with bile and blood, and she remembered what happened.

She went back into her room, showered and changed her clothes. These episodes were becoming all too familiar. And she knew they were hints of a darker future.

Later that night, Henry went out to replace the food. They enjoyed it sitting at her kitchen table. Now he was working on the computer and Jett lay in her bed. She just lay there awhile, staring at the ceiling, letting her mind wander, letting it explore. She found in those moments a freedom she had never experienced before. She knew that death was out there. Death was coming closer. But at that moment she felt pretty good. She didn't know why. But she did.

The ceiling shifted slightly and she shut her eyes. She felt her soul lift out of her body and upward. She saw herself lying on the bed. She drifted upward. Was this death? she wondered for a moment, but she knew it wasn't. She wasn't frightened. It was just a dream, just her mind turning in on itself, exploring . . .

In the dream, she walked into Robert Pearl's office. She was wearing a pair of black jeans, a worn leather flight jacket. She carried a well-traveled shoulder bag. Her long black hair flowed over her shoulders and down her back. She was a tall woman, lithe like a cat. Her legs were long and her muscles toned to perfection. An air of utter sophistication hung about her, mixed with animalian beauty. Her eyes were absolutely black.

She stood across from Robert. He was sitting at his desk. Charcoal suit. White shirt. Smoke and rose paisley tie. Dark hair. He looked up, smiled. Green eyes. He stood. They shook hands. He gestured toward the couch near the book cases. They walked together and sat down.

"Hello, Jett, how have you been?" he asked her.

"Fine."

"Business good?"

"Yes, very good."

"Would you like a drink?"

"Sure, whatever you're having."

He got up, poured them each a glass of wine, and handed hers to her.

She sipped it and set it down.

His voice was gentle, confident, warm. "You know, Jett, I've got to confess that this project really doesn't deserve you."

"What do you mean?" she asked, a little confused.

He shrugged genuinely. "It's more of an excuse really. Don't get me wrong, it's a valid project and a valid delivery, but it doesn't really deserve you."

"I'm not sure what you're saying."

He looked up at her. For a moment their eyes met. Then he turned away. He was frustrated with himself, perhaps even ashamed.

The smile dissolved from her face.

A seriousness hung about them.

He seemed to lose his confidence in what he was trying to say. There was no anger in his next words, only a heartbreaking despondence. "Listen, the package is on my secretary's desk. She can give you the instructions . . ." he started to get up.

She reached out. Touched his arm. The most gentle of touches. Her fingers remained lightly pressed against the white cotton of his shirt.

"What is it, Robert?"

He glanced up at her, then averted his eyes again. "I just wanted to see you, to talk to you," he said, his voice nearly a whisper. "This job isn't important enough to warrant your expertise, I just wanted to see you."

She lowered her eyes. She knew how difficult that was for him. There were a hundred inhibitors telling him that he shouldn't. He did anyway. She clung to that for a moment. He said it. Even though it would change everything. Even though it was against everything in his life. Even though it might open up a totally different world. He said it.

She didn't look at him. She couldn't. She didn't know what would happen if she did. Instead she held his arm. "I know," she said. Nothing else came from her lips.

For a moment they did not move. They stayed in that position, sitting beside each other on the couch, her leg almost touching his thigh, her hand on his arm, both of their heads lowered. They searched what had happened in that tiny infinite moment. They searched what was happening right then, even as the silence grew. It wasn't an uncomfortable silence. It didn't want words to fill it. In that silence they were together. And the silence wanted eternity.

Finally, he put his hand on hers. He held it there. "I want you," he said.

She nodded, without raising her eyes.

"It's not a smart thing to do," he said.

"It doesn't matter."

"No, it doesn't. It feels right. That's more important than anything to me right now."

She nodded. She understood what he was saying. Even though they had only been business acquaintances, casual friends, she had seen and heard what was happening to his company. She had seen and heard what was happening with his wife. His world was falling apart. He was clinging to her, clinging to a tiny seed of hope, of excitement, of warmth.

"I remember when I first met you," he said.

"I remember that, too. You were so formal with me, like I wasn't even a person. You were giving everybody orders that night. Your big project was taking off."

He shook his head at her impression of it. "You were the most beautiful woman I had ever seen, yet you behaved with such professionalism, such austerity. I couldn't touch you, couldn't even look at you. Ever since then . . ."

"What . . ."

He shook his head. Then he smiled. "I like when you call me on the phone. I like hearing your voice. I can't even explain how I feel when you walk into my office . . . it's electrifying. It's the beginning of a lifetime. You know, I've known you for years now. Years. You've seen this company grow. You've seen it falter. You've seen my most desperate moments here in this office. Through all of this, while everything else has been crumbling around me, this incredible feeling of love has been growing within me. I don't even know you, but I've let myself fall in love with you, to build a whole world around you in my mind . . . it's incredible what a human mind will do . . . what it will think about . . . it's like an escape . . . the mind wanders . . . and it escapes. . ."

She leaned against him, wrapping her hands around him and holding him. For the first time in her life she smelled him, and felt his heat against her body. She fell into a warmth deeper than she had ever known before.

When she woke the sun had set and it was dark in her room. She was alone. For a few cruel minutes her heart ached for the reality of the dream. It was a dream of a beginning. What she faced in reality was an ending. She didn't have any answers. Life was rapidly drawing to a close without them.

There was a poison inside her. She had seen what it did to Mary. She thought about going to the hospital or to the police. She even thought about getting help from Robert Pearl. But she knew they couldn't help her. A hospital or a research lab wouldn't know what this stuff was. She knew that by the time the doctors finished with their tests and scratched their heads in confusion, she'd be dead.

CHAPTER THIRTY-FIVE

On Monday morning Jett and Henry arrived back at the Museum of Natural History. The curator recognized the odd couple and greeted them. "Well, hello there, you're back."

"Hello, is Dr. Sullivan in today?" Henry said.

"Yes, he is, but it's really not a good time. I suggest you come back tomorrow. I'll leave him a message that you stopped by."

"We would like to see him now if that's possible," Henry said.

"I think it would be best if you didn't."

"It's quite urgent," Henry persisted.

"I understand, but Dr. Sullivan is rather upset right now. You would have better luck talking to him tomorrow."

Jett touched the woman's arm and looked directly into her face, her black eyes blazing.

"We need to see him now."

The curator paused, lowered her eyes, and finally agreed. "Alright. It's your head he's going to bite off."

She led Jett and Henry down a corridor, through a door, and into what appeared to be a storeroom of expedition equipment.

A ragged, irritated voice erupted from behind a tall book case piled high with scientific journals and backpacking equipment: "What's the point of having an office if people are going to walk in at any given moment?"

"Dr. Sullivan, there is someone here to see you."

A tall, brawny man stepped out from behind the book case. He was about forty years old, with long greying brown hair and a grey beard. An ample beer belly hung over the thick leather belt that held up his loose-fitting, worn out jeans. His skin was tanned dark by equatorial sunshine. He had on black Wellies covered in dried mud and a Gore-Tex anorak that had seen better days.

When he stared out from behind the book case, his dark brown eyes blinked a couple of times, taken aback by Jett's appearance. Then he regained his aura of choice: abject cynicism.

"I'm not interested in visitors today," he said.

"Dr. Sullivan, please, she came last week and has been waiting for you all this time."

"That's her problem."

He dragged a duffle bag across the floor. He unzipped it and pulled out a high-powered spotting scope, which he set on the desk with a pile of other optics and a cleaning kit.

Irritated because the people in his office weren't going away, he rubbed and sniffed his nose, turned his back to them, and tried to focus on his work.

Jett turned to the curator and nodded, indicating that she had done all she could do. The curator smiled apologetically and then exited the office, leaving Jett and Henry alone with him.

"We won't take much of your time," Henry said apologetically. "We know you have other things on your mind."

When he stepped closer, Henry noticed the faint smell of linseed oil, and perhaps marijuana.

"What's so important? Who are you two? Scarecrow and Mrs. King in reverse? Some sort of exchange students looking to start a dissertation? What're your names?"

"My name is Henry. This is Jett."

"Jett? What sort of name is that? Are you hippies or something?" He laughed, then continued cleaning the lenses.

"Jetta Mendoza Santiago," she replied, her voice even. It was obvious that he didn't like strangers. So she gave him her name.

"Jetta Mendoza Santiago," he repeated. He said her name with a perfect Spanish accent. He rolled the words over his tongue like he enjoyed saying them. "*Jetta Mendoza Santiago.*"

Henry began. "Dr. Sullivan, We've come to ask–"

"–Egads!"

"What?" Henry cried. "What's the matter?" He thought he had stepped on some rare African bird or something.

"Don't call me that! It sounds disgusting!"

"Pardon me?" Henry said.

"Don't call me Dr. Sullivan. Just Sullivan. Nobody calls me anything but Sullivan."

"Ah, I'm sorry. OK. We've come to ask you about a bird. The curator told us you could help."

He frowned. "Don't tell me Cynthia has misidentified another white-crowned sparrow!" It was clear he was pretending not to be interested in their problem. This vexed Henry, and he knew it wasn't agreeing with Jett either. Her silence while Henry negotiated with this guy's antagonism was foreboding. After all they had been through, she was in no mood to play nice-nice. He glanced over at her. Henry wondered how Egads-Don't-Call-Me-Doctor Sullivan would feel about a Glock 17 shoved in his mouth.

Dispensing with diplomacy, Jett took out the bird and held it in her palm.

At first Sullivan didn't even look at it. He kept working. Then it caught his eye and he turned. "Now, that's a bird!"

Henry smiled: Sullivan was hooked. "What is it?" Henry asked.

"That's *Momotus momota* . . ." Sullivan said, then paused.

They waited, watching him.

Sullivan frowned. He set the scope down and put out his hand. "May I see the bird?" he asked politely. His anger and resentment toward the administration of the museum was forgotten, at least for the moment. Everything was the bird.

She set the bird in his outstretched palm.

"Well, it's certainly some kind of *Momotidae*. . ."

"A what?" Henry asked.

"A *Momotidae*."

"What's that?"

"It's a family of South American birds, commonly called motmots. It looks like a blue-crowned motmot, but there's something strange about it."

Sullivan walked out of the room, taking the bird with him. He didn't bother to ask them to follow, but they did anyway. The bird was all they had. They wouldn't let it out of their sight.

They followed him through a series of rooms and corridors until he reached what appeared to be some sort of biological archive. He walked along a wall of cabinets, then ran his finger down a vertical column of drawers until he reached the one labeled *Momotidae*. He pulled open the drawer. It was filled with a hundred dead birds very similar to the one he held in his hand. The inside of the birds had been removed, leaving only the treated skin and feathers. Each bird was identified with a narrow tag which contained the details of its collection, such as, "Momotus momota, adult male, Bret Whitney, Ecuador, 1994."

He investigated the minute details of the bird, checking each feather, the shape of the bill. The bird was about eighteen inches in length, nine inches of that being its long, slate blue tail. The tail had a strange, circular formation of feathers at the end. But all the motmots had that same trait. Henry assumed it was not a defect of this particular specimen, but a characteristic of the family. The bird's large black bill was serrated, as if for catching and holding slimy jungle things. The back was green and its breast cinnamon. The face was black, the crown a striking metallic blue, and the specimen tag indicated that the iris had been bright red.

Sullivan was agitated. His earlier bad mood had been totally replaced by this new aggravation: his inability to quickly identify the bird's species. It consumed him.

"What kind is it?" Henry prompted him.

"Give me a minute!" he snapped back.

Finally, he shook his head and just stared at the array of specimens. He was stumped.

"I'm sorry, Dr. Sullivan, we'll take the bird back and be on our way. We heard you might be able to help us, but–"

"–Wait a second!" He wanted silence.

He thought through the problem with deliberate concentration. "I should be able to do this. I've got every known species, subspecies and plumage variation of *Momotidae* in this drawer. Every motmot in the world. Do you understand what I'm saying?"

"Not exactly," Henry admitted.

"Where did you get this bird?" Sullivan asked.

"We believe it comes from South America," Henry told him.

"Of course it comes from South America!" When he screamed the spittle flew into Henry's face. Henry stepped away, a little frightened. He wasn't sure what he was frightened of. Was it Sullivan? Was it the fact that the bird was unknown, and therefore their future uncertain?

"You tell *us* where," Jett challenged him.

"I don't know. I can guess. I can guess, but I don't know."

"Is there anyone who would know?" Jett asked.

He shook his head. "You could take it to LSU or the

Smithsonian. They'd say the same thing. They wouldn't know either. Then they'd tell you to bring it to me."

"What are you saying?" Henry asked.

"I'm saying that either this is an individual aberration or this is an undescribed species."

"I don't know what that means," Henry said.

"I'm saying this bird is unknown to science."

"A new species?" Jett asked.

"Exactly."

"How is that possible?" Jett asked.

"Look, wrong as this may sound, there are still things out there we don't know about. Lots of things."

"Here be dragons. . . " she mumbled.

"What?"

"Here be dragons. That's what they used to put on old maps to designate unexplored territories."

"That's right. The tropical rain forests are unexplored biologically. Though they take up less than two percent of the earth's surface, we estimate that fifty percent of all plant and animal species live there. The Amazonian rain forest is the most biologically diverse ecosystem on the planet, bar none."

"And you think this is a new species?" Henry asked, amazed.

"It may be. That's all I'm saying. I want to know where this bird came from."

"We don't know," Henry said.

"Who collected it? Why didn't he tag it properly?"

"We don't know where it was collected or by whom. We're sorry. That's why we came here, to find you, and see if you could help us," Henry said.

"But who are you?" Sullivan turned to Jett. "Are you a field collector? I mean, I've never met you before and I know everybody in this business, at least I thought I did. Of course, I thought I knew all the birds, too. It's incredible. I don't think you realize what you've stumbled onto here."

"No, we're not field collectors. It's a long story, but it's very important that we find the purpose of this bird," Jett said.

"What do you mean 'purpose'? Purpose for what?"

"I'm not sure. First, we need to find its specific origin," Jett said.

"There's only one way you're going to do that."

"How?" Henry asked.

"Me, of course."

"You?"

"That's how you're going to find this bird," Sullivan said.

"But how?" Henry asked.

"Look, I know these birds. I've been studying the Neotropical avifauna for thirty years. If anybody can find your bird, I can."

"Tell us how," Henry said.

"Where did you first come in contact with this specimen?"

"Brazil," Jett answered.

"What part?"

"Manaus."

"That's a start. I can tell you already, though, that this bird didn't come from Brazil."

"How can you tell that?" Henry asked suspiciously.

"You see these specimens here," he pointed to a section of the birds in the drawer.

"See the rufous shading at the neck. Your bird has that, too."

"What does that tell us?" Henry asked, unimpressed.

"All the birds with the rufous patch around the throat come from the west side of the Río Napo."

"So?"

"All those other specimens come from the east side of the river."

"There's that much difference?" Henry asked.

"Sure, happens all the time. The Río Napo is a major tributary of the upper Amazon. It may be just a tributary, but it's wider than the Mississippi. Because the birds don't fly across it, it separates two distinct breeding populations. The two populations have evolved slightly different plumages. Some ornithologists think that they are actually two distinct species, but that's debatable of course. That's what annual conferences are for. But, you see, your bird didn't come from Brazil."

"Where did it come from?" Henry asked.

"Peru."

"Peru," Jett repeated the word. She shifted her feet. "Are you sure it's from Peru?" she asked.

"It's a good assumption. That's the place to start. Of course, Peru ain't Rhode Island. If memory serves, it's about three times bigger than California. We can rule out anything east of the Napo and south of the Amazon, but it's still a huge region. It'll be tough to find."

"You sound like you want to go look for it right now!" Henry cried.

Sullivan looked at him with sympathy for his innocence. "Look, Henry, I don't think you understand what you've got here. We're talking about a bird unknown to science. And not just an obscure flycatcher or sparrow. We're talking about a motmot. Among ornithologists this is big, very big. If I had the funds to set up an expedition, I wouldn't hesitate to go down there. To discover a new species is the dream of every ornithologist, especially this one."

"But your funds have been cut," Henry pointed out.

Sullivan's face soured. "Cynthia tell you that? I hate that bitch."

"Is it true?" Henry asked.

"Yeah, it's true." He handed the bird back to Jett. "I'm stuck here, cataloging specimens, collating maps. My butt gets sore just thinking about it."

Jett broke in. "Don't worry about your butt just yet. We've got a few things to do this afternoon, but I would like you to meet us for dinner."

"Dinner?" he looked up at her.

"Dinner. You remember what that is? Plates, silverware, food in the middle," Henry reminded him.

He smiled. "Yeah, I remember, kid. I can't stand restaurant food, though. You guys come to my place. I'll fix something."

CHAPTER THIRTY-SIX

That evening Sullivan greeted them at the door of his apartment and led them inside, where they were immediately surrounded by a disorganized collection of books, papers, equipment, maps, clothes, utensils and furniture. The place was thick with the smell of marijuana. He hadn't bothered to hide the living Cannabis sativa growing in the corner next to the case of empty rum bottles. As far as he was concerned, grass had been legal since the sixties.

There were books everywhere, crammed into every crack and crevice of the old place. There were boxes of them, and great piles, and dozens spread across what might have been the kitchen table, if it was given a chance. Maps covered many of the walls. On one side of the room was a beautiful painting of two magnificent red-crested woodpeckers. On the other side of the room stood an easel, brushes, a pallet, paint tubes, and a work in progress. Henry stared at the painting, astounded by the sheer audacity of its color.

"Scarlet," Sullivan said.

Henry blinked. "What?"

"Scarlet Macaws on Cecropia Tree. That's the name of the painting."

"Nobody told us you paint," he said.

"Doesn't surprise me."

Henry smiled at his cynicism, and turned his attention to something else.

Jett was studying the map of South America on the wall.

"I'm your answer," Sullivan said abruptly to her.

"What do you mean?" she said.

"I can find that bird for you." He kicked a bag of supplies out of her way so that she could get closer to the map. "You see these red pins. These are all the areas I've been. Look at all the pins in Peru. Nobody knows the birds in there like I do. I checked a few sources this afternoon. Your bird probably came from an area north of the Quebrada Sucusari which runs through here. You see, we're narrowing in on it."

"Why are you so interested in finding the origin of this bird?" she asked.

"You don't strike me as a light-weight. You ain't no tourist or list-chasing birder. In fact, I recognize your accent. You're from Peru. The other side of the Andes, probably Lima, right? Now, I don't know what you're up to, but I can tell you have a *serious* need to find this bird. I can find the bird. All I need is money. Call it a symbiotic relationship."

Jett smiled. "And you want to describe it. You want to discover a new species."

"Of course."

He turned away from the map and walked into the "kitchen," an area in the one room apartment where he kept some rudimentary kitchen supplies. He apparently did his cooking on a compact, aluminum butane burner like those used by backpackers in the field. He hadn't gotten around to hooking up the natural gas range on which it sat.

"Yeah, I've got money," she said. "I've got plenty of money to get us down to Peru, and start an expedition, but there are other things to consider."

"Like what?"

She shook her head. "We have a problem to solve. I have two different approaches. First, I could contact a friend of mine that works in the pharmaceutical industry. I know he would help me. He would research the problem in his lab and eventually he'd find some answers."

"That sounds like it would to take a while."

"That's right, and we don't have much time. In fact, we don't have *any* time. We have to attack this problem directly. Get to the source. That's where the answers are. And, if my suspicions are correct, that's where our enemy would be most vulnerable. This isn't a scientific expedition for us," she said.

"What is it then? What's this all about?" he said softly.

Jett paused.

Henry watched her, wondering what she was going to do. Could she say, I've been injected with some sort of drug. We must find out where it comes from, what it's for and what it's going to do to me . . . and the bird is our only clue, so you must help us find it.

Jett looked into Sullivan's face. "We need to find this bird and we need to find it immediately, no questions asked. You're either in or you're out."

Sullivan turned away and laughed in intense discomfort. "Wow, I've got to veg on this!" he said, and went back to preparing the meal. He began slicing pepperonies for a pizza he was going to make. After a few minutes, he said, "I'd go down to Peru with any sort of excuse. I didn't want to come back from Costa Rica either, but the entire human world is a bureaucracy, and I got screwed. What I don't understand is why you need to do this. I mean, it seems like you're in some kind of trouble. I don't like pigs any better than the next guy, but if you're in trouble, why don't you get some help?"

She looked over at Henry. Henry was looking back at her, listening intently.

She shook her head. "This is complicated, Sullivan. I can't get the police involved. Too complicated. Too many problems."

"You're not legal."

"I've got three or four names in this country, Sullivan, all of them with legal IDs, two with legal passports, but if anyone starts looking seriously into my past . . . I don't want to think about the consequences."

"What about in Peru? Maybe the government down there can help you."

"I'm worse off there," she said.

"Worse off?" he said.

"If we're going in, then we have to go quickly, quietly and now."

"Groovy!" he whispered conspiratorially. "You know, Jetta Mendoza Santiago, you're beautiful and you're my kind of woman! I've only known you about eight hours and I think I'm in love with you! Come on, Henry, let's cook up some pizza!"

CHAPTER THIRTY-SEVEN

Faucett Peruvian Airlines advertises itself as "Peru's First and Only Airline." Perhaps this is supposed to instill confidence in its customers. For Henry, it didn't.

Faucett leases its three planes from the United States, and is required by law to use U.S. mechanics, U.S.-regulated maintenance schedules, and U.S. pilots. The stewards on board, however, are Peruvian to the last, giving it the flavor of a truly Peruvian airline. Some would argue that the same approach was taken with the government of Peru itself.

Once a week, usually on Saturday, Faucett flew a round trip flight from Miami to Iquitos, Iquitos to Lima, Lima to Miami.

Jett, Sullivan and Henry flew down to Miami, then boarded one of Faucett's L1011s.

In the hurried two days of preparation and planning, they discovered that they had much in common: hatred for bureaucracy, mistrust for authority, and perhaps most importantly, a connoisseurs' taste for pizza.

Cruising at 33,000 feet over Cuba, Henry heard Jett explain to Sullivan that she was a professional courier, and that it was one of her clients that had involved her in this. She said nothing more.

Jay Sullivan was born in Buffalo, where he grew up watching birds in his back yard. He graduated from high school with fair grades and some disciplinary problems, but got into Cornell on an art scholarship. After scraping together enough credits to get a degree four years later, he proceeded to pursue a masters and eventually a Ph.D. in avian biology. He did his thesis on the orange-crowned tanager, a rare bird found only in the Desparsus region of central Peru. He stayed on at Cornell to become the laboratory's primary field researcher and a world-renowned expert on Neotropical avifauna. But due to certain "personality conflicts" at Cornell, Sullivan left there to take a position as a collector for the American Museum of Natural History.

A decade later, the Museum had the largest collection of bird skins in the country and was considered a chief center for avian research, especially zoogeography. Of the more than three thousand species of birds indigenous to South America, Jay Sullivan had taken specimens of almost ninety percent of them. He became acclimated to life in the tropics, and started spending more time there and less in the States. Soon he was spending eight months of the year in the field. He wasn't collating and publishing his results. Worst of all for the museum, he wasn't collecting any more skins. Instead, he spent countless hours in the rain forest, finding and observing live birds, compiling detailed notes on behavior and vocalizations. Wherever he traveled, he collected bird sounds on a tape recorder he carried with him. He focused his efforts on *Amazonia*–the region defined by the Amazon river basin and its tributaries. He had recorded and annotated several thousand vocalizations.

While Sullivan explained all of this, Henry noticed Jett was starting to look a little queasy. Disoriented, she unbuckled her seat belt and stood. The plane rocked to the side, then dropped slightly. She moved into the aisle. She tried to get to the bathroom, but she fell to the floor and started vomiting. Henry ran to her and held her.

"What's happening? What's wrong?" Sullivan asked, standing above them while stewards gathered around and began helping.

"Air sickness," Henry told him.

When she felt better, Henry helped her back to the seat. They had been flying over Peru for the last hour. The engines throttled down and the plane descended.

As the plane tilted for its final approach to the Iquitos airport, Jett shifted nervously.

Henry leaned toward her. "You OK?"

She shook her head. Henry didn't know why, but she dreaded what awaited her.

Henry gazed out the window. He could see the brown waters of the Amazon river glistening below. Although they were 2,300 miles from the mouth on the Atlantic, the upper Amazon was three miles wide. From the air it looked like a golden serpent twisting its way over a deep green sea. The city of Iquitos was a brown island of humanity in an ocean of rain forest.

"Is it the river?" he asked. He could not fathom her fear.

She shook her head as the plane banked and dropped abruptly.

"You feeling sick again?"

She shook her head. "When I left, I left in a hurry. I never thought I'd be coming back."

"How long ago was it?"

"Ten years."

"Were you in trouble?"

She nodded.

"Will they remember that long ago?"

"If they see me . . . they will remember."

"What about your name? Won't they recognize your name?"

"I changed it."

Henry was quiet, but he couldn't stop himself. "Was it the law?"

"No."

The pilot pulled up the nose and the plane bumped three times before it fell onto the ground and stayed there. It screeched toward the far end of the runway as the flaps went up and the brakes went on. Finally it fish-tailed and careened to a full stop. The passengers cheered, glad to be alive.

"Then what is it?" Henry persisted.

"Henry."

He stopped asking questions.

Six officials in loose-fitting, khaki uniforms boarded the plane and ushered people down the steel stair to the tarmac. Once inside the airport, the passenger's luggage was opened and searched.

As was her habit from many years of traveling, Jett carried what she needed in her leather bag. Likewise, Sullivan carried most of his personal belongings in his backpack. Using money he had borrowed from Jett, Henry bought some clothing and accouterments in New York for the trip to South America, all of which was now stuffed into two brightly colored plastic suit cases.

The customs agent pawed through Sullivan's backpack, which was full of optical equipment: binoculars, scope, camera. After looking suspiciously at each item, the agent wanted to know what it was all for.

"Pájaros," Sullivan told him.

The agent looked up at him strangely, then motioned him through.

Jett whispered to Sullivan as they went in. "We're married."

"What?"

"We're married, and Henry is your little brother."

"What are you talking about?"

She pulled out her American passport.

He snatched it out of her hand. He opened it just as they took their places in the line beneath the sign: **EXTRANJEROS/FOREIGNERS**. Two hundred sweaty and frazzled travelers pushed themselves into the fray toward an intimidating maze of red and yellow lines, uniformed officials, armed guards, interview desks, and holding cells. All the passengers on the plane were divided into two categories: residents and foreigners. The first line was long and slow-moving. The inspectors interrogated each of the dark-skinned residents extensively before allowing him or her to pass through a series of metal detectors, x-ray machines and drug-sniffing dogs.

The other line, for foreigners only, moved along quickly. There was only one metal detector. The inspector would ask each group a few questions, smile, then wave them through. The phrase "tourist" seemed to be synonymous with "I'm white, friendly and have lots of money, so please let me in."

As they moved through this line, Henry noted Jett's passport: Cathy Sullivan. His own said Henry Sullivan instead of Henry Beaufort. Henry was watching the customs inspector with the side arm interviewing each person in the line.

Jett smiled to Sullivan as he stared down at her passport. "Just a family from Buffalo, New York on a vacation. Nothing to worry about. Nothing to slow us down. Nothing to catch attention."

Henry was wondering if the inspector was going to talk to him. What should he say? Hi, we're here to find a magic bird.

"How did you get these passports?" Sullivan stammered to Jett.

She shrugged.

Henry noticed that sometimes the inspector put his hand on his gun. Behind him there were a couple of German shepards. And standing next to the wall a few yards away were three uniformed soldiers holding machine guns.

"How did you get this so fast?" Sullivan asked, astounded. It was a perfect fake. "Come on, Jett?"

"Hey, I had *two* days!"

Jett gathered up their passports, handed them to Sullivan and pushed him forward. "We're up next. You do the talking."

Much to Henry's relief, Sullivan moved past him and took the first place in line. The customs inspector was now interviewing the man in front of them.

Sullivan turned back to Jett. "You see those metal detectors up there?" he asked quietly.

"Yeah, I see them," she said.

"Well?"

"Just stay calm. We'll be OK if you just stay calm," she said.

"We'll never get through!" he whispered.

"Yes, we will. Stay calm. You're up. Get up there."

Sullivan stepped up in front of the inspector.

"Your passports, please," he said in his thick accent.

The inspector read the passports, checked the dates and looked at the pictures. Then he looked at each of the previous border stamps. He was mainly looking for the warning signals: Colombia, Nicaragua, El Salvador, Cuba, Russia, Iraq, China, South Africa, Northern Ireland, Bosnia. Anything to indicate a connection with drug trafficking, mercenary activity or political terrorism. Though Peru was supposedly a democracy, there was in fact a large-scale, long-term communist revolution taking place. The Soviet Union might have collapsed, but the spirit of the revolution in Peru had not. Not to mention the fact that Peru had exceeded Colombia in illegal drug exports.

Cathy Sullivan and her brother-in-law Henry had never been out of the United States. They had no stamps whatsoever. The inspector nodded his approval. He returned their passports, then looked at Dr. Sullivan's. As he flipped through the pages he started to frown. He called his supervisor over and showed him.

"Why have you traveled these many places, Dr. Sullivan?" he asked, flipping past Costa Rica, Ecuador, Trinidad, Brazil and Venezuela.

"I am an ornithologist."

"A what?"

"Científico de pájaros."

"Ah! Yes, yes. Pájaros."

"Yes, that's correct. I work with the American Museum of Natural History."

"And you are here on business, to study birds then, and perhaps take some home with you? How many will you be collecting and taking to the United States?"

"No. Actually, my family and I are on a vacation. I have been to your wonderful country many times and I wanted to show my wife and brother how beautiful it is!"

"Ah, yes! Yes it is! No birds this time?"

"Oh, I might point out one or two along the way."

"No collecting?"

"No. None."

"That's good. Very well, you may go!" he said, then he gestured for the inspector to stamp their passports and let them pass.

Sullivan led the way. But when he approached the metal detector he slowed down.

"Keep going," Jett whispered to him.

At this point, Henry had the distinct feeling he was going to pee his pants. He was watching the all too interested look on the face of the closest German shepherd. Henry knew he should've worn long sleeves that day.

"Just keep going," Jett urged them.

"I don't like it," Sullivan said under his breath.

"You've carried the ball this far. It's time to hand it off and let me carry it awhile. Trust me."

"OK, here goes . . . "

The moment he got anywhere near the metal detector the machine went crazy. Alarms went off. Lights started flashing. Three guards surrounded him with machine guns. The dog started barking and snarling at Henry. His life flashed before his eyes.

The supervisor rushed in. "Dr. Sullivan!" he cried, shouting over the dogs, grabbing his arm and pulling him firmly to the side. In the confusion, Henry tried to get out of the way, but he knocked into one of the guards that was pushed up against him, causing still more confusion. Jett moved easily, unobtrusively to her husband, stepping around the outside of the metal detector.

Once the officials had isolated Sullivan, they used their hand-held metal detector on him. They asked him to hold out his arms while they moved the detector up and down his body. The hand-held unit allowed them to quickly narrow in on the source of the disturbance: his steel belt buckle in the shape of a huge marijuana leaf.

"That gets me every time!" Sullivan said with a boisterous laugh that brought absolute silence to every agent in the room. Even the dogs were quiet. They were not amused.

They checked him again with the hand-held unit. Then they frisked him. Then they made him walk through the metal detector holding up his pants because he didn't have a belt. Finally, begrudgingly, they let him through. He joined his wife and brother on the other side of the barrier. They joined hands and started walking away. Henry was counting the steps to the outside door.

"Mrs. Sullivan!" the supervisor called.

They stopped. "Yes, sir?" She turned toward him.

"You didn't walk through the metal detector."

"Sir?"

"You must walk through the metal detector. You walked around it."

"Excuse me?" she said, pretending not to understand, going for her best New York accent, hoping they wouldn't notice that it was a lot more Manhattan than it was Buffalo.

"You must walk through the metal detector."

"I thought I did already," she said.

"Yeah, I think she already did," Henry piped in.

"You stay out of this!" the supervisor told Henry.

"OK!" he squeaked.

"No, you didn't walk through," the supervisor said graciously, but quite firmly to Jett. "You must walk through the metal detector."

Jett smiled. Without hesitation, she walked back to where the supervisor was standing and while all the guards and officials watched, she walked through the machine. No alarms sounded.

Henry was amazed. Now, for sure, he was utterly convinced Jetta Mendoza Santiago was a magical creature. Later, Jetta would laugh. "Thank God for the Glock 17!" she would say. Designed to be light-weight and ultra-concealable, most components of the weapon are made from polymers. Out of the factory, it is about seven inches long and weighs just 1.9 pounds with a loaded 17-round magazine; only the barrel and some of the internal mechanisms are steel. These she had replaced with custom components made of high-strength composite materials. Sometimes she missed the heavy feel of a Makarov pistol at her side, but ever since discovering the "traveling characteristics" of the Glock when she first came to the United States, it had been her weapon of choice. She never left home without it.

A few minutes later they were out of the airport.

"My heart was pounding out of my chest back there!" Henry cried.

A young boy approached them: "¿Necestra usted un taxi, señor?"

Since there were no roads to the city, there were precious few cars in Iquitos. Instead the inhabitants traveled by foot, pedaled bicycles, or drove motorbikes. This boy had attached a small chariot to the back of his motorbike. Now he was a taxi driver. Entrepreneurialism at its best.

Henry looked down at the dilapidated little buggy. "Better than some of the taxis in New York," he said and they crammed themselves in.

"¿Están preparados?" the boy asked.

"Andale," Sullivan said.

With a kick and a sputter, they sped into the dusty streets of the city.

Unlike all other major cities in Peru, Iquitos is located on the eastern side of the Andes mountains, five hundred miles from everything else. Despite the four hundred thousand people who live there, there are no roads leading into or out of the city. The city of Iquitos is truly an island within an ocean of rain forest, reachable only by boat and plane.

The one and two-story buildings that line the street are made of cinder block, brick, stucco, or sheet metal–all shipped up the river. The buildings are painted in greys, off whites, and sometimes blue or green. Though clean and well-maintained, the city is undeniably poor. The buildings are simple, without glass in the windows. There are no street lights. No advertisements. People everywhere are going about their business, casually dressed in bright colors. They are dark-complected Hispanic people, invariably dark-haired and stout. Everywhere you look a couple dozen motorbikes compete for space on the road or at one of the few petrol stations. The exhaust from the motorbikes swirls upward, casting a fuliginous gloom over the streets. Black vultures sit like pigeons on the overhangs of buildings. How nice, Henry thought.

The side streets, though, were empty of motor traffic. Here the Peruvian people set up their market, selling fruit, coffee, fish, vegetables, monkeys, and Coca-cola. Wild palm trees protrude from the boulevard. Tropical bushes grow everywhere. Brilliantly colored flowering vines creep uninvited into people's windows. Jewel-like hummingbirds circled them.

Sullivan was still talking about the airport. "Thank God they didn't look at my pack any closer!"

"I've never done anything like that in my life!" Henry agreed.

"If they had checked my pack any closer we would have been in a world of hurt!" Sullivan cried.

Jett interrupted him. "It was just a few 9mm cartridges sewn into your pack lining. What are they going to do to you?"

"Throw him in jail and torture him until he died," Henry suggested.

"Yeah, but what else?" Jett smiled.

Sullivan grimaced at them.

"Marcos gran Hotel," Sullivan said to the driver after they had loaded into his motorized bike. The boy nodded his head, punched the accelerator and cranked up the radio to send himself back into oblivion. Henry noticed that he had used a piece of rope to tie a boom box onto the handle bars.

"How did you get past them?" Jay Sullivan asked.

"I told you it probably wouldn't be a problem. There are always ways to do things. That was one of the easier ones. Peru's problems are on the inside, not the outside."

"What's the big deal about the gun though? Why bring it? Why risk it?"

"You call carrying a weapon a risk?"

"Sure. What if you get caught?"

"Not carrying a weapon is a greater risk, at least in my experience. Things are never too bad if I have the Glock in my hand and plenty of clips in my pockets."

"It's when you run out of bullets that life really goes down hill," Henry said.

Sullivan shrugged and shook his head. "What pals I have!"

"Have you been to this hotel before?" Jett asked.

"I stayed there last time I was here."

"Who runs it?"

"Some Gringo."

"Talkative sort of guy?"

"Nope. He won't give us any grief."

"What part of town?"

"East, along the river." In Iquitos one seldom used the word "Amazon." People referred to the river as "el río" or "agua."

The taxi motored through the crowded streets. There were people and vehicles everywhere.

It had just rained. The sun was shining, but sinking low in the sky. The streets glistened with puddles of rain water.

Many of the streets were steep and the little two-stroke engine struggled against gravity, sucking in air that already had more carbon monoxide than it should.

A boy passed them on a scooter. His girlfriend straddled the seat behind him, her arms around his waist, her light skirt blowing in the wind, her face smiling. She smiled and waved at Henry.

Finally, they reached the outskirts of the city and turned onto a narrow road. They began to leave the urban sprawl behind them. Large-leafed palm trees grew on either side, their leaves whooshing loudly as they swept by.

The road descended into the forest. Soon the canopy blocked the sunlight and only the high-beam headlight led the way.

A couple of peccary ran across the road, startling the driver. He hit the brakes, slamming the passengers forward. "¡Cerdos de la maldición!" he spat, then punched the accelerator again and proceeded on.

The taxi stopped in front of the hotel. The driver hopped off his bike and opened the door for them.

Speaking in Spanish to the boy, Sullivan arranged for him to pick them up early the next morning, then he handed him several bills. Apparently more than satisfied with the payment, the boy left happily. He cranked up the volume on the boom box and sped away, his music blaring into the surrounding forest. He waved as he turned out of sight.

The travel-weary companions entered the hotel and walked up to the man at the desk.

"Hola, señor," Sullivan said, wrapping his arm around a surprised Jett. "The missus and I would like a room with a nice soft bed."

CHAPTER THIRTY-EIGHT

"That was a cute trick," Jett said as Sullivan put the key in the lock. They walked into a small room with two beds.

"It's all part of our cover," Sullivan said with a wry grin. "Besides, you're the one that's so paranoid. One room makes more sense from a security standpoint."

"Where am I gonna sleep?" Henry wanted to know.

"In here with us, Henry," Jett answered.

As they went into the room, Sullivan groaned and rubbed his back. "You don't have to worry about me. I'm dead tired. I'll be asleep before Henry's done brushing his teeth."

He wasn't exaggerating. He tossed his pack in the corner, took off most of his clothes and lay on top of the bed. "Wake me up if a flock of orange-crowned tanagers flies by!" he mumbled before he drifted into unconsciousness. A few minutes later, he was snoring loudly.

Henry got out his bathroom kit. He washed his hands. He cut his finger nails. He clipped his nose hairs. He checked his face for zits (nothing to do there, adventure appeared to be good for his complexion). He combed his hair. He began brushing his teeth.

Jett heard him turn on the tap water.

"Henry, don't drink that water."

"What?" He came into the room with a mouth full of tooth paste and a tooth brush in his hand. "What did you say?"

"Don't put that water in your mouth."

"Why not?"

"You'll get sick."

"But what am I supposed to do now?" he cried. "I've got to rinse my mouth!" There was so much toothpaste in his mouth he could barely talk.

"Don't do it," she said.

"Aw, man!" he cried and went back in the bathroom.

She was wondering what he was doing. Then she heard him spitting what toothpaste he could out of his mouth. A few seconds later he came stomping out of the room. "This calls for drastic measures," he declared. "Time to break out the emergency rations!"

Henry knelt down beside his gear, dug into his camouflage vinyl backpack and pulled out a 16 oz. plastic bottle of Mountain Dew. "I knew this would come in handy!" he said triumphantly.

"Where did you get that?" Jett laughed. "How did you get that through customs?"

"You have your ways and I have *my* ways!" he said mysteriously.

After rinsing out his mouth with Mountain Dew, flossing his teeth, using the toilet, blowing his allergy-congested nose, selecting and laying out a striped shirt and a pair of Boy Scout-like khaki shorts for the next day, Henry was finally ready for bed. He pulled down the sheets and crawled underneath. He fell asleep almost immediately.

Jett sat in the darkness, on the floor, facing the door. Only a few shafts of moonlight cut between the drapes into the room.

She disassembled and re-assembled her Glock piece by piece in the darkness. She knew the individual parts by feel. She required no tools. She assembled the weapon automatically, without thinking.

She was back in Peru: that's what she was thinking about.

She wondered how long before they would find her. She knew it wouldn't take long. Maybe it'd be the taxi driver, or the hotel man, or a merchant on the street. Somebody would talk to somebody. Word would get to them. Then they would come. That much was certain. How long would it take them? That was the question.

She sat there a while, trying to look at the situation objectively. Peru is one of South America's poorest countries, much of it disrupted by the Andes Mountains, and *most* of it covered by dense rain forest. These remote areas are sparsely populated with semi-acculturated Indians, if they are populated at all. The vast share of Peru's twenty-two million people are crammed into a tiny percentage of its land, a narrow strip of irrigated desert plain wedged between the Pacific Ocean and the western slopes of the Andes. There they built their capital, developed their industries. That is the Peru known to the outside world: Lima, terrorist violence, drug trafficking, epidemic cholera. It's a third-world country trying to scratch its way into the twentieth century–and will get there just about when everybody else moves into the twenty-first. That was the Peru Jett feared. That's where she came from. The ancient memories flooded into her mind. She tried to block them. She reminded herself she was far away from there, hundreds of miles and the Andes Mountains were between her and the history she left behind in Lima. She was in Amazonia: a river world with peaceful Indian tribes, thick rain forest, unexplored wilderness.

She could hear someone walking down the corridor. The walk was fast and heavy, an American, probably the man who ran the hotel. What was he doing in Peru? she wondered.

How long did she have to find the answers she was looking for? How would she find them?

She had asked Sullivan to take her to the place where this special bird lived. There she hoped to find a lead to the substance that Dracon Industries had injected into her body. There she hoped to find some clue to what would happen to her. Was it possible to reverse the effects? She hadn't been sick in a few hours. Would the effects ever go away? Would she die? She couldn't even tell if her condition was getting better or worse. Sitting in a little hotel in Peru, she had trouble remaining objective about herself and her surroundings: she felt danger.

She heard a set of feet skitter across the roof, then heard the animal drop to the ground next to the exterior wall.

A little later, she heard from the forest the cry of a potoo.

These sounds didn't bother her. Her mind filtered them out, drawing upon survival patterns from a decade earlier. She was listening for unnatural sounds. Metal. Footsteps. Cloth. The whine of a distant boat motor. The scrape of a hull on the river shore. The click of a weapon.

She filled the Glock's magazine with cartridges, then loaded the clip into the grip. It created a very distinct, metallic sound. Had she heard that sort of sound anywhere within a quarter of a mile it would have awakened her from a coma. She looked over at Sullivan and Henry. They were sound asleep.

Maybe Sullivan's right. I am paranoid. This isn't Lima. I'm far away from my past. I'm safe here. They can't get me here.

Just in case, she slept with her back against the wall and the 9mm automatic resting comfortably between her thighs.

CHAPTER THIRTY-NINE

Just before sunrise the next morning, the travelers woke and checked out of the Marcos gran Hotel. The taxi driver was sitting on his motorbike outside, asleep, waiting for them. When they got into his vehicle he woke up. "¡Buenos dias!" he said happily.

He started the bike's motor, turned on the boom box, and stomped on the accelerator.

They whooshed between the trees on the narrow road, climbed the hill, and started the trek back into Iquitos proper.

The taxi driver navigated aggressively through the crowded streets, beeping his horn and shouting, doing whatever was necessary to get his passengers to their destination.

The sun was rising, illuminating the buildings. Shafts of rosy pink light fell through the open half-walls of a crowded dance hall, where gay and exhausted young boys and girls in fancy clothes were streaming onto the street. It was not unusual for dance halls to open at midnight and close at dawn. Arm in arm, laughing, the dancers whooped their goodbyes to one another.

Farther along, a little boy sat on a step in front of his house. He waved excitedly to the Americans and pointed them out to his small puppy, which sat on the step beside him.

These images brought smiles to Jett's face, and for a little while she forgot where she was. Then she saw the graffiti:

¡Vida larga por Abimael Guzmán! ¡Sol rojo! Sendero Luminoso!

The words were painted in red on the side of a building, and were accompanied by a crude rendition of the "hammer and sickle." Despite the seeming normalcy of the events around her, much had happened since she had left Peru ten years before. What had begun as a "quiet struggle for communism" had escalated into an open war.

She saw something scribbled in English:

Death to the government! Long live Abimael Guzmán! Red Sun! Burn brightly the Shining Path!

On another building, she read similar slogans written in Quechua, a language that she had not seen since her departure from western Peru. The Quechua did not live in Iquitos. They came from the west, from the mountains and the cities.

Destroy the government! Kill the imperialists!

The open hostility of these images stunned her. They would have frightened her no matter where she saw them, but to see them in distant and peaceful Iquitos was at once heartbreaking and terrifying. It meant that the revolutionary forces had spread.

As a child she had been well versed in the six military plans. She left at the height of the Third Plan: the wholesale disruption of all government services. In 1986, the guerrillas notched 28,000 actions designed to interfere with everything from public transportation, utility services, and postal deliveries to police activities. Four of Peru's districts–known as departments–were put under a "state of emergency." Thousands of people died from the violence in that year alone.

The Fourth Plan was the next step. It entailed the infiltration of the now severely eroded economic infrastructure: unions, state companies, local governments, schools, colleges, universities, and the judiciary. Where the Third Plan called for disruption, the Fourth Plan called for control. It not only involved traditional rebel areas such as the south and west, but all areas of Peru, including the rain forests of remote Amazonia.

The official government, ill-equipped to deal with the effective and well-organized guerrillas, struggled to defend its most important districts. Remote areas in the Andes mountains and the Amazon basin were left unguarded and were easily overrun by revolutionaries. Whole cities were now under revolutionary control: Ayacucho, Apurimac, Huncavelica. By this time, the guerrillas had engaged in over 100,000 attack initiatives. Nine of the country's districts were under a state of emergency. The number of people killed could no longer be determined and the screams of the murderers covered every wall in the city. It sickened her. Sendero Luminoso: The Shining Path.

"If the drug traffickers don't get us, the revolutionaries will, that's what I always say!" joked Sullivan to Henry when he noticed him trying to read the slogans. He touched Henry's arm, "Don't worry about it. We'll be out of here before you know it."

"Not soon enough," he said.

At that moment, Jett looked up. The driver was waiting at a corner for a group of elderly merchants to cross the street with their goats. The air became momentarily calm. That's when she noticed it. The smell of tobacco. Perplexed, she looked at the driver. The young boy was smoking an expensive cigar.

"¿Qué estu fumando?" she asked.–What's that your smoking?

"¡Cigarro! !cansado de masticar coca!"–Cigar! Tired of chewing coca!

"¿Dónde lo consigio?"–Where did you get it?

"¡Era un consejo!"–It was a tip.

"¿De quién?"–From who?

"Gringo."–A Gringo.

"¿Se parecia a mi marido?"–Did he look like my husband?

"No, ninguno que no era un científico. Pareció más igual un a . . "–No, he wasn't a scientist. He looked more like a . . .

"¿Un qué?"–A what?

"No sé, como un soldado quizá."–I don't know, like a soldier maybe.

"¿Como se parecia?"–What did he look like?

"Blanco."–White.

"Sí, pero. . . ¿a dónde lo tomó?"–Yes, but where did you take him?

"Al Elmunque en el mercado."–I took them to the Elmunque, in the market.

"¿Va a recogerlos?"–Are you going to pick them up?

"Ya lo hice."–I already did.

"¿A dónde los tomó depues de eso?"–Where did you take them after that?

"Al rio como la voy a tomar usted."–To the river, just like I'm taking you.

CHAPTER FORTY

On the shore of the river, they found a man who would take them down the Amazon toward their destination. The boatman owned and operated a 40-foot long wooden riverboat, powered by a single outboard motor. Though of primitive construction and open to the air, the riverboat was complete with a thatched-roof sunshade and benches to sit on. It was the kind of boat used along the river for carrying everything: people, luggage, livestock, lumber, whiskey, bananas, tropical fish. Ten million neon tetras, popular with aquarium enthusiasts, are scooped into Styrofoam boxes, moved down the river on boats like this one, and shipped over the Atlantic to the United States every year.

Henry boarded the boat uncertainly.

"What if I have to go to the bathroom?" he asked.

Sullivan pointed to the board with a hole in it extending over the stern.

"Nevermind," Henry said.

Normally, a riverboat leaving Iquitos would be crowded beyond safe capacity, stuffed with Peruvians returning to their villages. Sullivan indicated to the boatman that they preferred to travel with no other passengers, that they would need the boat for several days and that they would pay in American dollars or Peruvian soles, whichever he preferred.

After a long delay because the motor wouldn't start and the boatman had to send his ten year old son running up into the city to find a spark plug, they were ready to disembark. But they were not alone. Four other people managed to get aboard, not including the boatman and his young son.

A somber old Indian boarded the boat and sat quietly on the floor at the bow. He didn't seem like he was going to bother anyone. They were inclined to let the old man ride along for a while.

Then a group of three young men also boarded. For some reason, the boatman didn't even challenge them. They were nothing more than teenagers, but they were dressed in dark green trousers, black t-shirts, and AK-47's. The venerable AK-47 assault rifle, designed by the Russian Mikhail Kalashnikov, was the standard-issue weapon of the Shining Path. The Kalashnikov boys took their places at the stern of the boat, their rifles slung casually over their shoulders. Apparently "alone" was a relative term for a river boatman. The young men looked around, surveying Sullivan, Henry and Jett with some interest, but not objecting to their presence. Then they noticed the Indian.

The elder of the three walked over to him. He wore a grimace on his face, like he could smell the Indian and it offended him. His comrades laughed. The Indian didn't seem to notice.

The guerilla pretended he didn't see the Indian and tripped over him, kicking him hard in the side. Once again his comrades laughed.

Then he pulled the rifle off his shoulder and pretended he didn't notice that he accidentally pointed it at the Indian's head.

Still the Indian didn't move. If the finger on that trigger even twitched, he'd be dead.

Jett stood.

The man with the drawn AK-47 glanced over at her. The others stopped laughing.

She walked straight toward him.

She ignored the rifle. She put her hand on the Indian's shoulder and sat beside him.

The guerrilla suddenly lost interest in his little game. Scowling, he returned to his comrades at the stern.

The boatman called for his son to throw off the tie. The motor pulled, gurgled, complained profusely, coughed a few times, then heaved the boat into the current. Once started, the motor seemed to run steady, and it was clear that the trusty Johnson had served the boatman well for many years. It broke down often, but when it did it was easy to fix and parts were available in Iquitos —when he could get there. The boatman sat in his thatched-roof wheelhouse. He took out a little bag, stuffed some coca leaves under his tongue, and drifted into day-dreaming as he steered down the river.

They traveled northward between the great islands off Santa Maria de Nanay. Iquitos disappeared behind them and was soon forgotten. The powerful flow of the golden brown river was bounded by the green wall of the forest on either side. Due to the large islands in midstream, the flow here was no more than a mile or so across and they could make out the features of the shore. Mud cliffs rose upward toward the trees, broken only occasionally by the wooden houses of the *ribereños*. The river people built their wooden platform homes on stilts. The Amazon could rise or fall twenty feet in a single night.

The river here was about ninety feet deep, and moved at six knots in an immensely powerful flow. The water was brown, opaque with the richness of the lands it traveled through. It brought with it the faces of distant mountains, the souls of vanquished glaciers, and the strength of its own muddy banks. The earth along the river shore was pulled into the river on a daily basis. The river wasn't a static geographical feature, it was a process. Sometimes they could actually see the earth moving, dirt falling, mud sliding into the flow. Eventually, everything gave way to it. It flowed where it flowed. There was no stopping it.

The driver of the boat decelerated to half speed. They looked ahead to see why. There, floating in the river, was a full-sized tree, branches, trunk, roots and all. Days or perhaps months before, the tree had been standing in the rain forest. Now that part of the terra firma had succumbed to the Amazon and was flowing toward the Atlantic ocean.

The early Atlantic explorers discovered fresh water and a vast field of terrestrial debris floating in the middle of the ocean. They had been more than two hundred fifty miles distant from land when they first encountered the plume of the great river and hypothesized its existence.

Once past the danger, the boatman pushed the throttle forward and continued at full speed.

Jett watched a flock of scarlet macaws flying raucously from an island to the western shore. They were returning from their nightly roost. At first the birds were just a red splotch and a little noise on the horizon, not even identifiable. But as they approached, everyone on the boat recognized the magnificent birds and turned to watch them.

"Ara macao," Sullivan mumbled the Latin name to himself. He smiled broadly, watching the birds with obvious enthusiasm. The Ara macao is mostly bright red, but has blue wings with large yellow patches, and a tail tipped in cyan blue. Each bird nearly a meter long, a flock of ten crossing the river was strikingly beautiful. The birds flew directly overhead, providing the passengers a breathtaking view as they crossed through the sunrise. The serenity of the moment shattered with the cracking report of the three AK-47 assault rifles. Three birds exploded. The guerrillas laughed as they bulleted the sky and watched the birds fall.

Outraged, Henry looked at Sullivan. Sullivan watched the guerrillas in silence, obviously sickened by what they were doing, but unable to stop them.

"Aren't we going to do anything? Doesn't that bother you?" Henry asked him, but Sullivan wasn't listening.

Henry watched the birds with utter fascination, unable to turn away, like somebody watching a horrible car crash on a race course. Jett saw Henry dig into his backpack. What was he going to do? she wondered.

Four more macaws fell in great blazing somersaults of scarlet feathers. The guerrillas reloaded their weapons and continued firing. Henry found what he was looking for.

Three more birds remained in the air. They had crossed over the boat and were now only a few hundred yards from shore. The guerrillas raised their weapons.

"¡Alto!" Henry screamed. He had found his little yellow Spanish-English Dictionary and looked up the word *stop*. "¡Alto!" he said.

By the time they stopped firing and looked over at him, only one bird remained. One round had clipped off part of its streaming tail feathers, and another had injured one of its wings, but it was flying fast and steady away from them. Jett watched the bird escape into the distance. Soon it became a dot against the trees. It would survive. That's me, she thought. *That's me.*

The guerrillas stared Henry. Why did he tell them to stop? they wondered.

Henry, who had stood at some point during the excitement, sat back down, and tried to look as obsequious as possible. He put his little yellow dictionary away, put his hands in his lap and lowered his eyes.

Jett continued to watch the guerrillas, and when they turned to look at her she did not look away. They met eye to eye and measured one another. Her stare said: The boy is with me. If you mess with him you mess with me, and I don't think you want to do that. Eventually, the guerillas backed off and gave orders to the boatman to retrieve the birds.

The boatman didn't need to be told. He knew the birds' value. He turned the wheel around, and started a wide circle back to retrieve them. He throttled the engine, knowing that the birds would float only a few minutes before they sunk, or were taken down by caiman. One of the guerrillas grabbed a pole from the deck and fetched the birds out of the water.

It was true that scarlet macaws were worth much more alive than dead. They sold for thousands of dollars in the United States. But the Kalashnikov boys couldn't catch the birds, only shoot them down. They began plucking the feathers from the bodies immediately. The next time they went up river, they could sell those feathers for a lot of money. In the meanwhile, nine macaws would feed them and their comrades at the local post for quite a while. They would be much congratulated when they arrived at their base. These days the birds were getting a little scarce.

"Happens all the time," Sullivan said to Henry. "It's not just the macaws, it's all the big birds, monkeys too. They sell them and they eat them. People have been eating those animals for thousands of years. True, they haven't been taking them down with machine guns, but they have been *eating* them. In Trinidad it's the scarlet ibis. The locals love 'em. In Venezuela it's the piping guan. It's the same all over. These birds are exotic to us, but nothing more than pheasant to them, meant for shooting and eating."

Henry did not disturb Sullivan further or urge him into action. Picking on the Indian had been mere amusement, easy to distract them from. But the birds were meat, survival. They would fight for that right. And Henry knew they couldn't afford to fight them. He watched with a grotesque fascination as the rebels stripped the birds down. The boatman's son found a burlap bag for them to store the feathers, and another for the meat.

The Indian at the bow had remained still and silent throughout this episode. Jett guessed that he was one of the *ribereños*, the river people that lived on the banks of the Amazon and its tributaries. The *ribereños* were a peaceful people. While the boat moved down the river, they passed their stilted houses, with thatched-palm roofs and low or no walls. In front of each of the houses was a dugout canoe.

Invariably, a scattering of little kids would be playing, fishing or washing clothes on the river bank. The river was everything to the *ribereños*. It was their source of sustenance, their only means of travel, the flow of their life.

The *ribereños* had no need for private property: people lived where they wished. They had no locks on their doors if they had doors at all. They had no plumbing, no electricity, no televisions, no telephones, no computers. In Amazonia there were no political borders, no government presence, no laws, no crime, no violence. The *ribereños* did not carry or own guns.

Then the Shining Path arrived. The guerrillas of the Sendero Luminoso infiltrated the Amazon as certainly as they infiltrated the other districts of Peru. The revolution's soldiers, most of whom were young men from the other side of the Andes mountains, were known locally as Senderos. They were now a common sight in Iquitos and along the great river. Yet, for the peaceful *ribereños* the Senderos were not "liberators"; they were an occupying army.

The Indian at the bow of the boat was wearing a breechcloth and long tattered cloak. He was carrying a small satchel at his side. He had long black hair, piled in a disheveled mess all around his head and tied loosely by a vine at his brow. He sat squat with his feet flat on the deck and his back against the gunwale boards. He, too, had watched the birds flying, and then the Senderos kill them. He said nothing. No one even knew if he spoke.

They reached Francisco de Orellana by nightfall, an old missionary village on the north bank, where the boatman picked up cargo and proceeded directly onward. He told the passengers that they shouldn't get off the boat. He didn't like the missionary. "Thieves," he grumbled.

After taking on several wooden crates, they were soon underway again. They left the Amazon now and traveled up the Río Napo, into the tranquil world of the *ribereños*. In the local language, "Napo" meant peace. River of Peace.

The boatman slept for brief periods while his son steered the boat.

The Sendero guerrillas were resting now, lying in hammocks which swung inside the little thatched hut. They were smoking cigarettes and talking idly. They were talking about the revolution, about different "initiatives" that had taken place. Though the revolutionary movement was still very much in control of about forty percent of the country's districts, the rebels were in a somber mood.

The Shining Path had been fighting a guerrilla war for twenty years. They were part of a movement, a successful, well-organized attack on all forms of existing government. So many similar movements all over the world had failed. Even the Soviet Union itself had failed, and China was under a barrage of international diplomatic attacks for its civil rights abuses. Peru's Shining Path was successful for one and only one reason, and his name was Guzmán.

Abimael Guzmán was originally a philosophy professor. He started teaching leftist ideals to his students, then to his colleagues. He eventually took over the entire university, then the district, then the country. He began the revolution single handedly, and many were still convinced he would end it.

Ever since the Fourth Plan, which called for the open seizing of governmental offices throughout the country, rebels referred to their leader as President Guzmán, though he had no legal authority whatsoever. The entire Shining Path movement, also known as the Communist Party of Peru, was organized and ruled dictatorially through him.

The Peruvian government had of course been searching for Guzmán for many years, often with the assistance of covert intelligence agencies such as the CIA. Guzmán's exploits and escapes were so famous in Peru that even the general populace held a special place for him in their hearts. He had taken on folkloric attributes and many fables were retold with him as the main character. Though photographs of him were rare, stylized paintings of him were everywhere. To the members of the Shining Path, Abimael Guzmán had taken on the supernatural status of a god. They called him the Red Sun.

Just six months before Jett, Henry and Sullivan arrived in Peru, detectives from the anti-terrorist unit DINCOTE had uncovered a lead in Lima, right under their noses. They had discovered in the rubbish of a small house some medicine for psoriasis, a skin disease from which Guzmán was thought to suffer, and cigarette butts of a brand known to be favored by him. After weeks of careful surveillance work, they moved in. They attacked at night and with force.

The police met no resistance. They found Guzmán working at

his desk. They also captured Elena Iparraguirre, his lover, and Maria Pantoja, who was believed to be his secretary and in charge of his computer. The computer contained member lists, detailed attack plans for both past and future initiatives, and long essays about communism in Peru and throughout the world.

Though the Red Sun's behavior that night has been greatly mythologized, the entire arrest and subsequent interrogation was recorded and remains on record. His words upon arrest were: "You can take anything away from a man, except what he has here in his head. This cannot be removed even if he is killed. And even if they do kill him, the rest of his followers will remain."

On October 7 he was condemned to life imprisonment by hooded judges. The threat of execution still hung over him, but the government didn't want to make a martyr of him. There was a stronger lesson in keeping him alive, keeping him captive. Many Peruvians attributed Guzmán with supernatural powers. Most people agreed he could turn himself into smoke and escape from any danger. This had been proven many times because the government could not catch him. This time, though, they *did* catch him. And they put him on television in a black and white convict uniform. And they proved to all that he was just a man.

Guzmán took his arrest with great serenity. In his last public interview he declared that the Shining Path was to go ahead as planned with the Fifth and Sixth military campaigns. "My arrest will make no difference. All the guidelines are already laid."

One of the Sendero leaned down from his hammock. He pushed a cigarette butt into the floor of the boat. Every once in a while he would look over at Jett. His eyes would rest on Jett for long periods of time, until she would turn toward him and then he'd turn away.

The Senderos were obviously wondering about her. They had seen white men, prospectors and scientists like Sullivan and Henry. But who was *she?* She looked Peruvian, but she was in American clothes and traveling with American men. How come she wasn't frightened of them when they looked at her? How come she didn't lower her eyes when they stared? There was a fire in her black eyes and a confidence in her face that mystified them. "El tigre," they whispered.–the Jaguar.

CHAPTER FORTY-ONE

Henry felt like he was on a jungle ride at Disneyland.

For several days they traveled down the river. The forest had been an unbroken wall of green. Then they came upon the Quebrada Sucusari, a small tributary of the Napo River. Apparently, *Quebrada* was the local word used for a small river. Literally it meant "gulch" or "break"–and represents a break in the otherwise dense and unending forest. So, a small river isn't named for the water that's in it, but for the trees that aren't.

At the mouth of the quebrada, where it flowed into the Napo, a pod of pink river dolphins circled them, surfaced near the boat in curiosity, then proceeded on their way. Henry had just enough time to reach out his bare hand, dip it into the water, and touch their pink rubbery skin.

Farther up the Sucusari they reached the *ribereños* village of Omaguas, a traditional stop for the boatman. Here he took on more cargo that he promised to deliver to Iquitos on his way back. They proceeded downstream, re-met the Río Napo, and continued northward.

Sullivan said that he had paid the boatman to take them up the Río Pucara to the village of Maranon. But the Senderos' base was in Copal Urco, farther up the main river and well beyond the turn off to Maranon. An argument erupted between the boatman and the Sendero, the Sendero insisting that they be dropped off at their destination first. They were tired of waiting around on the stupid boat, and even though Maranon was the next logical stopping point, they demanded that the boatman pass the turnoff and proceed directly to their destination.

Though certainly intimidated by the three rebels, the boatman knew the river and knew his business well, and would not accept their demands. A loud and animated debate ensued that included Spanish, Quechua and even a little English when the proper swear words could be employed. The elder Sendero reckoned himself the officer in charge, and the captain of the boat too, though he was at least thirty years younger than the boatman himself.

During the entire exchange, Henry remained as unobtrusive as he could, attempting to blend into the woodwork much like the Indian. No one had even *asked* him where he wanted to go.

The engine was idling. The boat was drifting. The men argued whether to turn west up the Pucara or continue north up the Napo. The eyes of the boatman drifted away from the discussion, transfixed on some distant point. He stopped listening to the Sendero.

Henry turned to look in that direction. There was another boat, similar to their own, approaching at great speed.

There was plenty of river to travel on, and not another boat in sight.

Ignoring the argument, Jett said to the boatman, "Let's head for shore."

"¿Qué? ¿Vamos a la orilla?" the Sendero cried.

The boatman ignored the Sendero. Instead, he nodded his head in agreement with Jett. He put one hand on the wheel, then engaged the motor. The boat began to turn. The closest shore was an island in the middle of the river.

"What's going on?" Henry asked, bewildered.

"I don't know," Sullivan admitted.

Jett's eyes marked the approaching boat.

"Why did you tell him to land?" Sullivan asked her. "He's got three people with machine guns telling him what to do. Why in God's sake did he listen to *you*?"

"He's thinking what I'm thinking," Jett said simply.

"What's that?" Sullivan asked.

The boatman's boy had climbed atop the roof in an attempt to get a better look at the approaching boat. Henry thought he was insanely brave. Even the Senderos had stopped and turned to look at it.

"Trouble," Jett said.

The Senderos turned and looked at Jett.

"¿Están esos amigos tuyos?" she asked them.

They shook their heads. No, not friends of theirs. The Senderos had forgotten their grievance with the boatman. "¡Vaya a la orilla!" the elder Sendero ordered him. Henry figured he was repeating in Spanish what Jett had said in English: Go to the shore now!

The boatman nodded and continued in that direction.

The Senderos checked their weapons.

"You got any binoculars?" Henry asked Sullivan.

"What kind of ornithologist would I be without binoculars?" he asked as he dug through his pack. "I know they're in here somewhere . . ." The boat was gaining on them.

"¿No va mas rápido este barco?" the Sendero cried, urging the boatman to go faster.

"Just a second, I'll find them . . ." Sullivan was saying.

With the binoculars finally in hand Henry studied the approaching boat. He marked the radio antenna sticking up from the wheelhouse, and the two powerful engines on the rear of the boat. Six white men with rifles. The men were watching them, waiting until they were in range.

"Better hurry!" Henry cried.

"I'm hurrying, I'm hurrying!" Everyone sensed the danger. No one knew who they were or what they wanted, but everyone sensed the danger.

"Ustedes dos," Jett said to the Senderos, "Ponganse de abajo atrás las tablas de la popa. Amartillen y cierren. No desparen hasta que están bien dentro de alcance."

"What's happening?" Henry asked her.

"I told the Senderos to get down behind the stern boards. Cock and lock. Don't fire until we're well within range."

The soldiers of the revolution complied with her orders immediately. They were sensible orders, and this was no time for arguing about who was in charge.

Sullivan and Jett stayed near the bow, huddled close to the deck, peering over the gunwale. Immediately beside them, Henry took cover behind the wheelhouse.

"Who are they?" Sullivan asked. Being the most knowledgeable about birds, Sullivan thought *he was the one* leading the expedition, but suddenly he had no idea what was going on.

"I don't know," Jett said, but Henry could see her mind working, her eyes locked on the coming boat. Henry felt completely useless. He didn't know what was going on. He didn't have a gun. He wouldn't even know how to shoot it if he did. He was beginning to wonder why he even came on this expedition. Disneyland would have suited him fine.

The boatman opened the throttle, hoping to outrun the other boat. The engine coughed. "Not now!" the boatman cried. He tossed a little red plastic bottle to his son and told him to go to the back of the boat and pour some of the liquid into the carburetor. "And stay down there!" he said. "Don't come back up here!"

Henry heard cracks in the distance. Bullets whirred over his head.

Jett hit the deck, pulling Henry with her. She didn't draw her weapon. Her eyes were on the Senderos. They were terrified.

Another set of rounds sang past, leaving a distinct ringing in the air. "30 calibre M1 carbines," Jett said.

"How much farther?" Jett yelled to the boatman. She was laying absolutely flat so she couldn't see the shore.

"Not much farther, missus! Not much farther! Why are they shooting at us?"

"Keep going toward the shore!"

The elder Sendero started inching his way up the boards of the stern.

"¡Quedate abajo!" she screamed at him and motioned for him to stay down.

He immediately went flat, clutching his weapon to his chest. He stared directly at her.

Bullets started flying again, this time more than a dozen ripping through the roof of the cabin and the walls of the outhouse. The boy below screamed. Henry jumped when an explosion of splinters sprang up in front of him. He crawled quickly to what was hopefully a safer spot and lay flat again.

"How much farther?" Jett called.

Henry wished he could see the shore, but he knew it would be foolish to peek above the boards. Following Jett's lead, Henry buried his face in arms.

"Not much farther!" the boatman screamed.

"Can you see the trunks of the trees?"

"No, we're not that close yet!"

A spray of bullets slashed across the deck and into the water.

They lay flat, and waited, and let the rumble of the engine take them toward safety. They put all their trust in the engine. They had nothing else to hope for.

"How much farther, boatman?"

"Not much father! We're almost there! Almost there!"

"Can you see the trunks of the trees?"

"Oh, yes, very clearly now. I see a sandy shore! Many trees! Good place to land!"

"Perfect. Cut the engine and fall!"

"What?"

"Cut the engine and fall! Now!"

"I don't understand. Cut the engine? But why?"

"Just do it!" she screamed.

Henry looked over at the Senderos. They were pointing their AK-47's right at the boatman's chest.

"¡Haga lo que dice!" they ordered him.–Do as she says!

The boatman cut the throttle, the boat lurched, and he fell to the deck.

"¡Nadien mueve!" she whispered in the quiet that surrounded them. "No one move!"

All Henry could hear now was the distant rumble of the coming boat. The boatman and three Senderos were watching her carefully, frightened, but obedient. Henry craned his neck around. The Indian at the bow hadn't moved an inch. He hadn't even taken cover.

"They're going to catch up with us for sure!" whimpered the boatman. "My son is going to die!"

"Quiet!" Jett demanded. "Don't you have weapons?"

"No, I have no use for guns!"

"I'd say this was a use, wouldn't you?" Henry said to Sullivan.

Henry watched as Jett made eye contact with the Senderos, using those few remaining seconds to lock them into her will. They stared back at her with utter obedience. They watched in silence as she drew the Glock 17 from beneath her jacket. She moved on her belly to the opposite side of the boat.

Henry could hear the voices of the men on the other boat now. They were speaking English, American accents. Henry recognized the voice. "Watch yourself boys," their leader was saying as the boat came along side. "Watch yourself. She's a wily one. I don't trust this bitch any farther than I can throw her."

Jett marked the location of the sound. She rose onto one knee and made a single shot. The 9mm round struck him square in the chest, knocking him flat.

The Senderos stood and opened fire. The ack-ack of AK-47's and the pops of M1 carbines suddenly filled the air. Rounds were flying everywhere. The oldest Sendero went down. The boatman screamed. Following orders as best he could, Henry cowered.

Then, in the midst of all the chaos, Henry heard her screaming. Jett was calling to him. "Henry! Get the wheel!"

Henry peeked out. The boatman was dead. The boat was drifting. For a reason Henry did not understand, Jett was crawling rapidly on her belly across the deck toward the stern. "Get us closer to their boat!" she called back to him.

Henry rose to a crouch, stepped gingerly over the bloody body of the boatman, and slipped into the wheelhouse. Surprising himself, he figured out how to start the thing. He throttled it forward. He closed the distance that had drifted between them, and then his boat smashed into the other with a satisfying thud.

While the Senderos kept the gunmen busy, Jett crawled the length of the boat. During this time, even in the midst of that horrific firefight, she didn't fire another shot. She dropped out of everything, and maybe the enemy thought she was dead. Then, from behind the protection of the engine at the stern, she rose up and emptied her clip into them. They were no more than a few yards away, a deadly range for any weapon, let alone the Glock 17. By the time her first clip was empty, the men on the other boat were dead.

CHAPTER FORTY-TWO

Henry managed to turn their crippled boat to the island. There were no posted speed limits on the river. And there was no speedometer on the boat. He pushed the accelerator and kept on pushing until he ran the boat aground on the sandy shore.

The two eldest Senderos, the boatman, and his son were dead. Sullivan had been grazed across the shoulder blade.

The other boat was dead in the water, drifting a hundred yards off shore. No one survived.

The only people who remained uninjured besides Henry after the twenty five second firefight were Jett, the youngest Sendero and the Indian man. Henry gazed at the Indian in disbelief. How did he avoid the bullets?

The battle had wreaked havoc on the confidence of the surviving Sendero. A look of abject terror contorted his face, even though the battle was very clearly over. The horror of gunfire and the trauma of seeing his comrades killed was more than he could bear. He stared after the drifting two-engine boat like it housed the dogs of Satan. "Imperialist cerdos!" he spat. Speaking in a mix of Spanish and English slang, his tirade continued: "Imperialist pigs! Stay out of our country! This is our business! This is not American business! This is our war, our country! Not CIA!"

Somehow the young Sendero had confused "American" with "CIA." To him the words were interchangeable. Henry had read that the CIA had been in Peru since the early eighties to help the so-called democratic government deal with the insurgence of terrorism and drug trafficking, but Henry didn't think these men were CIA.

Sullivan agreed. "If these guys were from the CIA, we'd be caiman bait before we knew what happened."

These were Americans with low-class hired guns. Corporate interests.

Henry remembered what the leader said, "I don't trust this bitch any farther than I can throw her." He knew those words. Outside the impoundment yard of the Southfield Police Station. The goons from Jensen-Bishop Corporation. The significance of this connection suddenly dawned on him . . . that was weeks before, long before they were captured by Dracon. Had Jensen-Bishop been waiting all that time for her? Had they followed her down here? Or had they been down here already? Whatever they're after, it must be incredibly important if Jensen-Bishop was sending people to Peru for it.

Or perhaps it was Dracon. Henry imagined all sorts of things that could explain it.

Dracon or Jensen-Bishop. Either way, he came up with the same answer: Whatever it was they were searching for, they were getting closer.

The young Sendero turned his anguished face away from the drifting boat and looked at Jett, who was standing beside him. They were very similar in appearance, these two individuals. Their skin was the same color. Their hair was the same color. The shape of their body was nearly identical, both lean, strong and youthful. The Sendero looked at her in admiration. "Hija del Sol Rojo," he mumbled and turned away. Jett remained by the river, gazing toward the rain forest on the other side.

"What's that mean, Sullivan?" Henry asked.

"Daughter of the Red Sun," he said.

PART FOUR: Sapo

CHAPTER FORTY-THREE

Jett ordered the Sendero to swim out to the other boat and bring it to shore. Since he was from Lima and a long way from home, he was inclined to complain about the possibility of caiman and suggest that he didn't want to swim in the river, but Jett's words did not invite discussion.

When she turned inland, she found Henry, Sullivan and the Indian situated among the trees. Sullivan was laying on his stomach, his shirt off, his back exposed.

The Indian huddled over him, attending to his wound. He had cleaned the area with water. Now he was applying some sort of poultice. Still the Indian had not spoken.

"How did you arrange such excellent care for yourself?" Jett asked Sullivan with a smile. She sat down with the others.

"Oh, he just winced a few times, maybe a little screaming," Henry answered.

Sullivan opened his eyes and squinted up at them. "The little man ran into the forest and returned with a bunch of leaves. Then he smashed them up, mixed them with something in his satchel, and pointed at the ground for me to lie down. Strangest thing I ever saw."

"I think you're in good hands," she said, watching the Indian work.

"I hope he knows what he's doing."

"He appears to. His hands move with the confidence of experience."

"Who do you think he is?" Henry asked.

"I don't know, probably just one of the local *ribereños*," Jett said.

"I had assumed by his silence that he was far from home," Sullivan said.

"Not too far. He knows the indigenous plants well enough," Jett said.

"That's true. Well, whoever he is, I appreciate his efforts," Sullivan said.

She touched Sullivan's arm to reassure him. "You sit tight. We'll look around and get a camp situated."

"Roger, captain! Hey, this is a nice place. I like the neighbors, too!"

"There don't seem to be any," Henry remarked, gazing around the thick forest.

"Exactly."

When the Sendero returned with the other boat, Jett boarded and looked around. They collected the four M1's and two revolvers. They didn't know what to do with the bodies, so they gave them to the river. Jett checked the cabin, looking for any sort of clue to help them in their quest, but found nothing. Locally hired boat. Six dead Americans. Apparently someone had thought to leave their passports and wallets somewhere else. Nothing to help. Jett turned to disembark. The young Sendero touched her arm, unable to contain himself. "Mi nombre es Luis. Salvo mi vida. Estoy agradecido a usted."–My name is Luis. You saved my life. I am grateful to you.

She ignored him and got off the boat.

The Sendero followed her. For having fought bravely in the battle, and for having saved his life, young Luis held her in high esteem.

Finally she said, "Toma el otro barco y sige en tu curso." –Take the other boat and proceed on your course.

The Sendero thought about this, knowing it was the right thing to do.

Jett urged him. "Toma las armas con tigo . . . "–Take the guns with you. We can't carry them all. Your comrades will congratulate you. Both guns and macaws.

"Sí," he agreed reluctantly. He lowered his head. He was uncertain. "Eran mis camaradas que querían regresar a el Copal Urco." –It was my comrades who wanted to go back to Copal Urco.

"¿No es ese su base?"–Is that not your base?

"Sí, sí es," he said, ashamed.–Yes, yes it is.

"¿Qué tiene?"–What's the matter?

"Hay nada allí ahora."–There's nothing there now.

"¿Qué quieres decir?–What do you mean?

"Hay nadie . . ." he began.–There's no one. I mean, there are others there, just like before, but it's not the same now. My comrades wanted to pretend it was, even though Guzmán is in prison, but it's just not the same. There is no leader. We have lost our direction.

"El camino ha hecho oscuro," she said seriously to him. –The path has become dark.

"¡Ése tiene razón!" he cried, elated that she understood. That's right! You understand! The path is dark now. I don't want to go back there. I am ashamed. There is nothing there for me. These two were my only friends. I was going to the base because of the them. They wanted to.

"Acampamos aquí esta noche . . ."–We are camping here tonight. We will go up the Pucara tomorrow.

"Sí, muy muchos. Gracias," he said, taking Jett's statements as an invitation, then he looked around suspiciously. "La selva me molesta . . ."–The jungle disturbs me. I don't like to be alone out here. I was born in the city, not the jungle.

She did not reply.

"Tomaré la primera vigilia. No se me canso," he said to her as she walked away.–I'll take the first watch. I'm not tired.

Later that night Luis cooked up one of the macaws on a little gasoline stove they found in the boat. They also managed to catch a dorado, a giant golden catfish, out of the shallows. The Indian contributed several roots, which he indicated could be eaten raw or cooked with the birds. He gestured toward Sullivan's wound, seeming to indicate that the roots would dull the pain and give him strength, but nobody was sure. Henry contributed two Milky Way bars.

During the night, after the others had gone to sleep and Luis did his first watch, Jett sat down with her back against a tree and gazed across the river. She watched bats skim across the water. Every once in a while one would splash down. A second later it would flap upward again, a fish in its feet.

"What are you thinking about?" Sullivan asked softly from behind her.

She shrugged and cleared her mind.

Without turning to look at him, she said, "You sure you're ready for this?"

"For what?"

"Going after this thing. I mean, after all that's happened, are you sure you want to go after this bird? Is it worth risking your life for?"

Sullivan paused for a long time. Perhaps he was thinking about her question. Perhaps he was trying to figure out how to phrase the answer. "Look, I've spent my life studying birds. Sometimes, when I get really arrogant, I think that maybe, just maybe, I'll discover and document a new species someday. That's a dream for me. I've been fantasizing about that since I was a kid. That's why I came here."

"We're not talking about dreams coming true anymore. We're talking about—"

"—I know what we're talking about. I'm not stupid. I know what's happening. We're talking about life and death. Your life, Henry's life, and maybe my life. I know that." Sullivan was silent for a long time, then he continued. "I know your not out here because you're interested in birds. You're sick all the time. There's something wrong with you. The bird is important. And other people know it, too. I can see that. I know it's dangerous, but this my only chance. I've always dreamed of discovering a new species. I don't think I'll be able to live with myself if I turn back now."

Jett lowered her head. She nodded and agreed. He would remain with them. She was relieved to have him. He was their guide into the rain forest, a world as alien to her as it was to Luis. Though she and Luis had been born in Peru, they did not understand the forest, not like Sullivan did.

"I'm gonna find this bird," he told her. For Sullivan it was more a mantra of determination than a personal promise to her.

"We must, or I think it's the end for me," she confided.

He nodded, accepting that as fact, then he said: "One last question: why did Luis call you that? Daughter of the Red Sun. That's what he said. Why?"

CHAPTER FORTY-FOUR

Jett heard Sullivan's question, but she did not answer it. To accept the question would be to accept the answer. Years ago she had put Peru and its problems out of her mind. She didn't care about Peru anymore. Peru was her past. She was an American now.

Perhaps she didn't fit in America either, she admitted to herself, but she knew she wasn't Peruvian. She was an *individual*. She was independent from all governments, all revolutions, all corruptions. She didn't want to think about anything else, so she didn't answer the question.

A tinamou called in the darkness, a plaintive, crystal-clear note.

She shook her head, turned away from Sullivan and stared across the silvery black surface of the midnight river.

After a while the Indian took the next watch. She walked over and lay down beside her companions. They slept by the river shore.

In the morning they woke to the wild cacophony of the Neotropical birds. They ate a small breakfast of fruit, then loaded up the boat and departed.

Motoring upstream, they arrived in the late afternoon at the village of Maranon where the Río Pucara and Río Tacshacurara met as one. The *ribereños* villagers came out to the river bank to greet them.

Luis gathered up his supplies, slung the rifles over his shoulders, and ambled off.

Sullivan left the boat in search of a place to stay for the night, thankful that the Indian's medicines had dulled the pain of his wound.

Only Jett, Henry and the Indian remained on the boat.

Sitting with the Indian, Jett wondered about him. Where was he going? Why was he staying with them? Were they still going the direction he wanted to go? He didn't appear to understand their language. He just squatted at the bow of the boat and waited.

When Sullivan returned, he was visibly frustrated.

"I couldn't find anything." He was chewing on a hunk of fruit the *ribereños* had given him. "We'll have to camp outside the village."

"Alright, that's no problem," Jett said.

"Where are we going tomorrow?" Henry asked.

"I've been working on that," he said. He boarded the boat, went to his pack and pulled out a map of the area. "Here's the Río Napo," he said, pointing at the thick blue ribbon winding across the page. "Here's the Pucara, and right about here is the village of Maranon." It was too small to be on the map, so he penciled it in. "LSU did a study up here a few years ago." He made a circle to indicate the spot. "They used Maranon as their base for a while. They're gone now, but they gathered some good data. Of all the Momotidae specimens I've seen, our bird looks the most similar to the ones they collected north of here."

"But where?" Henry said.

"Well, that's the trick. LSU surveyed this whole area. Look at their location chart." He brought out another map, this one populated with dozens of tiny dots. "Those are all the areas where they collected data and specimens."

"But there are hundreds of them. Too many to check. We don't have time," Henry said.

"You're missing the point. LSU never found our bird. I said they found birds *similar* to ours, but they weren't our bird. That means all these dots are places we shouldn't look."

"What's that area there?" Jett asked. Her finger pointed to the middle of the map, to a blank area that had no dots.

He smiled. "That's the place. The Andean Divisor."

"What is it? How come there's no dots?" Henry asked.

"It's a geological oddity. It's a piece of the Andes mountains that came up in the wrong place, isolated from the rest of the range."

"How come LSU didn't study that area?" Henry asked.

"Couldn't find a way in. It's an alpine valley with sheer mountains all around it."

"And that's where our bird is?" Henry asked.

"That's my theory. Remember how I told you about the rivers playing a role in the evolution of bird species?"

"Yes, some species of birds can't cross the wide rivers, so the populations on each side evolve independently, eventually creating different species," Henry said.

"Right. Classic Darwinism. Just like Galápagos, but instead of islands in the ocean, it's big rivers that isolate the populations. And the Divisor, it does the same thing. The mountains isolate the flora and fauna in that area. It might not just be our Momotidae we find there. It may be a whole new habitat type. Nobody's been up there."

"This valley, how big a place are we talking about? A mile across?" Henry asked.

"About the size of Massachusetts," Sullivan said.

"What?" Henry exclaimed. "And totally unexplored? That's impossible."

He shook his head. "It's not unusual in this part of the world. Some say that there are rivers as wide as the Mississippi here that don't even have names yet."

"Did LSU know about it?" Jett asked.

"The Andean Divisor?" Sullivan asked.

"Yes, did they know about it?" Jett repeated.

"They discovered it when they were here, after seeing it on satellite photos. That's how I know about it."

"Why didn't they survey it?" Henry asked.

"I told you: no way in. The birds aren't the only animals the mountains keep out."

"No one's been in there at all?" Henry asked.

"Not that we know of," Sullivan said.

His words were interrupted by a troop of twenty armed soldiers marching down the street and approaching the riverboat. The *ribereños* children and their parents that had collected on the river bank fled immediately when they saw the guerrilla soldiers. Soldiers of the Shining Path. They had established an outpost in Maranon Village.

"¡Bajese del barco!" the lieutenant ordered. –Get off the boat.

Sullivan and Henry looked at Jett.

Jett nodded, indicating that they should do as he said.

After they disembarked, the soldiers–with their rifles held at chest level–surrounded them.

Several of the soldiers noticed the old Indian sitting on the boat.

"¡Banjese del barco!" they ordered him.

He did not seem to understand them. They boarded and moved toward him.

"¡Levantese!" they ordered him.–Get up!

He did not move.

"¡Levantese Indio cochino!"–Get up you filthy Indian.

With the rest of their comrades watching, the two Sendero soldiers grew impatient. They kicked the old man.

"¡Por favor alto!" Jett said. She turned to the lieutenant. –We'll come peaceably, but leave the old man alone. He has nothing to do with us.

The lieutenant agreed and motioned to his men to back off.

Jett boarded the boat, helped the old man to his feet and asked him to walk with her.

"¡Venga por aqui!" the lieutenant ordered.–Come this way.

They followed him up the river bank, into the village and to a small wooden house. The lieutenant went into the building, motioning for them to follow.

Inside, they found several other men, one of them older than the rest and probably the commander. He sat at a wooden table in the center of the small room. He wore an oversized black beret on his head.

Luis stood at attention in the corner, facing them with an expression cold and lifeless.

The lieutenant sat down and motioned that they should do the same. Henry, Sullivan and Jett sat before him.

The commander, stern-faced and uncomfortable, spoke to him privately in Quechua for several minutes.

Finally, the lieutenant turned to them: "¿Cómo se llama?" –What is your name?

Jett spoke quietly to Sullivan in English. "You should answer his questions. They'll expect the man to speak, not the woman." She noted that no one in the room appeared to understand what she was saying. "When they whisper among themselves, they are talking in Quechua, Sullivan, which I know from years ago. Speak to the lieutenant, even if he is just translating. Let the commander watch you. Don't look at him directly."

"My name is Jay Sullivan," he told the lieutenant in Spanish. "This is my wife Cathy Sullivan."

The lieutenant said, "I will translate," and he did, though he used the word "woman" not "wife", which was an important difference. His knowledge of Spanish was either rudimentary, or he had purposely made the change.

"What are you doing here?" he asked.

"We are ornithologists. We study birds."

The commander frowned until this was translated, then he laughed and made a reply, which was then translated. "Birds? We have many birds! What good are birds except for eating? And there is much to eat! Where do you come from?"

"Should I tell them?" Sullivan asked Jett in English.

"Yes."

He turned to the lieutenant: "We come from the United States," he told him in Spanish.

"Do you work for the CIA?"

Startled, Sullivan couldn't help but glance momentarily at Jett. "No we do not," he said firmly.

The commander interrupted the lieutenant. The lieutenant translated his question: "How come you look to the woman?"

"Pardon me, I do not understand your question," Sullivan replied.

"How come you look to the woman for answers?" the lieutenant repeated.

Sullivan paused.

Jett spoke softly to him, once again in English: "Tell him that you are not a translator. Tell him that it is customary in the United States that the most experienced person remain quiet while the less experienced person speaks, and that is apparently the custom in Peru also."

Sullivan smiled. He saw the cleverness in the hidden compliment. He repeated her words.

Once the words were translated, the Quechua commander nodded, satisfied. Then he turned to face Jett directly, and through the translator said: "Comrade Luis has told us of the great battle on the water."

Jett nodded, although she wasn't sure what to make out of this statement. What had Luis told them?

The commander continued, interpreting her quietness as humility. "Comrade Luis has showered you with praise. He speaks highly of you and said that you led him and his comrades from Copal Urco base with great courage and tactical knowledge."

Jett nodded again, accepting this compliment. She didn't know what else to do.

"All who have seen you here have remarked that you are both familiar and strange to us. Tell me, how does a bird woman from the United States gain this knowledge of guerrilla warfare?"

"I come from a dangerous city in the United States and have learned to defend myself, that is all, commander. Perhaps Luis exaggerated my role in the battle, out of humility, in order not to take all the credit for himself, which is where it is actually due."

When she said these words, Luis stepped forward with an objection. The commander looked at him sternly. Luis shrunk back into the corner.

The commander returned his attention back to Jett. He shook his head. "No, Luis said that he was very frightened during the battle, and it is clear that he was. There is no shame in being frightened. But he said that you were calm. You fought like you had fought many such battles, and that you even used a tactic prescribed by the generals of the Sendero Luminoso."

"I think he must be mistaken, commander."

"No, I see now the quality in you he was talking about. You resemble in character and form the Chairman himself."

When these words were translated into Spanish, Sullivan asked Jett in a whisper, "What's this guy talking about?"

She shook her head, indicating that Sullivan should quiet himself. She was doing everything she could to concentrate on the conversation with the commander.

"I thank you for that compliment, commander, though it is not warranted. I wish only for my husband–make sure you translate that husband– and I to proceed with our research."

The translator frowned. If she knew that he had made a mistake with "wife" then she must know Quechua, and if she knew Quechua why didn't she speak in it directly?

After hearing her answer, the commander stopped, obviously frustrated by her unwillingness to discuss the battle on the water. And he was perturbed by the translation process. It put a barrier between them. He had no intention of harming the visitors. In fact he was very interested in who they were and what they were doing. He placed special significance in their presence. He didn't want to let them go. He felt like he had stumbled onto something very important and that he would be a fool to let it go.

"Can you explain this resemblance I see?" he asked, ignoring her request for them to leave the village.

When she did not answer, Luis burst out, "¡Es la Hija del Sol Rojo! ¡Ha regresado a Perú! ¡La revolución seguirá!"–She is the Daughter of the Red Sun! She has come back to Peru! The revolution will go on!

"¡Que queme brillante Sendero Luminoso!" another Sendero cried.–Burn bright the Shining Path!

Everyone started talking at once. Quechua, Spanish and English were flying around the room, everyone trying to figure out what was going on. In Quechua she was hearing: "Has the Chairman asked you to come home? Has he put you in charge? Or perhaps you have taken charge, knowing that since he is in prison the revolution cannot go on without you." In Spanish she was hearing: "Burn bright the Shining Path!" and in English she was hearing: "What is going on, Jett? Why are they all chanting like this? What's happened? Who do they think you are?"

Many questions were being asked of her, but she did not answer them.

"Stop!" she screamed. She startled everyone. Everyone stared at her in shock. She began speaking rapidly in Quechua: "Quiet! Luis, calm the men outside! Stop their chanting! Then shut the door! There is much to discuss!"

CHAPTER FORTY-FIVE

"What's going on?" Sullivan demanded. Henry was equally confused.

Jett and the commander had spent over an hour talking, all in Quechua, a language that neither Sullivan nor Henry understood.

After that, the entire village seemed to change. Suddenly the residents of the best house in the village were voluntarily vacating themselves from it so that Jett, Sullivan and Henry could have a comfortable place to sleep. Sendero guards were posted around the house. Long into the night, the village's campfires roared, and all the *ribereños* and all the Sendero gathered around to hear the stories that Luis and the commander told. Stories of the revolution.

"What is going on?" Sullivan asked again. Henry was quiet, but was just as anxious to know what was happening. Everything seemed to be moving so fast. People were talking in all sorts of languages he didn't understand. It was driving him crazy. He missed the safe, familiar world of his computer. Of course, a computer in the middle of the Amazon rain forest was an impossibility. There wasn't even an outlet to plug it into, let alone a telephone system on which to call out on.

Sullivan continued, trying to get Jett to explain: "Why are they treating us like kings all of a sudden? What did you tell them?"

"I didn't tell them anything. The lies weren't working."

"What do you mean? What lies?" Sullivan asked.

"They know I'm not American."

"So what if you're not American? Lots of people aren't American. It's not a crime, exactly."

"I'm Peruvian."

When Jett said this Henry remained very still. He realized that Jett wanted to tell them something, but she hesitated.

Sullivan pushed her. "So what if you're Peruvian! What's the difference?"

Jett wasn't going to explain. "I have arranged for the Senderos to help us. That's all there is."

"Help us? Why would they help us? Help us how?" Sullivan asked.

"You said that it was going to be difficult to get up the Pucara and into the Andean Divisor. The Sendero soldiers can help us. They have boats, supplies, weapons."

"Weapons?" Henry repeated before he could stop himself. "We need weapons?"

"I'm concerned that someone has gotten to the Divisor before us," Jett said.

"Like who?" Sullivan asked. Henry was nervous, but Sullivan was almost angry. Only Jett was calm.

"Dracon Industries. The Sendero report that there have been Americans in the area for months, that they have established a base camp upriver, and that they are searching for something. They have been intimidating the local population trying to find out where it is. The Sendero Luminoso has infiltrated this area very recently. Unlike on the Western side of the Andes mountains, they are having difficulty convincing the peaceful *ribereños* people to support their cause. They came to this village specifically because they see it as a perfect opportunity to defend the *ribereños* from the "violent oppressors." They think that the Americans are CIA, or counter-insurgency forces, or maybe drug traffickers. I think it's Dracon. If your guesses are right about the location of this bird, and if Dracon knows about it too, then the secret is up there, and I think they'll have it well guarded."

"The Senderos are going to help us?" Henry asked.

"Yes. Tomorrow we will take canoes up the Pucara as far as we can go. The Senderos will go with us, fully armed."

"Then what? Do they know the way? We need a guide to get up there," Sullivan said.

"They will take us up the river, but they will go no farther."

"Why not? Why can't they take us up there?" Sullivan asked.

"They are frightened," Jett said. That was the exact answer Henry didn't want to hear. Jett continued: "They will not go into the mountains and they will not cross into the Divisor."

"Frightened?" Sullivan said. "What are they frightened of? They've got M1s, for God's sake."

"Actually, they've got AK-47's. We have the M1s."

"Jett!"

She shook her head and shrugged. "They are very frightened.

They say that the land beyond the Divisor is evil, full of 'bad fates.'"

"Full of bad fates?" Henry whimpered.

"What exactly is that supposed to mean?" Sullivan demanded.

"I don't know what they're talking about, but they are clearly frightened and completely unwilling to go up there. The local *ribereños* refer to the valley as the Cloud Forest and have filled them with superstitious stories. They say that the forest is shrouded in perpetual clouds, that navigation is impossible, sunlight is seldom seen and black magic is commonplace."

"Black magic?" Henry repeated. "Like what kind of . . ."

"Unbelievable!" Sullivan shouted. "They're fighting a war for independence armed with machine guns and rocket launchers, yet they believe in black magic!"

"They believe what they believe," she shrugged. "We can't force them. We'll go on our own from there."

"Well, maybe we should . . . " Henry tried to cut in.

"How can we trust them?" Sullivan interrupted. "Why do you believe them? They're revolutionaries!"

"That's why I believe them. They're loyal to the core."

"Loyal to you," Henry observed.

Jett nodded. "Yes, loyal to me." She did not elaborate on how that could be. That's what Henry was wondering: why all of a sudden were the Senderos loyal to Jett? "Tomorrow we'll talk on the boat, but right now we've got to get some sleep. Our journey has just begun."

"I want to know now," Sullivan demanded.

"Sullivan, we've got to get some sleep."

"I don't want to go to sleep," Sullivan said.

"I can't sleep either," Henry agreed. He felt like he had drank a whole case of Mountain Dew. He couldn't get his hands to stop trembling.

"Tell us what's going on. You're not being honest with us," Sullivan said. "What about Peru? Why did you leave? Why didn't you want to come back?" Sullivan said.

She didn't answer.

Henry wasn't sure what to do. He watched all this and he felt agitated. He, too, wanted answers to the questions Sullivan was asking. But he didn't think it was right to push her. She didn't want to tell them. It was deep inside her. He did everything he could to respect that, but more than anything he wanted to *know*.

Jett spoke harshly to Sullivan. "Sit down, Sullivan. I don't want you pacing around. You're making me nervous."

"*I'm* making *you* nervous? *You* don't know nervous, woman!" Sullivan shouted.

"Just sit down."

"I'm going for a walk!" he declared and stomped out of the room.

Henry sat perfectly still. For a long time he didn't say a word. Jett sat beside him, silent, consumed by her own thoughts. Henry didn't know what she was going to do right then, but he knew that whatever she did, he would accept it and side with her.

Then she started talking.

"I was born in Ayacucho, a district of southern Peru. I grew up like any other Peruvian kid, loving my mother, my brothers and sisters, and my father. I went to school, got a good education. My father saw to that. Then, when I was still very young, I started working for him. I delivered packages. I didn't know what was in the packages. He would give me a package and tell me where to take it. As a little girl, I loved working for him. He treated me with such respect and honor and love. The harder I worked, the more attention he gave me. Soon, I was delivering packages great distances, to Lima and Junin and Cuzco. For a child, these were exotic and wonderful places. As the years went by, I became quite well known among my father's colleagues. I started delivering packages for all of them. I went into dangerous places where no one else would go. These men trusted me with their most important runs. I was a but a slip of a girl and could move through enemy territory undetected."

"When I became a teenager I started to become more aware of the politics of what was going on around me. We were beginning to learn in class about world geography, places like China and the Soviet Union, and about the world-wide communist revolution."

"The world-wide communist revolution?" Henry said.

She nodded. "That's when I began to realize that my country was at war and that I was a guerrilla."

"What was in the packages?" Henry asked.

"I told you. I didn't open the packages."

"Why not? Didn't you want to know what was inside?" Henry asked.

"It would have been a severe breach of trust with my father, which I could not do."

"But what were you carrying? You must know now," Henry said.

She hesitated. "I suspect they were lists of *soplón*, and–"

"–*soplón*? What's a *soplón*?" Henry asked.

"An informer or traitor," she said. "And I'm sure I also carried tactical instructions. Sometimes even bombs."

"Bombs?" Henry cried.

"Dynamite."

"How old were you?" Henry asked.

"I was about fourteen when I realized what I was involved in."

"Then what happened?"

"By this time I was completely and utterly a Sendero. I was a revolutionary, a committed member of the Shining Path. I had always been. I had never known any other truth. We could have all been Nazis and it would not have mattered. I loved my family and my family was Shining Path, so I was Shining Path."

"Did you believe in the cause?"

"Yes, very much so, with all my heart."

"Do you now?"

"No."

"What changed?"

"I'm getting there," she said flashing her eyes up at him. "When I was about fifteen we had entered the Second Plan. Government soldiers were everywhere. Violence was commonplace. For my protection, my father gave me a Makarov–"

"–What's that?" Henry asked.

"A pistol."

"Oh. Fun for the whole family," Henry said.

"My brothers taught me how to use it. I started carrying it with me wherever I went."

"Did you ever use it for real?" Henry asked.

"First, when I was sixteen . . . and many times since."

"Sixteen?" Henry repeated.

"I shot a policeman. By the time I was seventeen I had graduated to an AK-47 like the one Luis carries, though it had a nice modified double-clip that–"

"–OK, I get the picture," Henry said, impatient to hear the rest of the story.

"By the time I was nineteen I had a courier team under my command and was training soldiers in marksmanship and subterfuge."

"And what did your parents think of all this?" Henry wanted to know.

"I was their pride and joy."

"What?" Henry couldn't believe it. One time when he was a teenager, an older kid grabbed his clarinet case and threw it in a ditch. So later that day, Henry found out where the older kid was hanging out with his friends. He rode past on his Schwinn Bomber and threw an egg at him. The egg hit him in the face, splattering all over his hair and clothing. Henry never peddled so hard in his life! Then, when he got home, after he thought he had gotten away with it, he found his parents waiting for him. The older kid had called his parents and told on him. They were furious. Sweet little Jetta kills people with a Makarov and that's OK. Henry throws an egg and he gets grounded for two weeks. Henry turned his attention back to Jett and her story.

"I represented the spirit of the revolution in every sense. You see, my mother was an active member of the party. She played an important role."

"And how long did all this continue? What happened?"

Jett paused. She did not want to continue.

"I want to know," Henry said.

"Yes, but I've never told anyone before. No one. You understand? This is history I want erased."

"What about your father?"

"My father was Abimael Guzmán, the leader of the Shining Path. My mother was his second in command. What started out as an intellectual movement had become a war. The casualties on both sides were staggering. But my father was not phased by the many deaths. Even when they were his own sons. Eventually, when my second brother was killed, my mother suggested that the movement proceed with more moderation. She hated the killing and wanted to look for other ways to fight the government. My father ignored her suggestions. Over time her arguments became more vocal, more public."

"Well, what happened?"

"The news reports in Lima said, as did all the rumors within the movement, that my mother killed herself."

"She killed herself? A woman that strong?"

Jett shook her head. "I saw my father kill her."

"Kill her?" Henry whispered, sickened by what he was hearing. His heart was pounding in his chest.

"She was no longer a loyal follower. She was a *soplón*, a traitor. He silenced her."

Henry couldn't speak. He looked up at her and saw only the stone cold face of the Jetta Santiago that he had always known. There were no tears, no outward emotion, only a calm determination.

"That's when I left," she said.

"What did you do? Did you come to the United States?" Henry asked.

"Not at first. I escaped across the southern border, through Bolivia to Mendoza, Argentina. I stayed there a while, waiting. Then, when I sensed the time was right, I fled to Santiago, Chile and flew from there to Miami. In Peru it is custom that a young girl take as her middle name the name of her mother, and as her last name the name of her father. So I took Mendoza as my mother and Santiago as my father. I invented my first name from the hard, glossy, black stone called jet. Maria La Torre Guzmán became Jetta Mendoza Santiago. I left with the intention of never coming back."

"What happened once you got there? I mean, how did you survive? Did you know people?" Henry asked.

"No. I spoke Spanish. That was enough to get me through."

"In the United States?" Henry said, confused.

"I worked in Miami. I delivered packages."

"Drugs?" Henry asked, trying to get to the truth, however frightening.

"I never opened the packages."

"But they were drugs," Henry said.

"Probably. When I made enough money, I moved to New York and set up a business. I began developing a new client base, legitimate clients, wealthy people, institutions, corporations. I became known as the person who would deliver anything anywhere."

"So you were still delivering packages, just like when you were a girl . . ." Henry said, remembering when he first met Jett on the highway.

"But instead of delivering bombs and military orders, I deliver the plans for secret inventions and the financial reports of Fortune-Five-Hundred companies."

"The Red Sun? The Chairman? President Guzmán? They are all your father?"

"Yes."

"And the Senderos know it now?"

"I have not admitted it. That would start a resurgence that I'm not willing to take responsibility for. The movement is dying. Already the momentum is lost, and its ranks are dissipating. Amazonia is a peaceful place. The *ribereños* are a peaceful people. That peace will overwhelm the troubled Senderos here, and as they return to their homes far away, that peace will spread across the mountains and into the cities on the coast. The revolution will die. That is my hope."

"How do you know all that? How do you know what's going to happen?" Henry asked.

"It's only a hope. The Sendero are still fighting, still searching for hope that the movement will regain its momentum."

"That's why they're looking to you."

She nodded. "They are hoping beyond all hope that I will lead them to their previous prominence and beyond."

"But you told them you weren't Maria Guzmán?"

"They don't believe me. Their hope is too great . . . and we shall use that hope."

"They'll follow you no matter what you say," Henry said.

"Yes, even though I deny that I am the Daughter of the Red Sun, and they agree to this, they will do whatever I ask. They will be very useful to us."

"They are desperate for a leader aren't they?" Henry said. "Your appearance is like a gift from God for them."

She nodded. "Though I have told them that I am not his daughter and that I have no intention of taking over the Shining Path, they are sure I am and that I will. My insistence that I'm not is being interpreted as a need for absolute secrecy about this mission. They are sure that the Divisor has great significance to the revolution."

"And does it?" Henry asked.

"None whatsoever. It has great significance only to us."

The two of them sat there together in the dim light of the candle. They silently pondered the alliance that had jelled between them. Henry had never felt like this before. He was connected to her.

He was part of a team. He had a real companion, a companion that would risk her life for him, and that he would risk his life for. They were companions pulled together by their strengths, their weaknesses, their secret needs. For the first time in his life Henry felt like a powerful human being.

Sullivan did not return. He found a place to sleep in one of the other huts. Later that night, Jett and Henry finally tried to go to sleep. They were happy to have comfortable beds to sleep in. When they blew out the candle, neither said anything more. There had been too much talking.

The sounds of the forest surrounded them. They heard the call of a pygmy owl outside their window, tree frogs singing, potoos calling. In the darkness of the Amazonian night, they lay beside each other, listened, and wondered.

In the distance they could hear the mountain flutes and home-made guitars of the Quechua. The Quechua soldiers were playing to the *ribereños* who gathered around the fire to hear them. Accompanied by *quena*, *charango* and mandolin, they sang the ancient songs of their people, the songs of the Andes Mountains. They danced the *huayno* to the chords and voices of Peruvian history.

As the companions fell asleep, the Southern Cross spiraled above them toward another dawn.

CHAPTER FORTY-SIX

The next morning they climbed into dugout canoes and began the journey up the Río Pucara. Sullivan and Luis led the way. Jett, Henry, and the silent Indian were second, followed by the canoes of a dozen well-armed Sendero soldiers.

They traveled without event for most of the day, paddling slowly up the shallow river.

In the late afternoon, they came upon a small house. Like all the houses of the *ribereños* people, it was made of hewn logs. The floor consisted of a platform supported six feet off the ground by sturdy posts. The roof was made of tightly-woven thatched palm. The inhabitants had planted a few fruit trees and vegetables in the surrounding area. The homestead appeared deserted, except there was a small, lonesome puppy gazing out at them from the bank.

The Indian studied the little house with interest.

Jett noticed this and looked at the house again, but she saw nothing out of the ordinary, except that there were several yellow-headed caracaras circling overhead.

She looked back at the Indian. His eyes were locked on the house.

Jett told the Sendero, "Pon los barcos en la orilla allí."–Put the boats to shore there.

The Indian stepped out of the canoe and climbed up the bank.

Curious, Jett followed him. "I'll be back in a minute," she told Henry.

Some crude steps had been cut into the dirt, but they were worn by the recent rains. The Indian and Jett clambered up the bank with their hands.

It suddenly occurred to Jett what was missing from this place. Perhaps it seemed strange to the Indian as well, and that's why he wanted to stop. There were no children. Whenever they had passed a house, there had always been children playing, sometimes eight or ten. Here there were none.

When they gained the level of the house, they found the children. Their dead bodies were strewn across the yard.

The Indian was on his knees, crying. He held a woman in his arms. The woman was holding a tiny child to her chest. There were bullet holes in their heads.

The Indian held the dead woman and her child and he wept.

After a while he picked up the child, even as her mother had, and held her to his chest.

Jett watched in silence.

After a long time, the old man turned and looked at her.

"I wish I could help you," she said. She knew he didn't understand, but she didn't know what else to say. The words just came out. Perhaps he would sense the tone of voice, and understand that she cared.

"I've never heard her so quiet . . ." the Indian said in English. He looked down at the child. "Tara was always getting scared and crying. She was three years old. Just before I left, one of the chickens scared her and she cried. And when she would cry, everybody in the family would start crying with her. She had tears like the rains."

He was speaking perfect English. Jett stepped closer to him. She knelt down beside him. "Who has done this to your family?"

"The men up the river," he said.

"The white men at the camp that the Sendero spoke of?"

"Yes. In the forest north of here."

"Why would they do this?"

"A man named Traymore has told me many times that I must take him to the Cloud Forest. I refused to take him. It is the home of the Leopard Ghost, a very special place. I would not take him or tell him where it is. I think that he waited until I left, then came back here with his men. I didn't think he would do this! If I thought he would do this, I would have never left them! Never! He came back . . ."

"He came back to get the information from your wife?"

He nodded.

"He shot each of the children in front of her in order to get her to tell him how to get to the Cloud Forest," Jett surmised.

The Indian didn't reply. He was looking down at his little girl Tara. He shook his head. "My wife never left the our home except to gather fruit from the forest. She didn't know where the Cloud Forest was."

Jett remained quiet, trying to comprehend.

The Indian shook his head again. "Tears like the rains," he said, and stroked Tara's long black hair.

After a while, he looked up at Jett.

"My name is Boa Movaca. I am of the Yagua tribe." He gazed down at the Sendero soldiers waiting on the shore, and he was thinking about the men from the camp, the men who had killed his family. "The River People once lived in peace."

He was quiet a moment, thinking slowly through the course of time. "The government, the Sendero Luminoso, the white men . . . with their strange souls . . . they do not know about the River of Peace. Though they are here, and it is all around them, it is invisible to them."

Jett looked ashamedly at the ground, for she knew she was very much a part of the disruption he was referring to. "Yes, it is . . ." she agreed. "But, I–"

"–I have watched you," he interrupted her. "I have watched all that you have said and all that you have done. You need not explain yourself to me, Jetta Mendoza."

"You speak of the Sendero Luminoso and the white men from the camp. I want to rid your world of these intruders, Boa Movaca. I want the Sendero Luminoso to leave Amazonia, and I want to destroy the people who did this. But–"

"–What are you frightened of?" he asked her.

"I am going die."

"We're all going to die. Whatever we choose to do we must do before that time."

"But I'm going to die soon, very soon. There is a sickness in me."

"What kind of sickness?"

"I do not know. That's what I must find out. I am searching for a very special bird that may lead me to the answers. The bird is my only hope for survival. The men who did this to your family put a poison inside me and it has caused me great sickness. I feel its effects even now."

He shook his head in harsh recognition: "These are indeed evil men that have come."

"Yes! And there are others. I must destroy them all. Even if I cannot find the bird in time to save myself, I must destroy these men so that they can't go on hurting people."

"And the man who travels with you– Sullivan– he knows how to find the bird you seek?"

"We think it may live in the Cloud Forest."

"The Cloud Forest is a very different place than this, Jetta Mendoza."

"Do you know the way? Can you help us get there?"

"I have not been there in many years. I may get lost if I try to take you, but I know a very old, very wise man who knows. He was once the shaman of our tribe when we still traveled together through the forest. He knows the secret path into the Cloud Forest, for he collects much of his medicine there."

"How can we find him?"

"His name is Leopard Ghost. If we go into the forest and look for him, and we are careful, we will be able to find him."

"You'll come with me?"

The Indian gazed around the homestead. He didn't say a word.

A slight breeze began to sweep across the river and its banks. For a moment she thought that the poison inside her had once again taken a grip on her brain: maybe the Indian hadn't spoken to her at all, maybe he didn't know English at all, maybe she had hallucinated the entire conversation. Where there had been hope there was hopelessness.

Then he nodded. It was the most minute of gestures, a whisper of an acknowledgment. "It is said that when the prey is too large for one hunter to kill, then others must join him. If my people and I are to have tranquility, then I must help you. I have watched you, Jetta Mendoza, and I know what's in your soul: you are a leopard, cornered and desperate to survive–there is no more powerful animal in the forest. I will go with you. And I will show you the way. And I will help you fight them."

CHAPTER FORTY-SEVEN

A black hawk sat on the limb of a large tree that hung over the river, and peered at Henry as he paddled beneath it. Henry watched it with as much suspicion as it watched him.

They continued on their journey, paddling another day, camping for the night, then continuing on the next morning. In all this time Henry saw no other human beings, no settlements, no signs of the deforestation that he had heard so much about back in the States, just miles of seemingly endless rain forest. Near dusk on the third day, the Indian looked toward the western bank.

"Pon los barcos allí," Jett told the Senderos. They began moving the boats toward shore.

Jett and the Indian got out. Henry sat in the canoe, a paddle over his knees.

"What are we stopping for?" Sullivan asked from the other canoe.

"Boa knows the way," Jett explained.

"He does? How do you know? He didn't say anything," Sullivan said.

"Come on," Jett said.

"Alright, alright. You say he knows the way."

Gathering his Planet of the Apes canteen and other gear, Henry stepped onto the muddy shore. He watched Jett as she said goodbye to Luis. Though he did not understand all the words they had exchanged in the past few days, he knew Luis felt a certain loyalty to Jett. Henry didn't speak his language, but he liked Luis, mostly because he could see he was frightened, too.

Jett walked to meet Luis at the water's edge. She put her hand on his shoulder. Seeing Henry's interest in their conversation, Sullivan translated some it for him.

"Boa dice que el Bosque de las Nubes esta sobre . . ." –Boa says that the Cloud Forest is up this slope.

"Vengo con tigo si quieres, hasta dentro el Bosque de las

Nubes," he told her.—I shall come with you if you ask me to, even into the Cloud Forest.

"No, vuelve al pueblo . . ."—No, go back to the village. Later, I shall need your help again, but for this part of the journey I will go on without you.

Henry saw that Luis nodded his agreement. "Estaré listo."—I shall be ready.

Jett turned and began climbing.

Henry gazed upward. All he could see were trees, trees reaching upward for a thousand feet or more.

"I don't know about you guys, but I've never actually climbed a mountain before," he admitted, but no one was listening. He hurried after them, last in line behind Boa Movaca, Jett and Sullivan.

The Senderos had provided them each with a sharp machete for bushwhacking through the thick undergrowth, but Boa led the way and he showed them how to walk through the forest without cutting it.

Boa moved quickly and with confidence. They climbed for two days. After the third day the vines and trees of the forest surrounded them still, but now Henry could see the jagged ridges of the stony Andean Divisor.

"You sure he knows where he's going?" Sullivan asked a couple of times. Even he was huffing and puffing to keep up with the sinewy old man. For Henry, who was more used to sitting in a computer chair than clawing his way up a mountain, it was only the fear of being left alone that gave him the strength to keep up.

"Boa Movaca, will we go over the ridge?" Jett asked their guide.

"No, not over the ridge, Jetta Mendoza. There is a secret way."

"What's that mean?" Henry wanted to know. "Haven't we had enough excitement?"

"Some sort of pass maybe," Jett suggested.

"What did he call you?" Sullivan asked Jett. "Jetta Mendoza? Is that what he said?"

"What kind of pass?" Henry was asking.

"A way to get through the mountain," Jett said, ignoring Sullivan's question.

"Did I mention that I've never actually climbed a mountain before?" Henry said.

"Does anyone else know about this passage?" Sullivan asked Boa.

"The Leopard Ghost showed it to me and one other in my tribe when we were young men. The elder of our tribe had become very ill. The other apprentice and I came here with him in search of medicine."

The trail became steep. Henry had to use his hands to climb, holding onto the roots of trees, and the vines which hung down from the canopy. Boa climbed quickly and spoke softly. Henry could hardly hear what he was saying. The higher they climbed, the more difficult it was for Henry to remember exactly why he had come on this trip and what possible role he could play. They were in Boa's world now.

That night, while sitting around the campfire, Jett turned to Boa, "Tell us more about the Leopard Ghost."

"He is a great shaman who lives up here in the mountains near the Cloud Forest. He was an ancient man even when I knew him as a boy, and now he is older than the giant trees themselves. When we don't know what to do, we seek his advice. He knows all that there is to know about the forest."

"And you approached him when your elder was sick?"

"Yes, many years ago, when I was but a boy."

"And did he help you?"

"Yes, he gave us the medicine we needed, which we took back to our people and healed the elder. Ever since then we dance a dance for the Leopard Ghost each year."

"How long ago was that?" Jett asked. "How many years?"

"I cannot remember. A long time. A lifetime."

"Do other tribes know about the pass into the Andean Divisor?"

"We have kept the pass a secret. No other tribes know."

"What about Americans? What about scientists? Have any come up here?"

"The white men do not know. My children are dead, but the white men do not know."

A powerful and ancient instinct had kept Boa Movaca steadfast in his refusal to share that secret with outsiders. Now his wife and children were dead. Dracon had killed them.

The next day they proceeded. As they climbed the great slope, a new set of questions began to form in Henry's mind. Dracon's camp was north of Boa's house. Why didn't they establish their base inside the Andean Divisor? Could it be that they still hadn't found it? If the bird came from there, how did they get hold of the specimen that she delivered? Why couldn't they get more? And what connection did the bird have to their new drug?

That afternoon their route led straight into a rock wall. A cliff rose upward out of the forest toward the summit of the ridge's highest peak, some six thousand feet above sea level. They walked in the shadow of the wall for the rest of the day, then camped beside it that night.

"We don't have any climbing equipment. How are we going to get over that ridge?" Sullivan asked.

Henry was wondering the same thing. He was pretty sure even Boa couldn't ascend sheer rock.

Henry looked over at Boa. "We're in his hands." Boa was sitting a little distance from the campfire, eyes closed, apparently asleep. "We'd be hopelessly lost out here without him."

Sullivan nodded gravely, in sober agreement with that assessment.

None of this was making Henry feel any better.

Restless, but not knowing what else to do, they eventually lay down, rested their heads on their bundled up jackets, and fell asleep exhausted.

When Henry woke, the Indian was gone.

CHAPTER FORTY-EIGHT

"Where is he?" Sullivan shouted, more than willing to express his anger and his fear.

"I don't know," Jett replied, scanning through the trees for any sign of Boa.

"I woke up and he wasn't here!" Henry said.

"He just left!" Sullivan shouted. "He didn't say a word! We're screwed. I wish I had some marijuana. I've always said that death would be a lot more tolerable with a goodly portion of grass."

"Just sit down for a minute," Jett suggested. "Have some breakfast."

"I would rather know where our guide is before I eat, if you don't mind. First things first. We all agreed we're lost without him! So where is he?"

"I don't know," Jett said and began making preparations for breakfast.

"I have to use the facilities," Henry said. He wandered off into the forest and out of sight.

"Was this his plan all along, just to desert us out here?" was the last thing he heard Sullivan say.

Henry couldn't pee when there were other people around. It made him nervous. He had to be well out of sight, and well out of ear shot, before it would work. In a rain forest, it doesn't take long to hide yourself.

He found what seemed like a suitable spot among some bushes and behind a bunch of trees. He unzipped his pants, got himself out, and proceeded with his business. Then he noticed something crawling on his hand. He looked down at it, not quite sure what it was. He brushed it off. Then he noticed something on his other hand. Crawling. He brushed it off. Then there was something on his arm. He felt something drop into his hair. Then something ran across the back of his neck. There were spiders all over him!

Screaming at the top of his lungs, he ran away. He tried to kill the spiders, tried to escape them. Wild with panic, he was brushing himself off like a school kid that thinks he has the cooties, screaming all the while .

Hearing his scream, Jett came running with the Glock 17 in hand. She pointed it into the forest, then turned, then turned again, searching for a target to shoot. "What's wrong?" she asked, bewildered. She couldn't see anything.

Henry pulled shreds of grey stuff from his body, and brushed spiders off his limbs. He scraped spiders out of his hair, squishing bodies and legs between his fingers. He had cleared himself of the strands of web, but he was still checking himself, sure that spiders were crawling up his pant legs and down his shirt.

"Did I get them all?" he cried. "God, I hate spiders! Come 'ere. Check me. Did I get them all? They were all over me! I think one's crawling up my pant leg!"

Then he felt something on his arm. A small black spider was crawling slowly toward his shirt sleeve. He brushed the spider away. Finally, after several minutes, he managed to clean himself off, and he felt a little safer, although he'd be checking himself for days.

Bewildered and amused, Jett looked at him, then stared down at his open trousers. As if in defense of the spider attack, Henry's penis had shrunk into a tiny nub. He quickly tucked himself away and zipped up."Looking good, Henry, looking good." She thrust the Glock 17 back into its holster and smiled.

They turned to the cause of all the trouble.

A silver white wall of spider webs rose above them. The spiders had spun the webs between bushes, rocks, limbs of trees, anything that would hold the weight. When Henry looked upward he couldn't see the top of it. Twenty five feet, he guessed, but couldn't quite make out where the web stopped and the leaves of the trees began. And it stretched thirty or forty feet either side of him. It was a huge community web, built together and shared by thousands of spiders, each about as large as a green, fuzzy, crawling grape.

Shuddering, and stepping well away from the web, he gazed into it. The sunlight filtered through its silvery filaments. In one area, he could see a yellow-gold butterfly caught and immobile. In another, he could see a grasshopper. Yet another, a cicada. Deeper he saw small black orbs hanging, each one filled with millions of tiny baby spiders.

He took a few steps farther, seeing entrapped ants, beetles, even a tiny hummingbird.

A shiver ran down Henry's spine.

"Let's get out of here," Jett suggested.

Henry followed her back to camp and did not leave it again.

They ate breakfast, talked awhile, and waited anxiously for Boa to return. At about noon, he suddenly appeared. He had a worried and haggard expression on his face, but he didn't say anything. He sat down beside them.

"What happened to you?" Sullivan cried.

Boa sat calmly, and other than the fact that he looked extremely tired, he acted as if they should not be surprised at all at seeing him there. He shook his head with concern. "I have been walking all night," he said.

"What for?" Sullivan asked.

"I cannot find the pass."

"What do you mean, you can't find it?"

"When I came here as a boy, I remember we camped along this wall. During that night we ate and we drank, and when we slept we had a dream. In our dream a leopard visited us and he showed us the way."

"In your dream?" Sullivan's face was white with shock, like a man who has abruptly realized he has been the victim of a brutal and embarrassing joke. But this was the kind of joke that killed you. "You dreamed about a leopard? Are you saying you dreamed it?"

The Indian nodded his head, not sensing Sullivan's scorn. "Yes, and it was a particularly powerful dream. I remember it vividly, even now. But it's strange, I still cannot find the pass." He turned to Henry with complete seriousness: "Did a leopard visit you in camp last night?"

Henry shook his head. "Oh, no, you would've heard the scream quite clearly, don't worry."

Sullivan got up angry. He turned and walked away.

"Sullivan, where are you going?" Jett called after him.

"I'm not going anyplace!" he shouted back at her. "I can't believe my ears and I want to get as far away from this ridiculous charade as possible. I'll just bang my head on a tree for a while, just to get myself centered again. This old Indian has taken a little bit too much juju acid!"

Once Sullivan had left in disgust, Jett said, "Don't worry about him." Her voice was serious. She was trying desperately to understand what Boa was saying. She knew that animals, and cloud forests, and mysticism, were part of his symbology, his language. "I didn't dream last night either," she told him.

"That's the problem," he said. "We need to dream. Then we will find the way."

Jett nodded. She understood. "How can we dream, Boa?"

"It is the Leopard Ghost who makes us dream so that he can visit us in the night and show us the way."

"What do you think is wrong?"

"There can only be one answer," he said gravely.

"What is it?"

"I fear that the Leopard Ghost is dead."

"Dead?" Jett asked.

"Yes," Boa said.

There was no doubt in Henry's mind that Boa felt this. He felt the sadness in the old man sitting before him. His world had changed. A hitherto immutable aspect of the universe had been altered. The Leopard Ghost was dead.

"I must find the way myself," Boa said abruptly. "I am sad that the Leopard Ghost is no longer in our world. The trees will miss him, for he was their father. But I learned much from him and I will find the way."

He stood.

"Call Sullivan, Jetta Mendoza. We must go. We cannot dream our way to this place."

"Then how are we going to get there?" Henry asked as he got up and gathered his gear.

"We'll have to walk."

CHAPTER FORTY-NINE

As he had explained, Boa could not divine the location of the pass as he had hoped. Instead, this man who had mystified them in so many ways, suddenly became practical. He began walking. Having no other choice, they followed him.

Well into the afternoon, Boa Movaca stopped. Exhausted and confused, the others stopped behind him. "We are here," he said, triumphantly.

"Where?" Sullivan cried.

"I have found the passage of the Leopard Ghost."

They looked around.

"I don't see anything!" Sullivan cried. "Are you sure you're OK, old man?"

"Where do you see it?" Henry asked Boa Movaca.

"Do you see the angle of that branch hanging down from that tree?"

"Yes."

"That is a clear signal to me." He was reading the details of the forest in a way that Henry would never understand. Suddenly Boa Movaca turned. "And over there is the passage." He pointed toward the sheer rock wall that had for many miles been blocking their passage. Henry didn't see anything, not at first. Then, after a long time, he made it out. It was not a gaping hole. It was not a passage in the normal sense of the word. It was a mere discontinuity in the flow of green and grey of the forest.

"Wow!" Henry cried. "Look at that!" A crack, no wider than a narrow doorway, severed the mountain to the core. And yet it had been this way for so long and its edges were so worn, that it was nearly indiscernible from any other part of the rock.

Henry imagined the geological transformations that must have taken place to create such a structure. Two hundred million years ago the great land mass of Pangaea began to drift. Over the aeons, it separated into seven massive pieces, known now as the continents. When the tectonic plates shifted, their edges met, butted against each other and pushed upward. The collision of the Nazca and American Plates formed the Andes cordillera, a massive fault-block mountain range running north and south along the western side of South America. The land around the range wrinkled and contorted, like a rug being shoved up against a wall. The Andean Divisor was formed—an enclosed pattern of mountain ridges with a hidden alpine valley in the center.

Then, a hundred million years later, the jolt of a second major tectonic shift reverberated through the earth's crust and cracked one of the mountain ridges like an ice cube in a tray. Slow, powerful forces drew the two massive sections apart, widening the crack into a fissure. Storms weathered its sharp edges. Erosion rounded its surfaces. Now, a narrow, but well-smoothed crevice reached through the mountain.

Boa Movaca stepped into the crevice, disappearing within seconds. "Come... this is the way," his whisper echoed back to them.

Navigating a narrow river of stone, they followed the flow of the crevice walls. They climbed across the smooth grey stone, sometimes on hands and knees, sometimes running like children up a slide.

The chasm reached a high point of twelve thousand feet, where the air was brisk. Henry's short breaths did not fill his lungs with the oxygen he needed to make his way. Luckily, they rested often in the smoothed-out stone hollows of the ravine, sheer walls rising on either side of them. Though he tended to be a little claustrophobic, being inside the stone fissure didn't bother Henry. The stone walls provided a powerful feeling of shelter.

After a while the travelers began to descend. The crevice slipped inevitably toward the inner valley. Finally, the walls fell away completely and they came out on the other side of the Divisor, into a place few human beings had ever been.

They found themselves beneath the canopy of a great forest. The air was warmer now, and dense with the humidity of the jungle. Henry could no longer see the sun through the lushness of the vegetation. An explosion of yellow flowers clung to the draping vines, and there among them climbed an iguana, chewing each blossom in turn.

Following the others, Henry pushed his way into the verdure, brushing aside great palm leaves and tropical bushes. Mauve and white-spotted fungi grew at his feet, mixing with the many-colored lichen and mosses that grew on the trunks of the trees.

Above him, aracaris and toucans clamored in the tree tops.

Boa led the way, somehow finding a course through the understory. They followed the slope downward, deeper into the valley.

A bat falcon zoomed past them, chasing a bronzy Inca sunangel. Once it had eluded the predator, the little bird returned to its territory, high among the trees, where it hovered over and sucked nectar from long, red, tubular flowers.

They encountered a stream flowing down from the ridge. They walked with the stream for a while, accompanied by its babbling whispers.

Henry watched a bright, luminescent blue butterfly with wings as big as dinner plates flutter past. Soon another followed, nearly as large as the first. They came upon a small fruiting tree. There on the forest floor, beneath its outstretched limbs, a dozen giant blue butterflies sucked the nectar from rotting, orange-colored fruit. When they rose up again, the giant blue butterflies tilted and spun in the air, as if drunken on the fermented nectar.

As the travelers pressed on, a mist surrounded them. The water of the streams and vegetation continually evaporated and hung about them, forming terrestrial clouds; Henry understood now why the local people called this place the Cloud Forest.

Sometimes the mist was so thick that they held hands, lest they become separated.

When they stopped to rest, an owl-eyed butterfly landed on Henry's leg. It appeared as if it had been caught in a rain storm. The rain had worn the color off its wings and now they were completely transparent. Only the minute wiring of the wing's structural frame remained. A clear-winged butterfly.

They came then to a cocha, an oxbow lake, formed many years before by an ancient river. They worked their way around the lake, gazing across the victoria regia–giant water lilies–that covered its surface. Their green pads were as big as water beds, their white blossoms as big as footballs. The wattled jacana tip-toed across the lily pads with ease, hunting for the tiny crustacea that lived beneath. As he moved, Henry startled striated herons that flew for a short distance across the brilliant green waterscape, then landed again ahead of them. At times there were dozens of birds in the sky.

The mood of the company was good. They had found the place they were looking for. "Now we're getting somewhere!" Sullivan said, finally satisfied that the Indian knew what he was talking about.

Jett put his arm around Boa Movaca: "You don't need the Leopard Ghost after all! You did it!"

Boa nodded. "Yes, we are here. We must be careful not to get lost."

Jett smiled and agreed. "Yes, we must be careful."

They continued onward, exploring the forest. "Hey, Sullivan, what kind of bird is that?" Henry would ask when something would fly by. Henry was like a child in a new playground. "Look at that!" he cried when a fork-tailed wood nymph collided in mid air with a lazuline sabrewing. The two hummingbirds engaged in a fantastic aerial battle. Then they separated, hovered eye to hairy eyeball for a second, chirped angrily at one another, and darted off in opposite directions.

Sullivan ran after the sabrewing, the rarer of the two birds. As he moved through the forest, he pulled out a small pocket recorder he carried with him. His hope was to capture the "battle chirp" of the sabrewing on tape. He went far ahead of the others, and they soon lost sight of him.

A few minutes later, they found Sullivan kneeling in the dirt and studying something. His tape recorder sat on the ground beside him, the birds forgotten.

"What is it?" Henry asked as they approached.

"Look," he said, gesturing at the ground.

Henry saw them now. All around him. Thousands of them. Perhaps millions. There were four or five different types, two different colors. They were crawling on everything. They seemed to be engaged in some sort of conflict. Green against brown. A sort of war. He could see skirmishes taking place right at his feet, one soldier locked in mortal combat with another. And over there he could see the main lines of defense. But the greens were losing ground to the browns. The browns had fought their way into the nest. They were killing, looting, taking slaves, raiding aphid livestock. A steady stream of the victors were making off with the spoils. They marched in single file, each one carrying a huge leg, or wing, or thorax from their enemy's food stash. And the gargantuan soldiers stood guarding the line of workers against counter attacks. All around him raged a war of epic proportions –between two colonies of ants.

"Cup your hands to your ears," Sullivan suggested to Henry.

When Henry did so he was immediately startled. He could hear them. He could hear thousands of tiny mandibles, millions of tiny feet, and it sounded like rain on the leaves.

"The army ants are attacking the leaf cutter ants. The leaf cutters are losing. You see, here's a line of workers carrying away the larvae."

As the army ants swarmed around the colony, they devoured everything in their path, including the many incidental insects and spiders living in the leaf litter that covered the forest floor. Normally the arthropods hid beneath the vegetative debris, but now they fled to escape the swarm. This in turn had attracted the antbirds, birds that ate not ants, but the insects they stirred up. A white-cheeked antbird swooped in, nabbed a cicada, and swooped out. An antwren fluttered about the lower branches of the bushes, gleaning insects from the disrupted foliage. An antpitta ran along the ground, snapping up spiders as fast as they fled.

A cloud of gnats collected above the ant swarm, laying eggs on the spiders backs as they scuttled away. Some of the spiders would escape the birds, and these would provide new homes for the larvae of the gnats. Female butterflies came by the hundreds, feeding on the excrement of the birds, which was rich with the nitrates they required to produce eggs.

Eventually the human beings moved on, letting the ant swarm continue behind them.

As they traveled, Henry gazed around, wondering what amazing thing was going to happen next.

CHAPTER FIFTY

As they walked, Jett thought about the bird she had stolen from Caldwell's laboratory.

"What do blue-crowned motmots eat?" Jett asked Sullivan. "Are they antbirds like the ones we just saw?" She was trying to learn everything she could about this place because she knew that somewhere, deep in its complexities, it contained the solution to her problem.

"No, they're not considered antbirds. They eat insects, reptiles and amphibians. They're hunters."

"When are we going to see one?" Henry asked.

"I don't know. We'll just keep looking. We need to get into the right type of habitat, farther down the slope," Sullivan explained and he pointed the way.

As the day went on, the travelers grew tired and eventually began to spread out. Sometimes Henry would lag behind. Other times he would get a burst of energy and push ahead. Then Sullivan would be the one, stopping along the trail to study a bird. Boa was always ahead, always pushing forward.

Jett was making her way alone through an area of rough terrain. Great, gnarled trees grew all around her, their thick branches hanging over the path. The irregularity of the path had separated the travelers as they walked. Boa was quite a distance up ahead. Sullivan and Henry were falling behind. What are they doing back there? Jett wondered. Then something grabbed her. She bent over in intense pain. Teeth latched onto her side and held her with frightening force. The snake reared up, pulling her off her feet. She hit the ground. Scaly muscles twisted around her. She felt them on her feet first, then coiling up her legs. She tried to push the snake away. It wrapped around her hips, the coils tightening.

She lifted a boot heel and kicked it, even as she drew her Glock. Suddenly the snake released her. For a moment she thought that it had decided to leave. Then she realized that it just wanted to get a better grip. It wrapped around her in one swift, instantaneous contraction. She shot and missed. She shot again, blasting a hole through it. She struggled wildly. Irritated by her attempts to escape, the snake became all the more powerful. The harder she fought it, the harder it fought back. And its anger terrified her. She slammed the Glock into its head, then tried to shoot it in the eye. Its head jerked upward, then bent inward again. A twist of its body flipped her over and slammed her to the ground.

The pressure hit her stomach. She vomited, spewing in every direction as she fought. Struggling to breathe through the contents of her own stomach, she felt like she was drowning. Blood was pouring out of her mouth now. The coils wrapped around her rib cage. Panic-stricken, she exploded with an incredible burst of strength. She expanded herself, pushing the snake away. She got one arm free. She slammed a closed fist into its head. She could breath again, and the oxygen gave her renewed hope.

The snake redoubled its efforts. Her struggle became a childishly weak force against its power. The coil constricted around her, squeezing every wisp of air from her lungs, slowly stealing the life from her. "Sullivan!" she screamed. "Henry!" She felt her diaphragm collapsing. Her screams became gasps. Suffocation was imminent. "Henry!" she cried, a silent whisper from her evacuated lungs. Those were her last words. Cries for help. But there was no one there. No rescue. Only death.

CHAPTER FIFTY-ONE

Henry looked down at the motionless body of Jetta Mendoza Santiago.

Sullivan came up behind him. "What happened?" He had heard the gun shots, and her scream, and came running. "She's blue. Why is she blue, Henry? God . . . she looks dead."

Boa, who had also come running, knelt on the ground beside her.

Henry made space for him. "She's not dead, is she?" He noticed the vomit and blood on the ground.

"I cannot feel her heat," Boa said.

Henry touched her skin. She was cold like a cadaver. Her arms looked purplish and bruised. He put his head to her chest and listened for her heart. He couldn't hear anything. He tried for a pulse, couldn't find one.

"She's not breathing!" Henry cried.

Sullivan ripped open her shirt and began pumping her heart. "Quick, get her straightened out!" he said.

Henry and Boa laid out her wrinkled up body, as if to let her lungs unfold and fill with air. Her body lay limp in their hands, like a rag doll.

"No!" Henry said, tears streaming down his face.

"Jett!" Sullivan screamed. He kept pumping.

Henry's world was changing around him. Suddenly, it was becoming a grotesquely dark and lonely place. Jett was dead. It was too late.

"Jett!" Sullivan shouted. Angered, he stopped pumping and punched her in the chest again. "Jett! Wake up!"

Suddenly, Henry imagined he was sitting in his dingy little office. His bosses had given him another boring assignment. He was writing another program. Jett was dead. There was nothing to do anymore. There was no point anymore. The world was dark. He could not bear it.

She woke with a blood-curdling scream: "S n a a a a a k e !"

Horror-struck, she scrambled away. White as a ghost and blue around the lips, she was panic-stricken, fleeing a snake they couldn't see. She crawled wildly through the undergrowth.

"Snake!"

They ran after her, and held her down, and soothed her. "There's no snake. The snake's gone, Jett. There's no snake. You're OK."

She gazed around, bewildered.

Everybody stared at her like she was insane.

"Where'd the snake go?" she asked.

"There's no snake," Sullivan said.

Frustrated with that answer she looked at Boa.

"I saw no sign of a snake," Boa agreed.

She shook her head. "I was attacked by a giant snake."

"No, you weren't," Sullivan said.

She rubbed her head, wiped her eyes, pushed her hand through her hair. "I was attacked by a snake! I'm telling you! I got squished! I was dead! Anaconda bait!"

"You weren't. There was no snake. You were in some sort of coma when we found you, but there was no snake."

She ran her hand through her hair again, then gazed around the forest floor and the lower tree limbs for signs of giant slinking serpents. She pulled up her shirt and looked at her side: no massive snake bite.

She looked up at the sky, trying to check the time of day. She couldn't tell what time it was. She couldn't see the sun. The canopy was too thick. The mist was moving in on them now.

"I imagined it?" her voice trembled. She was terrified.

"'Hallucinated' would be a more accurate term I think. You had an attack, just like on the plane," Sullivan said.

"Like on the plane?"

"The drug. You know, like a bad acid trip."

She shook her head. She stood up. Her clothes were torn, and stained with vomit, blood, and urine.

"The poison has done this to you?" Boa asked.

She nodded. "The poison," she agreed finally.

She started walking again in the direction they had been traveling. She rubbed her legs, tried to recompose herself. "Let's stick closer together. If you guys see a giant anaconda, you'll warn me, right?"

Boa looked at her with concern. "We must find your bird for you. It is not good to be attacked by giant snakes in one's mind."

"No, it's not good," Jett agreed, and laughed.

"Quiet!" Sullivan whispered. He held up his hand, holding his companions in their places while he listened. "Did you hear that?"

Henry shook his head. He didn't hear anything.

Sullivan put his finger to his thumb, curled his hand into the shape of a cylinder, and placed his hand to his lips, like a trumpeter might his instrument. But instead of blowing outward to create a sound, Sullivan pulled air rapidly inward, in swift gasps of breath. The rush of air through his cupped hand created a loud and peculiar sound. He repeated the call.

He walked a short distance, then stopped and made the sound again. He listened intently, filtering out a hundred other sounds to find the motmot. A haunting reply floated through the forest back to them. Only then, after hearing the call of the bird, did Henry understand that the name "motmot" was an onomatopoeia for its vocalization. Just like the blue jay at home, the motmot got its name from the sound it makes.

With his keen and well-trained ears, Sullivan had heard a vocalization he was not familiar with. It was extremely similar to the known blue-crowned motmot, but there was a subtle difference to its tone. He was using it now to call the bird to him.

Sullivan took the lead. He made the peculiar call as he walked. In the world of birds it was he who knew the way.

"Each species of bird uses a different set of vocalizations to establish territories, attract mates, maintain flock cohesion, and alarm other birds of predators," he told them. "These vocalizations are the key to finding and understanding birds. What differentiates one individual from another as being a different "species" is its evolutionary history. If two birds come from the same breeding population they are by definition the same species. If they come from different breeding populations, which have evolved independently, they may be a different species."

"How does that help?" Henry asked.

"Since male birds use vocalizations to attract female birds, the vocalization itself determines which birds mate with other birds. The call is how the two birds get together. So birds with different calls never meet, never mate. Two flycatchers may appear almost identical in the field, and may live in the same place, but they will have two very different vocalizations, and therefore represent two different breeding populations, two different branches on the evolutionary tree, two different species. They may look similar to the human eye, but they have been separate for thousands of years and occupy a different niche of the ecosystem."

Then he shut up suddenly. "Did you hear it?"

"I didn't hear it," Henry admitted. Then added, "Somebody was talking."

Sullivan repeated the call, waited, and listened. "Yes!" he whispered. "This way!"

Henry glanced at Boa, wondering if he had heard it.

They pursued the sound several hundred yards, then came to the edge of a wide gorge. From the edge, they gazed through and across the tops of the trees that grew in the gorge's floor. A carpet of forest canopy covered the valley. Ornate hawk eagles soared high overhead. A river ran down the center.

Sullivan repeated the call of the motmot.

This time Henry heard the response, a quick "mot mot" sound. The sound was low and tentative in its character, muffled by the dense forest through which it floated.

"We've got him. He's coming in . . . "

Soon the call surrounded them. The bird was close. Remaining perfectly still, they searched the trees. The mist flowed down the slope and poured in great furling waves over the edge of the gorge. The ghostly sound of the motmot explored the air around them.

Henry watched a large bird fly into view and land on a branch a few feet away. It gazed down at them with its vermillion eye.

"There it is!" he cried.

"That's it!" Sullivan whispered, keeping his voice low so as not to disturb the elusive creature.

The motmot looked around quizzically, wondering where the other bird was. As it tilted its head in bewilderment, its jewel-blue helmet sparkled in the sunlight. Then it burst upward and flew away.

"I know that bird," Boa said after it had gone.

"How do you know about that bird, Boa?" Jett asked.

"The Leopard Ghost taught me."

"What did he teach you about it? Did he say that the bird was medicine?"

"No," Boa replied. "That bird has no medicine inside it."

Hearing these words, Henry's heart sank. They had come all this way only to learn that the bird meant nothing. Henry glanced over at Jett. He could see the disappointment in her face.

"Are you sure that's our bird, Sullivan?" Henry asked.

"Positive."

"Boa, are you sure it doesn't contain any magic?" Henry asked.

"Maybe he just doesn't know about it. Maybe Dracon knew something the Leopard Ghost didn't." Sullivan said these words, but they were desperate. Even he didn't believe them.

"I am sure, Jetta Mendoza. This bird has no medicine inside it. It has no special magic except that it is connected to all the other animals of the forest."

"That doesn't help us here," Sullivan said, depressed. "Doesn't help at all."

Henry wouldn't give up. "What do you mean by 'it is connected to all the other animals of the forest'?"

Boa continued: "The Leopard Ghost taught me that this bird is the way to find Sapo."

Jett broke in: "What did you say?" she asked, grabbing his arm. "*Boa, what did you say?*"

"Sapo is small and difficult to find. But the bird is large and loud, and easy to find. The bird will lead you to Sapo."

"But what is Sapo? That's what we came here to find out! *What is Sapo?*"

Boa shrugged. "Sapo is the magic."

"Sapo is magic?" Henry asked, confused.

"The Leopard Ghost used Sapo for medicine?" Jett asked.

"It's the most powerful magic I've ever seen," Boa said.

"How do we find it? How do we find the Sapo?" Jett asked.

"We must sleep first."

"Not this again!" Sullivan cried. "I can't take this! Where's a tree I can bang my head on!"

"I can't sleep, Boa. I'm going to die!" Jett cried.

Boa reached up and put his hands on her shoulders. "Calm yourself, Jetta Mendoza. Find tranquility. In the morning we will follow the bird and find Sapo." Boa smiled. "Go to sleep. Maybe the bird will come to you in your dream."

Jett looked sharply at him. "There are no birds in my dreams! There are giant snakes!"

CHAPTER FIFTY-TWO

When Jett opened her eyes early the next morning Sullivan was standing over her. He was fully dressed and had his boots on. At first she thought he was on his way out of camp, then she realized he was just returning. He was carrying his tape recorder and microphone slung over his shoulder. His binoculars hung around his neck. His face was beaming with a childlike wonder. "I got 'em on tape, Jett!" he told her, his voice ringing with the resonance of victory. He had been up for hours, documenting the behavior of the motmots and recording their vocalizations. "Look!" he said and pointed upward.

There were a pair of motmots high in the canopy. They were moving from one tree top flower to the next, looking inside each one.

"What are they doing?" she asked.

"They're hunting!" he said.

"What are they hunting for? What did you say motmots eat?" Jett asked.

"Normally they're opportunistic predators," he said. "They sit stationary and wait for something to go by, then grab it."

"Those two up there are looking in the flowers that are growing in the tops of the ceiba trees."

"I know! That's strange behavior for a Momotidae, but that's definitely what they're doing. They're foraging for something."

"What's up there?" she asked. "What are they hunting for?"

"I don't know." He raised his binoculars and studied them. "There! He just snapped something out of a flower!"

Henry groaned and rolled over. "Hey, what's going on?" he asked sleepily.

"What are they eating?" Jett asked.

"I can't tell," Sullivan said.

"We need to find out. How can we get up there?" Jett said.

Sullivan shook his head. "There's no way. It's got to be more than a hundred feet!"

"What about the gorge?" Jett suggested.

"Hey, what are you guys talking about?" Henry asked. He got up and looked around. "What's happening?"

"What about the gorge?" Sullivan said.

"Yeah, what about it?" Henry said.

"The motmots are moving toward the gorge. The tops of the trees growing in the gorge are at about the same level as us. All we have to do is go to the edge of the gorge and climb out on a tree limb and get to the flowers."

"That sounds like a really bad idea," Henry said.

"I agree," Sullivan said.

"You got a better idea?" Jett said.

"No," Sullivan said, "But I'm sure that's a bad one. Boa, can't you talk some sense into her?"

Boa nodded in the direction of the tree. "There is your answer, Jetta Mendoza."

"Telling her that isn't going to help!" Sullivan shouted.

Ignoring them, Jett began walking toward the gorge.

Henry followed nervously. "Jett, you're not really gonna do that, are you?"

Jett stood on the edge of the cliff, a few feet beneath the branches of a ceiba tree growing a hundred feet up from the bottom of the gorge. She climbed onto the branches of the giant tree. They bowed under her weight and she tried not to think about the ten story drop below.

"Are you out of your mind?!" Sullivan shouted.

"I've seen her do stuff like this before," Henry said, remembering the fence around the police impoundment lot.

"Jett, you're gonna break your neck! Come back here!" Sullivan shouted after her.

Jett didn't answer. She was too far away. She was clinging to a tree limb as thick as her own body. If she slipped or lost her grip she would fall to certain death. The alternative though (not finding the answer) would mean *uncertain* death–a worse fate. She climbed with total commitment, without fear. It was her only course and she took it without hesitation.

She grabbed a small branch as a hand hold. It snapped off in her hand, tumbling downward, hitting other branches as it fell, until finally it disappeared. A long moment later, she heard it hit the ground.

As she climbed, she began to hear a hissing noise in the

distance.

Soon the hiss came closer.

She heard a rustling sound, like a light wind moving through the tree tops. But there was no wind.

She clung with one arm to the tree limb and rubbed her face with the other. Was this another hallucination?

The sound of wind in the trees became louder.

The hissing surrounded her.

Something leaped from a tree top.

Agile brown shapes moved through the trees. The sound of twisting branches and rustling leaves suddenly exploded all around her.

She shut her eyes. She held them shut. She guarded every ounce of her soul from the hallucination and the pain that she knew would follow. If she went into convulsions, or lost consciousness as she had before, she would fall to her death.

The hissing sound, the moving tree limbs, the wind, none of it was going away. It all seemed very real, but so had the snake!

Then there was total silence.

She waited.

Something was going to happen.

She opened her eyes.

A small tamarin sat on the tree limb in front of her. Its tiny humanoid body was covered with smooth, dark brown fur. Its tail was curled behind it, hanging over an upper branch. Its sentient eyes stared upon her with unabashed curiosity. In its hand it held something. She couldn't tell what it was. Completely at ease with their precarious position on the tree limb, the tamarin sat and studied her.

There were about thirty tamarin in the troop. They had surrounded her and now stared at her with great interest. Though they moved with startling quickness through the tree tops, they were in no way violent or threatening. The hissing noise she had heard was simply their alarm to one another, their language. It was their way of saying: "Hey, what's that big tamarin-like thing crawling in the tree over there? Let's go see!"

Behind the first tamarin sat another, a female. She clutched to her breast a small baby, which suckled on her breast as she watched the intruder. Even when the mother leaped to another branch and climbed to a higher position, the baby remained clinging to her. Then the baby stopped and turned its little head. She met the gaze of a miniature face, its huge eyes black as the Amazonian night.

The mother crawled up to one of the giant flowers. The flowers were epiphytes, or air plants. They were growing on the mossy limbs of the trees, and drew their sustenance from the humid air around them. This species was a large bromeliad, with thick green leaves splayed in all directions, forming a hollow pitcher in the center. A bright pink stalk stuck upward with a spiny, brilliant flower at its top. The mother tamarin stuck her hand into the water that had collected in the plant's hollow center. She grabbed something and dropped it down her throat with delight.

The tamarin in front of her jumped back when Jett moved. Then the whole troop jolted in response, hiding wherever they could find cover. Suddenly there was a panic. The males hissed, as if preparing to defend the troop. After a moment, Jett saw the shadow of a harpy eagle pass overhead and realized it wasn't she who scared the tamarin. It was the predator. In a few moments the eagle was gone and the troop returned to normal. The males settled down again. The females and youngsters came out of hiding, realizing the danger had past.

Nervous, Jett decided that it was best to remain where she was. But she was desperate to find out what was in those flowers.

As if reading her mind, the tamarin sitting beside her crawled to a flower, snatched something out of it, then returned to her. It reached out to her. Its tiny hand was but inches away. When it opened its fingers she saw that it held a small black fish.

She accepted the fish from the tamarin's hand.

She studied it as it squirmed in her palm. Then she realized it had legs. It wasn't a fish at all. It was a tadpole, a baby frog. There were tadpoles swimming in the pitchers of rain water formed by the bromeliad plants.

She heard the call of the motmot. She looked up just in time to see the male motmot snap up a tadpole and fly off.

Becoming more daring, she moved forward along the tree limb. She searched the outside, then the inside of the plant's leaves. Eventually, she found an adult frog clinging to the flower stalk. The small tree frog was green above with blue and cream below, and a head shaped strangely like a snake. It was the same frog she had seen in the laboratory. The green serum had been labeled "Phyllomedusa bicolor."

She was now able to translate properly: two-color, snake-headed frog.

She turned back to the tamarin, who was still watching her. "Thank you, my friend," she said in a language it did not understand.

She stuck the frog in her pocket and started the climb back to her companions.

"What did you find out there?" Henry asked.

"Everything is connected," she said. Her mind was consumed with the complexity of what she was dealing with. "Just like Boa said, one thing leads to another . . . and everything is connected . . . everything . . . ."

"Jett, you're not making sense," Sullivan said. "What did you find?"

She took the frog out of her pocket and showed it to them.

"Sapo," Boa said.

"Sapo," she repeated. She had heard the word before. *1% Sapo solution.*

"What's Sapo? I don't understand," Sullivan said.

"In my language, Sapo means frog," Boa told him.

"What is Sapo used for, Boa?" Jett asked. "You said that Sapo was powerful magic. What sort of magic?"

"The Leopard Ghost taught me how to draw the slime from the cupped toes of the Sapo. Then you put the slime into a small bag. Then poke a stick into the bag. Burn the end of the stick and push it into your wrist."

"While it's still hot?" Henry said.

"Yes, it must burn the skin."

"A crude form of injection," Sullivan said. "forced through the skin."

"But what does it do?" Henry said.

"It has many uses."

"What's its primary use?" Jett asked.

"Once, when the hunters could not find game, the Leopard Ghost burned the slime of the Sapo into their skins and they dreamed to see where the game was."

"He's talking about dreams again," Sullivan said.

"Not dreams in the sleeping sense," Jett said. "Hallucinations. That's what he means. Waking dreams."

"Like getting attacked by a giant snake? You mean Dracon put a Sapo serum inside you? That's what's causing your attacks?" Henry said.

"That stuff has been wreaking havoc on you," Sullivan said.

"What good is a medicine like that?" Henry said.

"Depends on how bad the disease is," Jett said. "Boa, besides making you dream, what else does Sapo do?"

"It gives you the strength of many men. You can go without food for five days. It gives you the senses of the forest . . . hearing, sight, smell."

"What else?"

"When people got very sick with the purple splotches, the Leopard Ghost used Sapo to ward off diseases."

Jett was trying to interpret what the Indian was saying. "It sounds like it fortifies the immune system." Everything was coming together in her mind. "I was wrong," she said abruptly. "I was wrong about everything!"

"What do you mean? Wrong about what?" Henry asked.

"I thought the green liquid they injected inside me was some sort of exotic disease. I thought the green stuff killed Mary. But it was the cure! Sapo is the cure!"

She thought back to her weeks in the laboratory, trying to figure out everything that happened, trying to figure out what was going to happen to her now.

"OK," Henry said. "Sapo is the cure for the disease, but what's the disease? And what's going to happen to you?" Henry asked.

"Good question," Jett said. "We know what Sapo is now, but we still don't know the whole story."

The answer was inside Dracon Industries, her old enemy. She had to get back in there, somehow penetrate their defenses. But how could she?

Henry had lost interest in the frog. He was staring across the gorge and into the distance where they could see the walls of the Andean Divisor.

"What's on your mind, Henry?" Jett said.

"Nothing, just thinking . . . " he said, not even realizing his answer didn't make sense. He was up to something.

"What's up, whiz kid, you look like you've got a brainstorm going," Sullivan said.

Henry ignored them both. He turned to Boa. "Boa, have you

been to the white men's base camp?" he asked.

"Just what are you thinking about now?" Sullivan looked at him suspiciously.

Jett touched Sullivan's arm, quieting him.

Boa nodded to Henry. "Yes, I've seen the camp through the trees, from a distance."

"How big is it?"

Boa thought a moment about this question, then answered, "Like a small village."

"There are buildings then."

"Yes, there are buildings."

"How many buildings?"

Boa thought a moment, then answered "Eleven I think, including two small ones."

"Was the base camp quiet?"

"No," Boa said.

"Did you ever hear a loud rumbling noise at night?"

Boa nodded.

"Did all the buildings look the same?"

"Yes."

"Were they all the same size?"

"Yes."

"Did any of the buildings have strange silver objects on the roof tops?"

"What are you talking about, Henry?" Sullivan asked.

"Let him go, Sullivan," Jett told him.

Henry repeated his question: "Did any of the buildings have a big silvery structure on the roof?"

"Yes, one of the buildings had a strange thing on the top. I did not know what it was."

"Was it like a giant bowl?"

Boa nodded, remembering.

"Satellite dish," Jett said, making the connection.

Henry nodded. "If they're doing biomedical or biological research, they're probably using a computer and a generator. They must have some sort of connection to the real world. There are no phones here, so the only possibility is a satellite link."

Jett knew where he was going and took over the questioning:

"Boa, how many men are there in the base camp?"

"About thirty."

"Thirty!" cried Sullivan. "You're not thinking—"

"—OK," Jett said, interrupting him. "That shouldn't be a problem. We've done all we can here. Let's go."

"OK?" Sullivan cried. "What do you mean, OK? That doesn't sound OK to me!"

CHAPTER FIFTY-THREE

Dr. Raymond M. Caldwell sat down at his desk. He turned on his computer. While it booted up, he sat back in his chair and rubbed his eyes. It had been a long, hard struggle. Getting filthy rich and famous was hard work.

The patients were acting up again, making demands, doing harm to herself. It seemed that captivity caused a sort of insanity in these people. It had gotten worse since the two had escaped. All the patients had their personal quirks, their annoying habits, their individual problems that caused constant irritation to him.

He had gone into research for one simple reason: he hated patients. He hated dealing with their irrelevant complaints, their sniveling explanations of what *they* thought was wrong with them, their incessant need to know the details of this procedure or that possible side effect. Patients treated everything like it was brain surgery, like it was something important.

General practice was boring, and there were too many patients. In research, you could set up an experiment, do your work, and get the results. If you worked very hard, for a long time–and you were very lucky– you could discover something new. And if you applied every bit of science you knew, you could eke out something useful, and perhaps introduce a drug 2% more effective than the previous one. This process normally took many years.

He was fifty seven now. Many years had already gone by. Nothing much had come of them. He had spent his life for the betterment of medical science, but he hadn't bettered anything, especially not himself. He was convinced he was utterly brilliant, but there were just too many obstacles in his way, too many things preventing him from getting his job done and coming out with something really spectacular.

Chief among his enemies was PETA, the People for the Ethical Treatment of Animals. He couldn't even count on two hands the number of times they had halted crucial experiments just weeks before a breakthrough. How many times had they infiltrated his labs and ruined everything? They even got him fired from Jensen-Bishop a few years ago, just for experimenting on cats and dogs (which he found in ample supply at the local animal shelter).

PETA didn't make sense. Ethical treatment of animals? Concern for a few little mice and monkeys? What about the ethical treatment of human beings? What about concern for human life, for science, for progress, for money, for his career? He hated PETA, and everything it stood for.

People have to improve. We have to get better. We have to experiment on things so that we can figure out how they work and how we can make them better. We can't just leave things up in the air, just let things be the way they are. We can't just accept death, and anonymous poverty, in exchange for the well being of a few rodents.

After that, he was frustrated, looking for a job, looking for a new project. That's when he heard about the explorer who had recently returned from the Amazon rain forest with news of a "magic drug" that had powerful effects on the human body. No medical professionals took the explorer seriously. He couldn't even get an article published in the New England Journal of Medicine. Voodoo magic hardly competed with national health, cancer research and the long list of other critical subjects. Yet, the explorer's claims intrigued Caldwell. He contacted the man personally. That's when he saw Sapo for the first time. He knew he was onto something, something powerful. He was determined to do it right, do it his way.

Initial tests determined that six percent of the frog's body weight consisted of chemical peptides. Of the several dozen different peptides found, seven were bioactive: bradykinins, tachykinins, caerulein, sauvagine, tryptophyllins, dermorphins and bombesins. Each one had a selective affinity for binding with receptor sites in humans. In other words, they were seven keys to the locks that controlled the chemical reactions in the human body.

As a pathologist, Caldwell knew the power of these keys. He knew that if he had the right environment for experimentation he could develop a drug of incredible power. Of course, he had his own ideas on how a lab should be run. He was fed up with the antivivisectionists. He was fed up with the federal government, lab supervisors, the State Medical Board, and the American Medical Association. He didn't like laymen and bureaucrats telling him what *was* and *was not* ethical. This drug, if developed and produced properly, would not only make him the most famous scientist of his time, it would make him incredibly rich. There was no sense getting bogged down in rules for something that important. Bending the rules a little made sense in his mind. It was mandatory. What were a few dozen people's lives compared to the millions of lives he would save, the millions of dollars he would make?

Playing on the recent success of upstart bioresearch companies on the stock market, Caldwell found a series of over-anxious, money-hungry investors, promising them an incredible return on their investment when the new drug came to market.

By forming his own company, Caldwell knew that he could do what he wanted. He set up his lab in secret. He called it a "psychiatric research" center. That explained the monkeys, the strange experiments, the unusual patients.

He screened the employees very carefully and bound them into his service in such a way that he was positive they were not disguised members of PETA. He would make sure nobody got any cameras in the place. He would use only standard lab monkeys instead of chimps, which were his preference. It turned out that the rhesus monkey's immune system was incredibly close to the human immune system anyway. It was a better choice in the end. There wasn't another animal alive that made a better vehicle for experimentation. Except for human beings, of course.

He had used the monkeys to isolate the critical factors. Sure, he had lost a few, and a few had exhibited truly bizarre psychotic behavior, but in the end he had his answers, at least enough to move to the next step.

That's where the street people came in. He picked up the homeless, the drug addicts, people who society didn't need or want anymore. He got his "cats and dogs" and this time nobody would know or care. What better experimental vehicles than human beings? And what did people possibly care about the homeless? They were all drug addicts, drunkards and illegal aliens anyway. They were free, readily available, and there wasn't a People for the Ethical Treatment of People, thank God.

After months of careful work, everything was coming together. He had almost isolated the correct concentration of the drug in his human specimens and he had found suitable mixing agents. There were still a few undesirable side effects that he was concerned about, but he was confident he could nullify those with a little more experimentation. It was true that two of his test specimens had escaped through a hole in the bathroom piping system, and this concerned him, but he had people combing the city for them. As soon as they showed up, he'd nab them.

Last year one of the rhesus monkeys had escaped. Nothing ever came of it. The monkey got out into the city, probably crawled around for a few days and got hit by a car. There wasn't much difference in this case. At least one of the human specimens that escaped had been insane. He wasn't sure if the poor woman had gone crazy from her captivity, the drug itself, or some wound to her head. If the woman from Room 13 did manage to find someone to listen to her, they would soon conclude she was psychotic. She was no danger to the project, so he forgot about her. Like all patients, she was just an annoyance.

Once he formed the company and began experimentation, Caldwell soon realized that he needed help. It was a full time job running the lab, another full time job handling security, and another administering the computer system. He needed intelligent people to work with him, people he could trust, people who shared his sense of priorities when it came to human life and US dollars. He put his old friend Curtis Traymore in charge of security. Traymore was a ex-green-beret, ex-Vietnam vet, ex-con, schizophrenic . . . perfect. Then he hired an old buddy from college, the guy he used to pay to hack into the school mainframe and change his grades. Perfect. The three musketeers.

He sent Traymore down to South America with the explorer. He was to establish a good supply of Sapo extract and establish a safe route for shipments to the United States. Traymore wired back that they had found the frog in northern Peru. That's when they learned about the Leopard Ghost. Apparently the explorer hadn't discovered Sapo himself. Over the years, he had developed a rapport with a native witch doctor down there, some sort of shaman who showed him how to find and use the drug. It was from the shaman that they learned that although the Sapo frog was rare and very difficult to locate, they could use a special bird as a guide. It was a reliable method. The Leopard Ghost had been using it for eighty years.

Understanding the importance of the bird, Caldwell ordered Traymore to ship him a specimen for safe keeping. Knowing that security was critical, Traymore took a boat from Iquitos to Manaus, thinking that if the bird was traced it would be traced to the wrong country. Then he hired a "special courier" to get it to the United States, somebody that he knew could elude their arch-enemy Jensen-Bishop Corporation.

Once the link to the original source was made, Caldwell gave orders to Traymore for the explorer and his shaman friend to "have an accident." Caldwell knew those two wouldn't agree with the "methods and procedures" he was going to use to develop the drug. Besides, when cutting a pie, fewer slices means bigger slices.

Killing the shaman, of course, was a critical mistake. Using the bird to find the frog was fine . . . if you could find the bird! Without the Leopard Ghost's assistance, Traymore couldn't find a single specimen of the bird, let alone the frog.

Just weeks after Traymore dispatched the explorer and shaman, Caldwell began running short on the original sample. He would soon need more to continue his experiments.

All Caldwell's attempts to synthesize the drug in the laboratory had failed. He could not reproduce it.

Then he attempted to raise the Sapo frogs in captivity. He had marginal success, and managed to get two of the frogs to mate and yield offspring . . . only to find that the offspring did not possess the necessary toxins. They didn't contain the peptides. The frogs had to come from the rain forest.

Traymore had established a base camp north of the Río Pucara. Knowing that the entire project relied on re-establishing the link to the original source, Caldwell provided Traymore with all the resources he asked for. They hired men. They set up a computer station powered by solar collectors that could link into the Draconius Network and access the latest satellite photographs as they were released by the Weather Bureau and NASA. For the last three months Traymore and Caldwell had exchanged electronic mail nearly every week. Caldwell would bring Traymore up to date on the latest experimental results and Traymore would send Caldwell news from the Peruvian front. Each day Traymore sent out search parties for the blue-crowned motmot, but it was an elusive bird that sat in the branches of the canopy and remained very still. Of course, none of them knew its call. There were more than sixteen hundred species of birds in Peru. Five hundred species of frogs. Only one of them was Sapo.

Caldwell looked at the computer screen. He clicked on the network icon. His PC logged itself into the UNIX computer in the Data Center down the hall. That's where everything was stored: test results, chemical analysis, control parameters, and his personal log. The screen presented a login prompt:

DRACONIUS LOGIN:

He typed in "caldwell" and a password of "miracle drug." He liked that password because it was easy to remember and because it would be extremely difficult to break. His UNIX guru showed him the trick of putting in the space. It makes the password nearly impossible to guess or decipher. Very few people even know that UNIX will accept a space character in the password string.

Once into the system, he pulled up his experimental log and reviewed the last test. Then he retrieved the data from the liquid chromatograph, summarized the results, and established a new set of initiation parameters which downloaded from the main system into the machine. After completing the log entry and setting up the next test, Caldwell created and e-mail message to Traymore in South America:

TRAYMORE:

THE LAST BATCH OF TEST RESULTS WAS VERY PROMISING OTHER THAN THE USUAL VOMITING, CONVULSIONS, HALLUCINATIONS, BLACKOUTS AND ACUTE TACHYCARDIA, THERE WERE NO ADVERSE SIDE EFFECTS. VERY PROMISING.

YOU MENTIONED IN YOUR LAST MESSAGE THAT YOU HAD A STRONG LEAD FOR FINDING THE SOURCE, SOMETHING ABOUT A SECRET VALLEY THAT THE LOCALS ARE TRYING TO HIDE FROM YOU. YES, I AGREE, USE WHATEVER FORCE NECESSARY TO EXTRACT THE INFORMATION FROM THEM. THEY'RE RIVER PEOPLE, INDIANS, EXPENDABLE. WE ONLY HAVE A FEW WEEKS SUPPLY OF THE ORIGINAL SAMPLE LEFT, SO DO ANYTHING NECESSARY TO DELIVER ASAP.

KARL SAYS THAT HE'S TIGHTENING SECURITY ON THE SYSTEM. ALL PASSWORDS ARE BEING RESET AT MIDNIGHT TONIGHT. YOU'LL HAVE A NEW ONE ISSUED TO YOU. HE HAS MANAGED TO ENCRYPT THE DOWNLINK TRANSMISSION, SO YOU NEED NOT WORRY ABOUT THAT ANYMORE. KARL'S AN ASSET TO THIS COMPANY. YOU TWO SHOULD LEARN TO GET ALONG. JUST

BECAUSE HE DOESN'T KNOW A "PISTOL FROM A REVOLVER" (AS YOU SAY), DOESN'T MEAN WE DON'T NEED HIM. I'M SURE HE'S GOT THINGS TO SAY ABOUT YOU. SOMETHING ABOUT NOT KNOWING A "BIT FROM A BYTE". COOL IT.

AS FOR ME COMING DOWN, I'M CONSIDERING IT. I CAN'T BELIEVE WE'VE COME THIS FAR ONLY TO LOSE OUR CONNECTION TO THE ORIGINAL SOURCE. THE ACCIDENT WITH THE LEOPARD GHOST IS THE STUPIDEST THING WE'VE EVER DONE! WHO'D A THOUGHT A CRAZY OLD WITCH DOCTOR WOULD EVER BE SO IMPORTANT TO US! NEVERTHELESS, I'M SURE YOU'LL FIND THE SAPO FROG SOON. I AM NOT SURE WHAT I CAN DO TO HELP YOU THERE. IT SEEMS WE NEED A FIELD BIOLOGIST, NOT A PATHOLOGIST. ONCE YOU'VE FOUND THE SOURCE, I'LL COME DOWN AND HELP WITH THE PREPARATIONS FOR TRANSPORT.

CALDWELL.

CHAPTER FIFTY-FOUR

Henry followed behind Boa. The Indian walked quietly, softly, following an invisible path that moved with the twists and turns of the stream. Sometimes during the journey he talked, telling them about his wife and his three little girls, but most of the time he was silent. Along the way he pulled a piece of bamboo from the ground, hollowed it out and showed them how to make a blow gun. He explained that his people used such a gun when they went hunting for tapir, the mightiest of the forest beasts. "Tapir get very mean when you jab them with a sharp stick," he explained matter-of-factly to Henry.

"So would I," Henry replied.

Boa continued: "That is why you must poison the tip of the dart," and he showed him how this was done.

Boa's language was not a written language. The lore of the land moved from generation to generation through personal contact, through stories and folklore. Leopard Ghost had taught Boa. Now Boa was teaching them.

They had climbed out of the Cloud Forest, then down the slope of the Andean Divisor. Several days later they crossed over the Río Pucara, traversed it, and headed into the lowland forests.

"How much farther?" Henry asked.

Boa paused momentarily and turned toward him, as if a little confused why he was asking. "Are we not going to the base camp?" he asked.

"Yes, we are," Henry said. "How much father is it?"

Boa showed him the broken branches and the foot prints which made it obvious to him that the base camp was just ahead. "It's right in front of us," he said, a little bewildered by Henry's ignorance.

Henry smiled. "Oh."

Sullivan came up from behind. "I didn't notice either," he told Henry quietly.

"We can't let them see us," Jett explained to Boa. "They are our enemy. Do you understand? If they catch us, they will kill us. Just like they killed your family."

Boa nodded thoughtfully. "I see," he said. "I did not realize this. Then we must not go farther."

Jett shook her head, frustrated. "We must go."

Boa shook his head in return. "Too dangerous. Instead, our spirits will go in our place and see for us. We shall walk unseen and unheard, yes?"

Finally Henry realized what Boa was saying, though he didn't fully understand it.

"I'm all for sending our spirits ahead," he said. "Spirits can't get shot."

Boa led them into a thicker area of the forest where they could prepare themselves. He asked them to sit down, then he disappeared.

Much later, he returned with his medicine bag full.

He sat cross-legged in front of Henry. "You stay still?" Boa asked.

Henry glanced at Jett, "What's he going to do to me?"

She shrugged. "I don't know," she admitted.

"Then how about he does Sullivan first?" Henry suggested. "Whatever it is, I'm sure Sullivan is better at it than me."

"Oh, thanks a lot, kid!"

"I'll go first," Jett volunteered.

Henry stood up gratefully and backed away, allowing Jett to sit down in front of Boa.

Boa took a single green berry from his bag and crushed it against her hand. Then he opened her shirt and exposed the bare skin of her chest. He used the berry to paint an emerald design across her neck and breasts. He followed this procedure by shadowing the emerald paint in scarlet, the color of the birds shot down by the Senderos. Next he took out a black colored berry and painted a lattice of thick lines across her face. With this he was particularly thorough, making sure the lines reached down onto her throat and around her neck. Finally, he took out a foul-smelling fruit and crushed it under her arms. The smell spread all around them. "You are now invisible," Boa told her. "As long as you stay in the forest, you cannot be seen and you cannot be smelled, by animal or by human being."

She nodded. "I understand."

"You understand?" Henry asked, flabbergasted. "What do you

understand? I missed this part in science class, the part about turning yourself invisible with berries!"

"You're next, my friend. Take off your shirt!" she told him.

"But . . ."

"Henry, take off your shirt," Jett ordered him. She got up and pointed for him to sit.

"OK, OK," he agreed, sitting down in front of Boa. Just like when he was getting his hair cut at the barber shop, Henry shut his eyes while Boa did his work. The last thing he remembered seeing before shutting his eyes was Jett. She was standing over him, painted in the colors of the rain forest, scanning the trees for signs of the enemy. She checked her Glock 17 and her ammunition. The sunlight filtering through the canopy had faded. Soon it would be evening.

CHAPTER FIFTY-FIVE

The travelers observed the Dracon base camp. The camp consisted of eleven cinder block and log buildings, all with sheet metal roofs, crude wooden doors and rudimentary windows. They were arranged in a rough circle, the center of which had been cleared of vegetation. The buildings appeared to serve a variety of purposes, including equipment storage, dormitory, kitchen, laboratory and outhouse. The men in the base had strung a series of flood lights around the clearing to provide some semblance of civilization during the long, dark nights. Henry smiled. He wasn't the only one scared of the Amazonian nights. The nights were so dark beneath the canopy of the forest, and filled with such eerie sounds, that it frightened most people, whether they had machine guns or not. Sitting in the dark and listening to those otherworldly sounds emanating from the void, you'd get to thinking that bullets and brawn would do little against the harpies. Indeed, with creatures like the "horned screamer" lurking about, who could help but want for a 1000 watt quartz halogen?

At dusk, a small group of men that had gone out on patrol returned to the camp. They had with them some "bounty" that they had collected during their travels.

"Food for everybody!" they called to their fellow Dracon employees.

"What'd you guys get?" somebody asked as he stumbled from the outhouse. "I'm sick of the crap we've been eating. Rice and beans! Beans and rice!"

"Meat for the tables tonight, boys!" The hunter lifted up a string of dead monkeys. "They look like they're going to be good-tasting little varmints."

"What are they?"

"I think the locals call them tamarins."

"I don't care what they call them. Let's eat!" another said.

"Hey, Traymore, what's that you got?"

The last of the party, a hulking man, walked into the clearing.

He had a rifle in one hand and was dragging something in the other.

"What is that?" somebody asked.

Traymore held it up for everyone to see. By now most of the men in the camp had stumbled out of their barracks. Some of the technicians had come from the laboratory when they heard the commotion. Traymore held up a dead female monkey. To its breast clung a small baby, still alive, terrified.

"You seem to have a hanger on!" somebody shouted.

"Kinda like your girlfriend, eh, Traymore!"

"Shut up about my girlfriend!" Traymore shouted in the direction of that comment.

"What you gonna do with the little creature?" one of the men asked him.

"Well, I don't know. It won't let go." He dropped the dead female on the ground. The baby whimpered and clung tighter. It didn't know what else to do. Its little eyes were looking everywhere. It was looking for other members of its troop, anyone to help its mother. Henry looked over at Jett. She watched in silence. There was nothing they could do.

"How long you been dragging that stupid thing, Traymore?"

"Couple a miles. No big deal."

One of the other hunters in the party jumped in: "Traymore, what are you talking about? We got these things early this morning! Mine's half the size of yours and my arm's killing me! You're a strong son of a bitch dragging that thing around all day!"

Traymore grabbed the baby tamarin and pulled. It screamed and clung tighter to its mother. Traymore shouted something at it. He handed his rifle to the guy next to him. He tried again, this time pulling with both hands. Finally, after sixty seconds of horrific screaming, he pried the little tamarin from its mother's breast. "This little guy's going to have to learn how to get along on its own now."

"What you gonna do, Traymore, keep it as a pet?"

"Yeah, right," Traymore said. He took the baby tamarin and heaved it airborne with all his might. The tamarin tumbled through the air and slammed into the branches of the nearby tree. Henry's whole body jumped, unconsciously struggling to escape with the baby tamarin.

"Run, little guy, run!" Henry whispered to himself.

"You're letting it go?" one of the hunters asked.

"Yeah, right," Traymore said.

When it was thrown into the air, the tamarin realized that it was falling and grabbed out for the limbs of the tree. It latched on to the leaves and scrambled to a thicker part of the branch. It moved with incredible agility. It had lost its mother and it had lost all the members of its troop, but it knew danger, and it moved with every ounce of speed it could muster, running for its life. Traymore took his rifle back from the man who had been holding it for him. He aimed at the tamarin and pulled the trigger.

At that very moment Henry couldn't bare to look, so he turned away. Then he saw Jett. She had moved next to a tree. Using the tree as a rest, she aimed the Glock 17 with both hands. Henry realized now that she had been aiming at Traymore for a long time. She had been watching, waiting, focusing on the aim. She had already pulled the trigger. Bang! The Glock 17 cracked into the forest. The bullet cut through the sky and blasted a hole in the center of Traymore's chest. Every man in the base camp ran for cover. The baby tamarin ran safely into the treetops.

CHAPTER FIFTY-SIX

In the moments that followed, the camp erupted with men and gunfire. They knew now they were under attack, and they were prepared for it. They fired randomly into the forest at first, then began streaming out of the buildings and up the paths that led into the hills.

Henry's first instinct was to run like the dickens. He was overjoyed when Jett killed Traymore and saved the tamarin, but he realized now the danger it put them in. When he turned to run, somebody grabbed his arm and held him firmly.

It was Boa. He had gathered the three others around him, and with eyes which demanded obedience, he told them to sit still and be silent.

They had learned to trust Boa. They didn't understand him all the time, but they had learned to trust him. Hours before Boa had made them "invisible," and now Henry was beginning to understand this strange, seemingly nonsensical ritual. If someone was looking for you, they would be looking for signs of movement, recognizable shapes, the shine of skin beneath the lights. Boa had fixed all this. The dark lines crossing their faces served to break up the pattern. Their faces became indiscernible from the leaves. Their chests were but branches swinging in the breeze.

Henry's heart was beating so heavily he was sure that its sound would betray them. But both Boa and Jett were holding him now. The hunters walked within yards of them, M1s in hand, but did not detect them.

The companions waited until the sun had set fully and darkness fell. They waited until the men had returned to their camp. Finally, after many hours of total stillness that left Henry's muscles aching, Jett gave the signal to move. She walked a little, gazing through the trees to mark the position of each guard.

"They have posted many guards tonight, perhaps double their normal number, but the others have gone to sleep. Thanks to Boa, we should be able to slip in without being detected. By the placement of their guards it seems they are more worried about their laboratory and their sleeping quarters than the Communication Building. Henry, are you ready?"

"I didn't actually realize there would be guns involved." Henry thought he should mention that.

"I don't know if I can hack into their computer under pressure!"

"Maybe we should back off and approach again tomorrow," Sullivan suggested.

"No. We're going in now," Jett said.

"Jetta Mendoza, you must remember, once you go inside the place of the white men, you are no longer invisible. The magic doesn't work there."

"Yes, I understand, Boa, but we must find the answers we are seeking." Jett turned and stepped into the forest. Almost immediately she became invisible and disappeared. Frightened of being left behind, Henry hurried after her.

Henry crept a dozen yards behind Jett, watching her. She moved swiftly and silently through the undergrowth. She approached one of the guards from behind, wrapped a steel wire around his neck, yanked him backward and brought him to the ground. He was dead in seconds.

Sullivan moved forward, running to the shadowed corner of a building. Then he turned and gave Jett and Henry the sign to move ahead. Boa had disappeared. Having gotten them this far, he knew that his work was done. He chose not to enter the "place of the white men." That was their world, not his. They knew their own way there.

Jett and Henry moved up behind Sullivan. Jett touched Sullivan's arm and pointed to the building with the satellite dish on top. "Comm building," she whispered.

He nodded, then gestured that he would move up first and they should follow.

Sullivan crept up to the back door of the building and listened. Nothing.

He glanced back at Jett and Henry. Henry noticed only then that he was carrying the guard's M1 assault rifle.

Sullivan tried the door. Henry was hoping it was locked and that they could go home.

"Locked!" Sullivan mouthed silently.

Jett moved forward and met Sullivan at the door.

"It's not going to open!" Sullivan whispered to her. "Maybe Boa's got a walk-through-doors spell."

She put her shoulder against the door and shoved. It didn't budge.

"Give me a hand," she said.

Jett and Sullivan both pressed their shoulders against the door and shoved. That didn't work either. Finally, Jett gave the door one good punch with the butt of Sullivan's M1 and the door came open. Henry was frozen, waiting for a response to the noise. It had been so loud he was sure that the entire camp would wake up and attack them within seconds.

Nothing.

The one-room cinderblock building was filled with electronic equipment, radios, computers, modems, data lines. There were two windows and another door out the other side.

"Keep watch at the window," she told Sullivan and moved to the main console with Henry. Other than the glow of the computer screens, the room was dark.

Henry, already sitting at the console, was staring at a login prompt:

`DRACONIUS LOGIN:`

"Can you do it, Henry? Can you find out what they're doing?"

First he had to get in. He started at the top of his mental list. He entered a login of "uucp" and a password of "uucp." That didn't work.

"Geez, I can't think like this!"

"What's happening?" Sullivan asked from his position at the window. They ignored him.

"OK, no UUCP. How about MMDF, you must get mail . . ." He entered a user name of "mmdf" and a password of "mmdf." The computer accepted that and provided him with a command prompt.

"Bingo! Now, what do I do? Let's take a look around, see what we're dealing with . . ."

He did a "pwd" command to see where he was and a "ls -l" command to list the files in that directory. Everything was just as expected. "No surprises," he said. "Somebody's got me stuck in a closed directory, which is where I should be because I'm using a general mail account. But not for long . . ."

"What's happening?" Sullivan asked again.

"He's in . . . " Jett told him.

"This kid's good!" Sullivan said. "He knows his stuff!"

"Just enough to be real dangerous . . ." Henry whispered.

"What are you trying to do?" Jett asked.

"I need to get system access first . . . there we go . . . the old VI-hole. No problem. Henry strikes again!"

"Is it going to work?" Jett asked.

"I'm just waiting for my egg to hatch . . . there!"

"You got it?"

"Yup. I am now a system administrator of the Draconius Network. I can do anything I want."

"Find Caldwell's files!"

Henry was already on his way. He pulled up Caldwell's personal records and paged through sections of his journal. He found entries to correspond to the date of their arrival in the laboratory and the subsequent experiments. He noticed the name "Mary" and stopped:

PATIENT 13a, HVGT POSITIVE SPECIMEN.
OBSERVED SIDE EFFECTS FROM PHYLLOMEDUSA BICOLOR
EXTRACT VERSION 12.4.2:
NAUSEA, VOMITING, FACIAL FLUSH, TACHYCARDIA, CHANGES IN
BLOOD PRESSURE, SWEATING, INTENSE ABDOMINAL PAIN,
DEFECATION—ASSUMED TO BE ASSOCIATED WITH CAERULEIN AND
THE EQUIACTIVE PHYLOOCAERULEIN, KNOWN TO BE RELATED TO
GASTRIC AND PANCREATIC SECRETIONS. SALIVATION, TEARING,
INTESTINAL TORSIONAL MOVEMENTS ASSOCIATED WITH
PHYLLOMEDUSIN PEPTIDE. CHRONIC LOSS OF BLOOD
PRESSURE, SEVERE TACHYCARDIA AND STIMULATION OF THE
ADRENAL CORTEX ASSOCIATED WITH SAUVAGINE. MAY ALSO
ACCOUNT FOR HEIGHTENED SENSORY PERCEPTION. ALL
EFFECTS CONSISTENT WITH RHESUS SPECIMENS THAT WERE
TREATED SUBCUTANEOUSLY WITH THE EXTRACT VERSION
7.3.0. INTENSE CONVULSIONS FOLLOWED BY COMA.
NORMAL BEHAVIOR AND READINGS RETURN AFTER 3 DAYS.
SPECIMEN SHOWS EARLY SIGNS OF INFECTION AFTER 17 DAYS.
SPECIMEN DIED 15:12. INCREASE CONCENTRATION.

Jett was reading with him. "That *monster!* He injected the

disease into her, then tried to see if the Sapo would cure her. But he didn't give her enough. I'm going to take him down if it's the last thing I do."

"They probably killed the Leopard Ghost, too," Henry figured.

"You believe in the Leopard Ghost?" Sullivan asked.

"Sure," Henry said. He believed in everything now. Most of all he believed in himself, in a way he never thought possible.

He paged through Caldwell's records. He saw the word "vaccine" and stopped. He read a few paragraphs and continued, taking in information at high speeds.

"How we doing out there, Sullivan?" Jett asked.

"Doing fine. No problems. Everybody's asleep or passed out. Those floodlights out there work nicely. I can see everything just fine."

"Any sign of Boa?"

"Are you kidding? He's invisible, remember?"

Henry smiled, and continued his work. He noticed the phrase "positive specimen" and he stopped. It was a log entry about Jett:

PATIENT 13B, HVGT POSITIVE SPECIMEN.
INJECTED WITH 15 CC'S OF HVGT ID-III BLOOD-BORNE PATHOGEN.
SPECIMEN TESTED POSITIVE FOR VIRAL INFECTION.
INJECTED WITH 5 CC'S OF PHYLLOMEDUSA BICOLOR EXTRACT 15.5.0.
OBSERVED SIDE EFFECTS: NAUSEA, VOMITING, TACHYCARDIA, SWEATING, INTENSE ABDOMINAL PAIN, AS IN PREVIOUS PATIENTS. INSTANTANEOUS OVER-STIMULATION OF ADRENAL CORTEX, IMMEDIATE AND ACUTE INCREASE IN SENSORY PERCEPTION AND PHYSICAL STRENGTH—ASSUMED TO BE RELATED TO SAUVAGINE. INTENSE BLOOD-VESSEL DILATION ASSOCIATED WITH PHYLLOKININ. ACTIVATION OF THE PITUITARY ADRENAL AXIS TRIGGERED THE SPECIMEN'S FIGHT-OR-FLIGHT MECHANISM. GENERALIZED ANALGESIC EFFECT POSSIBLY RELATED TO THE RELEASE OF BETA-ENDORPHINS. LONG TERM INCREASE IN STRENGTH. PATIENT RESTRAINED. STILL UNDER OBSERVATION.

Henry experienced the sensation of falling off a cliff. His body was falling. Soon he was going to hit the ground. *Injected with 15 cc's of HVGT ID-III blood-borne pathogen. Specimen tested positive for viral infection.* He kept paging through the screens, his mind wandering back to those words and what they meant. Now they knew for sure: *Jett was dead.*

"What's wrong?" Sullivan asked. Henry wasn't working anymore. He just stared into the screen. His fingers weren't moving. "For God's sake, Jett, what's wrong? What did you find out?"

Terrified by their panic-stricken faces, Sullivan moved toward them. He grabbed Jett's shoulders and turned her to face him. She was in a daze.

Henry told him: "The lab report says she was injected with the same virus that killed Mary. That means she's dead. It's just a matter of time."

Suddenly there were voices outside. Two guards on patrol had heard them. The door opened.

CHAPTER FIFTY-SEVEN

Jett reacted instantly. She stood up. She put the Glock to the guard's temple. She pulled the trigger. His body flew across the room. His weapon clattered down. He lay sprawled on the floor of the communications center.

The other guard gazed upon his dispatched companion, momentarily paralyzed by fear. Henry stared at him, wondering what was going to happen next.

Sullivan stepped behind the guard and struck him over the head with the M1.

The guard went down, swore, and got back up again.

Sullivan grabbed him and tried to wrestle him back to the ground. He hit him in the nose with his fist. This did nothing except give the guy a nose bleed and spray blood everywhere. Flecks of blood spattered Henry's keyboard.

The guard struck Sullivan, first in the chest, then in the face, sending him reeling away in confusion and pain.

Jett leaned over, aimed the Glock at the guard's head and pulled the trigger. Finally the man was still. Henry was staring down at him. He shivered violently, then turned his attention back to the computer. He realized, once he began working again, that he had inadvertently developed the same nerves of steel that he had noted in Jett. He knew he had a job to do, so he forgot about everything else and did it.

Jett was all ears now. She wasn't paying attention to the computer anymore. She had fired two gun shots in the night. What would it bring? It took only seconds for the reaction to come. They heard the camp stirring. Only minutes remained.

"Get those keys. Lock the door!" Jett ordered Sullivan.

Sullivan picked himself up, brushed off his clothes. Blood and bits of brain matter were all over him. He tried to wipe it off, but it didn't do any good. He was just spreading it around, getting it on his hands. Ignoring this, Henry kept working.

"Forget about the blood!" Jett told Sullivan. "Focus!"

Henry sat at the computer, concentrating more fiercely than ever, pretending that Jett's orders were for him. He began establishing network connections to other computers outside the Draconius system, computers all over the world.

"Stay quiet until they figure out what building we're in, then break the window and start firing like a madman." As Jett gave these instructions, she moved to the other window.

Henry linked into his own system. Here he would find the tools he needed:

WELCOME TO BEAUFORTLAND! LOGIN IF YOU DARE:

He typed in his user name and password.

SORRY. BETTER IMPROVE YOUR TYPING. HERE'S YOUR NEXT
AND PENULTIMATE TRY. . .
WELCOME TO BEAUFORTLAND! LOGIN IF YOU DARE:

He stared at the screen. Did he make a typo? Or did someone change the password?

"Henry, we've got to get out of here," Jett said.

"Just a second," he told her.

He typed it again. This time it let him in. He had indeed made a typing error.

"What are you doing, Henry? What's taking so long?"

He began gathering the programs he needed. He knew he didn't have enough time to do what he needed to do. He did it anyway. "I'm either going to get this or I'm not. I'm at the critical point."

"Well, we'll just start praying!" Sullivan cried.

Linked into the various systems, Henry found his bearings, then focused on his goal. With his personal collection of password crackers, decrypters, backward-encrypted dictionaries, cuckoos eggs, mockingbirds, time bombs, and viruses, there wasn't a system on the planet that wouldn't succumb to him. Of course, there were only two or three that he was interested in today, then it would be all over, over for Jett, over for everybody. He made his connections and did his dirty deeds. Then he jumped back to the Draconius Network. He accessed the contents of Caldwell's database, the chemical formulas, the test results, and his medical journal: everything that was important to the son of bitch. Everything Henry would destroy.

"There's a dozen of them out there now! They're checking every building!" Sullivan said. "We've got to get out of here!"

"Stay down. Wait until they know we're here. Then open fire." Jett told him. Seconds later she screamed: "Now!"

Henry jumped when the shattering of glass and roar of the automatic rifle erupted behind him.

"I think they know we're here!" Sullivan screamed over the horrific noise. He strafed with the elegance of a Marine. "They know we're here!"

Jett didn't reply. She aimed and fired, aimed and fired, one deadly shot after another in rapid sequence. Counting on her completely now, Henry blocked out the explosion of violence around him. He was just keystrokes away from victory. Then they would have what they came for, and Caldwell would know what it was like to be hurt forever.

"Come on, Henry! Let's get out of here!" Sullivan screamed.

"Go!" Henry said. "I'll catch up with you!"

Just as Henry was retreating from the system, a message about Patient 13B in Caldwell's e-mail files caught his eye. Knowing he didn't have time to read it, he copied the file to his system so that he could read it later.

Gunfire ripped through the door, sending splinters in every direction. A slug went through the laser printer, another through the back of a chair.

"Come on, Henry!"

"Sullivan, get of here! I'll follow Henry out!" Jett said.

Bullets were flying everywhere. The windows had shattered. The door had been riddled with holes. They could last no longer.

"Now!" Jett screamed. "Out the back door!"

Sullivan pulled away from the window. Henry got up to follow him.

Jett slammed a new clip into the Glock, then shoved it into her pants. She picked up two of the M1s. With one rifle in each hand, she gave them the signal to open the back door and make a run for it.

Then the front door opened. Henry heard a clicking sound and turned to look.

Jett didn't need to think about that sound or try to figure out what it was. She knew. She hit the deck immediately, and spun firing on the front door."Get down!" she screamed. A spray of bullets burst from her weapon.

Henry dove to the floor.

In the next second he peeked out. He saw Sullivan standing over him. Stunned, Sullivan looked down at his side. No blood was coming out of the little puncture there. The second and third rounds blasted through his neck, killing him instantly and splattering blood all over Henry.

Then, in the distance, Henry heard an explosion. It was followed immediately by a second explosion a little closer, and a third explosion that shook the ground. Outside, a whole new firefight began. Days before, Jett had left the young Sendero Luis behind at the canoes, telling him, 'Later, I shall need your help again.' Now, the soldiers of the Shining Path stormed into the campground, led on by Luis' battle cry.

CHAPTER FIFTY-EIGHT

Dr. Caldwell sat down in front of his computer and logged into the network. The system indicated that he had electronic mail, so he went to his mailbox and checked it. He had a couple of messages, but noticed an item from John Dennison, the second-in-command at the Peruvian base camp. Why is he sending me messages? Caldwell wondered. What happened to Traymore? He read that message first:

DR. CALDWELL:

I AM SAD TO REPORT THAT CURTIS TRAYMORE IS DEAD. THE SHINING PATH MADE A SURPRISE ATTACK ON THE BASE CAMP. IN THE END WE DEFEATED THEM, KILLING OR CAPTURING ALL, BUT NOT BEFORE THREE OF OUR MEN WERE KILLED, INCLUDING TRAYMORE.

THE COMMUNICATION CENTER WAS SEVERELY DAMAGED. FORTUNATELY, WE WERE ABLE TO GET THE DISH BACK UP AND THE COMPUTER WORKING. LABORATORY OK. SOME SOLAR COLLECTORS DAMAGED, BUT CRITICAL EQUIPMENT UNHARMED. WE CAN PUT THINGS BACK TOGETHER AGAIN AND CONTINUE OUR WORK. WE WILL DOUBLE OUR WATCHES AND SEND OUT PATROLS EACH NIGHT, ALTHOUGH I DON'T BELIEVE THERE IS STILL A THREAT FROM THE SHINING PATH.

AFTER THE ATTACK, WE PERSUADED ONE OF OUR PRISONERS TO TELL US HOW TO GET THROUGH THE ANDEAN DIVISOR. WE HAVE FINALLY FOUND THE SOURCE. THE SAPO FROG LIVES HIGH IN THE CLOUD FOREST. THE TRIP INTO THE DIVISOR IS DIFFICULT, BUT MANAGEABLE. WE WILL BEGIN HARVESTING THE FROGS IMMEDIATELY. ALL OUR INITIAL TESTS MATCH UP PERFECTLY. IT'S DEFINITELY SAPO.

SUGGEST YOU COME ASAP. THERE ARE QUESTIONS TO BE ANSWERED REGARDING THE COLLECTION AND STORAGE. UNTIL THEN, I WILL CONTINUE TO RUN THINGS, PER YOUR

INSTRUCTIONS.

BY THE TIME YOU ARRIVE WE WILL HAVE EVERYTHING BACK THE
WAY IT SHOULD BE. EVERYTHING WILL BE READY.

JOHN DENNISON.

Caldwell cheered aloud. "He's done it! John Dennison has done it!"
The Sapo extract is on the way! He typed in an immediate reply:

DENNISON:

WELL DONE! I AM VERY PLEASED! MAKE SURE THE LIQUID
CHROMATOGRAPH IS CALIBRATED BEFORE YOU DO YOUR
TESTS. WATCH FOR PEAK 3 AND PEAK 17. THEY'VE GOT TO
MATCH UP EXACTLY. E-MAIL ME YOUR NEXT SET OF RESULTS.

I'LL MAKE RESERVATIONS IMMEDIATELY. SEND SOMEBODY TO
PICK ME UP AT THE USUAL PLACE FOR THIS SATURDAY'S
FLIGHT.

CALDWELL.

He sent the message, then logged off and picked up the phone.
He dialed an extension down the hall. "Dennison has found the source.
Isn't that great? I'm going down. I'll be back with the first sample in
a week. Make sure you have everything ready by then."

Then he called the airline and made the reservation.

CHAPTER FIFTY-NINE

"Sir . . ."

Caldwell rubbed his eyes and looked around. He didn't even remember falling asleep. The last thing he knew he was thinking about accepting the Nobel Prize.

"Sir. . . the plane has landed. We've landed in Iquitos, sir."

"Oh, good," he told the bodyguard. He stood up, got his carry-on bag out of the overhead compartment and disembarked with the five men, all casually dressed, who made up his escort.

They walked from the plane across the concrete to the airport terminal. It was raining. As usual, he thought to himself. He didn't like Peru much, except that it would make him a millionaire.

Once inside the scummy little airport he made his way through customs. No problems there. They weren't carrying anything and they were only going to stay a few days. "Tourist" they said. Thanks to Dennison, they had a ready stash of weapons in the city.

They walked down the row of taxi drivers and beggars until they came to an individual Dr. Caldwell thought he recognized.

"Are you the boy who took me to the hotel before?" he asked the boy. He knew enough about Peru to know that he had to be careful.

The driver nodded, and in a thick accent he replied, "I'm him, Dr. Caldwell. Dennison sent me to pick you up and take you to the hotel."

"Very good, lead the way, young man. These gentlemen are with me."

"I'll signal for another car, sir."

The driver picked up his bags and put them in his motorcycle-taxi. Then he opened the tiny door for him.

It didn't take long to get to the hotel. Just long enough to give Caldwell an upset stomach from the twisty roads and the wild driving.

He gave the driver a dollar bill and stumbled half asleep into the lobby.

"Dr. Caldwell?" asked the little man at the desk.

"Yes."

"We have your room all ready for you, sir. Best in the house. Mr. Dennison called ahead for you."

"Great, point the way, I'm bushed."

"A bad flight, sir?"

"As always."

"Well, sir, I'm sorry to hear that. A little rest and I'm sure you'll be fine."

"Certainly. Has a taxi been arranged for the morning?"

"Oh, yes sir. A driver will be waiting for you at six tomorrow morning to take you to the boat."

"Very well, thank you." He took the key and made his way down the vaguely familiar corridor of the hotel. He found his room and went to bed immediately. His bodyguards slept in the adjacent rooms.

CHAPTER SIXTY

The next morning Caldwell woke early. Outside his door he found two of his men waiting for him. They wore camo pants, olive drab t-shirts and black army boots. They carried assault rifles slung over their shoulders.

They went together to the cars, where they met the other men. Feeling much refreshed, he tossed his own bags in and climbed into the little vehicle.

"Good morning, my good man," he said.

"Good morning, Dr. Caldwell. How are you this morning?"

"Feeling much better, thank you."

The driver shoved it into gear and sped down the driveway. Once into the city, he followed a circuitous route around the more congested parts and brought Caldwell to the docks with surprising efficiency.

"There's your boat, Dr. Caldwell," the driver said, then hopped off the bike, grabbed the bags, and led Caldwell to the riverboat roped to the shore. The captain of the boat had laid a few planks of wood across the mud to make a crude gangway for the passengers.

"Who are all these people?" asked the senior bodyguard, suspicious of the many faces crowded with them onto the boat. There was a whole family of *ribereños*, including seven children, who had purchased a new goat in the city and were now taking it back down the river with them. There were also two Senderos, one man and one woman, both with short black hair, typical black t-shirts and AK-47's draped over their shoulders.

"Those are the other passengers, sir," the captain said.

"Tell them to get off," the bodyguard ordered him, then he gestured rudely for all the passengers to get off the boat. They stared back at him in confusion.

"I'm sorry, sir, they've already paid."

"Tell them to get off the boat!"

The captain looked at Caldwell and the taxi driver. "But . . ."

"You had better do what he says."

The captain shook his head in anger, but complied, requesting the other passengers to disembark. The two Senderos were angry and uncooperative until the bodyguard agreed to pay them double the amount they had paid the captain. Finally the boat was vacated. Caldwell and the bodyguards got on.

Then the senior bodyguard noticed the little creature in dirty clothes crouched at the head of the boat. She looked liked some kind of witch doctor. Wild black hair tied in big knots. Spindly body. Eyes closed like in some sort of trance. "Who's that?" the guard demanded. "I want this boat cleared!"

"I can't do that, sir."

"Why not?"

"I can't, sir. That's your guide," the captain replied. "The base camp is deep in the forest. You will need a guide to get there. Mr. Dennison sent this shaman to lead you."

"This dirty old woman? Our guide?" the guard repeated.

"It's all right," Caldwell said, waving him off. "We had a native guide last time too. Nothing to worry about."

The guard agreed begrudgingly. It was his job to protect his boss. And he took his job seriously.

He approached the shaman and was immediately offended by her stench. The bodyguard shoved the shaman with his foot, indicating that she should get up. The shaman complied quietly. She wore a tattered cloak, with a hood which fit loosely around her head to protect her from the sun. The bodyguard checked the pockets, then pulled the folds of dark material away from the shaman's body, exposing the ragged clothes beneath. He searched the inside of the shaman's satchel. All he found was shriveled up herbs, dried leaves, a tiny leather skin and a hollow tube of bamboo.

"You satisfied?" Caldwell asked him, irritated with the delay.

"No gun on her," the guard admitted finally. "But the smell might kill ya!"

CHAPTER SIXTY-ONE

Three days later they arrived in Maranon. They took canoes up the Río Pucara, then moved on foot into the forest. Finally, they arrived exhausted at the base camp. They knew immediately something had gone terribly wrong.

The place was deserted. It appeared as if many explosions had occurred. Whole buildings were destroyed. Casings and shards of glass covered the ground, scattered with broken solar collectors, dead monkeys and damaged laboratory equipment. There were bodies lying everywhere. Curtis Traymore lay dead in the center of the compound.

None of this made sense. There was too much destruction. A large number of soldiers had attacked the camp. They had detonated explosives. And they had killed *everyone*.

He turned to his guards. "We need to check the Comsat link."

Weapons drawn, they walked as a group to the communications building. Although it was riddled with holes and had no door, it was one of the few buildings still intact.

Caldwell stopped before he went in. He looked toward the forest edge, sensing a trap. "Stay out here and keep watch," he told his men. Then he glanced at the shaman. "I'll take her in with me." He gestured for the Indian to walk into the building first. If it's a trap, Caldwell figured, then the Indian would be his cover. They wouldn't attack while he's got the woman. He'd keep her as a hostage, just in case.

Caldwell and the shaman went into the building. The communication room had been ransacked. Lights broken, equipment inoperable, furniture destroyed. On the floor he found the body of John Dennison. He had been shot in the temple. Another man Caldwell did not recognize lay beside him, shot in the neck.

Caldwell glanced at the shaman. She was standing quietly in the darkness of the corner, a strange little obsequious creature.

Caldwell sat down at the terminal. He flicked it on. Amazingly, there was power and it worked. He knew that Dennison or Traymore would have left something in the base journal. Dennison said he found the source. At least that much was assured. Certainly he had made maps and taken notes. If he made maps, then he did his job and Caldwell could get on with the project. That's all that mattered now.

Caldwell smiled. The familiar network login prompt appeared:

DRACONIUS LOGIN:

He entered his user name and password as usual. The normal login information came up on the screen, but then, instead of getting the main menu, he got the following message:

YOUR PARTNERS ARE DEAD.

YOUR FILES ARE GONE.

YOUR COMPANY HAS BEEN DESTROYED.

SHOCK THE MONKEY!

"What's this?" Caldwell cried. A feeling of nausea moved through him. What did the message mean? Was his work really gone?

"It can't be gone!" he cried, but he knew the terminal was patched directly to the central computer in the States. If somebody had gotten in, then . . . he did not want to think about it. It couldn't happen.

He pressed the 'escape' key to make the message go away. Nothing happened. He pressed some other keys at random, demanding something to change. Years of work couldn't just disappear! Repeatedly, he slammed down the 'escape' key. Finally, a new message appeared:

RUN FOR YOUR LIFE.

YOU DON'T STAND A CHANCE.

"What?" What is this thing saying? This can't be happening! Who did this? Where are the maps? "We're so close! Dennison, where'd you put the maps!"

Suddenly he stopped raving.

A deadly silence surrounded him. He realized he didn't hear his men outside anymore.

He thought back to the electronic message that brought him to Peru. Was that really Dennison? He thought about the black-haired courier Traymore had hired. What was her name? *Shock the monkey.* Isn't that the phrase she used in the laboratory? *Shock the monkey.* What did she mean by that? *Shock the monkey.* Could she have anything to do with this? *Shock the monkey.* That's impossible. But then who's behind all this? A feeling of utter hopelessness and confusion overwhelmed him. He had lost everything. A dark and vile desperation filled his soul. He didn't know what to do. He pressed another key. One last message appeared:

LOOK BEHIND YOU . . .

A feeling of darkest fear flooded his heart. He turned uncertainly, trembling. The shaman was standing there in the corner. She was holding something, raising it to her mouth. A hollow piece of bamboo. She blew into it.

The dart stuck in Caldwell's neck. His mind grasped at reality, trying desperately to figure out what was happening. He looked at the shaman. The black eyes looked back at him, wild and unfathomable. Now he recognized the eyes, their wildness, their insanity. Everything else was different. The eyes were the same. They were Jett's!

His hand rose to his neck and pulled out the dart. He tried to throw it away, but at that moment he lost motor control in his fingers. His heart began to pound.

Then the numbness rose up through his arm. He paused and looked down at it quizzically. Then he looked up at his adversary. The blood vessels in his body began to swell.

"You were right about the Shining Path, Doctor. They attacked and destroyed your base camp. And you were right about the Indians. Their magic is powerful. And you were right about Jensen-Bishop. They're probably still out there looking for Sapo. You have many enemies in Peru."

She watched him struggle. His face flushed with the crimson pain rushing through his body. His body began to convulse.

"What you weren't right about was *me*."

When the pure Sapo extract reached his heart, Caldwell stopped moving altogether.

He slumped to the floor. Dead.

PART FIVE: The Courier

CHAPTER SIXTY-TWO

The taxi rolled down Broadway Avenue. It was three AM. The rain had just stopped. Streets were deserted, black, glistening. Lights reflected in shining puddles. Traffic lights turned red-green-yellow over empty avenues. Everything was still. Jett felt the comfortable numbness of experiencing a place for the hundredth time. She gazed ahead, not talking to the taxi driver. The taxi driver didn't care, and that made her smile.

The taxi driver stopped at the curb outside the Manhattan Wallren Building. Jett paid him, and she and Henry went in. The doorman was asleep. They walked past him and went up to the 15th floor, Suite 1a. Jett dropped her keys on the side table, hung her coat in the closet. She walked into her office. Henry sat down at her computer and turned it on. She watched anxiously. He called into his system and retrieved the files he had copied there from the Draconius Network. He paged through the files until he got to the very end of Caldwell's journal. In the last moments of the battle, just before he was forced to ditch the effort, Henry thought he saw something. He couldn't be sure until he found it again. Finally, he found the phrase he was looking for: *"Patient 13B. Positive Specimen. Sapo Solution 1.5% Version 15.5.0 effective. Patient tested negative for viral infection after six days."*

Henry smiled. He couldn't believe his eyes. He had to say it out loud to convince himself. "Caldwell infected you with a deadly virus just as we suspected, but what we didn't see in the Comm Building was that the Sapo actually cured you. Your concentration was .5% higher than Mary's. That made the difference. You have been feeling the many side effects of the drug, like Boa told us about."

Jett put her hand on Henry's shoulder, and squeezed it. That touch was love and gratitude and relief combined. A tremendous darkness leaked out of her, and in those seconds she felt her life exploding into the brightness of the future. *She would survive.* She would get to live some more. That's all that mattered to her. Survive. That's all she had been doing all her life.

Smiling broadly, Henry stood up. Suddenly they burst into wild celebration, hooting and screaming and embracing.

"You know, Henry, as I recall you really weren't appreciated by your previous employers, and by now, who knows, you might not even have a job back home."

"Well, at least I have a few more things to put on my resume: hacking under pressure, dodging bullets, computer system destruction, invisibility, bird watching, Amazon River exploration, familiarity with a Glock 17 . . ."

"And don't forget *lethal with a mechanical pencil*," Jett reminded him. "I was just thinking, I'm accepting resumes for a new partner, assuming he has the requisite skills and experience. What do you say?"

Henry just smiled.

* * *

The next morning, after a long deserved sleep, Jett woke. While Henry slept, she took a shower, washed her hair, got dressed. She pulled on a pair of back jeans and a simple cotton shirt. She found her old leather flight jacket. Picking up her keys and well-traveled shoulder bag, she left her apartment.

While she waited in the lobby for a taxi, she noticed an article in the *Times*:

POLICE BUST LAB ON TIP FOUND IN PRECINCT COMPUTER

The taxi arrived. The doorman Joseph smiled and opened the door for her.

Now the streets were filled with traffic. Stores full of shoppers. People bustling down the sidewalks. Suits, dresses, fancy clothes, fancy cars, advertisements, delis, bookstores, espresso shops. Everything was the same in the world. But everything was different for her. And she loved New York more than ever.

The taxi stopped in front of the Pearl Building.

She took the elevator to the top floor and convinced the secretary to let her enter unannounced.

She walked into Robert Pearl's office. Her long black hair flowed over her shoulders and down her back. She was a tall woman, lithe like a cat. An air of utter sophistication hung about her, mixed with animalian beauty. Her eyes were absolutely black.

Robert was working at his desk. He wore a charcoal suit, crisp white shirt, smoke and rose paisley tie.

On the table sat several legal documents: a signed copy of his divorce and a restraining order for his wife's attorneys to stop surveillance on him.

His desk was covered with papers and text books. At the corner of the desk sat two scientific articles. They had shown up mysteriously in the company's computer. The first had been submitted to the American Union of Ornithologists: *Description of a New Species: Momotus sullivanii. "Sullivan's Motmot."* The second paper had not yet been published, and Pearl Research appeared to have the only copy: *Advances in the Treatment of Immune Deficiency Diseases.* It had been credited to three people nobody had ever heard of: Mary Olsen, Tara Movaca, and Jay Sullivan. Although the paper was poorly written, hurriedly tossed-together material, the results of the study were astounding. The drug studied was an incredibly powerful, universal booster of the immune system, and could be used for all sorts of clinical purposes. Robert had dropped everything to pursue it, focusing all the efforts of his beleaguered company toward this one last hope. If the results were accurate, the authors of this paper would likely receive the Nobel Prize. Pearl Research would refine the drug and bring it to market. All he lacked, of course, was the physical article to support the paper's claims and begin development.

He looked up at her in surprise.

"Hello, Robert. I have a package for you."

She handed him a small brown package.

He was obviously astounded to see her, but he took the package and opened it, looking up at her as he did so. Once he had unwrapped it, he pulled the top off the box. Inside the box there was a small, colorful frog.